The English Heiress

Patricia Rice

The English Heiress

Patricia Rice

One

"Owning the most extensive pistol collection in the world won't feed your tenants, Aubry." Bored, Michael O'Toole leaned against a window frame and shifted his attention from Squire Aubry to a lamb gamboling in the field. "Prélat's newest percussion pistol might kill a man at fifty paces, but it's useless for shooting fowl."

"A man has the right to protect himself in these uncertain times!" his portly host blustered as he passed his newly-acquired weapon to a more appreciative guest.

"If a man surrounds himself with friends instead of enemies, he would have no need to protect himself." Idly, O'Toole juggled silver pieces between his fingers, assuming interest in coins and gamboling lambs.

A smart man would have heeded Michael's warning rather than his aloofness.

Beyond the high hedge shielding the lambs stood tenant houses with leaking thatch and mildewed walls and children running barefoot wiping runny noses—while the owner of the houses stood in his elegant room, bragging of his expensive weaponry.

O'Toole curled his lip in open derision as one of the guests asked if he might test a fowling piece. Collectors did not use their collections. They merely acquired and admired them. A fourth coin materialized amid the ones spinning between his fingers. He listened to the whispers about him but gave no indication that he heard, or cared.

"The man's got no title and little name to speak of. Why was he invited?" a particularly loud, querulous baronet asked.

"He's the brother of a marquess," the squire whispered back, "Or the adopted brother. I'm not quite clear. Effingham sent him in his place."

"The Marquess of Effingham? The American? He's little better than a savage himself," the baronet replied with scorn.

Savages were more polite than to insult guests, O'Toole mused, unoffended. Which was more unacceptable—being untitled, adopted, or American?

As the squire led his elderly guest away, O'Toole shifted his attention to the weapon cabinet. Simple lock. A thief wouldn't even need to break the glass.

He spun the coins so they sparkled in the sun while giving due consideration to the cabinet's contents. Expensive equipment really should be put to good use.

He shouldn't. He really shouldn't. He'd promised his high-and-mighty noble brother he wouldn't stir more mischief than necessary if he went in his place. But really, this was an opportunity begging to happen. It couldn't happen to a more deserving man. The squire could regale his dinner guests with the mournful tale for years to come. He would be doing his otherwise boring host a favor.

Cheerfully, O'Toole pocketed the coins to examine the valuable weaponry. More canny companions would be suspicious of his sudden geniality since it obviously didn't arise from the rum punch he wasn't consuming.

A gale of feminine laughter drifted from the hallway following a knock and bustle at the front door. The racket of more trunks and visitors arriving resounded through the hall. The old fellow had managed quite a house party before the Season reached full swing back in the city.

Always attuned to his surroundings, Michael listened to the feminine chatter while admiring a particularly clever pistol. He loved watching women in their frilly gowns, festive colors, and soft curls, loved listening to their cheerfully chirping voices. He'd discovered, however, that they were a serious obstacle to a man of his nature. Women saw men and thought nest. He preferred flight.

"Such an exciting journey we had! Let us freshen up and we'll tell you all about it. Would you believe...." The feminine voice trailed off as the speaker strolled out of range.

Michael froze and strained for another note of that once-familiar voice. It had been two long years— Maybe, if he eased closer to the door...

He daren't. Returning the pistol to its place, he eyed the casement overlooking the garden. His host wouldn't miss him. He had a well-known habit of never staying, one of many habits of which the lady disapproved, and rightfully so, did she know the half of them.

No longer able to hear her lilting voice, he returned to the heavy draperies of the open window.

He had plans for this household. It would be much safer if the gentle Lady Blanche didn't know of his presence. The wretched woman had the face of an angel and the character to go with it. Angels frowned upon theft.

"Borrowing," he called it, not theft. Thieves stole for ill-gotten gain. His intentions were as pure as the driven snow. Angels wouldn't see it that way, and he had no particular desire to waste his days in gaol.

* * *

"The entire weapons collection disappeared, Gavin! My word, a thief would have needed a cart to haul off that much armament." Dillian Lawrence, Marchioness of Effingham, shook her head in disapproval as she rocked her babe in her arms.

"I thought you told me Michael was supposed to attend the house party." Scribbling replies to the Season's invitations while the rain dripped outside the parlor windows, Lady Blanche Perceval raised her head as if she asked only an innocent question.

Both her cousin, Dillian, and Dillian's towering husband, the Marquess of Effingham, lifted their eyebrows in surprise. Blanche always felt fragile and insignificant next to her imposing relations. She didn't like being reminded of her resemblance to a porcelain figurine.

"Michael isn't a thief," Dillian protested Blanche's insinuation.

"The squire has more interest in his weapons than his tenants," Michael's formidable brother corrected with an air of resignation.

The accusation hung in the air. Michael was too clever to be caught by a country squire, but his relations knew his dangerous predilections.

"Will he never grow up?" Blanche asked in despair. "Or does he intend to play Robin Hood forever? Theft is theft, no matter what face he puts upon it. One of these days, he will hang."

The scar on the marquess's face wrinkled with his wry grimace.

"Michael just acts as others ought to act," Dillian defended him loyally.

"Men are fools, and Michael is no exception," Blanche replied, cutting her off. "Men think they can go about, doing as they please, without any responsibility to their families." As her father had, until he was lost at sea, casting her forever into the hands of servants. "Does he not consider what would happen to you and Gavin should he be caught?"

"He is not a thief—"

The slim figure of the Duke of Anglesey strolled into the room to interrupt Dillian's protest. "Creating dissension among the ranks, are we, Cuz?" he commented, raising unperturbed eyebrows at his relations as he regarded their frozen expressions. "Which of your suitors are we slandering today? You will not be content until all the bachelors of London stand with pistols drawn at one another's heads."

Blanche gave her paternal cousin a frosty look. "That is none of my concern, to be sure. If you've come to nag me some more, Neville, you may depart now."

The duke returned her look with a lofty smile. "It may be your coin that pays the staff, but the house is still mine, if you recollect rightly. I'll leave when I'm ready."

Dillian laughed, handed the infant to her husband, and rose from the sofa. "I think it time we depart the family argument. Really, Blanche, you shouldn't go about slandering suitors, or even poor Michael."

"I shouldn't?" Blanche inquired mockingly. "Shall you meet a few of my glittering beaus? They have no true care for what I think or feel. They merely see wealth begging to be taken. And if Michael wanted my wealth, he would merely help himself without bothering with the niceties of courtship."

His Grace helped himself to a cup of tea since neither of the women offered to pour. Like Blanche, he had come into his inheritance unexpectedly and had not yet learned the arrogance due his rank. He lifted his quizzing glass and peered with dubious interest at the infant in the marquess's arms. "Those things come dashed small, don't they? Hard to believe in a few years it will be a conniving female like any other."

"They wouldn't seem so small if you had to bear them," Dillian replied. "I'm making Gavin work on a bill for female emancipation so Madeline needn't marry."

The duke rolled his eyes at the prospect. "You did say you were leaving, didn't you?" he prompted. Before Blanche could protest, he held up his hand for silence. "I have some private matters to discuss with you, and I shan't leave until I have done with them."

"We're leaving now." Dillian brushed a kiss across Blanche's cheek. "Behave yourself for a change. Neville can't help who he is."

Blanche frowned but gave her godchild a wistful kiss. "I wish I could buy one of these for my own."

"Well, buy the proper husband, and you can have one, too," Gavin said crudely, pushing his wife toward the door. "We'll see you this evening."

Blanche waited until all sign of her maternal cousin and her husband disappeared before returning her regard to the duke. "I'm retiring to the country," she announced, forestalling Neville's offensive with her own.

"You can retire to Australia for all I care, but I need those papers signed allowing me to fence in the pasture before you go. We're losing sheep, and my hands are tied until you agree to purchase the fencing."

Blanche didn't like arguing with Neville, but someone must, since their grandfather had left his considerable wealth in her incapable hands. "If we fence the pasture, the Goodmans can't take their cows to water. And Nanny Smith is too old for climbing a stile every time she visits her daughter. Move your silly sheep elsewhere."

"Those sheep are the only thing keeping me in frock coats and cravats!" Neville replied. "This situation is no longer tolerable, Blanche. I am doing my damnedest to keep afloat with the meager profits of the entailed land, but you stand in the way of every opportunity to increase them. This cannot continue. Either find yourself a sensible husband who can deal with these matters on some rational basis, or marry me as grandfather intended. I cannot live my life tied by your golden chains."

Worn by what seemed like a lifetime of these arguments, Blanche fingered the faint scars at her hairline and stared into the distance. Neville usually had the patience of a saint. She had never seen him so frustrated and harassed before. She didn't like admitting that she was the cause, but she didn't like lying to herself either.

"Find a wealthy wife, Neville. Then your solicitors may talk to my solicitors and we'll never argue again," she answered, a shade too brightly.

"Your solicitor *is* my solicitor," Neville said with impatience, "And this is no time for facetiousness. If you've discarded all potential suitors and are down to considering that buffoon brother of Gavin's, I think your wisest choice is marrying me."

Mulishly, Blanche refused to consider her duty. Of course a society of men expected her to marry and hand over her trust to her husband. He could spend it as he chose while she would have no more purpose than producing his children on a regular basis.

Actually, she wanted the children. But should she marry, the children would belong to her husband. She'd had many long nights of convalescence, staring into the mirror as her scarred visage emerged from bandages, to understand that. Men did not want her for herself, but for what she represented. All those years of her father's neglect did not give her any aspirations to more. If she could not have love, she would not marry.

She might look like a fragile porcelain ornament, but she refused to break like one.

Blanche leveled a gaze on her cousin. "I have no desire to be your duchess, Neville. Court Lady Angela. She will suit you, and she has mountains of money."

Not pleased, Neville returned his tea cup to the table. "I cannot come begging every time I wish something done, Blanche. And Lady Angela laughs like a horse. I'm not that desperate yet."

He stalked out, leaving Blanche contemplating the newly arrived sun rays bleaching the color from her velvet cushions. She couldn't decide whether she felt more like the fading cushion or the dust motes dancing on the insubstantial beams.

Perhaps she should do as her mother had done, retire to her bed and let everyone wait on her and never be disturbed by another decision again.

Two

A light spring snow wafted through the golden lantern beams of the tavern, landing equally on man and beast, rich and poor as they scurried for the comfort of warm fires. Outside the tavern stood a gentleman in tall beaver hat and loose frock coat. The coat's sleeves had frayed at the hems, and shiny patches appeared at the elbows, but the gentleman did not look embarrassed by the lack of elegance. In fact, he appeared unconcerned by anything at all as he juggled three pebbles between gloved hands. The gloves had no fingers.

Passing by the tavern, a stout old gentleman wearing a muffler grunted amusement as the juggler added three silver coins into the configuration of pebbles. The older man held out another coin in appreciation for the trick.

The beggar's hat amazingly slipped from O'Toole's head to his hands while the glittering objects disappeared, along with the man's coin.

"Wasting your talents, son," the old man grumbled. "Ought to be a lawyer and juggle other people's money."

O'Toole grinned, and a gleam of light played along disheveled auburn hair. "People pay well for amusement. When I fail to amuse, I shall consider your advice, sir."

The old man grudgingly smiled at this impudence. "You consider this earning a living, then? Standing on street corners, hat in hand?"

"That I do, sir." Apparently devoid of the coins recently deposited into it, the hat again covered reddish-brown locks. A moment later the coins spun and gleamed in the light. "People pay for amusement as willingly as they pay for ale. I should prefer their coins spent on one than the other."

"An evangelist," the old man growled. "You fail to amuse when you begin to preach." With that, he turned on his heel and entered the tavern.

Undaunted, the young gentleman whistled happily, concentrating on setting all the coins spinning as they rotated up and down through the light, circling from one hand to the other. He had no intention of evangelizing, proselytizing, or orating in any manner. In his experience, actions spoke louder than words.

The rising voices within the tavern warned of the fracas he'd anticipated. O'Toole flipped another coin or two, but one-by-one, the collection disappeared into the pockets of his frayed coat. Human nature being what it was, his instinct for trouble seldom failed him.

"Out, you young lout! What do you think this here is, a poor house? Out with ye afore I call the magistrate!"

A ragged bundle of clothes tumbled head over heels into the frozen slush of the street at O'Toole's feet. A shriek of outrage revealed no harm done to more than pride, and O'Toole gently set his boot on a slender wrist before it could wield the soggy snowball forming between clenched fingers.

"And stay out!" The tavern owner shook his fist and slammed the door.

"Divil take ye, why didn't ye let me at him?" the youth asked angrily, shaking off O'Toole's hold and scrambling to his feet. "And after sayin' I'd work for the food! Is it stealing his miserable porridge, I am?"

Although the angry protest emerged as guttural growls, an interesting note caught O'Toole's ears. He cocked his head as he examined the slight figure straightening a much-darned coat and jerking a knitted cap further over a grubby forehead.

"And am I detectin' a note o' the old country?" he asked in a lilt mimicking that of his young companion.

The angry urchin halted his brushing to stare at the juggler now leaning on a handsome cane. "And what county do ye claim from?" the youngster asked with suspicion.

"All of them, my friend, all of them, but my spirit lingers in the grand green hills of Galway." This wasn't precisely a lie. O'Toole had never lived anywhere more than a year of his life. He'd felt a particular kinship with the inhabitants of County Galway at one time, as he had with many other people in many different places. But he thought he recognized the accent.

The starch wilted from the youth's stiff hide. "Well, then, and you're aftar knowing what it's like. Wretched Sassenachs think they own the ground we walk on. Not a farthing to be had for the likes of us."

"That is as it might be," O'Toole replied mildly. "I'll be taking it then that you're low on funds and have need of a place to stay. It seems as if you've already eaten," he added wryly.

The youth shot him another suspicious look. "I'll be doing just foyne on me own without the need of a pervert, thank ye."

O'Toole stifled a grin as one more engaging aspect of the little termagant appeared. He'd thought the young beggar oddly dressed and a little too deceitful in his speech to be as young as his size indicated. But if his instincts didn't lie, that slender wrist and occasional high-pitched note had little to do with the child's age.

O'Toole idly juggled the coins from his pocket. "And a foyne idea that is, too, me lad. The more for me, I say. But I'm not avarse to tipping back a wee one in front of a friendly fire on a night like this. Mayhap we can help each other. Is a foyne lad like yourself after having a name?"

"Mac," the young person answered reluctantly, eyeing the circling coins with respect. "A mug of something warm and a good song or two might be welcome."

Smiling to himself, O'Toole pocketed his coins and sauntered down the street toward a more hospitable inn. "Well, Mac, and I'm O'Toole."

Not until he had the "lad" in the lighted rooms of an inn did Michael discover the extent of the surprise concealed in this filthy package. Except for his companion's petite height and poorly disguised feminine curves, the image staring back at him could be his own sister.

Concealing his disbelief, O'Toole took a seat beside the roaring fire and gestured for the "lad" to do the same. "I think you'd best be telling me your real name," he suggested, trying to hide his curiosity from himself as well as his terrified companion.

He'd known people with red hair and green eyes before. The world abounded with them. Quite a few even shared his lean build. He'd never met any with all three features plus his striking lack of freckles. And while her chin was considerably narrower than his own, and her high forehead and marked cheekbones proportionately smaller, he would think her a younger version of himself were she not so obviously female.

"Mac" scowled and held the cup of heated cider between her

hands to warm them. "Mac is all they call me," she replied sullenly. "'Tis none of your consarn."

O'Toole debated calling her bluff, but he'd seen enough frightened youngsters to recognize one prepared to bolt. If she felt safer disguised as a boy, then so be it, for now.

He'd never known a home or had any particular desire for one, but he'd always wondered about his origins. Having no name of his own had its advantages, but his intellect couldn't abide ignorance. Gavin might claim him as brother, but that claim came from the circumstances they'd grown up in and not reality.

"P'raps it's none of my consarn," he replied with disinterest as he gnawed on a chicken leg, "but 'tis of some interest when you're after appearin' more like my brother than me own brother does."

She didn't look his way, so she'd noticed the resemblance also. He was inclined to believe what he wanted to believe, but he wasn't imagining the likeness.

"My family has produced bastards enough," she replied dryly. "Royalty is not alone in that habit."

He chuckled in appreciation of the observation. A young girl should have no such notions in her head, but he couldn't fault her acuity. "Well, and I'm flattered of your opinion of me and mine. Since we're neither of us from these parts, might I inquire as to your destination?"

He saw her shoulders tense beneath the thin wool coat. But she wasn't stupid. She knew travel in groups was safer than alone. He pushed the remaining chicken carcass in her direction and watched her eye it hungrily. One needed coins to travel safely. She would know that, too.

"To London," she replied, helping herself to the other leg. "To my aunt," she added with a shade of defiance, daring him to doubt her reply.

O'Toole brightened as if pleased with this discovery. "I have business in the city myself. We might help each other, after all. I just lost my assistant, you see."

He lied. More like, he fudged the truth considerably. He had no direction, no business, and no assistant, unless one counted the last stray he'd found a home. But he could easily manufacture all three with a sweep of his hat. He had twenty-eight years of experience in surviving in this world. He could be anything anyone wanted him to be.

She shot him a look of distrust. "And what might your business be? Horse trader?"

He grinned at her insult. "I'm an actor, lad, on my way to a new position in Drury Lane. But we're a long way from the city's glittering lights, and travel is expensive. I'll earn my way there. 'Tis an honest enough profession. I've paid for a bed in the common room. Why don't you take that fowl up and get some sleep? I've an eye on the serving lass over there for the evening."

She accepted that well enough. O'Toole watched as she gathered up the remains of the chicken and the bread rump. She looked too worn and weary for protest. If he treated her like a boy, she might linger. He would take precautions against her bolting at the first light of day. She didn't have a chance in hell on the road alone.

After she left, O'Toole stayed in his chair, sipping at his coffee and staring at the flames. In his experience, wealth created more evil than good. He had no desire to accumulate any. His goal in life had always been to see what there was to see, do what there was to do, and help the less fortunate along the way.

A family would inevitably ruin that footloose life.

He'd stumbled upon a crossroads he'd never expected to reach: should he continue down the direct path, delivering the lass to her aunt without further question, or should he explore the side road of that frightening resemblance and possibly uncover the family he'd never known?

The question was rhetorical. He'd never ignored an unexplored road in his life.

* * *

"This isn't the way to London," Mac announced as the hay wagon bounced in a rut.

After sitting in the farmer's barn all winter, the hay was redolent of rot, but Michael wouldn't complain of the odor or the ride. A hole in his companion's boot had broken through to match the one in her stocking.

"I have a stop to make first. We can't go into London looking like beggars." He'd thought long and hard on this as they'd traversed the roads from the lake country to Hampshire. Despite the similarities in their appearances, the chit couldn't possibly be his sister. They'd been born an ocean apart. Still, he couldn't ignore the possibility of a blood relation, or the instinct that told him she verged on desperation.

Days in her company hadn't imparted the information he wanted. He needed help. The melodic voice of a certain angelic female beckoned. If anyone could winkle information out of the chit, Lady Blanche could.

"What shall we go to London looking like?" Mac inquired idly, her brogue disappearing. He'd noticed that tendency as she grew more comfortable in his presence.

"That depends on what you mean to do when you get there, my lady," Michael replied, waiting for her reaction.

He watched her panic at his challenge, but she didn't speak her fear.

"I shall go to my aunt, just as I said," she answered without looking at him, not attempting to deny her disguise.

"You must have a very understanding aunt, Miss Mac," he said dryly. "A young lady traveling the length of England and breadth of Ireland, unaccompanied, and in boy's rags, would bring the stoutest of matrons of my acquaintance to their knees in horror."

"Whimpering Sassenach milksops," she returned sulkily. "I'll be getting off here, then, and making my own way, thank ye."

She tried to leap from the rolling wagon, but O'Toole caught her elbow. She struggled, but he dragged her farther into the cart with ease.

"I'll take you to the house of a lady friend of mine. She'll see that you're suitably attired. Then we'll discuss appropriate traveling arrangements. It would be best if I could give her a proper name."

O'Toole watched her war of emotions. To his dismay, he recognized real fear, along with indecision and determination. What could a mere child know of fear so great that she must run across two countries to escape it?

"Polly," she replied blithely, not looking at him again.

"Polly," he repeated with distaste. "I knew a sailor once who named his parrot that. It does not suit you. Wouldn't you rather choose something more interesting?"

The girl looked as if she might hit him. Eyeing him, she thought better of it. "Fiona," she tried carefully. "Fiona MacOwen."

"Fey-onah?" he pronounced with the proper Irish accent. "A

foyne old Irish name," he agreed with a grin. "I like it, though I think you ought to be a foot taller and much more mysterious to wear it. A red-headed cherub is more like a Molly than a Fiona."

She did hit him then, smacking his arm out from under him so he tumbled over backward into the smelly hay. O'Toole emerged laughing, his tall hat lost in the stack, and wisps of straw stuck in his hair.

"I'm that destroyed, I am!" he cried cheerfully, patting through the hay for his hat. "Taken down by a mere female. And a beggarly one at that. I'll never live down the shame."

Fiona smiled, and appearing less prepared to bolt, she sat with him as they let the fine sun seep into their bones.

The farm wagon turned from the main highway onto a private road, and Michael watched as his companion observed the rolling lawn with interest. Well-fed cattle roamed amid thick-wooled sheep ready for shearing. Stately oaks lined the gravel-paved drive. Her eyes widened when she saw the huge ridged mound the English ridiculously called a ha-ha separating the cattle from the main lawn, and she glanced over her shoulder at the "farm house" they approached.

It sprawled across the horizon, towering four stories high and sporting turrets, minarets, and a huge dome over the main block of the mansion.

She glanced at the flagpole above the entrance and sighed with relief, indicating she knew the lack of flag meant that the lord wasn't home.

Then she turned and socked O'Toole firmly in his middle with all the strength she possessed.

Three

Rubbing his midriff and grinning, Michael slipped down Anglesey's interior marble staircase. He hadn't expected interference from the servants when he'd brought the brat in the back way and ordered them to outfit her appropriately. He made it a point to know the servants in any place he visited, and Lady Blanche's servants in particular. They looked after her like the parents she didn't have, and they understood that Michael had the lady's best interests at heart. Of course, they didn't understand Fiona's presence, but that wasn't his immediate concern.

His immediate concern was the Lady Blanche herself. He was a trifle nervous about facing her after all this time. But if anyone could help him pry information out of his obstinate stray, Blanche could. They'd shared mischief in the past. He hoped she would enjoy a little adventure.

From the direction of the estate office drifted the lilting voice Michael remembered with such pleasure. "No, Beamis, I will not sell the Wilmington acreage. Did you not hear me clearly the first time?"

Michael frowned. He'd never heard the lady's voice raised in anger before. He distinctly remembered her as mild-mannered and ever courteous.

"But Lady Blanche, it is naught but rock and wood and of no use to anyone at all but poachers, His Grace said."

"You may remind the duke that the acreage is mine to do with as I wish, and I do not wish to sell it."

Michael hesitated, not wanting to interfere in a business discussion, but all his protective instincts clamored for him to halt the harassment of a lady in the name of her noble cousin. The intrusion of a third voice caused him further pause.

"My lady, we could use the proceeds from the sale for expanding the mine in Cornwall, as we discussed earlier. Your grandfather would have."

"I am not my grandfather, Barnaby! I have reason to keep the acreage and reason for not expanding the mine, and no need for explaining either. If you can do nothing better than badger me with the wishes of yourselves or my cousin or my grandfather with no care to what I want, than I shall be better off without the lot of you!"

Astonished, Michael presented himself at the office door. Two obviously harassed men, one in country tweed and the other in tradesman's drab, stood hats in hands before a wide desk. Behind the desk sat the dainty woman Michael remembered well.

Wisps of sunny hair drifted from her coiffeur, framing sky blue eyes. But the rounded cheeks he'd once admired had reddened into drawn, angry patches, and the blue eyes appeared a glacial gray as she glared at her steward and man of business. Rose lips formed a humorless line above a small chin tilted in defiance. Michael advanced into the room. "Why don't you just kick them in the balls and get it over with, my dear lady?" he asked with good cheer. "Men deal with physical pain much more stoically."

* * *

The startling appearance of her knight in tarnished armor dashed all thought of business out of Blanche's head. *Michael!* After almost two years, the wretched O'Toole dared to sweep back into her life as if he'd left only yesterday. She stifled an urge to dive over the desk and scratch his laughing eyes out.

He was more devastatingly handsome than she remembered. The years had sculpted his features into sharp cheekbones and lean jaw. Only the absurdity of his gloriously auburn hair and the laughing crinkle of his eyes softened his harsh features. She cast a quick glance at the breadth of strong shoulders she remembered too well, then forced herself to look away.

His ribald remark had left her men of business gaping with horror, but Blanche rose to his provocation. "Shall I take a pistol ball to your hide and discover the truth of that, O'Toole?"

Undeterred, Michael swept around the desk, produced a nosegay from his pocket, and flourished it before kissing the scar along her hairline. "Pistols at dawn, if you require, but I'd much rather take one to Neville than your dainty self."

He gestured toward their audience. "Wouldn't it be much simpler to just tell the gentlemen that you prefer feeding the poachers than letting your neighbors set traps for them? And I suppose the working conditions in the mine have deteriorated again to the point that you must visit the foreman and cut off his head before you give him one more ha'penny?"

"O'Toole, will you get away from me with your blarney and take these blasted flowers and shove them back in my garden where they belong?" Refusing to fall for Michael's charms as she so stupidly had once before, Blanche glared at their gaping audience. "You're both dismissed, and you may take this layabout with you when you go."

With that, she rose from her chair and glided toward the escape of her private apartments behind the public office.

Before the two burly men could manhandle him out the door, Michael called after her. "If I leave, you'll have to look after Fiona. I'm afraid she's a bit of a handful, but she's too far from home to return now!"

Blanche halted with her hand on the door to freedom. "Fiona? One of your strays, I presume?" she asked tartly.

He grinned. "Of course."

Unconsciously, she raised fingers to a brow knitted with the pain of this day and too many others like it. "Leave him, Beamis. I may as well deal with one more nodcock before this day's over."

Intelligently, the beefy steward dropped Michael's arm.

Michael waited until the two men closed the door behind them before speaking. "We meet again, my lady."

"It's been what? Two years?" she asked wearily. "And you just pop in and act as if it were yesterday. Who the devil is Fiona and what am I supposed to do with her?"

Michael rolled his shoulders beneath the ill-fitting frock coat. He knew he wasn't a careless person. He'd looked after the duke's wealthy granddaughter at a time when he'd thought she needed it, as Fiona did now. Of course, unlike his usual strays and orphans, Lady Blanche had any number of people who could have looked after her, but she'd been vulnerable after the fire that had almost taken her life. She couldn't trust anyone else back then, but she'd trusted him. And then, when she hadn't needed him anymore, he'd moved on.

He hadn't forgotten her, but he'd rather thought a titled lady would have forgotten him. But oddly enough, she seemed to be accusing him of neglect.

"I'm not entirely certain what Fiona is quite yet. I thought you might help me," he answered honestly, having no other reply.

"As if I have nothing else better to do," Blanche answered with bitterness. "Why bring her here? Surely you have any number of other women to whom you could take her."

For the first time in memory, Michael's instincts failed him. She possessed every treasure known to mankind: beauty, wealth, intelligence, the sunniest nature he'd ever been blessed to know. What had happened in the two years since he'd seen her last?

"I could take her to Gavin and Dillian, I suppose, but they're so wrapped up in the new addition to the family and the renovation of their mansion that I didn't like disturbing them. I thought you might enjoy a bit of adventure," he admitted. "If not, then I'll take her into London myself. She's a bit nervous about traveling with a strange man, so I've pretended to believe she's a boy until we arrived. She's utterly terrified of something, and I'm afraid she'll bolt now I've exposed her disguise."

"Tell me, O'Toole, do you make it a practice of rescuing every helpless female who crosses your path?"

"I thought you rather enjoyed learning to play hide-and-seek with me in Gavin's ridiculous fortress after the fire. Admittedly, you were never as terrified of your arsonists as you should have been, but you should appreciate the need to help those in trouble. And to answer your question, no, I don't limit my practices exclusively to females," he answered with pretended insouciance.

"Not exclusively females," she murmured, taking in his tattered state of dress.

Michael resisted shifting from one foot to the other beneath her contemptuous glare. He didn't remember her minding his carelessness before. He should have found a starched cravat and a more respectable coat. He knew where Neville kept his wardrobe.

"Do I have a choice?" she asked. "If I remember correctly, you go where you want and do as you please."

He leaned his hip against the sill, crossed his arms, and offered a bland smile. "I think you are in need of a little reprieve from your duties, my lady. A court jester is just the solution. Why don't you call for a nice cup of tea, and I'll bring Fiona to you?" He watched her waver.

"I'll be in the gold sitting room. Bring her there. And see if one of

Neville's coats won't fit you better. If they see you looking like that, the maids will think you a chimney sweep."

She swept out, apparently meaning to leave him feeling even smaller than before. Instead, Michael rubbed his jaw. Gavin hadn't mentioned anything amiss with his wife's lovely cousin, but then Gavin wasn't inclined to notice anything but his fields. Well, he had nothing better to do than dig to the bottom of the mystery while resolving Fiona's problems.

* * *

Blanche fought back the urge to cry as she gazed out on the lawn below. She had always considered tears a highly impractical solution and despised the vaporish maidens who gave into them.

She supposed she really didn't have a problem in the general run of things. She knew perfectly well that within a short walk lived people who struggled every minute of their lives just to put food into their mouths. Others fought terrible illnesses or barely survived with crippled or missing limbs. Napoleon's wars had destroyed so much. She had nothing to complain about other than too much wealth, too little respect, and an empty future bereft of love, family, or any of the things that gave life true meaning.

Michael couldn't know how much those few weeks after the fire had meant to her. He'd taken care of her as her family never had, taught her to play, and to protect herself. She'd never practiced deception in her foolish life until Michael had showed her how to hide in clear sight.

Blanche hadn't heard Michael enter, but she knew when he had. O'Toole's sudden appearance worsened her melancholy. Sometimes, she wasn't quite certain he was human. He had the most amazing way of knowing exactly what she thought and felt. Only Michael didn't offer comforting words and platitudes like everyone else. No, Michael tended to hurl things if she was angry, or twirl things in the air to make her smile, or kiss her when she needed to know she was still attractive. He meant nothing by any of it.

Blanche turned and watched as Michael finished pulling what looked like the Anglesey emeralds out of the ear of a petite waif wearing an old gown she'd given her maid. Blanche couldn't decide whether she should be more amazed at seeing the emeralds, which she'd thought locked in a box in her room, or at the laughing child/woman who so resembled Michael. She should scold him for playing fast and loose with her valuables, but the child held her fascination.

Not once did she think that a man who could rifle her jewelry box might help himself to more than the gems. Michael's eccentric propensities expanded with the years, but never had he harmed a friend. Blanche suspected he skirted the law with frequency, but only in what he considered the best of causes. Of course, should he decide someone else needed her emeralds more than she did, he was quite capable of rearranging her wealth to suit his Robin Hood idea of justice.

But she could almost read his mind when she saw the child who looked so like him. He was hoping he'd found family. A lump caught in her throat. "I trust the necklace will magically return to the box in the same way it appeared?"

"Repetition is so boring," Michael answered as he fastened the jewels around her throat.

He wasn't as tall as his brother, but his proximity unnerved her. She had forgotten what his skilled hands felt like against her skin.

"Baubles like these are meant for admiring, not keeping in darkness. There, now you look like a duchess." He stepped back to admire his handiwork.

"I am not a duchess. Will you please make the introductions?" Recovering her composure, Blanche nodded at the girl hiding behind him.

"Lady Blanche, Fiona MacOwen, Catholic, Irish, and if I do not mistake, a lass in dire need of a protector. Shall we give her to Neville?"

That would serve the damned duke right, but if Blanche read the excitement in Michael's eyes correctly, the protector he had in mind was himself, curse his Robin Hood hide.

Four

Not certain she hid her irritation well, Blanche gestured for Miss MacOwen to take a seat. She wished she could judge the girl's age, but the cynical green eyes didn't match the childishly smooth complexion, and the ill-fitting gown with the high, round neckline revealed nothing of her figure other than her lack of stature. She could be anywhere from fifteen to thirty.

"Now, Miss MacOwen, perhaps you would tell Lady Blanche why you thought to make London on your own," Michael suggested as he bounced on the balls of his feet. His restlessness seldom allowed him to alight anywhere. Blanche knew he shoved his fists in his pockets to keep from lifting the delicate bric-a-brac from the mantel and tossing it into the air. Since some of the figurines were a century old, she was grateful for his restraint.

Miss MacOwen blinked her wide green eyes with deceptive innocence. "I wish to visit my aunt, my lady. I meant no trouble for you or anyone, but Mr. O'Toole insisted we come here first."

Blanche could see the lie in her eyes. She sent Michael a questioning glance. He shrugged his shoulders in reply. Her curiosity demanded satisfaction. "All right, Miss MacOwen, we will endeavor to see you safely to your aunt's. London is no place for a lady on her own. Do you know your aunt's direction?"

Uncertainty flickered in Miss MacOwen's eyes, but she answered firmly enough. "Elton Avenue, just off Half Moon Street, I believe. I'm certain I'll have no difficulty finding it."

Blanche glanced at Michael for confirmation of her suspicions. Half Moon Street was in the Covent Garden area. It contained respectable enough houses, but some of the inhabitants were actresses from the theater, installed in the houses by their wealthy protectors. She had never heard of Elton Avenue, but if it led off Half Moon in the wrong direction, it could easily fall into the notorious slums of Seven Dials. Michael's grim expression confirmed her fears.

"Miss MacOwen, does your aunt expect your arrival?" Blanche

asked carefully. No decent aunt would lure a child to the nefarious confines of Seven Dials.

Miss MacOwen sat back in her chair, crossed her hands in her lap, and stared at Blanche defiantly. "That is unimportant. I must reach my aunt. If you cannot help me, I shall go on my own. I will happily reimburse your maid for the clothing as soon as I am able."

"That won't be necessary. Lily only gave you a gown that didn't look good on herself," Blanche answered wryly. With relief, she noted amusement lighten the girl's expression. Perhaps Miss MacOwen wasn't too thick-headed to realize they meant no harm. "Of course we'll help you. I'll have my coach and driver take you to your aunt as soon as they return. I just sent them off with my cousin, so it might be a day or so. I hope that doesn't matter."

Blanche watched the girl's gaze dart nervously from her to Michael. Michael would know she lied. She owned carriages and horses aplenty. But the longer they kept Miss MacOwen here, the more time they had for investigating this "aunt" and ensuring the girl's safety. Michael now hummed and tossed coins from his pockets into the air, apparently oblivious to their conversation.

Miss MacOwen nodded reluctantly. "Sure, and time is of the essence, my lady, but if you think it best."

"You wouldn't like walking all the way to London wearing boy's clothes and arriving at your aunt's looking like a ragamuffin would you? And that would certainly take as much time as waiting for the coach. It's decided then. Shall you have tea with us?"

Another hour passed before Blanche was able to send Miss MacOwen on a tour of the house with the housekeeper so she could confront Michael alone. She had learned Michael's tendency to disappear when things became complicated or emotions ran high. As Fiona left with the housekeeper, Blanche glared at the intelligent but elusive man immersed in an illustrated history of the Tudors. "Has no one taught you it is rude to read while entertaining guests?"

Michael looked up and in the blink of an eye, removed himself from the sixteenth century to the present. "Fiona isn't a guest. She's a disaster waiting to happen. There's no such thing as Elton Avenue. It's Elton Alley, and I'll not punish your ears with a description of the inhabitants. Suffice it to say, it's not a place for young girls. I'll ride into the city and see if I can find this aunt. I wish you could have pried a name from her."

"Since she's likely lying about the name she's given us, I don't imagine she'd tell the truth about her aunt, either. Did you see her hands? She's gently bred, Michael. They're red and cracked from whatever she's done lately, because they've never been submitted to such treatment before. And she's nervous, so nervous she clung to her teacup to keep from chewing her fingernails. At one point, she even shoved her hands under her to steady them."

"She doesn't have any fingernails left to chew," he said dryly, putting down the book and taking the seat beside Blanche. "I've tried all I know to work her tongue loose, but she keeps close guard on it. I tried ale, but she won't drink the stuff."

Blanche grimaced. "Can't blame her for that. Perhaps some sherry this evening, on top of wine at dinner. How long do you think we can hold her before she leaves on her own?"

"Not long. I'll leave for London this evening. I have the feeling she thinks someone is after her, and she may bolt to protect us from whatever she fears."

Blanche suffered a twinge of alarm, then realizing Michael would never have brought danger here, she calmed enough to answer sensibly. "Surely she must realize she's safe in Anglesey with an army of servants between her and the outside world."

Michael shrugged and idly shredded one of the tea cakes the maid had not yet removed. "Abused children never feel safe. Someone or something has terrified her."

His hostess sat hesitantly upon the gold sofa, her frail gown a bare wisp of material over curves so slender Michael longed to mold them in his hands. He stared down at his hands in incredulity. He'd used them for many things. Other men learned by reading books or listening to lectures, but he learned by touching. He could build a house of bricks and straw, or of jewels and gold. He'd molded clay and dough in his lifetime.

He'd never wasted time giving *thought* to molding breasts. But at the sight of this lady far beyond his limited means, physical desire flooded through him. Hastily, he rose and headed for the door.

"I think she'll talk more freely when we're in private," Blanche said, jarring him back from the dark alleys where his thoughts had strayed.

"That's what I hoped." With door latch safely in hand, he could think more clearly. He had hoped talk might reduce the evidence of his desire, but Blanche drifted closer, and his body reacted accordingly. He opened the door, prepared for escape.

"I'll see what I can do," she said. "We'll have an early supper, and I'll draw her out while you linger in the dining room."

Michael could feel Blanche's quizzical gaze, but he didn't dare meet her eyes. "Talk about her family. Usually, the trouble lies there. I'll check on the horses."

Michael fled the room. Dragging in a deep breath, he took the stairs to the stable. He never shared himself with others, not even Gavin. But with Blanche, it was too easy, like turning his face to the sun and burning it in consequence.

So he saddled a horse and fled into the dusk, leaving Blanche to deal with Fiona on her own. By tomorrow, perhaps he would have learned a few things about Elton Alley and its inhabitants and be better prepared for dealing with Fiona's problems. Nothing would prepare him for dealing with Lady Blanche.

* * *

Blanche wished she knew more curse words when Michael didn't appear for dinner. She knew perfectly well the scoundrel was capable of leaving without a farewell, but she couldn't believe he'd leave her alone with this Irish mystery. Miss MacOwen watched with curiosity as Blanche sent her butler in search of the missing guest.

"Mr. O'Toole tends to forget the time," Blanche explained, keeping a friendly smile on her lips. "I do believe he lives in a world of his own."

Miss MacOwen's cynical look matched her response. "From what I've noticed of Mr. O'Toole, he believes this world *is* his own. Do you know him well?"

Blanche offered her guest a glass of sherry since she felt in need of it herself. To her surprise, the girl accepted it. Perhaps she was a little beyond childhood after all.

"I suppose he's sort of a cousin-in-law," she replied in response to the question. "My cousin is married to his brother. But I can't say that anyone knows him well."

Miss MacOwen nodded in agreement. "He's that much like

Seamus, after all. The resemblance is remarkable. It's that surprising I find it hearing an O'Toole married to English aristocracy. Perhaps I should have visited your foyne country sooner."

Blanche heard the mockery in this speech, but she had no desire to explain O'Toole was the adopted brother of an American and not in the least Irish. Even she didn't understand his masquerade. Michael simply had many names and many appearances.

Nethers, the butler, returned quickly with the announcement that the gentleman had departed earlier in the afternoon. Wishing she could fling her glass into the fireplace and throw a royal tantrum, Blanche managed a polite nod of indifference and gestured toward the doorway to the dining chamber. "Shall we dine, then, Miss MacOwen? It seems we must entertain ourselves this evening."

The girl's eyes had narrowed in suspicion at Nether's announcement. "What does he mean, Mr. O'Toole has departed? I don't mean to be dumped here like a stray dog."

The mocking Irish accent quickly disappeared with the girl's rising ire, Blanche noticed. But she was too angry with O'Toole to take the youngster's bait. "You needn't fear for yourself, Miss MacOwen. Or shall I call you Fiona? You may call me Blanche, if you wish. There's not much point in formality if we're to deal with O'Toole together. The man is infuriating beyond all else, but he'll keep his word. He'll return to take you into the city. He'll just do it at his own time and pace."

"And you endure this?" Fiona asked, following her into the dining room.

Blanche took her time taking a seat and signaling the servants to begin serving while forming an answer. "Does one choose to endure thunderstorms, will-o'wisps, or other acts of nature?" she asked. "They happen. Michael is much the same."

She smiled in satisfaction as Fiona sipped thoughtfully at the excellent wine. She would have the girl talking before dinner ended.

"He is much more forceful than my brother, no doubt," Fiona said. "But he is still a bit of a leprechaun, isn't he? I would never suspect him of being gentry. No wonder I couldn't place him as beggar or actor or any of the other things I thought him."

Blanche tried thinking of Michael as forceful and widened her eyes as she realized the word fit. Back in the days after the fire when she feared everything and everyone, Michael had appeared no more than a laughing ne'er-do-well. But that was the appearance he'd wanted to give her. Now that she could look back on that time, she could see that Michael had been fierce in his protection, forcing even his aristocratic brother into doing his will.

She wasn't certain she liked that realization. She preferred thinking of Michael as a genial companion, one who could make her laugh and think at the same time. Frowning, she stabbed her fork into the delicate sole until it splintered. "Michael would be the first to tell you he isn't gentry. He's not even an O'Toole. And he doesn't claim his brother's name of Lawrence either. Michael is just Michael, as the wind is just the wind. Mostly, he is excessively annoying."

Blanche watched as the footman refilled Fiona's wine glass. "You spoke of a Seamus. Is he your brother? Is he as annoying as Michael?"

"And that's sartin," Fiona muttered. "Men have no heads a'tall, have they? 'Tis like God carved their faces out of trees and stuck them on their necks so they had something to talk through."

Blanche laughed. She couldn't help it. She doubted she had anything at all in common with this young Irish runaway, but they had much the same frame of mind: men were useless pieces of baggage.

"I'll be certain to pass that on to my cousin Neville. He's forever telling me to marry so he may deal with someone sensible. I suppose that means he needs another tree to talk to."

Fiona laughed. For a moment, Fiona was an the attractive, carefree young lady. Shiny copper curls framed her heart-shaped face, emphasizing eyes so much like Michael's it was eerie.

"I like you, my lady. I thought English ladies all stiff and proper and haughty, but I'm after seein' it's silly of me to make such generalizations. I'm thanking you for taking me in, but how do you know I'll not be robbing you blind during the night?"

Blanche signaled for the next remove. "I would say because Michael trusts you, but perhaps it is more practical to answer that you would fall over a dozen footmen before you could get out the door. Now let us find more pleasant topics. Is your brother younger or older than you are?"

Fiona grimaced. "Seamus is not a more pleasant topic. He is

years older in age, but years younger in mind. He thinks he can single-handedly save all of Ireland and return our lands to what they ought to be. Fool that he is, he believes the tales our uncle told us as children, of Irish earls and gallant knights and glory days gone by. He cannot understand that the past is dead, that we must look ahead and carve out a future instead."

Blanche hadn't been prepared for what sounded suspiciously like a political diatribe. She knew very little about Irish politics other than that the Irish had always caused trouble and that Catholics were unfairly despised by many. She had enough to deal with here in England without exploring the problems of Ireland, but it seemed as if she must listen if she were to help Michael learn more of his little stray.

"Glory can put bread in your mouths if it represents the glory of wealth or power," she said dryly. "We have enough of that thinking here. Does your brother attend school?"

Fiona sent her a bitter glance. "Hardly. But that is of little account now. When do you expect your coach's return?"

"That depends on too many things for me to answer, but I should hope by sometime tomorrow. Perhaps Michael seeks other transportation. If your aunt does not expect you, can there be any reason to hurry?" Blanche couldn't tell if two glasses of wine and a glass of sherry would loosen the girl's tongue sufficiently, but she signaled for more in precaution.

"The sooner I stop this, the sooner I can keep Seamus out of it. Each day brings us closer to destruction. As much as I despise your bloody English parliament, I would not see them..." Fiona abruptly shoved her chair from the table. "You must excuse me, my lady. I do not feel well." She fled from the room.

Startled by the hasty departure, Blanche stared at the grandiose doors through which her guest had flown. She would not see them what? The words sounded ominous.

She pushed back her chair and gestured to one of the footmen. "Send my maid to look after Miss MacOwen. And have tea sent into the salon."

In the salon, Blanche picked up the novel she'd been reading. She sipped her tea and tried to concentrate, but her mood wasn't on Sir Walter Scott's romantic fantasies. She wanted fantasies of her own. Babies like Dillian's. She thought she might make a good mother, certainly a better mother than an estate administrator.

Perhaps she *should* marry Neville. He could give her children, although she didn't like considering the act that would create those children with him. Dillian had explained the marriage bed with reference to soulful communication. Blanche couldn't fool herself into believing she had any soulful communication with Neville. Not like she had with Michael.

That thought so startled her that she dropped the book in her lap. *Michael?*

Rising, Blanche paced the rug just as Michael was wont to do, although she kept a careful distance from the fire. She'd been kissed by other men, but only that one kiss bestowed by Michael lingered in her memory. Could she possibly persuade him to kiss her again?

And what then? What if Michael aroused her as no one else did? That thought terrified her as much as the fire. Michael was not husband material. She wanted a home and family. Michael would go insane trapped by four walls and the enormous responsibilities of estate and family.

Sighing, she set aside the sherry. He didn't pursue her onto private balconies or into cozy mazes as her other suitors did. He didn't even stay to dinner when invited, the obstinate wretch.

Five

Clad once more in his baggy, frayed frock coat, Michael whistled his way through a London spring dusk. Coal fumes choked the moisture-laden air, but the hint of warm breezes carried laughter through lighted windows and lured strollers out to idle in the streets or sit on doorsteps. Michael didn't waste his time judging their habits any more than he wasted time judging his own. He was here to refresh his memory of Elton Alley. The fact that he should be sitting down to dinner with two lovely women had no relevance.

A painted woman called seductively from a doorway. Michael tipped his tall hat in greeting, gave her a quick, appreciative smile, and continued on his way. It annoyed him that he felt no tug of desire for a half-naked, obviously willing woman when he could scarcely look at a chaste lady like Blanche without feeling the pangs of lust. God had seen fit to play many jokes on him, but this one bothered him the most.

He had nothing against women. He had idly contemplated marrying someday should he find a woman willing to accept his eccentricities and vagabond life. He was more than a little jealous of his brother's rapport with his wife. But he could never support a woman like Blanche, or even treat her as she deserved. So why couldn't he find a more affordable woman to his liking?

His solemn vow to never chance leaving a woman with a child he'd never know ensured that he'd never be satisfied unless he married.

That was neither here nor there. He'd learned to walk through this world of woe without railing constantly at those things he could not change. He knew his limits. He couldn't have Blanche, but he could work his way through Elton Alley looking for any respectable creature resembling Fiona's aunt. The sooner he saw Fiona settled, the faster he could take himself from temptation. He didn't see much hope in it, but he could try.

He chatted with a ragged urchin selling wilting snowdrops obviously recently dug from someone's garden. The girl gave him a gap-toothed grin and in nearly incomprehensible English denied any knowledge of an Irish female living in these parts. Michael spun her a coin, and she dropped a pretty curtsy in return.

Still whistling, Michael filched a pocket watch from a drunken young lordling staggering from the doorway of his mistress. A large gold button disappeared from the coat tails of a liveried footman hurrying through the street to set up an assignation for his employer. A reticule of coins slipped from the pocket of a self-important old woman wearing the wig and copious skirts of a previous era. Michael knew her species well. It was her sort who trapped innocent young women into a profession that would ruin them.

Feeling no guilt for his depredations, he juggled his acquisitions as he sauntered through the narrow, crowded alley. No fancy gas lamps illuminated this corner of the world's wealthiest city. The occasional glitter of a linkboy's lantern or weak candlelight from a window provided all the illumination he needed to assess the inhabitants.

He lingered on a corner, juggling his wealth for all to see, and several ladies of the evening watched him. He grinned, and they called sultry comments. A coin dropped from the reticule he juggled, and he flung it in their direction, sending them in a laughing sprawl to catch it. Ultimately, they had no answers to his questions either.

Not until he reached the narrowest, darkest stretch of the lane did Michael find any clue to what he sought. By this time, he'd distributed his ill-gotten goods to various street urchins and young prostitutes who needed the gold more than the previous owners. None of them knew of the Irish woman. He hoped they would use the coins for food instead of gin, but he knew better than to ask. With his hands in his empty pockets, he traversed the most dangerous part of the street, whistling an Irish ditty.

"Seamus! Damn you, is it mad you are, coming here like this? Get your feckin' arse inside this minute." A rough hand grabbed Michael's shirt collar, shoving him toward an unlit doorway.

His captor smelled of ale, unwashed sweat, and mutton grease, Michael noted as he bounced off the solid door of the dilapidated brick residence. Without turning, he knew the man was broader and heavier than himself, with fists like small hams. Untroubled,

Michael dropped to his palms on the top step and shoved off with a quick flip. He landed neatly on the street at his attacker's side.

"Beg pardon, my good sir, but I believe you've mistaken me for someone else," he said in his prosiest tones. "My friends don't generally treat me like a sack of flour." Deftly, he brushed at his nearly trampled hat and returned it to his head, sizing up his opponent as he did so. The man was taller and had weight but no muscle on his side. Fully confident of his greater strength, Michael didn't bother seeking a weapon.

"Seamus, what the hell...." The burly man squinted in the poor light, seeking a better look at his captive. "What've ye done to yerself, lad?"

"Obviously found better companions," Michael responded cheerily, holding out his hand. "Michael O'Toole at your service, sir. May I help you find someone?" Was it possible if he looked like Fiona, he might also look like another member of the family?

The brute shook his head in confusion. "If ye ain't Seamus, did Seamus send ye? We need the gilt or all's lost."

A blowzy woman appeared in the window above them. Leaning out, she called, "Who're you talking to, Rob? Come on in now, the others are waiting."

The reddish color of her hair had no true resemblance to Fiona's naturally copper curls. Although not yet past her prime, this woman possessed the pasty gray coloring of unhealthy living. Her dull eyes focused on Michael.

"Seamus? Are you out of your mind, boy? Get yourself in here immediately."

She might have passed for pretty in a better light. Michael politely tipped his hat. "Michael O'Toole at your service. May I have the pleasure of your acquaintance?"

The woman gave his bulky companion a quizzical look. "Is he drunk?"

The man heaved his shoulders in a shrug. "Not the lad. Has he got some relation?"

When the woman looked puzzled, Michael had a good idea what would follow next. Grabbing his high-crowned hat, he ducked the man's outstretched hand. "I assure you, my good people, my name is not Seamus, and I'm not the least bit Irish. But I have come in search of a respectable lady who might go by the name of

MacOwen. Do you know aught of her?"

Now they both looked puzzled, and Michael sighed in resignation. Fiona had lied about her name or they'd recognize it.

If they were up to no good, as he suspected, they'd not be happy with his spying. The bloke still foolishly thought he had the upper hand. Time to disillusion him. With a cheerful grin, Michael bowed. "Sure and it's glad I am to make the acquaintance of both of ye. I'll be after seein' ye now."

And with that mocking speech he took to his heels even before the bully's roar of rage echoed down the alley.

Michael had no trouble darting in and out of the crowd, leaping over outstretched legs, dodging trash heaps, and merrily begging pardon as he leapt past the skirts of two soiled doves engaged in a loud dispute. The bulky man chasing after him had no such luck. Michael could hear him crashing into bins and tripping over deliberately positioned little feet. He'd salted the street well with his coins. The recipients would amuse themselves by not letting him come to any immediate harm.

Reaching the wider arena of Covent Garden, Michael slowed his pace, removing his hat and coat as he snaked through the crowd. Disappearing into a used clothing stall, he emerged a minute later wearing a loose smock and a cloth cap. As his pursuer shoved past, looking angrily from side to side, Michael whistled down another alley.

* * *

After a restless night during which she'd posted footmen at all the doors as a precaution against uncertainty, Blanche wearily descended the stairs to the breakfast parlor. Garbed in one of Neville's frock coats, Michael was already there. He greeted her with a bow and handed her a plate prepared with her favorite selections. He would make a splendid footman, but a perfectly wretched employee, she observed, as he took the seat at her elbow and returned to the paper he'd discarded with her arrival.

"How long do you think it would take for anyone to miss you should I shoot you between the eyes and bury your body in the garden?" she asked while sipping her coffee and eyeing the bow window that looked out over the garden she had in mind.

Without putting down his newssheet, Michael caught her fingers and pressed them to his lips, rubbing at her knuckles as he finished perusing the article that held his interest. The shiver of his touch traveled up her arm, tingling her elbow and all parts beyond. He laid the sheet aside and, freeing her hand, produced the smile that always melted her to her toes.

"Gavin would briefly wonder why I did not appear with some outrageous gift for his birthday. Dillian might put her head together with that irksome Cousin Marian and decide I haven't annoyed either of them lately and wonder if I've set up a mistress. You, my lady, would roast the devil out of them all until they admitted they hadn't seen me in ages, at which point they would immediately turn your garden upside down in search of my remains. Either that, or they'd just mount a headstone and save themselves the trouble."

Blanche fought back a laugh. Part of Michael's charm was that he wasn't insensible to his vexatious ways and didn't deliberately set out to annoy those who loved him. He just had very odd priorities.

"I don't suppose you would save me the mess and bother and just climb into that hole if I had the gardener dig one, would you? I promise you a very fine headstone."

He grinned and tilted her heavily sugared coffee to her lips. "A little more sweetening is needed, I believe. I won't get far with you in this humor."

Blanche snatched the cup from him and watched over the rim as she sipped. Michael had acquired a respectable cravat and a morning coat of bottle green kerseymere from Neville's wardrobe. His features were almost too strong for handsomeness. Unlike many redheads, he had no freckles, and his skin had weathered to a light brown she found more attractive than the pallor of most gentlemen. Deep-set eyes of laughing green watched her in a way that made her feel as if he saw right into her mind, which created a dangerous hum in her lower parts.

The sensuous fullness of his lower lip caught her interest, and she remembered that she wanted to know his kiss again.

Michael hastily stood up and poured himself a cup of coffee. "Did you sleep well?" he asked with seeming nonchalance.

His abrupt retreat startled Blanche. Had her thoughts been so very obvious? Hiding her embarrassment, she pursued a more important topic. "That's not important. Did you find Fiona's aunt?"

He returned to the table bearing a steaming cup. "I learned that she deals with dangerous people and knows nothing of the name MacOwen, providing the creature I uncovered was her aunt. Seems she thinks I resemble someone named Seamus."

"Her brother," Blanche admitted. "She gave me the name last night. Maybe we should just let her go. She could be a criminal of some sort."

"Can you really think so?" Michael chided. "Or is it just more convenient?"

Blanche poked at her sausage. "You can't always be right."

"Just take my word that I've had enough experience to know when a child is in trouble. This one's in over her head. What else did you learn of her last night?"

"That her brother's in trouble and she's in over her head," she said grudgingly. "But she's too bright to let me pry out more. She knew when she'd said too much and fled the room."

Michael whistled softly and drank half his coffee before replying. "I don't suppose she gave details. It's a pity we can't just tie people up and prevent them from hurting themselves until they see sense. What do we do now?"

Bemused that he actually asked her opinion, Blanche watched him warily. He seemed perfectly sincere. All the air left her lungs when he raised troubled eyes to meet hers. She desperately longed to be useful.

"Fiona gave me no details of her trouble. We could try taking her into London," she suggested. "Perhaps stay at my townhouse. Then we can take a carriage and footmen with us as far as Half Moon Street. How far can we take a carriage into Elton Alley?"

"Not far," he admitted. "It's a medieval cow path. I don't want you anywhere near the place. We'll travel in daylight with several husky footmen. I might call on Gavin's relations to accompany us. I don't know that I dare show my face." He grinned. "I had a bit of a ruckus with one of the fellows last night. He'll remember me."

Alarm shot through her. "You weren't hurt?"

He shrugged. "Not really. I wanted to draw them out and I did. Unfortunately, I apparently look too much like the lady's brother. They'll remember me no matter how I disguise myself. Do you think you could persuade her to send a card around to her aunt and wait for a reply?"

"We might try. Fiona's scared. She might agree if she thinks she's safe. The trick is persuading her to trust us. I don't think she's accustomed to trusting."

Michael frowned at his empty cup. "No, I don't think so, either. I wish she would give us her real name. I'd like to find her family."

Blanche signaled a footman. "Send my maid for Miss MacOwen. And tell her we'll leave for London shortly."

The footman disappeared down the narrow servants' corridor.

When she turned back to her plate, Michael asked abruptly, "Why haven't you married Neville yet?"

Blanche's heart skipped. Disconcerted, she looked away from his all-too discerning gaze and stared out the window again, wishing for some sight of nodding daffodil heads to distract her. "I see no purpose in it. We grew up together. It would be much like marrying a brother. I don't think I shall marry. Men are too much of a nuisance, and I enjoy doing as I will."

"No, you don't," he said. "You're not like Gavin's dragon lady. You want someone to look after you, someone you can care for in return. You've never had a proper family, and you want one."

Tears gathered in Blanche's eyes. Setting her chin, she glared at him. "I am not some helpless scatterwit who needs a caretaker, thank you. I'll have you know—"

The footman interrupted, returning with Blanche's maid in a panic. "Oh, my lady! She was asleep just moments ago, I assure you, ma'am. I checked on her myself. And then when she wasn't there, I thought she had come down to join you. I've sent Brown looking for her. Mayhap she became lost in the corridor?"

Before Blanche could reply, Michael rose and strode for the front hall.

With resignation, Blanche nodded to the maid. "Have the house and grounds searched, and check to see if anything is missing. I'm quite certain she's not lost." Rising, she followed Michael up the stairs, knowing perfectly well what they would find. Or wouldn't, as the case might be.

If she was anything like Michael at all, Fiona had presumably overheard their conversation. And like Michael, she'd escaped like a wisp on a breeze at the first sign of confrontation.

Six

Blanche examined Fiona's note for the hundredth time. "Can Parliament be made to close early? What can it possibly mean?" Nothing good, but she knew that.

"She cannot get far on foot, my lady. We will find her," Michael said reassuringly as Blanche paced the drawing room.

"It has been hours and no one has seen her! What if she has been abducted? What if someone came in this house and stole her away? She's little more than a child, Michael! I promised her safety." Blanche strode once more to the windows overlooking the carriage drive.

"Do you always hold yourself responsible for the acts of others?" he asked dryly. "The little brat took herself off. She didn't even take your maid's gown. And if your men can't find her on the road, I know where to look in town."

Blanche swung around and stared at him. Michael spun a walking stick of unknown origins between his fingers. In Neville's tailored coat, he looked too damned much like a gentleman, except for his glare. She wouldn't want to be Fiona when he found her.

"And what of that note?" she asked. "She said something of the sort last night, something about despising the men in Parliament but not wanting anything disastrous to come of it. Is she insane?"

"No, frightened out of her mind, possibly, but not insane. Parliament can take care of itself. I doubt our Fiona can say the same." He looked grim. "Let's not argue now, my lady. I'll take one of your horses and search the village. Even if she found a ride, she cannot have gone far. It's only been a few hours."

"With a good horse she could be in London in a few hours! I'm going with you. I'll have Nethers call my carriage around." Blanche tugged the bell rope.

"You will do no such fool thing," he exclaimed. "It is best if you stay where your men can report to you. There's no need for your haring off across the countryside."

"My men may report to Nethers. I know the people here,

O'Toole. They trust me. They'll confide in me if in no one else."
Striding back and forth, more confident now that she had a
direction, Blanche ignored Michael's furious expression.

"You are making a mountain out of a molehill," he declared.
"The chit isn't worth your time. Go argue with your steward and
keep your man of business from exploiting miners. That is of more
importance than a runaway."

"She's a child!" Blanche cried. "An unprotected, terrified child
heading for a city she doesn't know. What do you think I am that
you assume I would so heartlessly dismiss her?"

"I think you scarce older than she and less able to protect
yourself," he said dryly.

Furious, Blanche glanced up at the stoic butler waiting in the
doorway. "Have them fetch my carriage 'round, Nethers. I shall be
going into the village, and then following the London road." As the
butler departed, she vented her fury on her antagonist. "I daresay I
have a good many more years of experience than Miss MacOwen,
and I am not frightened." With that, she strode out of the room.

She showed no surprise half an hour later as she left the house to
enter her carriage and found Michael waiting with one of her best
geldings. She had traversed the road to London a million times in
her life. She didn't fear traveling alone. She hadn't asked for his
company.

She gave him no greeting and he returned the favor. He merely
mounted the horse as the carriage door closed behind her. She
couldn't recall ever seeing O'Toole on horseback. Actually, she
couldn't recall ever seeing him arrive or depart. He just appeared
and disappeared like the songbirds. She cast a surreptitious look in
his direction as the carriage rolled down the drive. He handled the
horse as well as any gentleman. Aware that she was admiring the
straight set of his back and the width of his shoulders, she sat back
and glared at the empty seat opposite.

She had the carriage stop in the village so she might climb out
and speak with the shopkeepers and housewives. She thought it
more likely that Fiona had taken to the fields, but her footmen and
grooms hadn't found a farmer who admitted seeing her. Perhaps
the child had boldly come into town looking for a ride.

Too small to boast a coaching inn, the village possessed one main
street of shops and a square of sorts where cattle grazed. Leaving

the carriage near the parsonage, Blanche began with the first shop and worked her way down the street. Michael left his horse grazing with the cattle and roamed idly in and out of the shops and alleys as she methodically worked her way through town.

She finally struck luck while talking with an elderly widow. The woman nodded her capped head. "Knew no good could come of them scoundrels sneaking about. Saw them when I milked Bossie this morn. They slinked back into the shadows, they did, but I knew they was up to no good. Told Melinda about them, but she didn't pay me no mind. Them young 'uns of hers got the croup and she can't attend to nothing else."

"What kind of scoundrels, Mrs. Blake? Did you get a good look at them?"

"City scoundrels is all I can say. They don't belong hereabouts. Big one had a cap pulled down, so I couldn't see more than that. My eyes ain't what they used to be."

"Where did you see them, Mrs. Blake? On the square?" If the widow had been milking the cow, it would have been too early for her to have seen Miss MacOwen. According to the maid, Fiona had been asleep when Blanche came down for breakfast. But the village seldom saw strangers.

"Over by the churchyard, they was. Vicar keeps that empty carriage house of his open. Mind you, I've told him time and again it's an invitation for trouble, but he thinks it's an inn for those down on their luck. Says the Lord was born in a stable, and he could do no less than offer his for others in need."

Blanche sympathized with the vicar's generosity, but she feared Mrs. Blake had the right of it. That empty carriage house would be an ideal hiding place. No one ever used it.

Seeing Michael step from the dim interior of the blacksmith shop, she reluctantly signaled him. She wasn't so foolish as to search the carriage house on her own.

"Mrs. Blake says she saw two strangers near the vicar's carriage house this morning. Do you think they may still be there?" she asked as Michael joined her. He'd removed his high-crowned hat, and the sun glinted off his thick locks, making them appear nearly as copper as Fiona's. Blanche struggled to breathe evenly.

"If not, they may have left clues," Michael answered. "I'll take your driver and search the place. It's possible someone followed me, but not likely."

He strode off in the direction of the carriage and the parsonage, leaving Blanche to thank Mrs. Blake and hurry after him. She wanted to curse Michael for his ungentlemanly behavior, but she much preferred a man of action. She just wished he wouldn't ignore her so completely when he acted.

Her driver had unhitched the horses from the carriage near the water trough on the square. At Blanche's signal, the driver led his horses across the grassy square to meet her and Michael. Holding her skirts, she was hurrying to catch up with Michael when he shouted in alarm.

"Get down, man! Cover your head!" Michael yelled, racing toward driver and horses.

Frightened, Blanche scanned the scene for the danger as heads popped from doorways all around, everyone eager for a little excitement to stir their day. The coachman dove for cover. And then Blanche saw what Michael had seen first: a snake of fire sizzling toward the underside of the carriage on the far side of the square.

Her first instinct cried for water to douse the flames as Michael raced toward the horses. Michael grabbed the bridles from the coachman and ran with them down the street.

The carriage exploded in a giant fireball.

Screaming, Blanche stood paralyzed in the middle of the street. In her mind, the conflagration roared around her, scorching her hair, blinding her eyes, filling her lungs with breath-stealing smoke. She couldn't bear it. She covered her eyes, screaming and praying for the fire and noise to go away, until reassuring hands caught her arms and shook her.

"Snap out of it, Blanche. It's just a coach. No one's hurt. You're all right. I won't let the fire touch you again."

The words held no meaning, but Michael's arms wrapping around her held her steady. Shaking, she clung to the cool unscorched cloth beneath her fingers.

Michael held her close and rocked her, repeating meaningless phrases until she quieted in the strength of his reassuring embrace.

"Come, let me take you inside. Someone will find you a glass of canary. Just hold on, my lady. It's all right. You're strong. You won't let anyone frighten you that easily."

Michael's words slowly sank in as he led her toward the village bake shop. The cool interior brushed her skin like a refreshing breeze. The fire had not touched her. Her clothing was unburnt. She was safe, just as Michael said. She wanted to cling to Michael's hand, but she'd already made fool enough of herself. She sank into the chair offered and sipped from the glass handed to her. Michael's look of concern vanished beneath his usual insouciance the moment she met his gaze.

"You're all right?" she whispered. "And the coachman?"

"Everyone is all right," he said firmly. "Even the horses. If you'll just sit here a moment, I'll see to everything. I suspect your driver was a trifle shaken and may need some reassurance that he did nothing wrong."

She didn't argue. The coach driver had more need of him than she did. Shame washed through her, and she could not meet the eyes of the concerned villagers. The vicar rushed in, murmuring comforting phrases as he attempted to persuade her from the shop to the safety of his home until she called for a new carriage. Blanche shook her head. She didn't want a new carriage. She wanted to childishly yell that she wanted her old carriage, but she held her tongue as an idea formed in her brain, spinning to conclusions she didn't like.

The driver entered the bake shop, holding his cap against his chest. "There's naught can be done for it, my lady, 'tis blown to bits, it is. They's some as gone to fetch the phaeton. 'Twill be but just a few minutes, my lady. I can't say as I know what happened. I didn't see nuthin'. It was there, and then it 'twasn't. Never saw the like in all my born days."

He would no doubt have rambled on in this fashion, but Blanche had recovered enough to know what she must do. Setting aside the glass of wine, she thanked the proprietor, murmured a few reassuring words to her driver and told him to sit and have a glass of the excellent wine. Then she strode past all her protesting protectors to the street outside.

As she expected, she found Michael crawling around the remains of the demolished vehicle. The horses calmly munched oats someone had provided. Kicking the sole of his boots, Blanche ignored his oath as Michael bumped his head on the underpinning. "What happened?" she demanded.

He slid from beneath the charred wheels, dusted himself off, and stood before answering. Michael wasn't a large man. He didn't tower over her as so many men did, but his chest had been wide and solid when she'd rested against it. And she shouldn't be thinking these things when she wanted to kick him.

"Someone planted gunpowder under the carriage, ran a fuse into the vicar's garden, and set fire to it," he stated bluntly.

The knowledge struck Blanche like a blow, even though she'd mentally prepared for it. "Why?" she asked.

"Neville may wish to wring your neck, but I can't think he would resort to blowing up your carriage," Michael said dryly. "It's not quite his style. Whoever blew it up knew you weren't in it. They just wanted to terrify you. Or slow you down. I don't like thinking I've led you into trouble by bringing Miss MacOwen to your home, but that's the way it looks right now."

Blanche studied his troubled expression. Michael didn't mind lying to suit his cause, but she didn't think he was lying now. "Fiona's in danger. I knew she was. We must find her, Michael."

"*I* must find her. You are going home and locking all the doors and windows and setting guards around the clock."

Two years ago, there had been a time when everyone had feared for her life, rightfully so, since she had almost died. But the villain had been caught and the reason for his villainy no longer existed. She would not return to those horrible days of hiding.

Blanche waved an impatient hand. "That's ridiculous. They don't want me. They want Fiona. If they think I have her, the first place they'll look is Anglesey. I'm going with you."

"You'll do no such thing. You can go to Dillian if you fear Anglesey."

Blanche couldn't remember ever actually arguing with Michael before. He usually avoided arguments by disappearing into the woodwork anytime someone disagreed with him. She supposed he could find no woodwork to hide behind here. His light eyes burned with the fire of determination, but she had no intention of standing around listening to male ultimatums. She would go with Michael, just as Dillian had once gone with Gavin. The idea buoyed her immediately.

"If you will not take me with you, Michael Lawrence O'Toole, I shall take myself. I know where Half Moon Street is as well as you. I'll find Elton Alley easily enough. I can hire Runners and search every house if I wish. I can do anything I blamed well want to. Now what do you think of that?"

"Faith, and I'm after thinking you're needing that caning your faither never gave ye," he mocked. "And I'm knowing just the man to do it."

"You wouldn't lift a gun to a tiger," Blanche answered scornfully. "I'll ask the vicar's wife for a habit and sidesaddle. It won't take me ten minutes. And if you don't wait for me, I'll go on my own. I have no intention of sitting here surrounded by Anglesey crests, waiting for someone to take another shot at me. I can assume a new identity as easily as you. I think I shall be your sister."

Wonderfully enough, no curses rang out over her head as she marched toward the vicarage. Michael never cursed. That was one of the marvelous things about him. Although right about now, his curses might reassure her a great deal more than his silence.

A silent Michael was a dangerous thing. She would best hurry before he devised some devious plan for ridding himself of her company.

Seven

She had the right of it. He couldn't stop her.

Watching morosely from the shadows of the apple orchard, idly fingering the coin that never left the chain at his neck, Michael saw Blanche mount a nag provided by the vicar. She had chosen to disguise herself in a shabby riding outfit, no doubt outgrown by the vicar's plump wife, and a flat cap with a veil for keeping the dust of the road from her eyes.

She appeared more the baker's daughter than aristocrat. But Michael's eyes saw beyond the obvious. Her straight, elegant seat in the saddle spoke of years of training. She had kept her own gloves, and the expensive lambskin clung to long shapely fingers holding the reins with practiced ease. The partial covering of the veil cast a shadow over delicate skin seldom kissed by sun, and did little to disguise the silken blonde locks carefully arranged beneath. Anyone with half an eye could see a duke's granddaughter.

Anyone with half an eye could see her groom, too, Michael snorted to himself. She'd concealed the man in shabby coat and trousers, but he sat his horse with as much confidence as his employer. The village men didn't own horses or know how to ride them. And if she had some funny notion she could play the man as a relation, she had bats in her belfry. The groom's harsh, weathered features, bandy legs, and rough hands belied any such possibility.

The pair stood out like songbirds on a winter's day. Scowling, Michael led his horse through the orchard. He wanted to get on with the business of finding Fiona, but he couldn't leave Blanche exposed and unprotected, not after what had happened today. He felt responsible for the incident, even if he had no proof of any relation between the explosion and Fiona. These were troubled times. He could think of any number of men angry at the wealth of a dukedom. There had been worse incidents throughout England.

Moreover, he couldn't forget the feeling of Blanche trembling and terrified in his arms. He'd once held a shivering and dying baby bird in the palm of his hand. The experience was much the same, except he knew Blanche, knew the brave woman who had rescued a house full of servants before saving herself, knew what it must have taken to reduce her to hysteria. He had a passion for fixing things, people as well as objects. He felt compelled to right wrongs. But with Blanche, it went well beyond that particular obsession. He wanted her whole again because she was the only perfection he had ever found in this world.

He wanted her whole because he couldn't imagine his arms around any other woman. Glumly, Michael accepted that unwelcome piece of knowledge. He had held her, and she had molded perfectly against him, her head bumping just along his chin, her slender waist swaying like a reed between his hands, her soft breasts pushing against his coat, and she aroused him as no other woman could.

He snorted in self-deprecation. Blanche could test the mettle of a monk.

He mounted his horse and followed behind the odd couple. There was no sense in torturing himself. If fate or the gods had any sympathy for him at all, they would arrange to discourage Blanche before she reached the city. A pity he had no confidence in either fate or gods.

She stopped and spoke with every farmer on every wagon, every housewife in every cottage along the road. They all greeted her warmly, spoke to her with deference, and every single one of them reluctantly shook their head in negative response to her questions. They all wanted to help, but none had help to offer.

Michael concluded the little brat had slipped across the fields, found herself a stranger passing through, and rode into town unnoticed in her boy's breeches and coat. For all he knew, Fiona could have stolen a few shillings and caught the mail coach. Someone might have noticed her, but Blanche hadn't seen Fiona in male garb. She wouldn't know how to describe the urchin she appeared.

When they reached a town with a coaching inn, Michael gave up his hidden pursuit and rode boldly into the inn yard behind Blanche and her groom. She gave him a look of annoyance and proceeded to question the ostler without acknowledging Michael's presence. As did everyone else, the ostler knew the Lady Blanche Perceval despite her disguise, and he tried desperately to find answers to please the lady, but he had none.

Michael swung down off his horse beside her. He hid a smile at her blue-eyed glare and doffed his cap at the ostler.

"The child the lady's looking for bears a strong resemblance to myself. She may well have dressed as a boy and covered herself with mud. She's a few inches shorter than my lady here. Would you have noticed her if she joined the mail coach?"

The ostler studied Michael's auburn-haired appearance a moment, scratching his beard stubble as he thought about it. "There's a youngster on the coach this morn, right enough. Didn't get a good look, but the size is right, I reckon. Had a boy through here some weeks ago looked just like you, exceptin' he wasn't so tan colored. Irish, I thought at the time. Didn't speak so fine as yourself."

Michael caught Blanche's arm, warning her to silence. He wanted to immediately jerk his hand away from the shock of electricity at the touch, but his fingers wouldn't let loose. "Did they both take the coach into London?"

"The one this morn did. T'other took a coach away."

Michael produced a coin from his pocket with his free hand and held it out to the fellow. "Thank you, sir, you've been a tremendous help. Where does the outbound London coach go from here?"

"Berkshire next. Don't know where it goes from there."

It didn't matter. There were other inns, other coaches, other directions. A man leaving London for Ireland could take many different roads. Michael couldn't possibly follow all of them, although if the other man who looked like him was Seamus, he'd liked to have followed.

Michael gently steered Blanche toward the inn. "This is as far as you go, my lady. She's on the coach. I'll check at the White Horse when I reach London, but it's a busy place. It's doubtful if anyone will have noticed her. We can just hope she arrived in Elton Alley safely. I'll find her there if that's the case."

"You may take your hand off me and go where you wish, Mr. O'Toole," she replied haughtily. "I shall have a sip of tea and go on to London." She turned a triumphant smile on him. "There isn't a blessed thing you can do about it."

He could cheerfully have wrung her neck. Or kissed her. It was a toss-up between the two. Michael released her arm. "You haven't disguised yourself. Every person on this road knows who you are, knows your direction, and knows who you look for. If the carriage fire was a warning, the ones who set it know you didn't heed it. You are a walking target, my lady. Do you expect your groom to shield you?"

Her glare died, replaced by uncertainty. He took advantage of her momentary silence to continue. "We can do nothing now. We'll hire a post chaise and go on to London. If they're following you, we won't lose them easily. We'd best pretend you have nothing to hide, go directly to a friend's house, and disappear from there."

The look of blatant admiration flaring in Blanche's eyes shook him. She swiftly covered it with suspicion.

"Why can't we go directly to my town house? I could find a disguise much easier there, and I wouldn't have to explain myself."

"If you are being followed, and I see no reason as yet to believe you are, they will expect you to go directly to your own home. They will have men stationed there, and escape will be exceedingly difficult. However, if we stop elsewhere, it will confuse them. If we stop at a modest home, say Cousin Marian's, that will confuse them more. They may fear you're not who they think you are, or that the real Lady Blanche has traded places with her companion, or some such."

He held up his hand to forestall her argument. "Illusions are created simply by doing the unexpected. Cousin Marian can send all her servants out on a lark and go out herself. With people going in all different directions, who will they follow?"

Michael saw the excitement in her eyes, even though she fought to hide it. A good confidence man would see her every thought. He needed to get her somewhere safe and leave her there. He rather thought he might have to tie her to a chair to do so. His self-proclaimed brother Gavin might be capable of tying his ladies to chairs, but Michael couldn't harm a hair of Blanche's head.

"But then where will I go?" she inquired. "I could disguise myself as a kitchen maid, I suppose, and meet you at Elton Alley. But even if we find Fiona, it may not be safe to take her home with us."

"I can just see you as a kitchen maid," Michael said dryly, looking down at the lovely soft skin of the hand she'd removed from her glove. "We might tart you out as an expensive ladybird, but we'd have some difficulty explaining that to Marian."

This conversation had taken too suggestive a turn. Lifting his hand in signal, he ordered the groom to find the lady some tea while he hired the post chaise.

Michael rode beside the carriage rather than join Blanche in the interior. His craving to sit beside her meant that his brain wouldn't work clearly. Just the faint fragrance of her herbal sachet had his pulse beating too fast.

A thick fog rolled in off the sea as they approached the city. The uncertain March light faded early, and Michael frowned at the implications. Even if it was only early afternoon, he couldn't allow Blanche anywhere near Half Moon Street in the fog. He itched with frustration at the responsibility of looking out for someone other than himself.

Michael guided the carriage down the street near Mayfair where Gavin's cousin Marian and her husband lived. They considered him a cousin, too, and he accepted the relationship with gratitude. He'd treated them abominably upon occasion, but family made excuses for family.

Michael swung down from his mount to help Blanche from the carriage. Once she placed her hand in his, he held her hand possessively to help her up the steps, following the groom who knocked at the door. Briefly, her fingers squeezed his and then the door opened and she freed herself.

The footman led them upstairs into Marian's parlor. Michael watched the skirt of Blanche's riding habit sway temptingly as he followed her up the stairs. He tried banishing the image of the legs beneath those heavy skirts, but he'd glimpsed their lovely curves when she'd jumped from the window to escape the fire.

"Michael! Blanche! What a delightful surprise." Marian rose from her seat to greet them. Like all other Lawrences, she possessed a darkly handsome complexion, thick chestnut hair, and sparkling brown eyes. Daughter of a marquess, married to the younger son of an earl, she could have moved in the highest society, but she chose to live in this modest townhouse, on the income her husband earned. Personally, Michael admired them all the more for their ambition.

It also made Marian and her husband, Reginald Montague, the ideal people to help them.

Marian sent him a swift look that said the lack of a chaperone didn't go unnoticed, but she didn't speak the words aloud. She merely hugged Blanche, sent for tea, and took her seat.

"I know perfectly well you didn't come all this way to visit for the mere pleasure of it. Michael has never once entered these portals without some request in mind," Marian said. "But you shall both keep me company and take some tea and talk no more of it until afterward, as advance payment for my cooperation."

Keeping an eye on the street outside, Michael paced the length of the room behind the sofa where the ladies sat. He recognized his cousin's perfume with indifference, but the more subtle temptation of Blanche's sachet drove him to stand as far away as he dared.

Frustrated, Michael jammed his hands into his pockets and wished himself to Hades. Blanche would make a queen look slovenly. Why didn't she just marry the duke and get it over with? They obviously belonged together: the slim, elegant duke with his cool indifference and the graceful, lovely Blanche with her passion for family. She would drag out Neville's better qualities, and Neville could give her the family she craved.

The idea of it drove a stake through Michael's heart. He couldn't eat the sandwiches offered him. The patter of small feet in the hallway outside filled him with immense relief.

"Cousin Michael!' The cheerful, small cry buoyed his hopes, and he grinned as he caught the bundle of energy hurtling toward him.

"Edwina!" Marian cried, scandalized by her daughter's behavior. "We have guests."

Lifting the toddler from the floor, Michael whispered in her ear, "The fairy princess, Lady Blanche, has come to visit, scamp. Make your curtsies, and I will take you for a horsie ride."

Grinning from ear to ear, the toddler planted a wet kiss on his cheek, scrambled from his arms, and ran to stand in front of their guest. Bobbing a wobbly curtsy, she lisped obediently, "Good day to you, Printheth Lady Blanche. Thank you for coming."

Then with a mischievous glint over her shoulder to Michael, she asked, "Is that good? Ride now?"

Even this toddler possessed the Lawrence dark good looks, and Michael felt his heart turn over in his chest at her winsome smile. He wanted a daughter just like her someday. He glanced back at Blanche, then wished he hadn't.

She looked at the child with such longing.

Insane, he muttered to himself. She would forget all about the child as soon as he took Edwina out of the room.

Out of the room.

Laughter once more dancing in his eyes, Michael held out his arms for the toddler. "Come on, scamp, I'll give you a horsie ride back to the nursery where you belong."

Squealing with delight, the child leapt at the offer. Swinging her up in his arms, Michael propped her on his shoulder, neighed at her command, and trotted out of the room in the direction of the nursery and escape.

Eight

Tears formed in Blanche's eyes as she watched Michael cradle the beautiful little girl in his arms. His whole face lit with pleasure as the toddler patted his cheeks and kissed his nose. She had seen many expressions on his face before. Michael didn't always hide his emotions as so many men did, but she'd never seen such love and devotion in his countenance as she saw now.

When they romped out of the room, Blanche couldn't face Marian immediately. She had to gain some control of herself. Her arms ached to hold Edwina. She should visit Dillian and hold her godchild for a little while to still the need. But she couldn't.

If she were to escape Michael's overprotective restraints and find Fiona on her own, she must disguise herself and slip away without endangering Marian or anyone. Michael had once showed her how to slip away...

Blanche gave the open doorway a suspicious glance and inquired urgently, "How far is it to the nursery?"

"Just up the stairs. Why...." Marian's eyes widened. She knew Michael even better than Blanche. Abruptly, she rose from the chair and led the way from the room.

Blanche followed, but she had no illusion about what they would find. Or wouldn't find. The blasted man had done it again.

In the nursery, Edwina rocked on a wooden horse, chattering excitedly to her nursemaid, with no sign of Michael anywhere.

"I shall feed him bells," Blanche declared ominously as she stalked back down the stairway. "I want to hear him clang every time he walks."

Marian giggled. "That is one solution, I suppose. It could be quite embarrassing upon several occasions I can think of, but we shan't mention them." Her laughter rang out at Blanche's puzzled expression, and she covered her mouth to stifle it. "Oh, dear. Dillian will have my head. I really shouldn't say such things in front of an unmarried lady."

Cheeks heating, Blanche swept into the parlor and scanned the street outside She didn't want to imagine Michael in bed with anyone, with or without bells.

"You might as well tell me what our elusive Michael did not. What kind of trouble are the two of you in this time?"

Marian's sensible tone drew Blanche back to the immediate. She wouldn't sit here like a useless turnip waiting for Michael to return. Or not to return, which was the more likely. The last time he'd disappeared, she hadn't seen him for two years.

Turning her back on the fog-shrouded street, Blanche faced her hostess. "A young woman ran away from my home this morning. We believe she is in some danger. Michael has taken it upon himself to go after her, but I believe I have considerably more resources than he does. I want to summon a Runner first. Then I shall call upon my servants for escort. I don't like involving you or your family any further, so I think it best if I'm seen leaving here. Send for my groom, will you?"

Marian frowned. "Michael didn't bring you here so you could go running home as soon as he turned his back. There's more to the story than that. I may deplore his methods, but I usually approve his intent. Let's hear the whole."

* * *

Sitting in the foggy shadows of Elton Alley, disguised in beggar's rags, Michael watched two fashionable fribbles lingering on the corner. The street possessed more than its fair share of actresses, he supposed. These fine fellows could very well be in search of one, but most gentlemen possessed the common sense to know the actress's direction and go straight there, not linger like cork-brained clunches in full view of every light-fingered rogue and dolly in the district.

The arrival of a hired hackney on that same corner stirred his suspicion more. He'd seen the Bow Street Runner—no doubt hired by Blanche—working his way down the street earlier. Michael had chosen this doorway to keep an eye on the blighter. He wished Blanche hadn't been in such a hurry to hire the officer, but from what he'd seen so far, the man knew his job. Michael just hoped he could find Fiona before the inhabitants of the house at the end of the alley noted the Runner's presence and fled. But the two fribbles and the hackney made him suspicious.

Michael buried his head against his arms and silently practiced widening his vocabulary of curses as an outlandishly garbed female descended from the carriage. he had no one but himself to blame. In the days after the fire he'd amused himself and Blanche by teaching her to disguise herself from Neville and society. She'd just carried his lessons a little too far this time.

Hoping he'd imagined the scene, Michael squeezed his eyes closed and opened them again. Even through the thickening fog he could see the scandalously low cut bodice sagging ridiculously over slender curves. A remnant of a different century, the purple satin skirt dragged in the mud, resembling a dressing gown more than any other female garment he recognized. He supposed she'd found it in Cousin Marian's attic, and he cursed Reginald's penchant for collecting antiquities.

He recognized the fops now — two of the foolish suitors who had been dangling after Blanche's wealth years ago. Mostly, they lay about quoting poetry and eating her food. Harmless, but stupid. When they joined her, offering their arms, Michael pulled his hair. Only this pair would be idiotic enough to play act with a lady, endangering her without thought. Blanche's neck was the one needing wringing. The lady was peeved at his escape and thought to teach him a lesson. She had, but it probably wasn't what she intended. Next time, he'd tie her to a chair.

Remaining seated, he leaned against the door behind him, draping his bare wrists over the tattered knees of his trousers as he watched the procession stroll down the alley. Even the usual inhabitants stared in disbelief, not knowing what to make of so lovely a lady in such out-dated dishabille. Her fashionable fribbles possessed the pale features and soft hands of aristocrats, not to mention an air of complete confusion at the noisy filth and chaos around them. He considered shooting them both for not having the brains to haul the lady straight back to a hackney.

Even the Runner blinked as he emerged and saw this marvel drifting up the street. Michael gave the fellow a mark for good sense when he merely continued about his business. Fiona was probably laughing herself silly if she watched from one of the windows above.

While the entire street watched the procession of Blanche and fribbles, a slight figure darted out of the fog to whisper in Michael's ear.

"She says as she's found her aunt and ye're not to worry."

The urchin made as if to dart back from whence he came, but Michael grabbed his coat and jerked him back. The boy didn't look frightened, just irritated that he'd been caught.

"Who said and where?" he demanded.

"She said as ye'd know," the lad declared boldly. "And she ain't there no more."

"And I'm to believe you?" Michael asked. "Do you take me for a fool? I want to see for myself she's all right."

Fear widened the boy's eyes, and he kicked at Michael. "I don't know no more than that. Let me go."

"Take me to where you saw her last." Keeping a tight hold on the boy's coat, Michael caught a skinny wrist with the other hand and rose from the street.

"She's gone to her brother, she says. I ain't knowin' nothin' more."

The boy lashed out with his foot. A cry from the other end of the alley distracted Michael into loosening his hold, and the urchin wriggled free, disappearing into the fog-shrouded dusk.

The growing fracas at the other end of the street kept him from caring. Michael couldn't see well enough through the haze to clearly discern events. He raced to the place where he'd last seen Blanche and her companions. He could find Blanche were he blindfolded and in the dark.

A wailing doxy holding a bundle of rags in her arms blocked Blanche's path. The taller fop admonished the beggar loudly, shaking his expensive walking stick in her face, but the woman knew a good mark when she saw one. She determinedly held her place, pouring forth her tale of woe. The shorter, fatter gentleman tugged on Blanche's elbow, sensibly attempting to turn her around. Blanche behaved as if she didn't know either man existed.

"The landlord threw us out, he did! My poor wee one hasn't eaten in weeks. There's naught for us but crumbs off the street. Her father died serving his country, he did, and this is what we gets in return! Please, my lady, a coin or two to ease our sufferin'. Just enough for the babe. I'll go without, but I can't bear to hear her cries."

Michael scowled at this self-serving nonsense. He might harbor a few idealistic tendencies, but he wasn't blind to reality. He despised the women who fed their filthy habits with the lives of the poor infants they bore. Fed gin from the day they were conceived, the infants had no chance of living long outside the womb. These women knew it and didn't care. They merely used the little inconveniences as sources of income until the babes died. By then, they could sell their bodies again and repeat the cycle.

"She's a thief and a doxy and she hasn't a notion of who the babe's father is," Michael muttered as he sidled up behind Blanche. "Get out of here before she starts a riot, which she will if she doesn't have her gin soon."

Blanche showed no surprise at his appearance. Indeed, she didn't even look at him. Her attention remained on the oddly limp infant in the woman's arms. "I can't leave that child here," she murmured, stark horror marring her features.

"That child is either dead or dying of gin. There's nothing either of us can do to save it. It never had a chance from the moment of its birth. Alcohol runs in its veins instead of blood." Michael grabbed the tall fop's walking stick and swung it at the beggar's skirts when she pressed too close. She let out a wail and jabbered at the top of her lungs, her gesticulations nearly toppling the infant from her arms.

A small crowd had already formed, eager for any kind of entertainment on a soggy night. More arrived to watch as the woman's cries escalated. Michael grabbed Blanche's arm and swung her around, shoving her toward the main street at the end of the alley. "Get out of here now!" He shoved the taller of her two companions in the same direction. "Get her out and don't let her come back or I'll break your head myself."

The fop grabbed Blanche's arm and half dragged her away. The beggar chased after them, shouting, followed by the crowd behind her. Michael waited until Blanche's back was turned before sticking his foot between the woman's legs and tripping her. The woman wailed louder, nearly dropping the ragged bundle in her arms.

Blanche instantly swung around, shaking off her captors.

Caught up in the crowd surging around the spectacle, Michael couldn't reach her in time. To his horror, he watched Blanche shove a purse at the woman, then grab the bundle of blankets as soon as the woman greedily stuck out her hand. Michael could do nothing more than heave a container of trash into the midst of the crowd to prevent them from chasing Blanche as she dashed down the alley, followed in close pursuit by her dandified escorts. A riot erupted behind them as the greedy denizens of the street fought over the bag of gold.

Not taking time to utter the litany of curses he'd practiced, Michael dashed after them, leaping over obstacles in pursuit of Blanche and her stolen babe.

Seeing her being helped into the hired carriage, Michael leapt up and grabbed the rear postilion, then scrambled over the wheel and caught the door before either of her escorts could join her. They couldn't help Blanche and this babe. He planted his foot firmly in the center of the taller man's chest, sending him sprawling backward across the cobblestones. The fat one merely shouted in dismay from the street as Michael slammed the door and ordered the driver to move.

Gasping for breath, Michael frowned as Blanche worriedly rocked the infant in her arms. She showed no shock or surprise at his appearance, not even bothering to scold him for his actions. He couldn't decide if it was because she cared so little for him or because she perfectly understood why he was here and what he had done.

With resignation, he pried the lifeless bundle from Blanche's arms and pulled the blanket back. The pain of that poor drawn face nearly crippled him, but heartlessly, he informed her, "The babe's dead, Blanche. The woman simply wanted the coins for gin. She's dead, and there's nothing you can do to save her."

Reluctantly, Michael surrendered the infant when Blanche snatched it from his arms. He watched in sorrow as she peeled back the blankets and desperately sought some sign of life. Even in the dim carriage light, he could see her grief.

He wanted to protect her from the horror of this world, but instead, he struck out with anger. "You could have got us all killed. If I ever see those addle-pated Bedlam lunatics again, I'll slam their heads together and see if it makes one whole brain between them for not flinging you right back in the hackney and shoving off the instant they caught sight of you."

He could scarcely see the pale swell of her flesh above the purple gown in the gloom of the carriage, but he could see it quite well in his mind's eye. He'd never been this angry in his life, so he had no idea how to handle it. He felt like tearing the carriage apart piece by little piece with his bare hands.

Blanche's reply indicated he'd surprised even her with his temper. "I'm tired of being treated like a helpless child. Fiona would have trusted a woman faster than any man, had you bothered to ask. And if you mean to behave like that odious brother of yours, you may get out now."

He ought to. He really ought to. She had finally driven him insane.

Nine

Having donned gentleman's attire from the wardrobe where he'd stored it the last time he'd invaded the Duke of Anglesey's London town home, Michael leaned against the cabinet and stared blindly at the unused bedchamber. The hasty patter of footsteps outside the door had long since died away. With luck, Neville's servants had taken charge of the child's corpse and returned the grief-stricken Blanche to bed. Even an angel with the wealth of aristocracy couldn't buy life from death.

Miracles and angels didn't exist in the world as he knew it. He'd learned that the hard way, accepted reality, and overcame the disappointment. Life was much simpler that way.

Blanche complicated all that. A goddess like Blanche ought to have a plump, smiling cherub of her own. She ought to be surrounded by loving family, singing lullabies to an armful of healthy children. Michael could see the picture more clearly than he could see the room around him.

He'd seen it the night she'd sailed out that second story window with flames licking around her. She'd saved every servant in that old house, saved their few wretched possessions, and nearly lost her life in the process. Someone should have married her then, grabbed her up and cuddled her and made her smile and laugh again. Instead, they'd let her retreat to lick her wounds behind a barricade of riches.

"Blanche, have you lost your mind?" Neville's shouts of fury echoed down the corridor. "When Allendale told me what happened tonight, I thought he was nicked in the nob. When the devil did you get to town anyway? No one told me you were here."

Hands in pockets, Michael strolled down the corridor into the blue sitting room. The usually imperturbable young duke stood wild-haired and frantic in the center of the Axminster carpet, ranting at his lovely Madonna of a cousin who sat on the ice-blue couch, carefully sewing a piece of linen. Blanche didn't look up. She said nothing to Neville's ravings. She merely continued her self-appointed task.

"Someone blew up the lady's carriage today. You haven't let any old friends out of the Tower, have you?" Michael asked, distracting the furious duke from his traumatized cousin.

Neville swung around and grabbed Michael's coat front. "I should have known you were involved in this! What do you mean by allowing her on that side of town?"

Michael knew how to use his fists, not to mention his feet, teeth, and any other weapon that came to hand. He simply had an aversion to violence when common sense could solve the problem. But after the day he'd had today, he teetered on the brink of losing what little poise he possessed. He dug his fingers deep into the duke's wrist and twisted until the other man's grip broke.

Watching calmly as the duke grabbed his injured wrist in pain, Michael stepped out of his reach. "I said, *someone blew up the lady's coach today.* If you won't do something about it, I will."

* * *

"What the hell are you talking about?" And why the devil are you wearing my coat?"

Neville glared at the wrinkled fabric of his expensively tailored frock coat as he signaled the butler. "Bring us some brandy. And find someone to haul that corpse out of the parlor." He would need a brandy to fortify him for whatever tale the Irishman would relate now. He knew he didn't want to hear it. He also knew he couldn't avoid it, not with Blanche withdrawing into that silent stupor she'd lived in after the fire.

Only the Irish had this flair for the dramatic, this damned empathy for every beaten dog in their path. The threatening dolt stood there in his black evening coat, looking like some caveman prepared to wrestle a tiger for his food. Neville had no particular desire to be that tiger.

"If you throw the child on the streets, the lady will follow. I didn't think you a stupid man, Your Grace," Michael replied harshly.

Neville noted that Michael didn't look at Blanche. He'd suspected there was something between these two back when they'd been in each other's pockets for weeks on end. Satisfied that at least O'Toole had retained enough sense to realize he had no place in Blanche's life, Neville took the brandy and gestured for his unwanted guest to do the same.

"Coffee, if you don't mind." Michael absently corrected the duke's order.

Neville raised his eyebrows. Gentlemen drank brandy, but he'd already ascertained O'Toole was no gentleman even if he ordered the servants about as if he were. "What the hell is this talk about explosions?"

"Someone planted gunpowder under your traveling coach and set a fuse to it," Michael reported tonelessly. "I assumed it had to do with Lady Blanche, but someone may have just taken a dislike to your family crest. Laborers across the country are rioting over poor wages and the high cost of bread. Our war heroes beg in the streets. Our mines are killing women and children. You might say there's some dissatisfaction with the aristocracy. The French didn't invent revolution."

"Confound it, O'Toole! I didn't ask for a lecture on political economics. I'm not the one with mines and factories. I barely scrape enough to buy cravats. If someone blew up the coach because of the crest, then they were after Blanche. She's the one who owns the factories and mines, although it sounds a lot of faradiddle to me. Where would any poor factory worker find that much gunpowder?"

He watched as the Irishman's eyes narrowed. He'd seen O'Toole do this before and knew his formidable mind was as dangerous as his swift fists.

"Excellent question, Your Grace, one I hadn't time to ask myself. Poor men with gunpowder. That does not bode well at all. If I were you, I would have someone begin investigating the sales of gunpowder manufactories, starting with the ones closest to home." Michael absently set his cup aside. "And since we'll not pry the lady from the house until she is satisfied the infant is decently buried, I suggest extra guards patrol the perimeters. If the lady is owner of those factories, then we have reason to fear. Her men of business will not have told her of the conditions there."

Neville quelled a shiver of alarm. Vowing to look into the factories on his own, he answered in a low whisper Blanche couldn't hear. "O'Toole, so help me, if you're making this up for your own reasons, I'll have you strung up by the ballocks."

Michael shot him a look of irritation. "If I wanted to be rid of you, I'd find a much more entertaining method than gunpowder. Question her groom if you doubt me. Then talk to a few of your stuffed shirts from the north and see if they haven't heard of the protests and riots. This country is coming apart at the seams, and the lot of you sit in the Lords with your silly wigs and robes and pretend we're living in Tudor times. Will you believe when they start building a guillotine in Hyde Park?"

"Damn and blast it." Neville glanced worriedly at the woman on the sofa. "If anything happens to her, I'm the one they'll hang," he replied.

Michael gave a fleeting grin. "I know. You'd best find yourself a wealthy wife. The authorities are less likely to suspect you of Blanche's murder once your debts are settled."

Neville scowled and stomped toward the door. "I will take care of that if you will see she finds a husband with more sense than she has, else she's likely to take a notion to let her employees run the factories."

* * *

As the duke departed, Michael wished he could go with him. The haunting sight of the lady tenderly sewing a garment for the dead child had him longing to run as far as he could in the opposite direction. At the same time, it nailed him to the floor.

He scowled at his coffee. He had seen the poison of strong drink and never felt the need for it, but he wished he could summon the solace of alcoholic oblivion now.

"Why would any woman treat her child so cruelly when there are so many women who would give everything they possessed to have her?" Blanche whispered in anguish once the duke left them alone.

"Would they now?" Michael asked as he sauntered across the room to stand beside her. "Sure, and it seems to me there's far too many children in this world as it is."

She sent him a scathing look. "And far too little wealth to take care of them. You needn't hide your thoughts from me behind that mocking tone, Michael Lawrence O'Toole."

He shoved his hands in his pockets. "Far be it from me to argue with your ladyship."

"Of course! Never argue, never disagree, just disappear and do as you please. Why are you still here? I've defied your wishes. You should be vanishing out the back door."

Michael winced. He supposed he did tend to leave at the point when others disagreed with him. He preferred relying on himself. Why argue? Still, he disliked the picture she drew.

"I pride myself on doing the unexpected," he answered insouciantly. He wandered to her bookshelves. That was one thing he truly liked about Blanche's many homes. Everywhere he turned, he saw books.

He found a tome of Shakespeare's poems and pulled it down. In general, he disliked poetry, but he'd discovered some fascinating plays on words in the works of the great bard. Sometimes, silence worked as well as disappearing when avoiding an argument.

He took a chair to the side of the sofa, where Blanche could not see him but he could keep an eye on her.

"Will you read aloud to me?" she asked.

The plea jarred Michael back to reality. He'd known he had no business making himself at home. He would only end up torturing himself with what he could not have. But he couldn't deny her this simple request.

He opened the book and began reading blindly where his eye first fell:

> *Shall I compare thee to a summer's day?*
> *Thou art more lovely and more temperate:*
> *Rough winds do shake the darling buds of May,*
> *And summer's lease hath all too short a date:*
> *Sometimes too hot the eye of heaven shines,*
> *And often is his gold complexion dimm'd;*
> *And every fair from fair sometime declines,*
> *By chance, or nature's changing course untrimm'd;*
> *But thy eternal summer shall not fade,*
> *Nor lose possession of that fair thou ow'st,*
> *Nor shall death brag thou wander'st in his shade,*
> *When in eternal lines to time thou row'st;*
> *So long as men can breathe, or eyes can see,*
> *So long lives this, and this gives life to thee.*

As the meaning of the words sank in, Michael nearly wept at his choice, but then he heard a whimper from the sofa, and his head jerked up.

Tears flooded Blanche's cheeks as she rocked back and forth. For a moment, he madly thought the poem had affected her as much as it had him.

But then he realized she poured out her grief and anguish on a lost child. The lady's emotionless shell had finally broken.

Ten

Blanche wept for herself as much as for the child who would never know sunlight and butterflies. She cried from loneliness. She wept for what she could have given that lost child.

Michael kneeled before her. She couldn't stop rocking, couldn't stop the tears flooding her face.

"She would have suffered all her life should she have lived, Blanche," he murmured. "God spared her the pain. Let her go, my love. Let her go."

The soft caress of his words overwhelmed her, and she didn't know how to respond except with more tears. She'd missed her mother's loving kisses, a father's laughing hugs. She'd known nothing but orders and corrections from tutors and governesses, subservient bows from the army of employees surrounding her. Even her cousins treated her as if she were a porcelain figurine easily broken. Only Michael dared speak to her as if she were human, as if she were like everyone else. She cried harder as he rose to sit beside her and caressed her cheek, brushing away the tears.

"Oh, God, don't do that," he whispered, wrapping his arms around her. "Don't make me cry. I'm not man enough to cry, my love. I can't bear it."

At that foolish plea, she broke down completely, burying her face against his shoulder,. Muscled arms surrounded her, and she let Michael's wide chest carry the burden of her despair. "I'm all right. I'm sorry. It's just been such a long day." She sat up, wiping at her tears with the back of her hand until Michael handed her a handkerchief. She shivered at the touch of his finger wiping a wet streak from her cheek.

"I know. You've been terrified ever since the carriage exploded. I should have found a better way of keeping you safe. I'm not very good at taking care of people, my lady."

She smacked his hand away. "Stop calling me that, or I shall take to calling you 'my lord.' The brother of a marquess is generally given that title. You ought to feel its weight."

He smiled at her sharp tone instead of being irritated as he ought. "Then what shall I call you? Should anyone hear me call you Blanche, they will think us entirely too familiar."

"You are just trying to distract me." Gulping back a sob, she forced her chin up. She knew Michael's ways too well. "It won't work, you know. Pull the rope and see who it brings. There must be someone still up and about."

"I'll have them bring a hot bath to your room."

He spoke with such command that Blanche didn't bother arguing. She was too tired to object in any case. All her life, she'd had to give the orders, make the decisions. Let someone else take charge for a change. In the morning, she would take command again.

* * *

By morning, Blanche awakened with the realization that she'd given Michael ample opportunity to escape all over again. She pounded her pillow and cursed, then rang for a maid. She could tell by the shortness of the sunlight across the floor that the hour was late. Michael would be long gone. And she still had to make arrangements for the funeral of the poor infant who had no name.

She found the little girl already laid out in a small coffin, her wasted body garbed in the white linen shroud, the tiny black curl on her forehead neatly arranged with a ribbon pinned to it. She almost broke down and wept again but fought the weakness. She'd forgotten herself last night in Michael's arms, but she wouldn't forget again.

Blanche almost forgot her vow a moment later when, dressed in the black clothes of full mourning, Michael appeared out of nowhere. He just appeared and disappeared without sound, a quite annoying trait. Yet his presence was so welcome that she nearly cried with the relief of it.

"I thought you'd left," she said, grabbing his hands before she realized the impropriety of her action. The shock of his ungloved palms against hers was enough to remind her, yet she didn't want to let go. The emerald glow of his gaze dissolved her grief and turned it to warmth.

"I told you I'd help. I thought it best if we kept the funeral private. The carriage is waiting. Are you ready?"

Once they'd seen the infant buried and left a generous donation with the vicar who managed the orphanage near the gravesite, Blanche concentrated on the view outside the carriage window rather than on the man seated across from her. He'd called her *his love*. He'd held her in his arms and touched her with more tenderness than she'd ever experienced. Her cheeks warmed with just the thought.

Yet this morning he seemed as distant as always. Incapable of sitting still, he now played with a length of string threaded between his fingers, looping it around and around and pulling at it until it came out straight. She wanted to see how he did it. At the same time, she wanted to smack his hands and make him talk to her. But of course, he could not, not while the maid listened.

Frustrated, Blanche clenched her gloved fingers. She had the feeling that Michael could converse upon the most fascinating subjects had he the inclination, but it took a brickbat over the head to persuade him to anything beyond what needed saying.

When they reached the house, she groaned inwardly at the sight of two men descending the front stairs, returning their tall beaver hats to their heads. Allendale and Benington were fools who occupied her parlor like bookends, but she had always relied on their loyal discretion. Michael obviously did not see them that way.

Blanche considered telling the driver to move on, but Michael had already seen the pair. His jaw set and a vengeful gleam lit his eyes at sight of the men waiting upon the carriage's arrival.

Michael climbed down first, turning his back on the waiting visitors as he extended his hand to help her down. She squeezed his fingers and whispered, "Behave," but Michael had never obeyed a direct order in his life unless so inclined. She bit her lip in resignation when he turned that belligerent look on the two gentlemen.

Lord Benington's eyes narrowed in suspicion as he took in Michael's hostile stance. He glanced at Blanche in her black gown, and showed relief when her maid descended from the carriage. "We came to see if you arrived home safely, my lady." He returned his glance to Michael. "I say, you look familiar. Have we met?"

"Are these the two muttonbrains who allowed you in Elton Alley last night?" Michael asked in a dangerously polite tone.

"I say, that's unfair! We were there to protect the lady," the taller gentleman protested.

"They will say nothing of it," Blanche insisted, closing her fingers over Michael's elbow and steering him toward the stairs. She may as well have tried moving mountains. "Lords Allendale and Benington are friends of Neville's who understand loyalty and discretion. Let us go inside. It is chilly out here."

Michael politely took her arm and guided her up the stairs, but she distrusted his solicitous smile. Allendale and Benington followed them up. She wished she could send the pair away. Michael had ridiculous ideas of protecting her, and he was spoiling for a fight. Although with Michael, one could expect anything.

While the butler helped Blanche with her bonnet and cloak, Michael generously offered their visitors help with their accouterments.

When Michael took Allendale's hat, an extremely large feather appeared behind the gentleman's ear. Blanche choked back a cry and covered her laugh as a drooping nosegay of half dead roses peered out of the young lord's vest pocket after he handed over his cane. Somehow, Allendale's coat pockets became lining side out and his cravat fell unfastened. His elaborately ornate pocket watch disappeared from the chain across his vest and came to rest— Blanche blinked in astonishment as she discovered the watch dangling from the belt on the back of Benington's coat.

Benington fared little better. With his back toward the others so Blanche's maid could divest him of his great coat, he hadn't yet noticed Allendale's newly rearranged attire. Aside from the pocket watch dangling from his back and the knob of a walking stick protruding from his coat neck, he didn't appear seriously harmed until he turned around. This time, Blanche couldn't bite back a gasp of laughter at the lady's red sash replacing his usually pristine white cravat. How in the world had Michael come across that sash? She'd thought it safely in her wardrobe with the gown to which it belonged.

She didn't have much time to muffle her giggles before Allendale and Benington came face to face and stared at one another in incredulity.

"What the devil are you wearing on your neck, Bennie?" Allendale asked peevishly.

Benington snatched at the back of his neck, seeking the object prodding him between his shoulder blades. Grabbing the knob and pulling, he gave Allendale a stare of disbelief. "*My* neck! What is that dangling from *your* collar? An ostrich feather? And what do you mean coming into a lady's presence with your cravat like that? I swear...."

Blanche's peal of laughter swiveled both men in her direction. She couldn't help it. Her eyes watered, and she nearly bent double in her attempt to contain her chortles. If Michael had hoped to assuage her grief while telling her suitors they were unwanted, he'd succeeded.

The ostrich feather swayed over Allendale's eye, and the ostentatious pocket watch chose that moment to play its merry chimes. Even Blanche's maid bit back a grin, and the butler covered his mouth, hiding his mirth. Allendale and Benington looked at each other again as if questioning the sanity of the house's inhabitants.

"Ummm, that nosegay looks a little wilted, Allendale," Benington observed a trifle doubtfully.

"What nosegay? I...." Glancing down, his lordship pulled the wilted roses from his pocket, then frantically searched for the watch that he could hear but which didn't rest in its place of honor. "My watch! Where's my watch?" When the giggling maid pointed at Benington's back, he swung the other man around and cried out loud. "My watch! What the devil....?"

Both men caught on at once, swinging around to glare at Michael. Blanche erupted in another gale of giggles when she realized Michael, naturally, was nowhere in the vicinity.

"Oh, please. Oh, please...." She couldn't get the words out through her laughter. "There's a mirror in the parlor, so you may straighten yourselves out. Please forgive him. He thought I needed a jester today." She pointed at the room on her left, covering her mouth again as a soft tenor singing an Irish ballad drifted from the hallways above. Michael hadn't left then, just conveniently misplaced himself.

She was going to kill him, if she didn't die laughing first.

Eleven

By the time Blanche had Benington and Allendale straightened out and laughing with her, Michael had divested himself of his black mourning coat and breeches. After her old friends had departed, he strolled in wearing an immaculate gray scissor-tailed coat and neatly pressed trousers. He'd tamed his hair into some semblance of order and wore a frilled cravat rivaling any the Beau might have worn in his day.

Blanche eyed the emerald stickpin with suspicion, but since Neville seldom wore jewelry, and she suspected Michael never owned jewelry of any kind, she couldn't be certain of its origins.

The fleeting illusions with which he disguised himself and distracted others reminded her of the time after the fire, a time when she thought herself lost and alone, with Michael the only certainty in her world. She didn't like being reminded of her helplessness. She was much stronger now. She could resist Michael's wiles this time. If she felt like it.

He leaned against the closed door, crossing his arms and inadvertently revealing more muscles than most gentlemen. Awareness of his physical proximity unsettled her.

"You had no reason to treat Benington and Allendale like idiots," she admonished.

"One must treat idiots like sane men?" Michael asked without rancor. "They should have told Neville at once that you aimed for Elton Alley. Do you dangle them on your puppet strings that easily?"

Blanche had known she wouldn't like the path of this conversation. Glaring, she rang the bell for tea. "That is none of your concern. I refuse to hide in the country, if that is your plan. I have already hired a Runner. I expect a report from him shortly."

"He will report that our suspects are fled. If you had not appeared when you did last night, I might have questioned the boy who carried a message from Fiona. As it is, he escaped before I could find out more."

Blanche stared at him. "You didn't tell me this."

He shrugged. "When had I the opportunity? It makes little difference. I've paid spies up and down the alley for information. If she's there, or if she returns, they will send word. In the meantime, they can tell me little other than the red-haired woman has lived there some time, and the rough-looking men have come recently. The only one who seems to know Fiona is the lad, and he could have been lying."

Blanche twisted her fingers in her lap. "That doesn't leave much for me to do."

"On the contrary, if you're truly interested in finding her, your unlimited funds might have a use. I have a feeling we must trace Fiona's origins to settle this matter. With your Runner and my spies working in London, we can do naught else on this end. But we can trace her from whence she came."

That *we* grabbed Blanche's attention. She watched as the grim, straight line of his eyebrows relaxed and his features returned to their usual laughing structure. "Caught your interest, did I? Should the way lead there, would you be after seein' the old country with me, now?"

Blanche waited until the maid brought in tea, arranged the table, and departed. She no doubt scandalized the household by entertaining Michael alone. The butler would be at the door shortly, keeping an eye on the proprieties. She could just imagine what the world would say should she depart in Michael's company for parts unknown.

"Are you more interested in Fiona, or her family?" she asked, stalling. "The resemblance is admittedly striking, but you cannot persuade me that you are not Gavin's brother. The two of you are too much alike in too many ways."

"We were raised by the same parents. Of course we're alike in many ways. I made it perfectly clear long ago, my lady, that I am not the grandson of a marquess," he said firmly. "And as curious as I am to find Fiona's family for my own sake, it's for hers that I go. Someone or something sent her fleeing far from home. The answer is back there, not here. Were it not for that explosion yesterday, I would leave you here. As it is, I can see no help for it but that you come with me. For the sake of propriety, I suppose you should bring a maid, but she must be discreet."

71

He actually meant for her to travel with him! She would probably have insisted on it in any case, but she couldn't believe he'd suggested it first. Despite every opportunity to take advantage of weeks spent hiding together, he'd never made an improper advance, except for the one kiss to restore her confidence. Michael had that kind of honor. Unfortunately, he also possessed a rather peculiar morality that warred with the prevailing beliefs of society. He knew his offer was improper. He simply didn't care.

"What will I tell Neville?" she whispered, still disbelieving.

"I didn't think you told Neville much of anything," he replied dryly. "He'll think you've gone back to Anglesey. As we travel, you could send messages to your man of business so no one doubts you are alive and well. You might give some explanation to Dillian and Gavin. I would hate for them to chase after us. Other than that, we must travel incognito so your journey cannot be traced."

"It sounds too simple," Blanche said. "Why all of a sudden are you willing to take me with you?"

He shrugged his shoulders impatiently. "I told you, I cannot be certain of your safety except in my company. I dislike borrowing funds to speed my travel, so your coins are convenient, and people are more likely to respond to my questioning with a lady by my side. I have a feeling time is of the essence."

The urgency of his tone convinced her. Blanche rose from the chair and approached the door he blocked with his masculine frame. "I will have a bag packed at once. I suppose we cannot use the town carriage?"

Michael stepped away from the door. "You will take the town carriage to Dillian's and send it away. Take only a bag your maid can carry. You will leave Dillian's through the back gate and catch a hackney by the park. Have the hackney take you to the White Horse. I'll meet you there. By the time we are finished, it will be impossible for anyone to trace your steps."

Blanche shivered with anticipation. Blanche kissed Michael's cheek. "I don't care who you are, Michael Lawrence, you're a gem among men."

Twelve

Garbed in a country gentleman's careless tweed and knee high leather boots, Michael twitched his riding crop in his gloved fingers and anxiously watched the inn yard. He tried reminding himself that he should peruse the second-hand clothing shops more frequently — this coat had seen better days — but his concentration focused on the arriving coaches and not the disrepair of his disguise.

He hoped Blanche had understood his instructions. If she arrived in full aristocratic regalia, she would make hiding their trail difficult.

He had already decided he'd lost his mind to even contemplate this journey. He should hop the next mail coach and save himself no end of grief, but he wouldn't. He'd seen the despair in Blanche's eyes, felt her grasping for some token of human warmth, and knew Neville couldn't provide what she needed.

He would take her away to safety, give her an adventure to make her smile and forget the responsibility piled on her frail shoulders, and return her to Anglesey. With any luck, she would adopt an orphanage and find happiness with the children there. Right now, she wasn't strong enough to accept the death of any more children, and that happened too frequently even in the best of orphanages. First, he must make her strong.

No, first he must make himself strong. He paced like a nervous bridegroom, aware that he seldom set about a task with less than full assurance of his ability to accomplish it, but Blanche made him second guess everything he did.

Michael hurried into the inn yard at sight of a small leather-clad boot stepping daintily from a coach.

She had wrapped herself in a coarse brown cloak and covered her hair with a brown bonnet adorned with brown roses. Brown roses. Michael shuddered at the abomination while admiring her choice. She had made herself as mousy and nondescript as a woman of her beauty could. The elongated bonnet brim successfully

disguised the revealing scars as well as her hair. Thick mittens hid
delicate fingers. She could be a governess or a squire's wife.

Only when he reached her side did Michael realize Blanche
arrived alone. Scowling, he caught her mittened hand, paid the
coach driver, and hastily led her through the chaos of the inn yard.
Arriving mail coach passengers shoved and shouted around them,
yelling for their luggage, for post chaises, at each other and the
animals. Blanche seemed startled by the confusion as he led her to a
quiet corner inside, out of the immediate uproar.

"Where is your maid?" he whispered heatedly. He didn't like
lingering. Her family would start searching at posting inns once
they discovered Blanche missing.

"I left her at home," Blanche replied defiantly. "She had no
desire to travel. I told her I would borrow one of Dillian's maids.
She could not help but talk, Michael. I have enough wealth to care
nothing for gossip, but Neville would see you hung. It seemed
safest this way."

"And Dillian?" Michael asked with dismay.

"She thinks I just want to be left alone. She thinks I go to my
cottage in Dorset. She has too many other things on her mind to
worry overmuch. The baby has a cold, and Gavin has the Lords in
an uproar over his bill for better working conditions for children.
Dillian has angry men stalking through the house all day and
night."

Michael ran his hand through his hair and bit back a groan.
Traveling alone with Blanche was the ultimate foolishness.
Desperately, he wondered where he could leave her, but the eager
face she turned to him prevented his thinking of it long.

"I have brought a great deal of cash, Michael. I've sewn some in
my cloak, and my skirt, and in the lining of my bag. Shall we
pretend we're the children of a rich nabob?"

He grinned. The innocent, eager young woman he remembered
emerged with this plunge into fantasy. "The children of a wealthy
nabob would wear silks and satins more outlandish than your court
dress. No, we shall be the offspring of a well-to-do Northumberland
Methodist squire returning home, quite dismayed at the scandalous
activities of the city. I shall insist that you marry the lordling who
owns the land adjoining ours."

"And I shall protest that he is too bookish and not to my taste."

Blanche's conspiratorial smile was nearly blinding.

"Right. I suppose you want the rakehell younger son, blackguard that he is. Women are like that." Grabbing her arm, Michael led her to his hired carriage. Just touching her through the layers of clothes scorched him. Smoke fogged his brain. He had difficulty even recalling Fiona.

The ennui he'd been suffering of late vanished. He wanted the lady to himself for a while. He craved it with every inch of his misbegotten soul.

He hadn't lost all sense however. He'd reserved the coach in the name of MacDermot, the name of an old family friend Gavin's father had often mentioned. Gavin would recognize the pseudonym should anything happen that required he find them. Michael would never involve Blanche in anything dangerous. But he knew the ways of the world too well to believe everything would go as planned. He always left a bolt hole.

Climbing into the coach behind Blanche, Michael wished he'd included a horse in his plans. The soft feminine scents of her sachet assailed him, and he closed his eyes to enjoy it.

"Why Northumberland?" she inquired as soon as the driver sprang the horses. "I thought Fiona came from Ireland."

"And would we wish to let our pursuers know our direction?" Michael asked, opening his eyes in time to see Blanche remove her confining bonnet. She had pulled her hair into a prim knot at her nape, but baby-fine tendrils escaped in profusion around her ears and neck. He fought back a strong desire to stroke them.

Her smile reflected her delight. "We will go north for a while under this guise, then switch directions under another one!"

"Actually, we will go north to the lake country where I met her so we can trace Fiona's steps. From her accent, I suspect she traveled from the area of Belfast to Scotland. I should think she took a fishing boat to one of the lochs off Scotland's west coast."

"Scotland and Ireland! How lovely. I've never seen much of anything but southern England. Will the roads be safe for travel this time of year?"

She seemed content pretending he was her brother and they did no more than travel for the pleasure of it. If she knew of his decidedly unbrotherly urges, she would stop the coach and run screaming in the other direction.

Unsettled, Michael stared out the window. "The highwaymen are not so thick as they once were, but the roads can be impassable in bad weather. The inns are fraught with unsavory characters who may take a fancy to your pretty face. I've tried making certain we have a good driver, but I'm not infallible. And I can't control fate. I've seen mail coaches turned over in ditches because some mutton-head couldn't manage his cattle. So do not think we are on a little pleasure jaunt. Any time you want out, let me know. I'll arrange for a place of safety for you until I return."

Blanche stuck out her tongue at him. For a wild, heated moment, Michael considered what he could do with that delicacy.

"You'll sound just like Neville if you continue. I 'm not in the least missish, you know." She opened her reticule and pulled out a small pistol. "And I borrowed this from Dillian. I'm quite prepared to slay anyone who stands in my way."

"Oh, gad." Covering his eyes, Michael slumped back against the seat. "Put that thing away and don't ever let me see it again. I'm in more danger from it than any highwayman."

"Good. Then you shall not have any fancy ideas as we travel," she said with satisfaction.

So much for innocence if her version of "fancy ideas" meant she'd guessed his lustful thoughts. Keeping his eyes closed, Michael pretended to sleep.

* * *

Blanche watched Michael's face in repose. She seldom had opportunity to study a man in this proximity. Aside from Neville, she saw them only when they had tricked themselves out in all their finery, disguised themselves behind nosegays and snuffboxes, and acted the roles of smitten gallants.

The cloudy day lent little light to the interior, but she could distinctly see the masculine cut of his jaw, the intelligence of his wide brow, and the boyish dishevelment of the hank of hair falling in his eyes. She thought she even saw the beginnings of dark bristles under his skin, although she supposed with his coloring, his beard would be more red than dark. His long legs stretched crosswise over the carriage floor, revealing the muscularity beneath tight buckskins. When her knee brushed close to his, the muscles in her midsection tightened.

She wanted Michael to kiss her. She knew he was completely unsuitable as a suitor. Since she had no intention of marrying, it didn't matter. She just wanted someone to kiss her. She tried not thinking beyond that. First, she must persuade him. In her experience, men liked touching her. Or at least pretended they did. It had taken tears to bring Michael to her side. What would it take to make him go a step further? A direct command? Not likely.

She mulled it over as the shadows lengthened on the countryside. They would be fortunate to reach Oxford by nightfall. Chilly as it was, they could see snow by tomorrow. She shifted restlessly.

Apparently the driver had been given thorough instructions. While Michael slept, the carriage surged on through the early darkness. He'd hired a footman as well as a driver, and the man lit the carriage lights when the sun dipped low, but the meager light did not ease her anxiety.

She wished she knew why Fiona had left that note asking if parliament could be dismissed early. How early? Did Fiona have family in government who needed to come home? How foolish to think an urchin like that would have family in parliament, yet why else would it matter when they adjourned? And did any of this have aught to do with the exploding carriage?

Instinct said it did, but she didn't rely on instincts as Michael did. She wanted concrete facts, and she had none.

The horses ran faster, as if they knew food and warmth waited ahead. She kicked Michael's boots to wake him.

She could feel him peering at her from beneath his hat, even if she couldn't see him in the darkness. She wanted to kick him again for not speaking, but Michael was impervious to insult or injury.

She produced a small pouch of coins and threw it across the carriage at him. He caught it deftly, as she knew he would. "You should carry some of these. It would look odd were I to pay all the tabs."

The purse disappeared into the depths of one of his pockets. "How can you be angry already when I haven't done anything but sleep?"

Damn his ability to discern every nuance of her voice. Gritting her teeth, Blanche didn't honor his question with a reply. "Doesn't it bother you to take a lady's coins?" She could see the shrug of his silhouette in the darkness.

"They're just bits of metal. I have no fondness for them. I could earn what I needed in a few hours in the tavern, but I didn't think it wise leaving you alone that long."

She could supply the words he did not speak. In essence, she paid for her own comfort and safety, not his. For some reason, that response irked her. "You were the one who wished to travel quickly."

Again, she could feel his grin more than see it. "And did you think I would travel slowly on my own? I need only borrow one of Montague's remarkable steeds and I could travel all night."

"Then why did you bring me along if you don't need me?" she asked irritably as the coach slowed for the inn ahead.

"I didn't say I didn't need you. I merely said your coins are a convenience." He glanced out the window. "I gambled by telling the driver to come here. I wanted to make a good start, and I thought you might like this place better than some others. But it's late. The rooms may already be taken."

"Oh, thank you," she answered huffily. "And what do we do then? Sleep in here?"

"Bribe the proprietor with your coins," he replied cheerfully as the carriage drew to a halt. "Wait here, and I shall see what we can do."

He opened the door and leapt down from the carriage without waiting for the footman to lay the steps. Whistling, he disappeared into the interior of the well-lighted inn as the first flakes of snow fell.

Blanche glanced up at the clouded night sky and basked in the warmth of anticipation. She would show the blasted brash Irishman that she wasn't completely helpless. Tonight, she would make him kiss her.

And if she enjoyed that, tomorrow, she would venture even further.

Thirteen

The snow turned to rain after that first day, but Michael insisted on riding outside. Blanche thought she knew why. She had caught him by surprise that first night of their journey, turning abruptly and practically landing in his arms. He'd only had to lean over, and he could have kissed her. Instead, he'd caught her shoulders in a grip so hard it had caused bruises. He'd stared down at her as if debating strangling her or making mad love to her. And then he'd abruptly let her go and left the room.

He'd left her dining alone ever since. Since then, Michael had averted every opportunity for seduction. Fuming, she watched him ride the horse he'd purchased with her money, while she sat bored and ready to kill inside the rocking carriage. Michael, the man with no scruples, apparently possessed a passionate degree of propriety when it applied to women.

She thought she should know more of the pleasures of physical passion before retiring to spinsterhood, and the more Michael denied her, the more determined she became that he be the one to teach her.

Blanche reached that decision on the outskirts of Manchester. The carriage slowed, and she pushed her nose against the window to see what delayed them. Michael generally rode alongside and made himself available to explain the sights, but she saw no sign of him now. Lifting the window, she stuck her head out to see ahead.

An angry mob gathered outside a tall desolate building set in a field by itself. Ragged men and women wrapped in wool scarves and old coats spilled across the road, blocking travel. They shook their fists and raged at something or someone beyond her field of vision. It did not seem very likely that the carriage could get through the milling crowd, so she ordered the driver to halt, opened the door, and jumped down to the rutted road.

Dismounted, Michael hastened back through the throng, pushing his way until he reached her side. "Get back in. I'll order the driver to turn around and find another route."

Blanche looked at the narrow, rutted road, up at the wide coach, and back to Michael with incredulity. "Unless you lift the carriage and horses in the air and turn them yourself, I don't think that's likely. What is happening?"

Michael scowled, most likely because she was right and not because of her question. "The mill owner insisted the workers extend their day to sixteen hours for an order he needs immediately. They refused to do it without extra pay. When he said he'd turn off anyone who wouldn't stay, they all walked out. The situation is growing ugly. I better put you on the horse and get you out of here."

"You found all that out in these few minutes?" Blanche replied in admiration.

Michael shrugged. "They are not exactly hiding their complaints. The owner stands to make a large profit if he can get those orders out on time. They saw no reason why they should suffer and not share in those profits. But if he closes the mill, they will all be out of work. Most of these people are the sole support of their families. They'll starve."

"But if he closes the mill, he won't get out the orders, and nobody profits."

"It would seem that way, but I suspect the real owners of the mill also own other manufactories that could supply the order. It would just mean putting aside their current projects to produce this one. It will only take a week without wages to drive these people begging back again. I've seen it happen."

An angry shout rose into a wave of terrifying screams rippling backward from near the mill. People at the front of the crowd broke away and sprinted across the field, with others close behind. Some fell, and others trampled over them. Blanche heard glass breaking and the sharp report of what sounded like firecrackers. More people screamed and ran.

"Damn and blast it, you need to leave, *now!*" He grabbed her by the waist and threw her up on his horse. Blanche grabbed the reins as the mob surged around them, tilting the carriage and driving its horses to rearing panic.

From her vantage point atop the horse, she could see over the heads of the mob, and she gave a gasp of horror. "Militia! They've called the militia. They're shooting, Michael. We have to stop them.

There are children in this crush! They'll all be killed."

Without waiting for Michael's reply, Blanche grabbed the horse's reins and kicked with her soft boot. She had no side saddle to grab with her knee, so her sideways position was shaky, but she'd grown up on the back of a horse. She could hold on.

She nearly fell when Michael leaped up behind her, cursing fluently under his breath. He kneed the horse into the crowd, and she could only hang on.

The firing had stopped now that the mob fled across the fields, but the damage had already been done. Ill-clothed bodies of every shape and size lay strewn across the trampled grass and mud, whether victims of the fleeing mob or gunfire, Blanche couldn't determine. A woman's sobs caught her ear, but Michael kept the horse at a steady gallop toward town, away from the fleeing mob and the soldiers.

Blanche screamed in rage when she understood his purpose. She didn't want to go toward town. She wanted to run down those soldiers and shoot the owner of that wretched mill. She needed to help the wounded. She wanted to tear out the throats of whoever was responsible for this catastrophe. She certainly had no intention of running for safety.

She pounded Michael's hands on the reins with her fists. "Stop this instant, you blasted beast! Let me off!" She beat upon his thigh when he didn't rein in.

He caught her wrists with one hand and gripped the reins in the other. "We're not going anywhere near those soldiers. They won't know you from the rest of the mob. We're running to safety before the mob returns and tears the mill down."

"You'd stop if it were just you!" she accused him tearfully, struggling against his imprisoning hold. "I'll buy the damned mill! Just let me down from here."

With a muttered imprecation at her contrariness, Michael reined the horse through a broken gate some distance past the carnage. He couldn't hold on to a kicking, screaming female for long, not and keep his grip on the horse too. Sooner or later she would slide off, and probably fall beneath the horse's hooves.

And she was right. If it were not for her, he'd be storming through that field prepared to rip someone apart. The idea of buying the mill and firing the management suited his sense of justice. He wondered if she really could do that. He didn't know, but between them, perhaps they could equalize the situation.

Checking the scene behind them for danger, Michael turned the horse toward the mill.

The untrained militia stood uncertainly on the front steps, their muskets aimed at the road. As a few women crawled through the scene of battle, searching out the bodies scattered there, the soldiers waited for further orders, unwilling to shoot directly at women or the injured. Michael suspected some were already prepared to lay down their guns and retreat with disgust, but soldiers with weapons often possessed a thirst for power. He couldn't trust appearances.

"Stand back!" one shouted as Michael rode boldly toward the mill's front door.

He released Blanche's waist. Reining in the horse, he groaned as she immediately slid to the ground and ran to a fallen child. So much for buying a mill. She would be sending for the carriage and hauling bodies off to her townhouse, where she might mother and nurse an entire mob to her heart's content.

Michael focused on the frock-coated gentleman appearing in the mill doorway. "You'll have to post guards around the clock," Michael remarked when the gentleman's gaze turned in his direction. "They'll come back and tear the place apart elsewise."

The man scowled and diverted his gaze to Blanche, who now consulted with another woman over the child's unconscious form. "Who's that, and what the hell's she doing?"

Michael had known it was impossible to disguise Blanche's air of privilege. Even though she wore the dowdy clothes of a squire's daughter, she carried herself with grace and dignity.

"Under the circumstances, I don't believe revealing her true identity wise. Just suffice it to say, she can make a great deal of trouble for whomever is responsible for this carnage. Are you the owner or the manager?"

"None of your damned business." The man muttered a few curt orders to the militia, and they set out across the mill yard, their firearms across their chests.

Blanche looked up. "Michael, send for the carriage. These people need transport to the hospital. I think they're all alive, but I don't know for how much longer."

Her bonnet had fallen back, revealing a cascade of flaxen hair. Her lovely oval face with the burn scars marring her cheeks and forehead gleamed in the dismal gray light of the cloudy day. The man standing on the doorstep paled at the sight, Michael noted with interest.

"I warned you," Michael said, gambling that this man at least suspected Blanche's identity. "Women detest violence. She'll have the man responsible for this by the short hairs as soon as she takes those people to town."

"I had my orders!" the man replied nervously. "I just do what I'm told. I'm to get that order out or close the mill. I can't let a mob dictate how I run the business. Where would we be if those barbarians started doing things their way? They'd arrive when they felt like it, leave when they'd the notion, and demand enough money to keep them drunk on gin around the clock. They can work as told or find work elsewhere."

Returning to Michael's side, Blanche apparently overheard this self-serving speech. "I demand to speak with the owner," she ordered.

"The owner isn't here," the manager responded nastily. "You didn't really think he'd stay in this godforsaken hole, did you? He's in London, with all the other swells."

"Truly? Then I'll be certain to meet him when I return. I'll have his name, please."

Blanche's slender fingers dug into Michael's arm. Instinct warned him not to pursue the subject of ownership. "My lady, I think it best if we call the carriage...."

Blanche glanced at the approaching vehicle. "I sent one of the women for it. We'll take your horse into town. There won't be room left. That child has a broken leg." She glared at the man in the doorway. "And it's all your fault. He'll most likely be crippled for life. There are others out there who might die from gunshot wounds. I'll have your name and the owner's name immediately, or I shall go to the magistrate and request them."

"Don't know the owner's name," the manager snarled. "I just deal with his man of business. Barnaby is the name, and good luck to you if you find him. He'll scale the hide off any interfering female. It's none of your damned concern what we do."

The fingers biting into his arm weakened. Michael held them in place. With a curt nod, he bade the manager farewell and hurried Blanche down the path toward his horse. The driver of the carriage seemed to have the women and the injured well in hand.

"Barnaby!" Blanche whispered. "Do you think there can be two of that name?"

"I should think there could be hundreds of that name," Michael answered soothingly.

"But not with the same profession," she returned with a scowl. "*My* Barnaby. *My* man of business. Do you think I own that mill?"

Michael didn't want to answer that. Unfortunately, she must have inherited Barnaby from her grandfather.

She didn't wait for his dilatory reply. "I'll have to dismiss him. I cannot believe he would order this...this *horror*."

Michael said nothing as he lifted her onto his horse. Absentee owners and landlords were the scourge of any number of countries. He'd condemn them all, but then he must condemn people like Blanche. She had done her best, but only someone who lived with the locals and knew how the operation worked could possibly understand what it took to run a company like this, or a mine in Cornwall, or a farm in Ireland.

"Is this what Fiona complained of?" Blanche whispered. "Have we become too removed from the people who work for us? Is that the problem?"

Since that was exactly what he had been thinking, Michael couldn't lie. "I don't know Fiona's complaints, but yes, that is much of the problem. Not all. I have seen factories run by local people who think human lives are expendable. The greed for gold is more important than their souls. They would work their employees all day and night if they could. We are not so terribly different from the slaveholders in the American South. We just don't buy and sell our employees."

"But we work them and beat them and starve them. I think I'm going to be sick."

She said it casually enough, but then she bent double and gagged. Alarmed, Michael halted the horse and lifted her down. He watched helplessly as she bent over the muddy ground while she emptied the contents of her stomach. He dipped his handkerchief in a creek and wiped her lips when she shakily sat back, her arms clasped around her middle.

He offered a sip of watered wine from the flask in his pocket. "There is only so much one person can do, my lady," he said as she drank. "We will stop in Manchester and you may send letters to your solicitor asking that he find a replacement for Barnaby. Or would you prefer that I return you to London?"

Michael held his breath against Blanche's reply. He'd tried not to touch her, avoided spending too much time in her presence, and ignored her lively questions so he wouldn't rely so much on her company. But it had happened anyway. He didn't want to let her go.

Still kneeling in the mud, Blanche returned the flask, and lifted her gaze to his.

Michael felt the impact like a bullet to the chest. He read the plea in her eyes, the quiver of her pale lips, and he couldn't resist. He never could. Terrified he would do it wrong and frighten her, he placed his lips on hers.

Her breath tasted of wine, and despite the cold, heat enveloped them. Gasping at the intensity of his reaction, Michael caught Blanche's waist with his hand, balancing their precarious position. Her lips parted and tentatively, she slid her arms around his shoulders. He held back a groan of pleasure and tasted of her again. Blanche responded with all the eagerness of his dreams.

Michael closed his eyes and conjured private bowers and whispered words of love as their mouths clung and drew hungrily on one another. Pure bliss flooded through him as he brushed his hand upward, to the softness of her breast. She offered no protest. Instead, she opened her mouth, inviting further exploration.

Michael nearly exploded with the need for that and more. Only the creak of a wagon returned him to his senses. Hastily, he stood and yanked Blanche to her feet.

Ducking her head with embarrassment, she wiped at the mud on her skirt.

"Night comes early. We'd best hurry into town." Michael cursed himself for the awkwardness of this speech, but he didn't possess a lover's words. He merely helped her back to the saddle, ignoring the throbbing in his loins as he climbed up behind her. He might as well try to ignore a manacle around his heart.

"I'll not turn back," she whispered.

She didn't say more, leaving Michael with the uneasy feeling that she spoke of more than the road to London.

Fourteen

"Michael, don't leave me here alone." Blanche caught Michael's sleeve as he prepared to leave her in a private parlor.

He hesitated. The knowledge that she owned a mill that worked people like slaves had shaken her, he understood. She had spent hours composing letters after they arrived at the inn. But the memory of the kiss obliged him to leave.

"I am tired of eating alone, Michael, and deserting me like this is ungentlemanly. What is the purpose, after all? Can't we cry friends?"

"And is it friends you're being with a penniless Irishman?" he asked mockingly. "'Tis not a puppy dog I am. I'll be off on the morrow or the next day, and you'll be returnin' to your real friends. Nay, 'tis better this way all around."

She jerked his coat sleeve again and gave him a look of exasperation. "Were I given to violence, I'd smack you, O'Toole, or whoever you are tonight. Your monetary status has no relevance to me, although admittedly, your tendency to disappear at will annoys me abominably. One of these days you'll do that to someone who will come after you with a big stick. But that's no matter now. I merely want some company besides my own tonight."

Only Gavin had ever cared enough to threaten him with a stick for disappearing. Michael kneaded his brow and closed the door. "Did you have something in particular you wished to discuss? Have you changed your mind about tracing Fiona? It's a long journey just to trace one little girl."

He strolled the planked floor rather than take the seat Blanche offered.

"I haven't changed my mind," she answered. "I do worry about what the Runner may have found by now. Perhaps we should have let someone else know what is happening." She took a seat at the polished table and adjusted her skirts around her.

"I told the Runner to go to Gavin if need be. He'll know what to do as well or better than we. With any luck, if any of my friends actually see Fiona, they'll most likely abduct her and drop her on Gavin's doorstep. You don't want to be there if that happens," Michael said wryly.

"Probably not, but I still worry. If she fears someone who is dangerous, and it involves Parliament, then we must find out more. Perhaps we should have notified government authorities."

Michael snorted impolitely. "Gavin and Neville *are* government authorities. How do you think they would react should we present them with our story?"

The dinner tray arrived, and Blanche didn't reply as the maid set their food upon the table. Michael had never eaten so well in his memory. He'd spent the better part of his life arbitrarily redistributing other people's wealth. It had never occurred to him to partake of it himself. But Blanche watched him expectantly, and he took the seat offered.

"I suppose you're right," she agreed reluctantly. "We know very little about her. I just hope she is all right somewhere."

Pouring the contents of a pitcher into his glass and discovering it was ale and not cider, Michael frowned. "Until she is found, there is nothing else we can do in London. I still think the problem lies where she comes from."

Blanche watched as he set aside his glass of ale. "Do you not drink ale? Should I have ordered brandy?"

"I'll have coffee later."

Blanche's brow pleated at his declaration but she did not press the issue. It was one of the things he liked about her. She accepted his idiosyncrasies. Thanking her for that, Michael produced a silk rose from an inner pocket and lay it across the table in front of her.

She blinked, then gave him one of those blinding smiles that had the impact of a sunrise at midnight. He had taught her some of his sleight of hand tricks when he'd kept her entertained after the fire. She understood the mechanics, but she'd never caught on to the swiftness of the illusion. He could still surprise her upon occasion.

She stroked the petals and tucked the flower into her sash. "Do you carry a supply of such things for special occasions?"

Michael grinned. "And you're not after believin' I pulled it from thin air? I'm that destroyed, I am."

"So, don't tell me. Tell me how I can find a man of business who will listen to me and not Neville or his peers. All men think women are fools. How will I ever know what is happening at places like the mill?"

"You cannot travel around the country like Barnaby. There is only so much you can do," Michael reminded her. "By getting rid of your grandfather's man, you are off to a new start. The next one should answer to you and not act by your grandfather's beliefs. Question every applicant carefully and see if he is willing to accept new ideas. Perhaps you could ask if they believe local management is preferable to absentee ownership. An honest answer to that question will tell you a great deal."

Blanche rewarded him with another heart-melting smile. "You're right! I have ordered my solicitor to find a list of applicants. I shall see how they respond to that question." She glanced at his untouched glass with concern. "Shall I order some wine?"

"Coffee or cider is fine." In truth, after that smile, he could drink turpentine and not know it. He could not look upon her face for long either, for fear his gaze would fall lower where his rose snuggled in the sash beneath her breasts. She wore no scarf to conceal the devil's own temptations curving her bodice. He had the urge to sit on his hands to prevent their straying.

She rang for the serving girl, and Michael was distracted by the soft curve of Blanche's bare arm, The maid returned with a heated bowl of punch. It wasn't coffee, but Michael took the cup. It was sweet with the taste of apples, not the usual potent grog, and it gave him something else to do with his hands. He'd already carved the entire leg of lamb into tiny slices.

"I have never been to Ireland," Blanche said.

Michael dragged his attention away from her physical assets. He had done himself no favors by avoiding the physical pleasures of women so long. He stretched his legs and sipped at the hot punch as he listened.

"If our road leads there, will we travel by ship? What will the weather be like?"

The aroma of roasted lamb in mint sauce blended with the herbal spices of Blanche's sachet. The fire crackled and popped, providing a musical rhythm to accompany a fiddle singing in the neighboring tavern. Lamplight flickered, casting mysterious and seductive shadows.

Desperately, Michael grasped the thread of conversation. "The journey across the Irish Sea is short in mild weather. 'Tis April now and the worst of the winter's storms have passed. Have you never traveled by water?"

Her eyes seemed luminous behind lashes too long for safety. Michael drank thirstily and poured more.

"I've never been on a ship of any kind," she said wistfully. "I grew up at Anglesey, completely land-locked. My grandfather never traveled, and it did not occur to him that I might like to try."

He'd spent his entire life on the road, while she'd never left home. If nothing else illustrated the chasm between them, this did.

"I think I would enjoy traveling," she said tentatively.

Michael shook his head. He was behaving like a complete oaf, not even keeping up his end of the conversation. "Travel does widen one's experience," he agreed. Having some difficulty persuading the words from his tongue, he glared at his nearly empty mug. "Now if you will excuse me, I think I had best retire. Let me escort you to your room."

She pouted, but when he staggered to his feet, she reluctantly followed. Michael thought his head might spin off his shoulders, and he cursed the punch and his own blindness in drinking it.

"They never brought your coffee," Blanche murmured near his ear. Michael glanced down, surprised to find her clinging to his arm, her small breasts nearly brushing his coat. "Shall I have them send it to your room?"

"I'll take care of it," he responded thickly, aware that her hair smelled of lemons. He inhaled the fresh scent amidst the odors of pipe smoke and stale ale in the inn corridor.

Somehow, he kept his head from falling off his shoulders as they climbed the stairs. All too aware of the sway of Blanche's hips and the scent of her hair, Michael counted himself fortunate to remain standing.

They halted before her door, and she stood on tip-toe and pressed a kiss to his cheek. "You are too much a gentleman," she whispered.

He could have grabbed her then, but years of training and the effect of drink prevented his hastiness. She smiled sadly, then disappeared into her room and closed the door.

Michael stared at the rough oak panel for a while before staggering down the corridor. In his current state, she was in far more danger of being disturbed by him than strangers.

Shutting his door, Michael removed his coat and splashed cold water on his face. Perhaps, as in the case of women, he should have partaken of more liquor during his lifetime and developed a better resistance. He didn't dislike either alcohol or women. He just deemed it wiser not to indulge in them.

He tore off his cravat, dropped to the bed, and sprawled against the pillows. Dimly, he registered a knock at his door. Unaware that he'd offered an invitation, Michael watched the serving girl enter with a tray of coffee. He grabbed the cup as the maid bobbed a curtsy and departed. He should lock the door after her, he mused. He'd never tasted better coffee in his life. Leaning back against the headboard, he could see how one would grow accustomed to a life of wealth.

The bed had towering mahogany posts draped in dark blue damask that he could pull closed against drafts. A down-filled satin counterpane provided warmth to keep a winter's night at bay. Michael yanked back the cover and admired the fine linen sheets. He felt too unclean for such finery.

He should have ordered a bath. He would make do with the cold water in the stand and the kettle over the fire.

Head still spinning, he struggled from his clothes. The coffee hadn't helped, but perhaps a bath would. Mixing the water in the bowl and sudsing a cloth with a French milled soap that smelled better than anything he'd encountered in a long time, he lathered all over.

The unaccustomed luxury of soap, warmth, and a full meal, aroused him despite his weariness. Or perhaps the unruly image of Blanche caressing where the towel touched unlocked his control. Whatever, he would have a devil of a time sleeping tonight.

After toweling himself in front of the fire, Michael sipped his coffee. Draining the dregs and with his member still standing at full attention, he staggered to the bed and slid naked between the cold sheets, but his loins burned hotter than ever. Damn the woman.

He doused the lamp, leaving only the fire's light for illumination. Now, if only he had a warm body to join with. He rubbed the cold empty place at his side and tried to imagine what it would be like having a woman like Blanche in bed with him, talking softly of the day past or the morrow's dawn. To feel her cuddle close and fit her flesh to his.

A cold draft doused those warm thoughts, and Michael sought a more comfortable position for his aching loins. The click of a door reminded him he hadn't turned the key in the lock. He tried dragging himself awake enough to rise to the task, but the bliss of too much alcohol wrapped around him, and the thought wandered off.

The bed creaked and sagged to one side, shifting the warm feathers of the mattress. Michael tossed again, seeking the warm spot. Instead, his hand encountered hot flesh, and he groaned with delight at the vividness of his dream.

He might wake to spilled seed upon the sheets, but for now, he needed the release of his dreams. His palm sought the soft haven he had desired for so long, and with an exhalation from deep in his soul, Michael hugged his dream closer. If naught else, he might conjure up the bliss of Blanche's kiss all over again.

Fifteen

Michael's hand gripped her waist and dragged her deeper into the bed. If she meant to turn back on her bold course, now was the time. The magnetism of his touch, however, possessed a pull stronger than fear or doubt. She slipped toward him at his urging.

Murmuring incoherently, he slid his hand down her side, grazing her breast, lovingly tracing the dip of her waist, and the rise of her hip, all covered by her nightshift. She caught her breath at the wave of sensation.

She knew her willfulness for what it was. She had wanted Michael's kisses again. She'd hoped ale would break down his resistance, and when it hadn't, she'd ordered the liquor-laced punch. She thought the heady brew must have stolen her own wits.

As Michael's hand explored more fully, caressing her curves, urging her closer, Blanche's senses reacted to the effects of alcohol, desire, and fear. Bliss, heady bliss swept through her as his lips finally reached her own. For weeks, years, she had coveted this tender exchange. Michael's mouth nibbled along hers. The heat and moisture stirred primitive responses. Daringly, she stroked his jaw while his kisses wandered from the corners of her lips and settled fully in the center. Blanche concentrated on the increasing urgency of his lips crushing hers, absorbing each new sensation, each caress, each moment as it came. She didn't want to give in to doubt or fear. Not now. Not with Michael.

The gentle stroke of his hand through her hair relaxed her. His lips turned soft, beseeching as he pulled her closer and plied her mouth more thoroughly. She felt protected, cherished while he fed her lips with sweet-flavored kisses.

Only when his hands strayed to her shoulders and held her more firmly, as his kisses deepened and his mouth parted over hers did Blanche recognize the depth of her danger. She hadn't expected the heated thrust of Michael's tongue between her teeth. His kiss deepened enticingly, their breaths mingled, and Blanche dug her fingers into his arm to prevent drowning in the tides of desire.

She could no longer deny the strength of the hands crushing her against the bed, the bare flesh of his muscled arms, and the response of her own body as she arched upward, needing the brush of his chest against hers. *His naked chest.* Naked! He wore no bed clothes. She had never imagined…

"You are so beautiful, so soft…"

The kisses she'd craved tasted sweeter than ever with Michael's whispered endearments. Blanche daringly invited further exploration as his tongue swept her inner lip. His hand roamed from her shoulder to her breast again, and she gasped. Even though protected by a thin cover of linen, her nipple responded, and she felt the tug straight to her womb.

"I need to touch you here, and here…" His fingers worked their magic across both her breasts and downward, exploring, arousing.

The combination of heady kisses, strumming fingers, and the hard, heated body pressed along hers undid her completely. Blanche stroked his chest.

In response, Michael plunged his tongue between her teeth without the earlier gentleness, but with an urgency that fired Blanche's blood. He wedged his leg between her knees and hovered over her, his sensitive hands wandering and exploring with a restless desire that matched her own.

Her breasts swelled beneath his ministrations. Her hips rose and fell, searching out the potent heat of his nakedness. His kisses wandered with his hands, discovering pockets of exquisite pleasure along her jaw and throat.

"Your hair smells of lemons," Michael murmured as he ransacked her tresses. Spreading the strands along the pillow, he kissed behind her ear, and Blanche cried out in pleasure and desperation.

The linen of her shift offered some protection, but she writhed impatiently against the encumbrance. Michael's knowing fingers unfastened the ribbons of her bodice.

A draft of cool air blew across her heated skin. She groaned in relief as his fingers slipped beneath the opening, finding the nakedness of her breast. Any doubt dissolved beneath Michael's gentle explorations of her swollen nipple. The intoxicating touch scorched her. The twin pleasures of mouth and hand pinned her to the bed more surely than his greater weight.

Her brain must surely have disintegrated because she could do no more than rub her hands up and down his taut arms, caress his shoulders, and submit to the demands of his mouth. When his lips slid away, she whimpered and urged him back.

Instead, his mouth covered her breast, and she emitted a high, keening cry of joy and surrender. She dug her fingers into his hair, and Michael lifted her other breast and took it equally, swirling his tongue around the tip. The heat forming between her legs had Blanche squirming against the weight of him. She didn't know if she needed him to move away or closer.

He shifted to one side, allowing her hips to rise without the interference of his greater weight. Blanche cried out against his departure, then froze as she realized Michael's hand now rested on her bare thigh.

His hand stroked higher, touching her between her legs, while he whispered words that both frightened and tantalized. Blanche tried fighting the sensation as her hips rose and fell beneath his caresses, but she was helpless against his insistent stroke. He obliterated all but the pleasure and the need and the urgency. When he moved over her again, spreading her legs wide with his knees, she no longer resisted.

Not until his male hardness branded its heat against her thigh did she truly panic. She accepted the gentle magic of his hands and fingers. In the haze of mindless lust, she had not considered the full extent of male demands. He'd always abided by her wishes before, never insisting upon his own.

But she didn't resist. Her hips arched eagerly upward, seeking solace for the aching void.

* * *

Groaning with long-denied desire, Michael accepted her invitation with the same mindless lust in which it was offered. Somewhere in the back of his mind he knew he no longer dreamed. But now that he had the object of those dreams in his arms, years of denial erupted in passion beyond control. With a shout of triumph, he thrust deeply.

Blanche's cry of pain pierced Michael's alcohol-sodden brain, but he'd gone well beyond any ability to heed anything other than attaining this exquisite pleasure. Even as she wept, he thrust and thrust again, pushing past the tense muscles and burying himself deep inside her.

With a thrill of possession, he cupped the tender weight of soft breasts, exciting her hips to the restless motion of earlier. Michael nearly wept in rapture when her tightness relaxed. With gratitude, he kissed her wet cheek and sank deeper.

He'd denied himself too long to last more than a few minutes. With the urgency of years of abstinence, he pulled back and thrust again. Blanche's inner muscles gripped and held him even as her hands pushed ineffectually at his arms in protest. Covering her mouth with his, Michael took one more mind-exploding plunge. With a cry of primeval triumph, he emptied all his hopes and dreams deep within her woman's body.

Gently, he kissed away her tears. Alcohol had robbed him of coherent speech, but instinct guided him. Unable to force his long-starved body from the haven it had found, he set about giving her the solace she deserved.

As Michael's roving hands once more strayed down her abdomen, Blanche tried summoning the energy to push him away. She felt wounded and shamed at the same time. The bliss-fogged ecstasy of earlier had dissipated. She had given herself to a man who didn't want her, who had taken her only because she'd made him drunk. Embarrassment stained her as much as the stickiness of his seed against her thigh. His kisses didn't relieve the deep pulsating pain where he'd penetrated her. She shoved futilely at his muscled chest, but he only adjusted his weight so he didn't burden her. He kissed her again, then lowered his head to suckle at her breast.

How quickly desire returned! All too aware of the pressure of Michael's heavy legs parting hers, she squirmed against him, seeking to evade the source of the heat. Instead, she only succeeded in recognizing the growing length of him inside her. Her aching soreness dissolved in a rush of renewed need.

Panicking at the ease with which he again bound her, Blanche struggled for her freedom. Michael teased her nipple with his tongue and slid his hand between their hips, seeking and finding another nub to entice. She nearly swooned when he fondled her there, then involuntarily raised her hips to give him access.

"I'll take care of you," he whispered against her ear as he

lowered his weight on her again. "You're mine now, and I'll treasure you forever. Let me pleasure you, Blanche."

Openly weeping, she surrendered. If she heeded her heart and not her head, she could revel in the delight of Michael's caresses. She knew they would lead her where she wanted to go.

And they did. Oh, how they did. This time, when he thrust, she accepted him fully, and cried out with joy at the joining. He took her slowly, gently this time, letting her adjust to his intrusion, then sweeping her to the same brink of desire he'd unleashed earlier.

With a wild cry of happiness, Blanche followed him over the edge, giving herself up to the freedom of weightlessness as they fell into the void together.

* * *

"There is a man at the door who is most insistent upon seeing you, my lord," the butler said with his usual note of disapproval.

Gavin, Marquess of Effingham, winced over the letter he was writing. He'd rented the Earl of Mellon's London house for the Season, but he royally wished he didn't have to rent the servants as well. Since the man wouldn't disappear even if he continued glaring at the paper beneath his fingers, the marquess gave a cursory acknowledgment of his presence, then sat back to trim his pen. "Who is it, Dickson?"

"He has no card, my lord. He looks a ruffian, but he insists he's from Bow Street and he must see you. I believe he referred to your brother."

Gavin grinned inwardly at the man's snide intonation on the word "brother." The last time Michael had flitted through here, he'd made the silverware disappear from the sideboard and reappear in various places on the butler's person. Dickson nearly had an apoplexy. Gavin had hoped he'd offer his resignation, but the man knew a comfortable position when he saw one. The Earl of Mellon never used his town home, so the place stayed empty and masterless the better part of the year. Gavin had long ago decided the earl had enough sense to keep Dickson from his country home but had too kind a heart to get rid of the obnoxious boor.

"Then I suppose you had best show him up, Dickson," Gavin said, cleaning the pen and returning it to his holder. A Bow Street Runner showing up at his door with word of Michael both angered and worried him. Michael was a grown man. Gavin had long since quit trying to tame him. Now he just prayed daily that his brother wouldn't get himself hanged. Or murdered.

The Runner smelled as if he hadn't indulged in soap in days. Gavin watched an unraveling thread from a buttonhole stretched taut across the man's ample girth, wondering what kept the entire waistcoat from splitting at the seams or sending buttons flying like missiles through the air.

"Gatsby, you say your name is?" Gavin inquired, trying to keep his attention on the topic.

"Mortimer Gatsby, at your service, your lordship," the man pronounced formally, making a painful bow. A button gave up its grip and popped across the rug.

"And you have word of my brother?" Gavin had come to accept the stumbling speech of newcomers introduced to his chambers. He didn't know if his title or his scarred jaw sent their brains into relapse, but he'd learned patience until they recovered their tongues.

"Not of your brother, my lord," the man answered crushing his cap in his hands. "He just says as to let you know when I've got somethin' to report. I've got somethin' to report."

Gavin prayed for more patience than he possessed, summoned Dickson to bring brandy, and ordered the Runner into a seat. The man nervously dusted off the chair with his filthy handkerchief, as if doing so would keep the chair from contamination. "Your report, sir?" Gavin prompted once the man sipped at his drink.

"Aye, your lordship. I've scouted every house in the alley, and there ain't no sign of the Irish female, but she knows I'm there. She's had a brat trailin' me from mornin' to sundown when I'm over that ways. Leastwise, I figger it's her. She sent me a message when I stopped at a tavern there last night. That's what I've come to tell you."

Gavin assumed Michael had lost one of his strays and employed this man to find her. That would be an odd thing for any normal person to do, but any normal person wouldn't go about the countryside picking up strays and finding them homes. Michael's activities made sense only to Michael.

"And the message?" he prompted again.

"She says as to tell your brother not to let the lady near the duke," the Runner recited with evident pride in his memory.

"What lady and what duke?" Gavin demanded, not feeling at all entertained by the direction of this conversation.

The Runner scratched his nearly bald pate. "Well, as to that, I can't say with certainty, but ain't it Anglesey's lady cousin what got her carriage blown to bits?"

Gavin sighed and tugged at his coat sleeve. Michael had once erroneously assumed the Duke of Anglesey meant to harm his cousin, Lady Blanche. Surely he had not returned to that insane theory again. Anglesey was a product of his proper upbringing: stiff-necked, stubborn, narrow-minded.... Gavin didn't bother completing the list for nowhere in it did it include "murderously inclined." Honorable gentlemen did not murder female relations no matter how much they might enjoy considering it. No more than Gavin considered murdering Michael, leastwise.

"I think you had best begin at the beginning, Mr. Gatsby. I seem to be missing a few pertinent facts."

The Runner nodded and began a horrifying recital involving exploding carriages, disappearing Irish waifs, a house of known treasonous activities, and ending with the fact that Michael wanted all this dumped on Gavin's door while Michael took off for parts unknown. Gavin thought murder too easy for his wretched relation by the time the recital concluded.

But he nodded as the man finished his tale and the brandy at the same time. "Thank you for illuminating the picture, Mr. Gatsby. I trust you will keep me informed of any other activity, and if you should catch this Fiona person, that you will bring her directly to me. My butler will see you adequately recompensed as you leave."

The Runner took up his cap and lumbered out. The minute the door closed behind him, Gavin ran his hands through his hair, rang for Dickson, ordered the sum paid for the Runner and that a maid find his wife. He had a notion that Dillian knew more of this than he did.

Dillian's dark curls bounced as she dashed into the room within seconds of the Runner's departure. She'd no doubt been listening at the other door the whole time. Gavin tried scowling at her, but she sat on his chair arm and kissed his scarred cheek. Pleasure shot down his spine every time she did that.

He curled his arm around her waist. "All right. Tell me what you know of this maze Michael has conjured," Gavin demanded gruffly.

She leaned against his shoulder and sighed. "I have no idea, but it involves Blanche. She came here one day with her maid in her own carriage, left the maid and the carriage, and departed out the back way as if eluding someone. She explained that Michael thought it best if she went to Dorset to avoid whoever had blown up her coach. I wanted her to take someone with her, but she assured me she stayed with friends and they would take care of her."

"And?" Gavin prompted, knowing he still didn't possess the whole story.

Dillian frowned. "Blanche owns a cottage in Dorset, but I don't believe she keeps any servants there. I've known her for years, and not once has she gone to visit. I can't imagine what friends she might have who live there. Blanche only knows people of society."

"And Michael? How is Michael involved?"

"Well-l-l," she drew out the word as she seemingly studied the carved-wood paneling of the ceiling. "I talked to Marian."

Gavin groaned. "If my cousin Marian is involved in this, it is worse than I thought."

Dillian nibbled on his ear before whispering into it. "Your cousin is a very nice lady, and she lets Michael run all over her just as you do. He brought Blanche to her after the exploding coach incident. He wanted Blanche to disguise herself and go away. Then he pulled one of his disappearing acts and Blanche became quite enraged."

Gavin tugged his wife from her tempting occupation and set her on her feet. "What did Lady Blanche do after my wretch of a brother dumped her on Marian?"

Dillian grinned. "What any sensible woman would do. She disguised herself and went to Elton Alley after him. That's where Fiona's aunt lives."

Gavin gave her a look askance. "I'm not going to like the rest of this story, am I?"

"I haven't heard from Blanche for a week. No, I don't think you'll like the rest of this story."

With a curse, Gavin rang for Dickson again. This time, the lady's damned cousin, the duke, could be in on the escapade. He had no intention of keeping Michael's secrets to himself if they involved Blanche. He'd seen the pair of them at work a few years ago, and the memory still gave him shudders.

Between Blanche and Michael, they would have the Tower of London carted off on a barge and London Bridge sold to the French. He wanted someone else to share the responsibility of stopping them. He didn't much care if he and the duke were at daggers drawn in Parliament. They needed a united front at home.

And then they needed to find their damned relations and lock them up somewhere until all of them were old and gray.

Sixteen

Blanche awakened feeling rested and content and to the odd sensation of something not quite right. Of course, feeling happy was odd enough in itself.

She delayed opening her eyes, letting the warmth of the bed enfold her. A maid must have stirred the fire. She snuggled deeper into the pillow. The place between her legs ached, but she sought sleep and the pleasant dreams of the past night.

She stirred restlessly, and realized her nightshift was not only wrapped about her waist, but open all the way down the front. She glanced down at her bare breasts and flushed. She definitely did not want to wake up. Maybe if she went back to sleep, she'd wake up in her own bed with her nightshift properly fastened and in place.

But the navy bed curtains pulled closed against the draft didn't resemble the rose hangings on the bed she'd been given last night. She knew perfectly well she had never lain between the sheets of that other bed. Instead, she had willfully decided to make Michael kiss her.

Blanche winced at the memory of that decision. She must have been drunk. She would never touch punch again, not after two glasses of wine, anyway.

Maybe it had been just some cup-shot dream. Her hand swept the bed and found it empty. Maybe Michael had never lain there. He was perfectly capable of letting her sleep it off in his room while he disappeared into the stable. Surely he had the sense to put her aside as he had done since the day they met.

But she'd plied him with more drink than she'd consumed. He would have been well-addled by the time she'd climbed into his bed. And if the evidence of her body gave any testimony, what she remembered was not a drunken dream. She had done it. She had finally experienced the marriage act. And she had enjoyed it, just as Dillian had said she would if the right man came along. Of course, Michael was scarcely the right man in any other sense of the word, but for this purpose, he was perfect. She wanted to try it again in the bright light of day.

That gave her pause. If Michael had wanted to couple with her again, he would still be lying at her side. That he had pulled one of his disappearing acts didn't bode well at all. Panic overcame any remaining shyness. She didn't want to be left alone in a strange inn days from her home. Hastily fastening the ribbons of her bodice, Blanche leaned across the bed and peeked out the curtains.

Michael sat, fully clothed, in a chair between the fire and the window, his arms crossed forbiddingly over his wide chest. She'd seen him do that before, and it never meant anything good. With the light behind him, she couldn't make much of his expression, and she was grateful for that reprieve. Michael set a high price on his principles.

"I've brought your clothes and ordered fresh water. You may dress while I call the carriage." He sounded murderous.

He rose, and Blanche swallowed, realizing just how large he was. His lean build concealed the strength of ten men.

She didn't object when he let himself out. She hadn't known what to expect from him, but she hadn't expect cold anger. Michael didn't know the meaning of cold, and his anger usually found outlet in action, not contemptuous words. She felt as if she'd fallen even lower than the man who ordered the militia to shoot yesterday. She *was* lower than that man. She owned the mill that had made wretched slaves of those people.

That didn't give Michael cause to treat her as if she were a piece of dirt. They had shared something beautiful last night. Why couldn't he just admit that and go on?

Because despite all appearances to the contrary, Michael was a gentleman, and gentlemen felt obligated to treat ladies with honor. That meant after what they'd done last night, he'd have to offer her marriage.

Soberly, Blanche dragged herself from bed to the dressing screen. While she washed, she contemplated what she'd done.

She didn't want to marry. Michael didn't want to marry. So why was there any problem? She would just explain things, make him understand. She'd enjoyed what they'd done. She would like knowing more. She didn't fear having a child out of wedlock. Her wealth could conceal anything. Michael had shown her how to create illusions by giving people what they expected to see, while he did as he pleased behind their backs. If he could do it, so could she.

Reaching that conclusion, Blanche recovered some of her equilibrium. She wanted to try coupling in the sunlight. In the carriage. Anywhere. Anytime. Her fingers grew clumsy with excitement as she tied her ribbons.

Michael didn't return. Uneasy, Blanche hurried as best she could. Michael had brought her valise to this room. She donned her blue velvet traveling gown and fastened her hair in a loop tied with matching ribbons. She covered her head with a jaunty hat that did nothing to disguise her gold tresses. She had little vanity, but she knew what men liked. She would make Michael want her again.

She stopped in front of the mirror and grimaced at the faint red scars along her hairline, but she didn't think Michael noticed them. Michael liked touching, and what he saw didn't matter to him as much as what his other senses told him. She dabbed a little cologne to her wrists. She seldom wore it, but she would try anything to ease his anger.

Sweeping down the stairs with heart pounding, Blanche didn't see anyone in the lobby, and she hastened to the inn door. The coach waited in the yard, the driver already in his seat. She was starved and would like breakfast, but she didn't want to escalate Michael's anger. Glancing around, she saw his horse tied to the back of the coach, and her heart lightened. He would ride with her today!

The innkeeper ran out bearing a brown paper-wrapped parcel that steamed in the early morning chill. Behind him a servant appeared with her trunk and tied it to the carriage.

"His lordship ordered up some ham and hot bread, my lady. And I've added some cheese and bacon with some of my wife's good jam. It will keep you going awhile. It's been a pleasure serving you and your lord, my lady. I hope you will return again."

Astonished, Blanche took the package, then accepted the hand of the footman to help her into the carriage. Hot bricks waited on the floor to warm her feet. Michael had thought of everything. So where was the damned man?

And why were they suddenly *her ladyship* and *his lordship*? They'd traveled incognito all this way, pretending to be the wealthy children of a Northumberland squire. What on earth had Michael told them? And why?

She caught her breath on a gasp as Michael appeared in the inn yard carrying a steaming jug. He wore his most elegant beaver hat, curled at the brim and polished to the same gloss as his high top boots. An emerald swallow-tailed coat enhanced the breadth of his shoulders, and its cutaway tailoring emphasized the flatness and narrowness of his hips. He had no fancy watch or fobs, but the shimmering white of his cravat spoke of expensive tailors and an army of servants. Except she knew he had neither.

She swallowed hard, realizing she now knew what lay beneath those gentlemanly clothes. She had never considered a man's naked body before, but now her thoughts couldn't travel past Michael's. Even as she flushed with embarrassment at the memory of what they'd done, she wanted to try it again.

Michael shook the innkeeper's hand and crossed the yard to enter the carriage. Silently, he took the seat across from her, shrinking the interior with his presence. The driver let his horses have their heads, and the coach jerked into motion, nearly upsetting Blanche from the seat. She grabbed the hand grip rather than fall into Michael's lap. The aroma of strong coffee struck her as she straightened.

Michael produced a pewter cup from thin air and poured coffee from the jug he'd carried. Blanche wanted to smack him for this nonchalant performance, but she'd already learned her lesson about instigating arguments with this man. He disliked drama or high emotion and disappeared in its wake. She must talk with him before he took it into his head to vanish again.

"I don't suppose you could produce another cup while you're at it?" she asked, eyeing the steaming mug with thirst.

He silently handed her his.

She looked down at it, then up at him. She couldn't ever remember drinking from the same cup as anyone else. Meeting his mocking eyes and remembering what they had done last night, she blushed. It scarcely mattered if they shared a cup after last night. They'd certainly shared everything else. She drank thirstily.

"Save some for me," he said dryly. "I don't think your head is as painful as mine."

Blanche returned the mug and dabbed at her lips with a handkerchief. "I am sorry for that. I think they made the punch recipe too strong." She kept her gaze lowered as she opened the parcel in her lap.

"That's stating it mildly."

She regretted the tension between them. Michael had always made her laugh or think or took her away from whatever bothered her most. Cautiously, she handed him some bread and ham on a linen napkin the innkeeper had thoughtfully provided. When he didn't take it, she was forced to look inquiringly at him.

"My stomach won't tolerate food right now," he told her honestly. "I don't hold my liquor well."

Blushing, Blanche glanced back at her lap. She took full responsibility for what had happened last night. But she didn't know how to explain that in the bright light of day.

"Why did the innkeeper call me *my lady*?" she asked instead.

"The maid thought you'd been kidnapped when you weren't in your room this morning. I had to convince them that we were just recently married and keeping it a secret until we reached our families. It also helped when I called myself Lord Michael. Apparently, the nobility are inclined to strange fits and starts."

Blanche smiled at this return of the Michael she knew. He had a tale covering any circumstance. But his tone remained empty and distant. Her apology hadn't begun to touch the surface of his anger.

"I am sorry I got you drunk, and I am sorry if I caused you any embarrassment." Not knowing what else to say, she bit off some of the ham and bread as an excuse for not saying more.

The silence in the carriage grew longer. The noise of the galloping horses drowned out any early morning birdsong. The trunk clattered against the back of the carriage. One of the rear wheels squeaked. But still, the silence was deafening.

When she'd finished chewing, Michael interrupted her before she could take a second. "Why did you do it?"

Startled, Blanche finally lifted her gaze to his. She read nothing in his expression. She didn't even see curiosity there. She'd never seen him quite so remote. The man across from her had become an enigmatic stranger. A handsome stranger, admittedly, but someone she could never have guessed existed inside the charismatic man she knew.

She dropped her gaze again. "I wanted you to kiss me again." She couldn't offer anything less than honesty, if this were her punishment. She owed him that.

"You wanted...." He cut off his astonishment and said with

practiced casualness, "You certainly found an odd way to go about it."

"Yes, well, perhaps I had a little too much of the punch also. Any other man would have kissed me in the parlor, or at the door. I would no doubt have had to fight off the advances of any man who'd imbibed as much as you did. But you wouldn't even kiss me."

She said the last angrily, almost convincing herself it was partially his fault for not indulging her in this one thing. But she knew better. She wasn't really spoiled enough to believe she deserved everything she wanted.

"I don't suppose you gave consideration to the possibility that there was a reason for that," he said dryly, sipping at his coffee again. He held up his hand when she glared at him. Finally, he showed some curiosity as he asked, "Why me? You could have the kisses of any man. Why must you have mine?"

That question set her aback. Blinking, Blanche tried to formulate an answer. The more obvious one was that she wanted his kisses because she couldn't have them. But that was a glib understatement. Finally, she admitted in a low voice, "Because I don't like anyone else's."

The silence that followed his noncommittal "Ahhh" nearly broke her.

When she glanced back at him, he had his eyes closed and seemed asleep. Gently, she took the jug of coffee and corked it.

She didn't know if he truly slept. He hadn't offered for her. Sighing, Blanche picked at the remains of her breakfast. Apparently, even Michael knew the impossibility of a match between them. She didn't suppose he'd be too willing to continue to share her bed without it, though. Why, of all the men she could have chosen, had she fallen for the one with enough honor to stay out of her bed?

Seventeen

Fiona sat cross-legged in front of the garret window, watching the Runner strolling along the trash-filled alley below, and wondered if she had been wrong to run away from O'Toole and Lady Blanche. Family loyalty required she protect Seamus and her uncle. They were all she had, and O'Toole had seemed intent on discovering all her secrets, drat the man. Only now, sitting here helpless, she wondered if she hadn't been just a bit hasty.

She'd sent the Runner a message when she'd heard the plans for picking off England's great nobles one at a time. At least Seamus and Uncle William hadn't been part of that discussion. They had apparently returned to Ireland to gather funds. She'd learned the other conspirators by appearance well enough to follow them to their meeting places. They seldom wandered farther than these back alleys of Covent Garden, and she had Little Jack helping her. Hiding in these musty old attics, she could almost always hear their plans.

Unfortunately, she feared they knew she lurked nearby. Seamus had received word that she'd gone missing. The men who had blown up the duke's carriage had heard the lady was looking for someone named Fiona. She should never have given O'Toole her real name. Now they had added Lady Blanche to their list of targets along with her cousin, the duke. She didn't dare go near either of them again.

It wasn't as if she didn't understand the need for Irishmen to control their own destiny. She certainly recognized the frustration and anger of the overworked poor. But she could not sympathize with violence. There had to be a better way.

At the moment, though, she was more concerned with her own neck. She couldn't continue hiding in one garret or cellar or another. She'd enlisted the aid of a homeless little boy who brought her what morsels he thieved. She shared her hiding places with him and helped him steal food from the poor larders of the houses she hid in. But ultimately, they would get caught. That was why she kept watch on the Runner.

He was searching for her, so she concluded Lady Blanche must have hired him. Seamus and O'Toole wouldn't have the funds. Fiona didn't want the lady harmed. She would warn her about the danger of this group of mad radicals except she couldn't figure out how to do it without involving Seamus and William.

She had to do something soon. Last night the madmen had decided they couldn't acquire enough gunpowder to blow up Parliament, but they almost had sufficient funds for a nobleman's house. They intended to wait until all the cabinet officials had one of their dinners together. The Duke of Anglesey had planned such a dinner the first week of May.

Fiona watched the Runner disappear around the corner and sighed. She owed the duke naught. Did she dare risk herself and her family to warn him?

* * *

Blanche allowed Michael to feign sleep for as long as she could. Perhaps he truly did doze upon occasion, but she knew he was awake now. Even Michael hadn't the willpower to stop his eyelids from flickering.

"Your coffee will grow cold if you don't finish it soon," she said aloud. "And you really should have something in your stomach to settle it."

He opened his eyes and glared at her, then closed them again. Perhaps the sunlight hurt his head. "I must go back, Michael. I can't leave those poor people out of work. It's an outrage. I shall just go in and tell that horrible man who I am, and set things right."

Michael groped for the cup without opening his eyes. "You'll ruin your reputation by appearing there without an appropriate escort, and you will do it for naught. He doesn't even know the mill owner's name. He'll demand written notification from Barnaby. You've done all you can. When you interview men for Barnaby's position, you can make certain they're prepared to travel at once. That's all you can do."

Blanche took his cup and filled it. She enjoyed the way Michael sipped gratefully at the coffee she handed him, as if making him happy mattered.

"It's not enough," she insisted. "Many of those people were injured because of me. They won't have any way of providing food for their tables. Children could go hungry. If nothing else, I must go back and distribute food."

He opened his eyes to narrow slits. "I took care of that. Our traveling funds are now quite limited. We won't be staying in such elegant inns from here on."

It didn't surprise Blanche that Michael had divested her of her money to provide for others without asking permission—or even discussing the matter. But still it frustrated her that she could do nothing else.

"I want that manager removed," she said. "And I want those people back to work."

Michael unbent his long legs and stretched them across the carriage. Blanche had the uneasy feeling that he was staring at her breasts. She squirmed at the thought.

"I've taken care of that, too," he admitted wearily. "I forged Barnaby's name on a letter remanding earlier orders. The mill will begin twelve hour work days and the workers are receiving a wage increase. Of course, the same needs to be done at every mill you own, but since I don't know the extent of your holdings, I could only correct the one situation."

She kicked his large boot with her small one. "You forged Barnaby's name! How could you? And shouldn't you have at least consulted me before going to such lengths?"

He shrugged. "I doubted you would approve of forgery and saw no reason to blot your pristine conscience with my actions."

"And here I thought you different from other men!" she exploded. "Why must you all think of me as some mush-brained ninnyhammer who can't do anything for herself? Isn't it possible that I might like to be consulted about things that affect my interests? Or must all of you believe that only a man knows what is best for a woman?"

Michael opened his eyes enough to glare at her. "I did precisely what you just suggested, only a little more effectively. Had I asked your permission to forge Barnaby's signature, you would have gone all proper on me, and nothing would have got done."

"How do you know what I would have done since you didn't bother asking?" she demanded. "And how could you have forged Barnaby's signature? You've never seen it."

With a scowl, he produced a rumpled piece of paper from an

inner coat pocket. "I stole this from your desk that day I heard you arguing with him."

Blanche swept the bill of sale from between his fingers, noted the familiar signature of her man of business, and slapped it back in Michael's hands. "Why in the name of heaven would you have stolen such a thing?"

The paper disappeared somewhere about his person. "I find such things useful from time to time. Gavin tries to correct inequities from his position in Parliament, but he might as well try carrying the world on his shoulders. Those stiff-necked aristocrats won't surrender one inch of their power unless someone holds a gun to their heads. I simply find more efficient, if less legal, means of achieving what Gavin wants. Of course, I can only do a little at a time, but that's better than nothing at all."

Blanche slumped against the carriage seat. "I don't suppose you were in Derbyshire earlier this year?"

Michael watched her warily. "Could be."

"When the squire discovered someone had sold his fabled gun collection and distributed the proceeds to his tenant farmers?"

Michael drained his cup, leaned his shoulders back against the seat, and closed his eyes. "Providential that someone wanted to buy the collection, I'd say."

"Providential that an entire armament room could empty itself overnight," she returned with sarcasm. "I had wondered at the time. It didn't seem the work of ordinary thieves."

He twitched his shoulders restlessly beneath his tight coat. "That's neither here nor there. Tonight, we'll reach the village where I found Fiona. My inquiries into how she arrived may take a while. Shall I arrange for a post chaise at the next inn and return you to London?"

The idea of returning to London alone chilled her. She'd enjoyed traveling with Michael, even if he was the most frustrating, irritating man alive. And last night...she couldn't stop thinking about last night. She didn't want to give up that beautiful connection. How could she find a way past Michael's remarkably odd code of honor? Forgery and theft didn't stop him, but he drew the line at bedding willing women. She would never understand the man.

"I thought it unsafe for me back there," she answered stiffly.

"It's obviously unsafe for you with me," he said dryly.

She caught a fleeting glimpse of remorse in his expression and hope rose. He wouldn't deny last night, then. "Or do you feel unsafe with me?" she asked with more boldness than she would have dared had she given her retort any thought at all.

His gaze lowered to her bodice. "I've spent these last hours wondering what else you wear between that pretty blue gown and your skin."

He said that deliberately to scare her. And it did, just a little, at the realization he'd been mentally stripping off her clothes. At the same time, her breasts tightened against the fabric of her chemise. She daringly rubbed a pointed nipple concealed in velvet. "I can feel you inside even when you aren't touching me," she said with wonder.

He groaned low in his throat, and closed his eyes again.

"Does your head still hurt?" she asked guiltily.

"Among other things," he muttered. "Unless you're willing to climb on my lap and service me now, I wouldn't repeat that little maneuver anytime soon. Why don't you read a book? We've a long day ahead."

Her cheeks flamed. Michael was no gentleman to say anything so crude, except she wasn't thinking like a lady. She actually tried to imagine his proposition, but she thought such a position would be more than a trifle awkward. Michael's stiffly uncomfortable posture warned her not to ask about kissing instead.

When he closed his eyes again, she darted a glance at his tight trousers, and the color rose in her cheeks again. He'd meant what he said, if the bulge there was any indication. He'd take her like a whore anytime she was ready.

* * *

The next inn they stopped at had only one room available, and Michael signed them in as Lord and Lady Michael Lawrence. Blanche watched with trepidation as he ordered their baggage carried up. The wheels of his formidable mind had had hours in which to spin plans he wouldn't explain to her. He seemed entirely too calm after the anger of earlier.

This inn lacked the amenities of their earlier stops. She wondered how many coins they had left. She supposed if she really wanted to know, she could check the hem of her skirt and cloak. She'd long since given him the money in her bag.

Michael escorted her upstairs and disappeared immediately thereafter. Since they'd reached the town where he'd found Fiona, Blanche had hoped she could help in his inquiries, but he didn't ask for her help, and she didn't dare put herself forward after what she'd already done. She eyed the lumpy mattress askance and removed her pelisse.

She ate her supper alone. No doubt she tried Michael's patience as much as he tried hers. They didn't suit, except in bed, she amended, glancing in that direction. And even then, she supposed he could find more compatible women. She was the one so isolated she could find no one to suit her taste but Michael.

After supper, she read for as long as she could stand it, then washed and donned her nightshift. She smoothed the soft linen over her body and wondered if she would ever feel Michael's touch again. Watching his hands as he juggled silverware, disappeared cards, and produced roses in winter had excited her imagination long, long ago. He had magic in his fingertips, and she coveted their touch.

Of course, she coveted a child, too. If he'd succeeded in giving her one, she would have to go to the Continent for a year or so. She could easily acquire a paper husband and become a paper widow while there. She'd known other women to do the same, although most just gave their children away and never admitted having them. She wouldn't do that. She would admit it for all to see. By that time, Michael would have gone on to other places, other activities, and would never know the difference.

But as the night grew late, Blanche gave up the hope that Michael meant to return to her bed. She watched out the window for a while but saw no sign of him in the sleepy little village. A tavern down the road spilled light onto the roadway. People came and went from there, but none resembled Michael's familiar silhouette.

She turned down the light and crawled between the fresh linens. The bed wasn't as large as the one last night. If Michael returned, he'd have to lie close to her. Only that thought let her drift into sleep.

Michael returned some hours later. His loins quickened as he stared longingly at the fall of golden hair across the pillow. He'd almost succeeded in shutting this amazing woman from his mind as he'd searched for Fiona's transport. For a short while, he'd almost felt himself again, wearing his juggler's clothes and taking handouts. But watching Blanche like this, he didn't know who he was any longer.

He'd welcomed a gentlewoman into his bed, filled her with his seed, and now he must pay the price. He'd given marriage an idle thought or two upon occasion, but he'd never dreamed of a wife so far above him. Well, he'd *dreamed* of Blanche. He'd done nothing but dream of her since he'd first laid eyes on her standing frail and wistful in her garden and immediately set out to put himself into her employ. He'd just never dreamed of her as wife.

Of course, he hadn't really won her. He knew how Blanche's mind worked. She didn't have marriage in mind. He didn't fit her plans any more than she fit his.

But there were some things in life that one had to do, regardless of the consequences. The minute he'd planted his seed in her body, he'd sealed their fate. He wouldn't renege on a solemn vow just because neither of them had known what they were doing. Blanche would be his wife, and any child she bore would be his own.

They would reach Scotland on the morrow.

Eighteen

The Duke of Anglesey paced up and down the richly hued Oriental carpet. "Dashitall, Effingham, if you are making up this sorry tale just to distract me from that labor bill, I will have you strung up! Men are entitled to make a profit as they will. It is none of our concern how they go about it. And if we raise wages, the cost of everything will escalate, and then no one will afford anything."

"You mean the cloth for your fine cravats will cost a penny more and you must find some better way of persuading the coins out of Blanche's bottomless purse," Gavin, the Marquess of Effingham replied, twisting a letter opener between his fingers. "That's nothing to do with anything at the moment. You have not told me: do you know where Lady Blanche is?"

"I'd thought her returned to the country," Neville replied crossly. "I'm not her keeper, after all. She's a headstrong baggage, thanks to your wife. She never consults me on any matter, and she particularly delights in thwarting me when she can. She hired that wretched aunt of hers as companion, then never takes her anywhere. The old hag is currently ensconced in one of my best guest rooms because she claims her rooms are being refurbished. And I have an important dinner planned in a few weeks. How does one go about telling a lady she is not welcome at the table?"

Effingham hid a grin at His Grace's dilemma. As the elder by some years, Gavin thought Neville as badly spoiled as his lady cousin, but the duke held a powerful position that Gavin did not. As an outsider, an American who had come into his title only recently, Gavin lacked influence.

"We will worry over the lady's companion after we've decided what to do with our wayward relations. I suggest you find out if Lady Blanche is at Anglesey or in Dorset. She can probably answer our questions." Effingham sent up a prayer that Lady Blanche was right where she should be, but in his heart, he knew better.

"And you think some of those radical labor leaders may have set that carriage explosion?" His Grace asked.

"I come from a country that became independent through such violence," Gavin reminded him. "England is ripe for revolution. If those old bastards in the Lords don't pull their collective heads out of the sand, the radicals will tear down the walls of parliament just as the mobs tore down the Bastille in France."

"That is why we must not give power to mobs!" the duke replied indignantly. "If we let them have what they want, they'll only demand more. We must use military strength to keep them under control and in their places."

The ivory letter opener in Gavin's hands snapped, and he rose angrily. "You damned conceited young pup! Do you not think mobs are made up of people? Why should those thousands of British citizens suffer to enable a few narrow-minded bigots like you to stay in power? Had you listened to their rational concerns from the start, there would be no mobs now. We're talking of men who have reached the point of desperation, women whose children die of exhaustion and starvation. They are not just mindless mobs!" He snorted in disgust. "I've half a mind to find the radicals and join forces with them."

His wife's bouncing dark curls and troubled eyes peered around the corner. "I just put Madeline to sleep. Must you shout? And I daresay the radicals need money more than your bluster. They would sooner welcome Blanche than you."

That ridiculous observation drained some of the tension. The duke bowed. "Lady Effingham, it is good to see you looking well. I understand you have not heard from my cousin recently?"

"It's not been quite a week, and the mails from the village can be dreadfully slow, you know. I should think you ought to take precautions for yourself more than for Blanche. The message from Fiona sounded as if anyone in your vicinity might be in danger."

"And that is another thing." The duke swung around to confront Gavin. "Why must your brother bring a dangerous Irish female into my household? I cannot believe he didn't know she was some part of this nefarious plot. I'm going to advise the Home Office to have that alley taken apart brick by brick until we find her."

Gavin sank tiredly into his seat. "We have no certainty that there is a plot. We only have an eccentric message from a Bow Street Runner and a few suspicions. I am sending a messenger after my brother as we speak. We might deploy a few more men in the alley to keep an eye on what's happening there. You must see if you can locate Lady Blanche."

The duke's glare didn't waver. "How long will it take to find your wretched brother?"

"Michael always leaves a trail I can follow should I need. It's just a matter of thinking as he does. My cousin Marian says her husband's stable is untouched. If none of your carriages or horses are gone, he's taken coach or shank's mare. I have men checking the coaching inns now. If you will start looking on your end, we might make some progress."

Dillian sent him a worried look as the duke bade his farewells and departed. "Do you think there is any chance that they're traveling together? If so, sending Neville looking for them is not a wise idea."

"Even Michael isn't that big an idiot," Gavin said. "Neville would cut out his throat. No, he's stashed her somewhere safe. It's this Fiona who concerns me. If Neville won't hire more men to help that Runner, then I will."

Dillian didn't look reassured.

* * *

"Rise and shine, my lady," the maid called cheerfully, setting a tray on the bedside table and pulling back the draperies. "His lordship's already eaten and gone to call up the carriage."

Prying her eyes open, Blanche scowled at the maid and the otherwise empty room. If Michael had come in last night, she'd seen or heard none of him. So much for any hopes of his taking advantage of their new disguise.

She frowned again after she'd dressed, broken her fast, and proceeded to the inn yard. Michael awaited her on the back of his horse. He wouldn't even ride inside with her.

Trying not to notice the way the sun played on the dancing auburn highlights of his hair, Blanche glared up at him. "You may as well send me home if you won't tell me what you found or where we're going."

"We're going to Scotland. It's a long day's ride to the coast where they picked her up. There's rumors of more unrest in London. I'll not send you back there." His posture was stiffly correct on the back of the prancing horse.

Blanche wanted to make him notice her the way she noticed him. She wanted him to talk to her, to discuss what had happened the other night. And if all else failed, she wanted to knock him off his high horse. Instead, she smiled, bobbed a docile curtsy, and stalked back to the carriage. She would get even somehow. It would just take thought.

Steaming, she sat in the carriage with arms crossed, not even glancing up as Michael rode beside her window. He hadn't needed her for this trip. He'd simply kept her out of trouble. She didn't suffer fools gladly, and men who thought they ran the world were fools.

Unable to keep from looking out as the coach rolled down the road, Blanche admired the way Michael's muscled thighs gripped the horse, emphasized by his tight breeches. She remembered how his naked legs had parted her knees without effort and held her positioned so she could have done nothing to fight him had she tried. She shivered and picked up her book.

She read the same page a dozen times before giving up. She watched the rolling hills and the bleak clouds scuttling in to obscure the sun. She prayed the rain held off until they arrived. The roads this far north were insufferable.

The innkeeper had provided a basket for a mid-day meal, but Michael didn't allow the coach to stop until they reached an inn to exchange horses. She had already nibbled her share of the meat pies, but she was thirsty. When they halted, she didn't wait for permission to leave the carriage. She signaled the driver to set down the steps.

She smelled rain, but a brisk wind held off the clouds. The ancient stone inn appeared as if it had stood since the Picts controlled the northern lands. No other carriages or horses idled in the yard. Picking her way across the mud, she headed for the door where she assumed she'd find Michael.

Inside she regarded stone walls scarred with fires of long ago and a rough plank floor worn from centuries of boots. A cheerful woman bustled out, wiping her hands on her apron.

"Aye, and it is your ladyship! Your man was to bring ye a wee dram shortly. Have a seat, my lady, and aren't ye the daintiest thing I've ever set eyes on?"

Unable to distinguish more than one word of three through the woman's heavy burr, Blanche took a seat on a long bench while the woman rushed to find a drink. A moment later, Michael appeared from the rear of the inn, followed by a burly man with a beard. The man nodded, holding out his hand and saying something in the same thick accent. She deciphered what sounded like "Lady Michael," but she saw no point in correcting his usage.

"Mr. Malcolm welcomes us to Scotland. We have crossed the border," Michael explained as the innkeeper's wife hurried out with glasses of water. He leaned over and whispered, "We're MacDermots here, for the record."

Unsurprised that he preferred to register under an anonymous name, delighted that she finally visited another country, Blanche listened as Michael spoke to the innkeeper, but she could understand little.

"Mr. Malcolm inquires if we will spend the night here. He has a clean room available, and the next inn is some distance. With the rain, we might not arrive until late."

She couldn't believe he actually asked her opinion. She stared, waiting for the jest, then responded warily to his tense eagerness in awaiting her response.

"If you think it best to stop early, of course," she agreed. "Do you think we might explore the countryside before it rains?"

"If you so desire, my lady. A brisk walk before we're confined to the inn, by all means." He helped her rise and nodded to the innkeeper. "We'll take the room, sir. My wife wishes to explore your hills. Is there a path you might recommend?"

Still suspicious of his sudden good humor, Blanche tried following the discussion. She gave it up after a while, letting her attention wander to the thick glass in the mullioned windows and to the huge book the innkeeper's wife laid on the table.

At a nod from the innkeeper, Michael signed them into the inn. The woman held out a pen for Blanche to do the same. Finding that quaint, Blanche boldly signed herself as Lady Blanche MacDermot. She refused to lower her rank for an imaginary husband.

The woman nodded and bustled off again, returning moments later with an armload of fresh linen she carried up the stairs. Well, at least they would have clean beds.

"Shall we bring the lunch basket with us then?" Michael asked, taking Blanche's arm and guiding her toward the door.

As they exited the cozy inn for the brisk, raw day, he brushed a kiss across her cheek, and smiled when she touched her cheek wonderingly. He retrieved the basket from the coach, took her hand again, and led her up the hill.

"You've been to Scotland before, haven't you?" she asked as they strolled up the path. She brushed an unruly strand of hair from her face to admire the luminous green of Michael's eyes against the background of billowing gray clouds.

"Aye, a dozen times or more, I ken," he answered mischievously. "It's a braw enou' country."

Blanche playfully slapped his arm. "And I suppose now you're a MacGregor or some such. When will you decide who you want to be when you grow up?"

"When I find out who I am, I suppose. Do you think we might stop here by this hedge to eat? I'm that famished, I am."

The rough hedgerow sported several flat stones at its base that would serve nicely as table and chairs. And the hedge formed a windbreak. With Michael's aid, she arranged herself on a wide ledge and set the basket on a rock. To her surprise, Michael sat beside her rather than on the other stone. While Michael ate, they gazed over a panoramic landscape. Blanche thought she might enjoy the life of a shepherdess if it meant living this simple beauty every day. The April wind carried the first scents of spring, and the signs of the earth's awakening appeared in patches of gold and green.

"'Tis a lovely sight, isn't it?" Michael asked, leaning back on his hand.

"Wild and lovely. I can't wait to see the sea. Shall we reach it tomorrow? Did you find out where Fiona landed?" Michael's closeness made her giddy. She luxuriated in the opportunity much as she admired the natural wonders spread before them.

"I have. It's no more than a fishing village. The accommodations will be poor. If we leave early in the morn, perhaps we can ask our questions, and be gone before we must spend the night there. I don't know that it will have a ship safe for your passage."

"Are you regretting that you brought me along?" she asked, not wanting to disturb this moment of peace but needing to know. She didn't want to leave him, but she must put Fiona ahead of herself.

"It may come a time that you'll regret it," Michael said, tracing a finger down her jaw. "But I'll not give up a moment of it to save the world."

Before Blanche could fully register his meaning, Michael leaned over and kissed her.

Shocked that he'd actually taken the initiative, Blanche reveled in his slow, tasting kiss. He almost seemed to be questioning her, waiting for her to accept him. She eagerly slid her arms around his broad shoulders, savoring his strength, his heat, and the way his kiss instantly deepened.

He hugged her close, crushing her breasts against his chest and urgently claiming her mouth. When his kisses traveled down her throat to nibble and caress, he whispered impassioned phrases and slid his hand down her spine to her bottom, lighting a fire between her thighs.

She needed to be closer, to feel him naked against her as she had before. The magical hands she so dearly loved explored daringly, molding her breasts, encompassing her waist, drawing her hips tighter as he ravished her mouth. She wanted to rip off his cravat and slide her hands beneath his shirt, but she had no idea how to go about it.

He lifted her long skirt and caressed sensitive skin. She cried out in surprise at the intimacy. He broke their kiss to meet her gaze with a heated question in his eyes. Blanche didn't know why he had changed his mind, but she welcomed the change with all her heart. Not knowing how else to reply, she leaned closer, kissing the corner of his mouth and whispering with excitement, "Please."

Wordlessly, he grabbed her hand, pulled her to her feet, and ran with her to the bottom of the hill, toward the welcoming inn and away from the impending storm.

Nineteen

Laughing, their hair and clothes rumpled by the wind, Michael and Blanche dashed through the inn door. The men waiting in the lobby smiled at them in understanding.

Blanche halted abruptly, aware of the appearance she must make running like a hoyden through a public place. Michael slid his arm around her waist and cheerfully greeted the innkeeper and his new guest, showing her that her appearance didn't matter. Her behavior would have scandalized Neville, but Michael could accept anything. She thought she might learn to love him just for that, except she was in a hurry to retire upstairs.

"Lord and Lady Michael MacDermot," the innkeeper acknowledged them with a bow, then gestured at his guest, "The pastor of our little church, Mr. MacGregor."

Blanche stifled a giggle at the coincidence of the local minister having the same Scots name she had just given Michael.

Michael teasingly pinched her waist and held out his other hand to shake MacGregor's. "It's good to make your acquaintance, sir. We're in for a bit of weather, I'm afraid. Do you stay until it blows over?"

"Aye, I might, but I dinna live far. Will you share a dram with me awhile?" The minister indicated the steaming mugs Mrs. Malcolm carried from the kitchen.

Blanche wanted nothing more than to escape to their private chamber, but doing so in front of a man of the cloth would no doubt be a mortal sin. She took the mug and let Michael lead the conversational path. "And have ye been married long?" the minister asked as she sipped the hearty drink.

Blanche quivered in panic at the direction of the conversation, but she had confidence in Michael's ability to lie their way through anything.

"Truth is, this is our wedding journey. My wife has never seen the north country, and I promised to show her what I could." Protectively, as if she were made of porcelain, Michael took

Blanche's elbow and helped her to the long bench there in the narrow lobby. She rather liked the security of someone taking care of her.

"Aye, and is it that way noo?" MacGregor answered with pleasure. "And Lady Michael, how do ye find our fair land?"

She saw only kindly interest in the minister's face. "It is lovely. I was wishing I was a shepherdess so I could live with that beauty every day."

Both men beamed at that statement. Mr. MacGregor was first to respond. "And would ye leave yer husband for such a chore?" he asked with a laugh.

Blanche darted Michael a look, and the warmth of his gaze gave her courage to carry on the deception. "No, sir, I could not. I suppose he would have to be a shepherd with me."

The men laughed at the sally, and the minister pounded Michael on the back. "Ye have a fine lady, my lord. Do ye have family waiting your return, or may ye linger as ye like?"

Michael's grin made Blanche blush and look to the floor again.

"We've no family to hurry us home. My lady lost her mother young and her father in the war. I was raised by my brother who just recently married. Blanche is my family now."

The minister gazed at them more soberly. With an understanding nod, he said, "May the blessings of the Lord be upon ye, then, and may your marriage be long and fruitful."

Blanche thought she might die of embarrassment right there and then, but Michael helped her to her feet and replied solemnly, "We thank you for the blessing, sir, and now I think we'd best repair to our chambers. We've journeyed long and hard to get here."

Blanche sighed gratefully as they hurried up the narrow wooden stairs to their chamber. She could hear the rain beating against the slate roof. Michael's hand was warm and comforting as they reached the landing and found the open door welcoming them.

He swept her through and closed the door before releasing her. Blanche's breath caught at the intensity of Michael's expression as he brushed her cheek with his nimble fingers and whispered wonderingly, "Mine."

They did this now with clear intent, not in a moment of mindless passion or drunkenness. She savored the reassurance of his caress.

"I've thought of how my wedding night would be," Michael said slowly, holding her gaze. "I've many dreams. But marriage is a sharing of dreams, and I would know yours. Would you have me go outside until you've readied yourself? Or may I have the honor and the pleasure of undressing you?"

Relief swept through Blanche in the same manner as the wind swept through the bare trees outside. She didn't feel shy or uncertain with Michael. He brought the power of the storm inside with his fiery, windswept hair, and the freshness of the wind perfuming him. Still, she did not fear what came next. Not with Michael. The chiseled bones of his handsome face might appear harsh and unforgiving, but not when he looked on her. Eagerness returning, she reached for the knot of his cravat. "I would not have you leave me."

Michael caught her in his arms then, crushing her gown and her mouth and bruising her ribs with the joyous strength of his embrace. Blanche surrendered to this possession, understanding that in some way, he surrendered something more vital to him than just his body. She wrapped her arms around his shoulders and returned his kisses.

Before she realized what he had done, her gown gaped at her back and fell loose across her shoulders. Blanche looked up, startled at his surety in this, and Michael grinned as he held the sleeves so she might slip her arms out.

"You have no idea how many times I have found those buttons in my dreams."

The heavy cloth pulled easily over her hips, falling in a puddle at their feet. In the small room with a cozy brazier, she felt no draft, but burned with the heat of Michael's hungry gaze as he took in the sight of her in only chemise and stockings.

"I had no chance to see you that other night," he murmured, tugging the ribbons of the chemise. "I would see all of you now."

Blanche resisted the urge to cross her arms over her breasts. Instead, she took the buttons of his waistcoat between her shaking fingers and pried them loose. Obligingly, Michael shook off his unfastened coat, then shrugged off his waistcoat. She already had his cravat unfastened, and it took little to untie the neck of his shirt. Clothes fell about them everywhere as they stripped each other and themselves.

Blanche stared in amazement at the broad bare chest revealed when Michael threw off his shirt. She had never seen a man's naked chest. It had nipples like her own, but the powerfully sculpted muscles beneath took her breath away. He wore a small silver coin on a necklace that nestled in a dark patch of curls. Her gaze followed the scattering of hair to his navel and beyond, but he still wore his trousers.

Michael caught her chin and urged her gaze upward. "If you touch those now, you will be on your back with me inside you before either of us knows what's good for us. I've waited a long time for this. Let's take it slow until we know our way."

That image shot a surge of heat through her, but Blanche offered no objection when Michael lifted her from the floor and laid her across the turned-down bed. When he rolled down her stockings, kissing her legs as he went, she thought she would come undone, but he had the silk off before she lost control. She wasn't certain when he removed his own shoes and stockings, but when he came to her, he wore only his trousers. She slid her hands over the smooth solidity of his back as he covered her against the cold.

His mouth took hers at the same time as his hands claimed her breasts, and she was truly lost after that. Blanche caressed him everywhere, discovering those places he liked to be touched, losing herself in the places he touched her.

They lost no time in returning to the heights of passion they had reached before, only now in the privacy of their chamber, the urgency was stronger, more demanding. When Michael finally stripped off his trousers, Blanche was more than ready for him.

She cried out when he finally surged into her, but then the familiarity of his possession claimed her, and she surrendered to his pace with ease. They belonged this way, joined together beneath the pounding rhythm of the rain, in the gloom of day, with the fire sending shadows across all the hills and valleys of their bodies, secure in their knowledge of each other.

When Michael cried her name and shuddered with his release, she went with him, clinging and weeping with the joy of their joining.

* * *

They slept briefly, waking with the roll of thunder as the rainy day gave way to rainy night. Michael rolled onto his side and stroked his hand over the fullness of Blanche's breast, scarcely believing he'd achieved this much-desired gift. After years of denial, he was acutely sensitive to every nuance of her beauty, from the shy delight of her smiling lips to the way her graceful fingers held a teacup.

Just the ability to touch where he wished aroused him to painful hardness. He would exhaust her with his demands. Fascinated, he watched the pale pink bud of her breast pucker and harden against his hand. Feeling her stir, he met her eyes.

"I wish I could be beautiful for you," she said sadly, catching him by surprise.

Startled at so insane a comment, Michael caressed the puckered skin of a scar. Brushing his fingertips over the old burn, he sought others, medals of her courage and heroism.

"I love the way you feel," he whispered as he brushed a kiss against her cheek. "I love the way you look and smell. You're everything beautiful I've ever known in this life. You've the softness of a kitten and the scent of hyacinths in spring. Your skin is the finest silk, and if I start upon your lips, we will do naught but talk for the rest of the evening." He slid down to press his kiss lower, murmuring, "I can find better things to do with my tongue, I think."

She gave in to him without hesitation, and joy flooded Michael's soul. He wouldn't consider the whys and wherefores. He only knew she had come to him, and she was his now. He had few illusions in life. A treasure as rare as Blanche could never fully belong to him. But he had done what he could to ensure that he would always be part of her life.

With tender care, he slid his hand down the flatness of her abdomen, marveling at her dainty build. She gasped as his fingers located the curls below, and he propped himself on one elbow to smile down at her.

"I love the way you respond so easily. I didn't think ladies could do that."

She made a face at him, then brushed his stubbled cheek with her fingers. "Dillian told me that was nonsense. It only requires the right man."

"Dillian's tongue runs away with her sometimes," he said wryly, stroking her breast, reveling in his freedom to do so. He watched her with curiosity, wondering if she had any understanding at all of what they did. "Did Dillian tell you what happens to ladies who find the right man to play with?"

Her gaze wavered, but her answer was bold enough. "They get with child. I'm not a total ninnyhammer, as I keep reminding you. But I have wealth enough to arrange anything, so you needn't worry about being tied down or trapped."

Michael didn't like the sounds of that, but he must tread carefully here. Even England recognized the Scots law under which they had just married. Declaring themselves married was a binding contact. He had witnesses and the inn's record book proving they entered into marriage willingly. MacGregor had promised to record the event in his church record.

Unfortunately, he now had a wife who didn't know she was married. A bit of a problem, that, but he'd not bring it up unless a child came of their lovemaking. He didn't mind bending or ignoring laws in Blanche's best interests, but he would never abandon his child.

Michael knew the impossibility of a real marriage between them. A duke's mansion and a king's ransom frightened him more than the idea of giving up his travels. Blanche's inevitable anger and frustration when she discovered what he'd done worried him even more. But he'd had no choice.

He'd made a vow when he was very young that no child of his would ever go without a name. Keeping that vow had ensured a life of near chastity. He saw no reason for breaking what he had endured so much to keep just because the woman he'd finally chosen had wealth beyond his comprehension.

"I don't consider myself trapped," he answered. "You're the woman I want, the only woman I'll ever need. You may find yourself uncomfortable with the bounds I set, however. I would not share you with any other man."

Michael thought he heard relief in the soft assurance of Blanche's reply. "I want no other man. I just want a child of my own to love and hold. Give me that, and I will be content. I'll not hold you to any other promise."

Michael couldn't prevent a twinge of anger at her reply. "You want my child but not me?"

She squirmed beneath him, but he did not let her go. He caught her hip and held her pinned to the bed.

"How can you say that?" she asked, pressing a hand to his chest. "Do I act as if I do not want you?"

"As lover, but nothing else," he reminded her.

Her chin firmed stubbornly. "I will not have a husband, neither you nor any other. And if you are honest, you know you do not want me as wife. You have no interest in the society in which I live. You don't know my friends and would probably despise them if you did. I do not accuse you of wanting my fortune. I know you better than that. You have no use for all my mansions and wealth. But if you had it, you would fritter it away on your orphaned waifs and lost causes. I cannot allow that. I have responsibilities, a word you do not comprehend."

So much for love and tenderness. Growling under his breath, Michael flattened his hand against her abdomen. "If I give you a child, I want full responsibility for raising him. I would have him know his father. There are some responsibilities other than those of wealth that I recognize."

Again, she looked slightly frightened by his vehemence. "You do not even have a name to give him," she protested. "I would go to the continent and buy him a name, then return as a widow. He will have all the advantages a loving mother and money can offer."

"He will have a father to teach him right from wrong," Michael insisted. "You will not shut me out of his life or I return you to London right now." He returned his fingers to the place between her thighs, brazenly reminding her of what she would miss.

Her hips rose, drawing his fingers deeper into her liquid warmth. A fire kindled in her eyes, and Michael recognized relief. She would not deny him this much, then. He would have dried up and blown away with the wind if she had.

Michael took Blanche's mouth with his and began the wondrous process of stoking her embers to roaring flames. When at last they reached that ultimate pleasure, when he felt his soul sink into hers with the blending of their bodies, he knew he had been right to save matrimony for this moment. The joy of Blanche's acceptance melded them more certainly than any mere physical release. She was his. It was done. Even eternity wouldn't separate them now.

Later, he would worry about what would happen when the world learned of their marriage.

Michael had no doubt that time would come much too soon for

their liking.

Twenty

Blanche sleepily noted the howl of the wind tearing at the slates on the inn roof. She considered discovering the cause of a tug at her hair, but instead, she found a warm spot, and wriggled nearer the source of heat in hopes of returning to sleep.

A hard naked leg wrapped around hers. Startled, she rolled over and brushed against a distinctly masculine appendage. She pried her eyelids open and blinked up at Michael.

"Sleepyhead," he murmured, smiling as his fingers continued their play in her hair. "Another few minutes, and I would have it all plaited."

His simplest gestures warmed pathways to her heart that no one else had ever touched. His fingers in her hair tingled her scalp and all parts south. And that wasn't even taking into account what happened when he tightened his leg around hers.

Michael pulled his handiwork over her shoulder, tickling her breasts with it. Magic fingers had somehow plaited her hair with sparkling gold and silver ribbons while she slept. She smiled at the festive effect. What other man would ever dream of adorning her hair with pretty ribbons? Most thought presenting a wife with the family jewels sufficient sentimentality for a lifetime. She stroked the flaxen braid admiringly. "Now I need only have a ball to attend to show off my finery."

Michael lifted the sheet and leered at her nakedness. "The only one you'll attend dressed like that is mine."

She found the ticklish spot beneath his arm and attacked it without mercy.

The tussle that followed resulted in her lying spread-eagled beneath Michael's strong body. Dancing green eyes laughed down at her before he tormented her with kisses just out of reach of her mouth.

"It's still raining," he murmured uselessly. She could hear the clatter as well as he.

"We won't reach the coast," she suggested. Thinking at all while he kissed her like that was nigh on to impossible, but she struggled to follow the path of his thoughts. She arched her hips slightly to remind him of his real purpose.

He obliged by rubbing his arousal where she wanted, but he went no farther. "I can make it on horseback," he whispered. "It's not far across country."

She thought she knew what he meant, but she was too mindless with lust to protest. When he suckled her breast, Blanche cried out with the pleasure and need of it.

"You can stay here and keep this bed snug and warm against my return." He nuzzled her other breast, and inched slowly inside her.

In truth, right at that moment, she could think of nothing she would like better. The day outside sounded cold and miserable, and she was warm and happy right here. And she would be even happier if Michael would attend to business. She shifted urgently upward, taking him a little deeper.

"I knew you'd understand," he whispered wickedly in her ear as he sank inside her, freeing her legs so she could meet him fully.

Blanche thought he probably deserved to have his ears boxed, but she was in no condition for anything but surrendering to the wild ride that followed. She hadn't understood that this act could forge her into a slavish tool of desire. She didn't understand it fully now. She only knew Michael could just touch her and she was lost.

She dozed, then woke to discover Michael up and dressing. She cursed her earlier acquiescence, Michael's unquenchable energy, Fiona, and any other topic crossing her mind as she untangled herself from the blankets and pushed her braid over her shoulder.

Michael tucked his shirt into his trousers and grinned at her scowl, then bent over to kiss her forehead. "Maybe Mrs. Malcolm will teach you how to bake some of those mouth-watering scones while I'm gone. I could eat a dozen when I return."

"If you return," Blanche replied gloomily. She doubted if she could tell flour from sugar and would be hopelessly lost should she venture in search of the kitchen. She didn't need this reminder of the chasm between herself and the wife Michael deserved.

Instead of donning one of his citified frock coats, Michael pulled a leather jerkin from his satchel and donned it before brushing a kiss across her cheek and cupping her bare breast in his palm. "Do you think me so stupid as to forget what is waiting for me here, my lady? I assure you, I am many things, but foolish is not one of them."

Her father had always proclaimed his love for her and then disappeared for years on end. She had no confidence in her power to draw him back.

She wished she could change her mind and go with him, but she was no fool either. She had no side saddle or riding habit, even if a carriage horse could be persuaded to accept a rider. And taking a carriage through mud-filled ruts endangered everyone. Frustrated, she wrapped warmly in the covers.

"I wish I were a man," she muttered.

Laughing, Michael finished dressing. "That would make things exceedingly awkward for me. I rather fancy you just as you are."

He kissed her and departed before she could offer further protest. Blanche flung a pillow at the solid oak panel separating her from his world, then fell back among the covers.

She might as well become accustomed to Michael's absence. He would soon grow tired of lugging her around with him and would find excuse to leave her somewhere. The only reason she'd had his company for this length of time was the newness of their physical intimacy and this journey on a mission that held his interest. Once they found Fiona or her family, she would become part of his past again.

She kept repeating that to herself for the rest of the day rather than remember Michael's possessiveness when he talked of a child. Michael had no possessions. He would lose interest in the novelty soon enough.

* * *

Exhausted, soaked to the bone, and covered head to toe in mud, Michael entered the inn late that evening in an oddly triumphant humor. The good Mrs. Malcolm took one look at him and bustled off in the direction of the kitchen muttering something about "buckets."

Grinning, he took the stairs two at a time, eager for the loving welcome of his wife after a hard day's work. He'd seldom considered the pleasantness of homecoming, but he succumbed to it now. Throwing open the door, he stood in all his muddy glory, relishing the sight of his own ray of sunshine occupying the chair beside the fire.

His ray of sunshine screeched and dropped her book at sight of him. "Michael Lawrence, how dare you drag such filth up here! Mrs. Malcolm spent the day scrubbing those floors."

For some inane reason, happiness welled at this wifely greeting and he laughed. He had half a mind to whirl her around in a muddy jig, but the wiser half decided he would have no head left did he dare try.

"And a pleasant good day to you too," he replied, sitting and tugging at his boots.

"You have got to be the most uncivilized, uncouth barbarian the good Lord ever made mistake to provide," Blanche muttered, skirting around him. She met Mrs. Malcolm preparing to knock, a hip bath resting at her feet. "I'll fetch the hot water," Blanche said through clenched teeth, slipping past the innkeeper and into the darkness beyond.

"I look that bad?" Michael asked as his hostess deftly arranged the large tub in front of the brazier and pulled the dressing screen around it.

"It's daft ye are," she agreed obliquely, "leaving your lady wife to amuse herself while ye traipse through gorse and broom, coming home looking like ye've seen the field of battle."

"And how did my lady wife occupy herself while I was gone?" Michael asked cheerfully, tugging at his other boot. He couldn't imagine Blanche baking scones as he'd suggested. He'd just done that to irritate and distract her. He was well aware he'd taken a delicate hothouse flower to bed. Her rarity fascinated him.

Before the old woman could answer, Blanche entered hauling two steaming buckets of water with their handles wrapped in towels. Michael thought his eyes might pop out of his head. Recovering his wits, he hurried to relieve her of the burden.

"Have you lost your mind? I can carry these. You just go back to whatever you were doing," he urged, splashing the tempting water into the bath. He hadn't realized how much he longed for heated water to soak the cold from his aching bones. Unaccustomed to such luxuries, he seldom thought of them. Having a wife to do so shook him more than he liked.

Mrs. Malcolm had already taken out the empty buckets, and ignoring Michael's protest, Blanche prepared to follow her. "Don't you go one step further in that filth. We'll be back shortly with the rest," she called over her shoulder.

He couldn't let her carry those heavy buckets. Glancing down, Michael grimaced at the filthy trail he'd left across the floor. He was a barbarian, just as she said. Still, Blanche was too fragile for heavy work. He should never have brought her to this out-of-the-way inn where their only servants were an elderly couple.

He met them coming up the stairs and took the buckets from Blanche. She promptly relieved Mrs. Malcolm of hers and sent the old woman back down the stairs with a commanding wave of her hand. Fuming, Michael led the way back to the tub. She at least had sense enough to let him pour.

"Don't you dare fetch anymore," he warned as he stripped off his filthy clothing behind the screen. "This is more than enough for my needs." In truth, the blazing brazier and hot steam felt like heaven. Not caring if he scalded off half his skin, he stepped in and sank beneath the water with a sigh of relief. Perhaps he was getting old.

"It's a wonder you didn't catch your death of cold," Blanche fussed, coming around the screen and gathering up his clothes. "You look as if you're soaked through. I'll take these down and bring you back some hot soup."

Angel song with harp accompaniment, Michael mused, thinking of a good steaming mug of hearty soup, but he hadn't lost all sense of propriety. "You need do no such thing. I'll fetch it when I'm done here. I'll not make a serving maid of you."

"A mistress but not a maid?" she asked with what sounded like amusement. Before he could admonish her, Michael heard the door closing. She'd completely ignored his command.

Idly soaping at his chest, Michael contemplated this new development. The delicate Lady Blanche, the lovely fairy queen who first enchanted him, had grown into a woman bent on having things her own way. Michael silently accepted the soup and coffee she brought, not knowing how to react to this turn of the tables. He'd never had a need for pampering, didn't know if he liked the idea of Lady Blanche waiting on him, but her willingness to do so filled an emptiness within him he hadn't known existed. Her hesitant look when he took the cup without a word of thanks returned some of his senses.

"I trust ye emptied me pockets afore abscondin' with me clothes, lass?" he inquired lightly, ignoring the strangeness of this ease and concentrating on the way her gaze narrowed at his taunting.

"I did, and it's a fine collection I found there," she mocked in return. "Did you keep the rabbit in your hat, then? I could not find it."

Feeling more cheerful now, Michael sank back in the tub, pulling his knees higher to disguise the extent of his arousal. The woman had no modesty whatsoever. "Then fetch that wee parcel tied in string, would ye now?"

He thought she might dump it on his head when she returned. Few women appreciated the characters he hid behind when uncomfortable with the emotions of a situation. But his lady wife had always understood as no other had. Rising from the tub, Michael wrapped a towel around his hips and untied the string with a single pull.

"For you." He handed her the package nervously, and began toweling dry rather than watch her reaction. He had a great deal of experience with the world, but he had little intimate experience with ladies. He could only hope his instincts served him well.

He couldn't resist watching when she opened the small wooden box and exposed the ring inside. Every muscle in his body froze, including the ones that worked his lungs.

Blanche reverently lifted the small gold band from the interior and slipped it on the proper finger, her face alight with the tenderness he so desperately craved.

"It's exquisite," she sighed, twisting the band to capture all the lovingly carved facets in the firelight. "It's like tiny clasped hands," she said in wonder. "Where did you...?" embarrassed, she gave him a hasty glance and tried again. "How did you...?"

Michael smiled at her ingenuousness. "I did not steal it, if that is what you ask. A man in the village had a rare piece of gold. I've done some goldsmithing, so I copied a ring I saw once in Ireland. Does it fit?"

She held her hand up for his inspection, turning it back and forth in the firelight, admiring the glitter. "It is so beautiful, Michael. I had no idea you could do such exquisite work. I've never seen the like. You did not have to. . ." Her gaze suddenly turned suspicious. "And what did you do to earn the gold?"

Michael laughed. Fastening his clean trousers, he took the few steps across to her and kissed her soundly. "At least you do not accuse me of using your own coins to buy it, like some crass fortune hunter."

She twisted out of his arms and stepped away, holding her hands behind her back in an oddly passive posture. "I know your character a shade too well for that, Michael Lawrence. You might use my coin for the less fortunate, but never for yourself. So if you did not steal the gold, you must have done something else to acquire it."

"Isn't that a bit like asking the cost, my dear?" he teased, closing in on her as she backed away. "Would you rather not hear what I discovered this day about our Fiona?"

He trapped her against the wall beside the window. The lamplight glittered along her sun-gold hair and the metallic-threaded ribbons he'd placed there that morning. He liked that she'd kept the braid he'd plaited for her, but now it was time for it to come undone. With deft fingers he unwrapped the strands.

She trembled beneath his touch. She was as slender as a willow wand, easily bent with any wind. Michael caressed her side, feeling each bone beneath his fingers. In all his imagination he could not conceive why he had dared take this fragile confection to his bed. Nor could he conceive of taking any other.

"Tell me what you discovered," she asked breathlessly, apparently dismissing the question of how he'd obtained the gold.

He could have told her he'd earned the gold by working himself half to death repairing thatch in the freezing rain for an old miser. The skinflint had then demanded Michael work another piece of gold that he might sell later before he allowed Michael the use of his jeweler's tools to create the ring. He'd earned that piece with the hard sweat of his brow, but he wasn't certain Blanche would appreciate the costliness. Instead, he distracted her with Fiona and his kisses. He did so enjoy the way her eyes glazed over with confusion when he kissed her.

"I had no trouble at all," he bragged happily. "I merely walked into the tavern and the men there told me they wouldn't go to Larne in this weather. It seems they mistook me for our stray's big brother."

"Larne? Is that in Ireland?" Blanche whispered as he tickled tiny kisses down her throat. Michael brushed aside the flimsy kerchief she wore around her shoulders and kissed the swell of her breasts above the muslin of her bodice. For good measure, he traced his tongue down the valley in between and had the pleasure of experiencing her shiver.

"A small village on the coast," he agreed, pleased at discovering this gown buttoned down the front. He had it open in a trice, the ribbon beneath untied in less. He sighed in happiness as he caressed the silken warmth of her full breast.

"We will sail there when the weather allows?" she murmured against his cheek as he divested her of her clothes.

He liked the way she went all soft and helpless beneath his touch, Michael decided as the gown slid off. With his vow to not create any bastards to hold him back, he'd never been a rake. They would learn together.

"The rain is already ending," he promised, gathering her into his arms and aiming for the bed. "Let us hope you make a good sailor."

Leaving his trousers on the floor, he climbed into the soft feather bed with her. When she daringly stroked his arousal, studying him with wonder, Michael decided he had a lot more to learn, and he proceeded to the next lesson with all alacrity.

Blanche's cries of pleasure rewarded him for his quickness as a student.

* * *

"Michael never dallies with females!" Gavin stormed, pacing up and down the much-abused carpet.

"Except Blanche," Dillian reminded him. "And she's not to be found anywhere."

"Why Blanche?" In frustration, Gavin pounded his fist against a paneled wall. "Heaven only knows, he could keep half a dozen women in that pile of rocks of ours and I would make no complaint. But not *Blanche*. She's the granddaughter of a damned duke, devil take it! Daughter of a marquess. She's slept on silk sheets all her life. Michael calls the stars his blanket. Where could he keep her?"

"Your messenger said he traveled with a woman," Dillian warned, bringing him back to the subject. "If Michael has no interest in dalliance, perhaps they observe the proprieties, if just in an improper fashion."

Gavin glared at her as if she spoke gibberish. "They travel to Scotland. Why in the name of all that is holy would they go to Scotland for any other reason but an elopement?"

"Blanche said Michael found Fiona in the lake district. Perhaps they only mean to go there," Dillian replied with doubt in her voice.

"And what will Neville do when he discovers his cousin has eloped with a man without a penny to his name?" Gavin continued his tirade, ignoring her suggestion.

"Go after him with his pen?" Dillian asked with amusement. "He wouldn't consider Michael gentleman enough to challenge to a duel, and Neville isn't much inclined toward sword and gun."

"I cannot believe it of him." Gavin dropped wearily into his leather desk chair. "Michael is not a womanizer. He will have to marry her."

Dillian laughed and slid her arms around his shoulders from behind. "Blanche is the one you must convince of that. She thinks all men fools, and Michael the biggest fool of all. She's of age, Gavin. No one can force her into a marriage she doesn't want."

Gavin's scarred face twisted into an ominous scowl. "Then Michael blamed well better be traveling with another sort of female entirely. All the world will know of his elopement soon enough if they're together."

Twenty-one

An unusual clatter in the early morning darkness stirred Michael from slumber. Instinctively, he reached for Blanche, pulling her closer. Snuggling her slenderness against him, he cupped one perfect breast, and slipped back toward sleep.

The violent crash against their bedchamber door jerked him rudely awake. With the wary experience born of years on the road, Michael rolled them off the far side of the bed. He muffled Blanche's scream with his hand as the door crashed in.

"Grab the bloody impostor and we'll have Fiona soon enough!" someone roared over the sound of splintering wood.

Michael dove under the bed and grabbed the leg of the first man who ventured near, jerking hard until a skinny shin cracked against the bed frame. Screaming in pain, the intruder flailed backward into his partner.

Michael rolled from beneath the bed, grabbed the water pitcher from the washstand, and cracked it soundly across the nearest skull. The pitcher shattered, and the man stumbled to his knees. The intruder with the bruised shinbone scrambled upright and swung at him, but Michael dodged in the opposite direction.

In the early dawn gloom, he could discern little more than size and shape as his assailant roared and rushed after him. The man probably had a good two stone on him, but he was slow on his feet. Grabbing the old washstand and grinning wickedly, Michael swung the heavy oak, connecting solidly with his attacker's shoulders. The pegged pieces of the old stand flew apart, but the man sprawled to the floor.

Mr. Malcolm appeared in the doorway, brandishing a cudgel, Mrs. Malcolm screaming behind him. Kicking at the ribs of the rogue trying to rise, Michael whipped a sheet from the bed and began trussing this more conscious intruder first.

"Knock the other one over the head if he moves," Michael ordered his host. He finished binding the first man and turned to the second.

"Knaves!" Malcolm thundered, standing aggressively over the cowed man lying between his feet. "Thieves! A man canna sleep in his own bed for the likes of these maggots!"

Behind him, Mrs. Malcolm whimpered something indistinct about her "beautiful china."

Michael spun around to check on Blanche. She'd wrapped the wool blanket around herself, tucking it up somehow so it left her delicate shoulders bare but her hands free. Michael grinned at the iron poker she wielded. "You'd make a marvelous Amazon, my love," he assured her as she hesitantly lowered her weapon. "But right now, I need something to tie up this other fowl. Unless you just wish to knock him out," he added thoughtfully.

The man at his feet screamed in protest.

"Are you all right?" she whispered, her eyes wide with fear.

With an embarrassed grin, he reached for the trousers he'd dropped on the floor the night before. "Best way to rouse a man's blood in the morning. I'm fine." He turned to the innkeeper and his wife. "Will you call the magistrate?"

"I'll have the laird fetched," Malcolm replied as his wife returned with rope.

Michael took the rope and firmly bound the second intruder. "Whatever you suggest. Help me roll the rogues out of here so my wife may dress."

With the door safely closed on their audience, Michael clasped Blanche in his arms and kissed her hair, offering prayers of gratitude that she wasn't shaking as she had the day of the carriage fire. "Someone realized I'm not Seamus," he murmured into the luxuriant thickness of her hair. "We need put some distance between us and the coast."

She nodded against his chin. "Must we wait for the laird?"

"Not if I can help it." After kissing her forehead, Michael hastily dressed. He'd gone far enough in registering their marriage lines. He wouldn't risk exposing Blanche to some noble who might know her and pass word of her to others. The scandal would break eventually, but not yet, he hoped.

Leaving Blanche alone to dress, Michael went downstairs and tried questioning his prisoners, but they were singularly uncooperative. That one of them still had his eyes crossed from the blow on his head didn't help. Of course, interrogation wasn't one of

Michael's strong suits, either. He'd always preferred hit and run.

"They obviously intended murdering us in our bed," Michael declared blithely as his host returned with a pot of coffee. "We'll have the fellows hanged for attempted murder, robbery, and worse," he added with enthusiasm, well aware his captives listened.

"You'll never hold us," the more conscious one growled. "We'll be out within a fortnight. May as well save yerselves the trouble."

Michael didn't like the sound of that. If someone sought to rescue these two, he wanted Blanche as far from the scene as possible. Taking their host aside, he handed him a quantity of their remaining coins. "We need to be leaving."

"Will ye not wait for the laird, my lord?" Malcolm asked with disappointment. "He'll not do much without ye to stand as witness."

"My lady longs for home," Michael lied. "Being set upon by thieves has shaken her. I heartily apologize for any damage I may have caused in my zeal to protect her."

"My missus will get over it when she sees your gilt." The innkeeper pocketed the coins with a smile on his rough face. "'Tis a shame you're ending your wedding journey so soon."

Michael shrugged and gave a knowing smile. "Perhaps I'll take her south through Bath and see if she changes her mind about returning home."

That would give anyone following them a wrong direction, Michael hoped as they brought out the carriage and loaded it. He counted their few remaining coins and wondered if he could slip away long enough to conjure up another purse or two.

But the idea of returning to his usual trade while in Blanche's company didn't sit well. That worried him, but he was more concerned with having Blanche well gone before the scoundrels' companions came looking for them.

Blanche clasped his gloved hand as he took the seat beside her and the horses started down the road. "You think they will follow?"

"They think we know where to find Fiona. Word must have traveled from London that Seamus has a look-alike. They didn't think I was him this time."

"But you said the men in the village did," she said with puzzlement.

"Yes, but they're not part of this gang, if gang is what they are.

The villagers are just poor fishermen. Fiona and her brother are not."

"What has Fiona got herself involved in?"

"I don't know, but it looks pretty grim from where I stand. Perhaps I'd best take you to Dorset. I may be mistaken in thinking you're safe with me."

But when Blanche trustingly rested her head against his shoulder so he had to circle her with his arm, Michael couldn't bear the thought of parting with her so soon.

"I'm safer with you than alone," she argued, "and you promised to take me to Ireland. Perhaps we'll meet this Seamus and find out if he's your real brother."

"It's been over a week," Michael protested weakly, knowing his argument held no substance. "The duke will be looking for you."

"No, he will not," Blanche replied scornfully, sliding her fingers beneath his waistcoat and rubbing the linen covering his chest. "He'll not miss me until the session ends."

"You grow bold, my lady," he murmured, unfastening her traveling cloak. "What must I do with you when we return to London?" Michael asked the question idly, trying to hide his concern.

"Let's not return to London," she suggested as her cloak fell from her shoulders. "Let's stay in Ireland and make babies."

Michael's laugh was short and painful as he lowered her bodice to take what she offered. Her breasts beckoned him like ripe peaches ready for plucking, and his loins took over from his brains. They would make babies of a certainty. Unfortunately, he didn't think the delicate, sophisticated Lady Blanche would be happy raising them on the road.

He took her nipple into his mouth and she moaned enchantingly. Michael thought no more about their predicament as the carriage jounced down the rutted road toward England and safer ports. If his vows of fidelity prevented his ever having another woman, he would have this one as often as possible before he must give her up.

* * *

Blanche had fallen asleep in his arms by the time they crossed the border into England and found another posting inn late that afternoon. Michael brushed a strand of hair from her forehead and straightened her bodice as the coach rocked to a halt. There were so many places he would take her if only he could. but right now, he couldn't even publicly call her his wife.

She blinked sleepily and stirred as Michael touched the ring she wore on her left hand. "The weather is clearing," he murmured. "I would like to go a little farther this day. Stay here while they change the horses. I'll inquire about the roads ahead."

She kissed his cheek and curled up with the carriage blanket around her. For a moment, Michael imagined her growing round with his child, and he panicked briefly. He knew better than to court fate, however, and he climbed down with only the next inn in mind.

Even that thought vanished when he entered the bustling front hall and caught sight of a familiar visage at the ticket desk, questioning the clerk. One of Gavin's men.

Michael debated escaping before the man saw him, but he couldn't run from Gavin. The messenger turned and shouted in relief and recognition.

"Mr. O'Toole," he called, hurrying through the milling crowd of people.

He'd grown accustomed to the Lord Michael address these last days, but not wanting to infringe on Gavin's titled legitimacy, he'd always insisted on the anonymity of O'Toole. Michael clasped the man's hand and led him toward a more private alcove. "What is it? Are the marquess and his family all right?"

"They're well, far as I know. It's the duke. His Grace can't find his cousin, and Lord Effingham thought you might know aught of her. There's been some threat against His Grace and his household, and they're concerned something may have happened to her ladyship."

"Threat?" Alarmed, Michael tried to keep his voice down

The duke had already missed Blanche. If Gavin had traced him, they may know Michael traveled with a woman. He couldn't let the scandal hit Blanche before she was ready to call him husband. And he couldn't send her back to London if it was unsafe.

A loud cry caused them to turn. In the room's center, a stout female, her apron thrown over her head wept loudly as a crowd gathered to watch.

Distracted, Michael lied without thinking. "I saw her ladyship off to Dorset and no more. What threat is there?"

The caterwauling continued, making conversation difficult.

"I don't know the whole of it," the messenger admitted. "But it's something to do with some radicals threatening His Grace. Lord Effingham has hired men to search some street in Seven Dials. He needs your aid in finding the radicals and Lady Blanche."

Michael was uncertain who Gavin protected with this garbled message: himself, Michael, Blanche, the duke, Fiona, or some combination of all. Gavin had never asked for Michael's help until now. Michael couldn't refuse. But he couldn't take that carriage into London with Blanche, either, not with Gavin's messenger watching.

The woman's wails became wrenching sobs as someone comforted her. Michael pounded the messenger's back and nodded toward the tavern.

"Let me buy you a drink while I find a fresh horse. Mine is too blown to continue. I'll come fetch you when I'm ready."

The messenger accepted the offer and disappeared through the tavern door as Michael listened to the animated conversation at the ticket counter.

"Her daughter's to have a babe and needs her mother," a gray-haired lady complained loudly to the ticket master for the hundredth time. "What's she to do if she cannot get to Wiltshire from here, I ask you? It's a fine day it is when His Majesty's mail does not go to Wiltshire!"

"It goes to Wiltshire, mum," the harassed clerk explained again, "but it does not go direct. And the southbound coach has just left. If you are in a hurry, you must hire a chaise."

"Do you think us nabobs, then? Hire a chaise and six, hire a driver and groom, and my daughter traveling all alone with strange men and not knowing when she'll be set upon next. The mail coach it must be, sirrah!"

Pulse escalating at the enormity of the lie he was about to perpetrate, Michael approached the women. "Ladies, pardon me for eavesdropping, but I see you are in some distress. Might I intrude a moment? My sister is just on her way to...." He hastily improvised a substitute for Dorset in case anyone attempted tracing Blanche later. "...Sussex, but her maid was overcome and cannot travel farther. We would be most appreciative if you could act as her chaperone as far as Wiltshire. We have friends she may call on there who can accompany her the rest of the way. I have business here, and it would save me a great deal of trouble."

The woman instantly fell into raptures as Michael spun his tale, renaming Blanche "Miss MacDermot" and praying she would understand when the woman used that name. With Gavin's messenger watching the inn yard from the tavern, Michael didn't dare approach the carriage to explain. Blanche would be furious when she learned what he'd done, but he saw no alternative. He must see her to safety while he answered Gavin's call.

He located his carriage driver, pressed the last of his coins on him and ordered a change of direction. The coachman had stoically accepted all his eccentric employer's commands for over a week now and didn't blink an eyelash. Michael gave him Gavin's address and promised his aid should he ever have need of it.

The driver tucked the card in his coat pocket and asked with interest, "Be yer lordship needin' a new groom anytime soon? I'm fixin' to wed, and this travelin' life must end."

Michael thought the driver's words strangely prophetic, but he merely nodded his head and agreed. "If not as groom, in some other capacity if you like. A wedded man cannot leave his family alone for long, can he now?" Just saying the words injected them with truth, and for a moment, Michael heard the nails pounding into his coffin. A married man could not leave his wife alone for long.

Beaming, the driver went about his business with an alacrity that assured Michael he'd done all he could to place Blanche in the best of hands.

Before the wailing woman could be foisted off on his unsuspecting wife, Michael pulled the messenger from the tavern, slipped out the back way to his waiting horse, and galloped off in the direction of London.

Twenty-two

Waking from a doze, Blanche stared with astonishment at the immense creature who opened the carriage door.

"Miss MacDermot, it's that kind of your brother to offer your carriage. I'm certain he's the most perfect gentleman I've ever laid eyes on. A rare treasure, and you must be most pleased to have him look after you so well. It's a pity it is about your maid and all, but fate has smiled on us both!"

The carriage tilted as the woman climbed in, the ostrich feather in her bonnet dipping and bowing as she struggled with her bulk, her cloak, her skirts, and a basket. Too stunned for immediate reply, Blanche watched the woman settle in the seat across from her.

As the constant stream of effusive gratitude continued to flow, her message slowly sank in. MacDermot—the name she and Michael had traveled under. Not coincidence. Nor was this chatter about her "brother."

"I must say a word to my brother before we depart," Blanche said with a menace in her voice. "If you would excuse me for a moment...." She reached for the door, but the driver was already tipping his hat to her as he walked toward the front. Blanche opened the glass as he took his seat and in a most unlady-like manner shouted, "Wait! I would speak with...." She hesitated, not knowing what name to call Michael by in these circumstances.

It didn't matter. The driver shook the reins and set his horses to a trot. "His lordship has made all the arrangements. I'm to see to your comforts. He says as you're not to worry, but he's had an urgent message. You're in good hands."

Blanche forcibly closed her mouth as the man steered his cattle to open road. She dropped back into her seat with fury boiling through her. She could not believe Michael had done this to her.

She could not believe that she hadn't known he would do this to her.

The chattering woman on the opposite seat didn't seem in the least perturbed by her silence. Opening up a basket, she produced a box full of sweets and kindly offered one to Blanche.

Without paying attention to what she did, Blanche blindly squeezed the confection into crumbs between her gloved fingers.

She would kill Michael, she decided. She would throttle him until he spluttered and keeled over dead. She would take a knife to his bloody heart. She would scratch her fingers into those laughing, tempting devil's eyes of his and pluck them out one by one. Remembering Michael's naked assault on the thieves this morning, she decided she would kick him where it hurt the most, where he had hurt her the most. She knew what to aim for now. But first, she would skin him alive.

Murderous plots took her well toward the next inn. By then, Blanche had a scheme to rid herself of her garrulous companion. She intended heading straight for London and to hell with Wiltshire or wherever the madman thought he was sending her. If he wanted trouble, she would show him where to find it.

* * *

Eamon O'Connor leaned back in his uncomfortable chair, stretching his long legs as much as possible in the narrow, dirty little room. The pipe smoke around the table suffocated a man accustomed to the brisk fresh air of an Irish countryside, and he removed himself as far as possible without leaving his companions. They nattered on incessantly about rights and power and other things well beyond his ken. When they needed his expertise, they would let him know. At the moment, he did his best to stay awake by sipping at the rotgut they served and staring at the ceiling, imagining his Jocelyn smiling at him while slipping off her kirtle.

He had her skirts on the floor and her petticoats down when a pair of fine Irish eyes blinked through the hole in the lathe above him. Startled, Eamon dropped his feet to the floor and nearly lost his mug. The eyes hastily disappeared along with his idle daydream.

Ignoring the startled expression of his companions, Eamon leapt up and rushed out the door, heading for the staircase he'd seen hidden down the back hall. A clatter of chairs and feet behind him warned his actions had not gone unheeded.

Upstairs, Fiona cursed her daring and ran for the attic stairs. That dratted Eamon would run a hound to the ground when necessary.

She had really destroyed herself this time.

She knew the ancient attic by heart now. Dodging the gaping hole in one floorboard despite the darkness, she ducked under the sagging beams near the window. She pounded the filthy frame at just the right angle so the panel would shove up without sagging and sticking. She heard Eamon's long legs reaching the landing just behind her.

She dropped off the window ledge into the fog-shrouded darkness, landing on the roof below just as Eamon reached the attic. With luck, he would fall through the hole in the floor and anyone following him would stumble over him before they reached the window. With even more luck, none of the lard-bellied asses would fit through the tiny garret window. She couldn't rely on luck, however. It had never stayed with her for any great length of time or she wouldn't be in this position now.

Fiona raced across the rooftop along her planned escape route, searching for alternate paths. If they had half a brain between them, they would send someone outside to look for the next break between buildings where she might come down. She heard the shouts below just as she reached the roof's edge. Cursing, she halted and scanned the rough tile for as far as she could see. Behind her, she heard another shout. Damn, but someone had crawled through the window. They had her coming and going.

She took the only way out that she knew. Sitting on the brick edging, she groped with her toes for the window ledge on the next floor down. She hoped the whore who worked that bed didn't have company.

She achieved the twisting turn onto the ledge, slammed open the loose window, and hopped in, pulling the sash closed behind her. Blinking her eyes to accustom them to even deeper darkness, she sighed in relief at the empty room, and headed for the door into the upper hall of the tavern.

Below her waited the Bow Street Runner. He'd positioned himself in the same tavern booth every night at the same hour since she'd sent Little Jack to him that first time. The man was persistent, if nothing else. Or someone paid him extremely well.

She could try escaping past him. He didn't know her by sight, after all. But she'd lost her cloth cap somewhere on the rooftop, and her hair was a dead giveaway. For the millionth time in these last weeks she wondered at her close resemblance to the extraordinary O'Toole. God had a mysterious sense of humor. If O'Toole had any intelligence, he'd told the Runner she looked like him. She didn't doubt O'Toole's intelligence one bit.

Perhaps it was time she gave it up. She couldn't go on like this forever. Seamus was out of reach. Perhaps she could arrange for someone to warn him. He could escape to France or America. He wouldn't be the first MacDermot to lose himself in a foreign country. She didn't want to see him go, but she must end this senseless plotting before the rebels killed people. Shivering at the thought of confronting a duke, Fiona ran her hand through her disheveled locks, made some effort to straighten the overlarge jerkin over her boy's trousers, and then marched down the stairs into the tavern.

The Runner looked up at her and grinned.

* * *

Michael arrived at Gavin's townhouse after three days of hard riding. He'd changed horses and napped in fields and barns when the horses needed resting. He'd eaten when he could raise a few coins. But mostly he'd just rode until both he had reached exhaustion. It kept him from imagining Blanche's reaction to his departure.

Dusting himself off as best he could, he climbed off his steed and allowed Gavin's groom to lead the mare away.

He thought grimly of Blanche's inevitable wrath as he climbed the steps to Gavin's townhouse. He had no solution to the problem of keeping Blanche while pretending they were not married. 'Twas a pity Blanche wasn't the sort to live with the Indians.

Not giving him time for a bath and a change of clothes, Gavin stormed out, grabbed him by the collar, and hauled him into his study. Too tired and discouraged to fight, Michael permitted the man-handling.

"Where the hell have you been? And where is Lady Blanche?" Gavin demanded as Michael collapsed onto the leather couch where he'd been shoved. He considered toppling over and falling asleep, but Gavin wouldn't allow that. When Gavin worked up a full head of steam, no one could stop him.

"Lady Blanche should be on the way to Dorset by way of

Wiltshire," Michael answered wearily, stretching his tired muscles. "If you think there is any danger to her, I would suggest having the duke send out a small army blocking all roads between Dorset and London to impede her progress. She'll not stay put for long."

She was most likely slitting her garrulous companion's throat and turning the carriage around on her own, Michael mused.

"There's danger enough if we're to believe your little Irish rapscallion," Gavin answered ominously.

Michael came fully alert. "You've found Fiona?"

"She found us, although she won't tell us why. And I won't guarantee she's where we left her, either. I'd have to put iron bars on all the windows to keep that one caged. Are you certain you haven't duplicated yourself in female form?"

Michael was on his feet and heading for the door.

"Michael!" Gavin didn't raise his voice, but his tone demanded obedience.

Impatiently, Michael swung around to face him.

Gavin toyed with the broken handle of a letter opener and eyed him with skepticism. "I've never known you to womanize. Would you care to explain what is happening here?"

"The hell if I know."

Since Michael seldom used swear words, his use of them now spoke of his confusion.

He didn't take long in locating Fiona. An Irish lullaby drifting from an upper room drew him up the stairs two at a time. He located Gavin's wife painting flowers on the nursery wall while Fiona crooned to the infant in her arms.

"And a pleasant good morning to you too, Michael," Dillian said, with only a touch of sarcasm at his abrupt entrance. "I presume you left Blanche safe and well?"

"I trust you do not malign the lady's reputation so crudely around her family." Michael scowled at the infant in Fiona's arms. Gavin's offspring slept soundly, a picture of innocence and helplessness. The sight terrified and stirred him at the same time. "Why did you run?" he demanded, glaring at Fiona.

Long-lashed green eyes glared right back at him. "I had my reasons."

"And did you find your aunt well?"

"Aye." Fiona threw the marchioness a nervous look, then rose from the stool and deposited the infant into Michael's arms. "'Tis not a subject for the ears of innocents."

With that, she walked out, leaving Michael with his hands full of wiggling fingers and toes. The infant chose that moment to open wide blue eyes and blink. Michael nearly dropped the entire package. Fascinated, he watched a puzzled, cherubic smile form on tiny pink lips and a fist wave tentatively toward his nose. A child this size had no choice but to trust the adults around her implicitly. How did parents handle such responsibility?

Dillian stood beside him, waiting patiently until he returned the child to her. Then she gave him a quizzical look. "Is it Blanche or Fiona who has you so befuddled?"

Michael looked at her blankly as he transferred his niece into her arms.

Then he smiled. "Your daughter, my lady, completely befuddles me. I find it amazing that so charming a child could come from such demanding, obstreperous parents. If you will excuse me, it's time I nail a certain female to a wall."

Dillian's laughter followed him as he wandered down the hall. Michael located Fiona in the front sitting room. She'd tied her thick auburn tresses into some kind of knot on top of her head, but she still looked little more than the urchin he remembered.

"Gavin said you came to him. I take it this is a recent development?"

She gave his rumpled appearance a cursory look. "I take it you came at breakneck pace at his call?"

"He sent a messenger saying Lady Blanche had gone missing. He did not mention finding you. I've been on the road for three days, so I'm not best pleased at exchanging pleasantries. Let's get on with it. Why did you seek Gavin?"

"Because I was about to be discovered and had no other choice," she replied. "I don't know your Gavin and didn't know whether to trust him. I'm not in the habit of trusting bloody English aristocrats."

"He's not English. He's American. And he's on our side. You can trust him. Now will you please hurry and tell me what brought you here? I have to head off an angry duke."

Fiona's eyes flared wider at this news. "There's a conspiracy by radical leaders to blow up the heads of British government. A dinner party at the Duke of Anglesey's was mentioned. I trust your Lady Blanche has removed herself from his presence?"

Michael clenched his fists against this confirmation of his suspicions. "Not unless a small army can keep her away."

Fiona smiled grimly. "Then find that army. Eamon O'Connor is the best gunpowder expert this side of Napoleon's finest. He was trained by the French, and he's in London now."

Michael would have preferred not to hear that. He would have preferred it even more if he hadn't turned to see the Duke of Anglesey standing in the hall right behind him.

Twenty-three

Michael was in no humor to appease an angry duke. He'd left Blanche in a fury and probably headed straight for London into the arms of an explosives expert. He scowled and waited for the first round of attack.

"Where the bloody hell is Blanche?" Neville demanded.

Crossing his arms over his chest, Michael shrugged. "Visiting friends in Wiltshire, last I heard. If I were you, I would find some way of keeping her there. Of course, if I were you, I wouldn't have a band of radicals hot on my heels."

"I'm not afraid of a bunch of sniveling cowards who hide in dirty back streets and mutter imprecations to keep themselves warm," the duke declared. "I just don't want them anywhere near Blanche."

Blind, deaf, and dumb, these bloody nobles. Michael closed his weary eyes and leaned against the doorjamb, knowing Fiona had left through the back the instant the duke had appeared. "Is Your Grace aware that Lady Blanche owns mills in the north that are currently targets of attack by radicals? And I suspect, if the mills are targeted, then so must be the mines and whatever. And it is your laws that permit the conditions leading to this unrest."

"We've already instructed authorities to read the Riot Act and send out the yeomanry if these rabble rousers cause any more trouble," the duke said coldly.

Michael flinched and rubbed his eyes. "Then you are personally responsible for any danger the lady is in. Go away and leave me alone."

Neville grabbed Michael's coat lapels and jerked him upward. "Where is she?"

They were evenly matched in height and weight, but Neville played fair by rules Michael had never bothered learning. He caught the duke's wrists and twisted. Neville yelped and released his grip.

Dusting his lapels back in place, Michael answered, "She attempted to stop a riot in Manchester. Ask her solicitor. And if you insist on remaining, then keep Fiona from escaping. I've better to do than stand here arguing."

As he departed, Michael didn't remind him it would take an army to stop Lady Blanche from coming to London. He would take care of that on his own.

* * *

"What do you mean you are in his lordship's employ and your orders are to take me to Dorset? I do not wish to go to Dorset. I wish to go to London. I order you to turn around and go back." Blanche balled her hands into gloved fists of frustration as the carriage driver held his cap and scratched his head. She had rid herself of her companion at Wiltshire. To her dismay, she had discovered that Michael had absconded with what remained of the coins she'd removed from her hems, and she must rely on the carriage driver for her accommodations.

"His lordship might change his mind about hiring me if I were to do that, my lady," he answered in dismay. "And I've a new wife who wants me to take a permanent position. I promised his lordship I would see you safe in Dorset."

"I will hire you!" Blanche declared. "You may name your position. I can find you a cottage at Anglesey. You will never worry about money again. Just take me to London now!"

The driver looked dubious. "If it's all the same to you, my lady, I'd rather take the gentleman's word and live in London. Dorset is naught but another two days journey. Once I see you safe there, you may do as you wish. I don't have my orders for more than that."

"The gentleman hasn't a ha'penny to his name!" Blanche nearly screamed in frustration. "Those are my coins he paid you with. He does not own horse nor carriage or even a roof over his head! You are much better off in my employ." They'd already spent five days of miserable back roads traveling to Wiltshire. Another two days and Michael could be on his way to America for all she knew.

The driver still didn't look convinced. Few wives had funds of their own. Even fewer held land or the power to dispense employment, and he thought her Michael's wife. She understood his dilemma.

That didn't mean she would make it easier for him. Throwing up her hands in anger, Blanche picked up her traveling skirts and started marching down the road toward the crossroads leading to London.

"My lady! You cannot go afoot. It will take you more than two days that way, and you'll be beset with thieves and the like. Let me take you to Dorset. Then we'll go to London if you choose." The driver hurried after her, leaving the groom holding the carriage horses.

"I...don't...want...to...go...to...Dorset," she muttered between clenched teeth, kicking up the dust of the road as she increased her pace. She knew she behaved like a fool. She couldn't possibly walk unmolested to London. She had no money. Her shoes were paper thin. But she couldn't let Michael win this battle.

"I'll drive the horses faster," the driver suggested helpfully. "The days are longer. We'll travel till dark. We'll make Dorset in one day. Then we may turn and go to London."

"We have all of Wiltshire to cross! And then we're even farther from London than now. If we hurry from here, we can be in London in two or three days. If we go to Dorset, it will be nearly a week before we're there. And if the rains start, it will be longer. Did he give you enough coins to last that long?"

She'd caught him on that one, Blanche noted.

"If your ladyship could explain to his lordship...." the driver answered hesitantly.

Heady with triumph, Blanche nodded her head grandly and turned back toward the carriage. "I will explain it all. And you will have your position as I promised. Just take us back as quickly as we can go."

Her triumph lasted only as far as the next posting inn, where fresh horses were mysteriously not available suitable for a lady and her coach. It took her until the next morning to bribe the innkeeper with promised money to let her use horses that had come in the evening before.

When the same thing happened again at the next inn, Blanche remembered that Michael had friends in low places all across the country. But she had acquaintances in high places. She ordered the driver to take her to the country estate of the nearest one. She would put an end to this nonsense.

* * *

Fiona sat idly in the window seat, petting a long-haired white kitten while staring out at the London street below and listening to the argument in the parlor. The two gentlemen O'Toole had summoned did not seem to like him very much, but she judged them less harmful than the terrible duke. So she listened for anything that might mean danger to her family and wondered if she would ever see them again.

"His Grace has explained all this," Michael said with unusual impatience. "There have been threats to blow up he duke's dinner party. We must keep Lady Blanche out of town until we find the terrorists."

The idle juggler Fiona had first met had disappeared behind this angry gentleman. She liked the entertainer better, but the gentleman was very good at commanding his troops. Of course, when his troops consisted of dimwits like these, he had some right for impatience.

"It still ain't right," Lord Allendale insisted, stretching his gangly legs and staring at his polished boot tops. "We can't just kidnap a lady like that. She'll not ever forgive us."

"Benington," Michael appealed to the shorter, fatter young lord, "Explain it to him, please. She counts you among her loyal friends and has always relied on your discretion."

Fiona smiled to herself as Benington gave the same reply he'd repeated in any number of different ways throughout the morning. "I still don't see how we can hold her against her will. She'll flay us alive, she will."

Michael flung his hands up in frustration. "Then stay and patrol Elton Alley while I stop her. If you cannot control a puny female, you should be ashamed to call yourselves men."

"Gentlemen," Allendale replied huffily. "We're gentlemen. And gentlemen don't kidnap ladies."

"But I'll be damned if I'll let you near her," Benington added. "We'll take our sisters along and stop her. But we can't hold her long. Blanche don't like our sisters by half."

From her window seat, Fiona asked with curiosity, "Who does she like?"

"Lady Effingham," both young lords answered in chorus.

Michael and Fiona exchanged glances. Without another word to his troops, Michael left the room in the direction of the nursery and

Dillian.

It took bribery, persuasion, coercion, and a modicum of blackmail to pry Dillian from her husband's side when it looked as if Gavin meant to endanger himself in the search for the radical leaders and attend the duke's dinner. But with Gavin's full approval, Michael accomplished it.

Benington and Allendale would lead Lady Blanche to Anglesey, and Dillian would keep her there in some manner or another. Michael didn't want to learn the details. Blanche would be angrier than a nest of hornets when she found she'd been tricked. He just couldn't take that into consideration. He had to keep her safe until he'd found the conspirators.

That they existed, Michael had no doubts. Even with their recently won representation in parliament, the Irish had no power, and they still despised English authority. If the radical English labor leaders came from farmers and industrial workers, they didn't have the military experience to carry on a real war. But the rebellious Irish had invented the pastime. And then there were the unemployed soldiers from Napoleon's wars....

Later that night, Michael rubbed his eyes wearily as he stared out over the dark London street.

"Will you find them in time?" Fiona asked softly from behind him.

"Neville has an entire army at his disposal. They'll find the bastards. I don't like to think what will happen when they do."

Fiona was silent, and Michael knew her thoughts traveled the same path.

In a country where a child could be hung for stealing a loaf of bread, treason of this immensity would result in swift and hideous punishment. Michael couldn't condone violence, but he couldn't exactly blame the radicals for their desperation either.

"Eamon used to push me in my swing when I was a lass," Fiona said quietly. "When they took his da's lands for taxes, he had no choice but to go into the army. The English army didn't want him. The French welcomed him with open arms."

"Is he kin of yours?" Michael asked. He knew somewhere behind Fiona's sorrow lay family of some sort, but she remained close-mouthed about them.

"Of the mind, perhaps. Not of blood. Could we not spirit them away somehow?"

"Neville's setting a trap. If they come anywhere near the townhouse before his dinner, they're dead men. I suppose they deserve death for thinking to take the lives of others. I just can't accept either alternative."

"Do ye love Lady Blanche?"

Michael swung around. "What has that to do with anything?"

She shrugged. She had donned boy's clothes again as if taunting them with her ability to disappear the instant they did something not to her liking. So far, she had only disappeared as far as the nursery. Michael didn't know how much longer that situation would last.

"The lady is not likely to approve if you side with the radicals," Fiona suggested.

"I'm not on the side of anyone who would harm a lady," Michael growled, feeling as irascible as Gavin usually behaved. "And Lady Blanche is more on the side of the radicals than her cousin. They do her grave injustice."

Fiona nodded understandingly. "I believe that, but Eamon and his friends will not. And that does not help all the others. The lady cannot change the laws."

Crossing his arms, Michael leaned his shoulders against the wall and stared at his nemesis. "So what are we discussing here?"

She faded into the shadows, out of the lamp light. "I can take you to their leaders. You can tell them their plot's come undone. But you must make them believe they can do nothing further. They have more plans than London has streets. It will not be easy."

Michael thought of Blanche somewhere between here and London. It had been nearly two weeks since he'd last seen her. Wishing he could hold her just once more, Michael sighed and pushed away from the wall. "All right. What do we have to do?"

He wondered if Blanche would visit him in the Tower if he was charged with treason.

Twenty-four

"Dillian, you know perfectly well you and Madeline are the only reasons I allowed those ninnyhammers to talk me into staying prisoner in my own home." Blanche pounded the bass keys of her pianoforte. "Madeline seems quite recovered and never looked peaked at all. And if you continue pacing that way, I'll become convinced this is all a hoax and take myself into London immediately."

"Anglesey's fresh air is doing me a world of good," Dillian replied absently, glancing at the ormolu clock on the mantel. "And you shouldn't speak so harshly of Allendale and Benington. They've done their best entertaining us while the Season is at its finest."

"That's because their creditors can't find them here and they're eating and sleeping for free," Blanche said dryly, picking out a tune on the pianoforte. "They're like the brothers I never had, but they're still harboring some foolish notion that I'll choose between them."

Dillian dropped into a damask-covered chair and clasped her hands. "And will you not? They're perfectly agreeable gentlemen and willing to permit you control of the purse strings. Isn't that what you wanted?

Blanche picked out a brief refrain. "Do I want a biddable husband? What is the point? I can do as I wish without marrying. Why should I saddle myself with someone who will only interfere with my life and expect things of me that I'm not willing to give?"

Dillian watched her shrewdly. "If you want children, you must take some man to bed. Did you have some other in mind?"

"Not Allendale or Benington," Blanche said curtly. "If you're feeling well enough to tax me with this nonsense, then you are feeling well enough to be left here alone. I really must go into London. The stewards my solicitor keeps sending for interviews are thoroughly hopeless. I must find someone who will listen to my ideas. I can't do that while sitting in the country."

"If I'm feeling stronger on the morrow, I will come with you,"

Dillian assured her. "I've asked Gavin to look around for someone. You do not set him an easy task."

An ominously low chord emanated from the pianoforte. "No, of course not. What sensible man would listen to a woman's opinion? And besides, Gavin no doubt concerns himself overmuch with Neville's dinner tonight, is that not so?"

Dillian started nervously, glancing at Blanche before reaching for her sewing basket. "Of course not. What makes you say that? I'm not even certain Gavin will attend."

"Dillian, you always were a poor liar." Giving up, Blanche slammed the pianoforte lid and rose from the bench. "Where are our incompetent bodyguards tonight? Stationing the militia on the grounds?" She didn't miss Dillian's nervous twitch as she hit the target. "Do you think me a complete imbecile? Admittedly, I foolishly fell for Michael's assurances that he needed my help in finding Fiona. But after spending weeks trying to reach London only to be carted off to Anglesey by you and my eager suitors, I'm not so deluded. I haven't been to town in well over a month. Neville's dinner party is tonight. And you expect Fiona's radicals to attend. Don't you?"

"I don't know what you're babbling about." Dillian fixed her with a glare. "And what is this about helping Michael find Fiona? You were with him that week, weren't you? Blanche, how could you?"

Blanche waved a hand in dismissal. "Don't distract me. I know that ploy too well. What is happening back there, Dillian? Is there really any danger?" She ran her hand over the pianoforte's lid, avoiding Dillian's watchful gaze. She'd removed Michael's ring weeks ago and had no intention of ever speaking to him again, but she couldn't help worrying. He'd gone far out of his way in seeing her safe at Anglesey and out of trouble. She would wring his neck for that. But she wanted to be the one murdering him. She didn't want anyone else doing it for her.

Dillian gave up her innocent pose now that nothing could be done. She dropped her sewing in her lap. "I don't think there's any danger, but Gavin wouldn't tell me if there were. They just don't want to take any chances. Fiona said you were a possible target, and they didn't want to worry about you while they went about stopping the others. Do you hate me terribly?"

"No, I'm just sorry everyone thinks I'm such a helpless goose that I must be protected at all costs. You've spent weeks here for no reason when I'm sure you'd much rather be with Gavin. And I could have been looking for a new man of business. And I would have liked to know more about Fiona. I suppose she'll disappear back to Ireland after this." Casually, Blanche asked, "Do you think Michael fancies her?"

Fiona was the only reason she could think of that would summon Michael back to London in such a hurry that he would leave her in the care of a coachman while he went rattling off on his own. She didn't like thinking it.

She didn't know Fiona well. She didn't even know the girl's age. But the resemblance between the two was unmistakable. Michael had grown up in America with the Lawrence family, so a family resemblance to the Irish girl wasn't likely. But she suspected a similarity of the soul called them together. She couldn't say that of Michael and herself. They had nothing in common but their physical desires.

Blanche stopped her hand from traveling to the flat space between her hip bones. It was too soon to tell. She'd missed monthlies before. Terror that they might have created a child warred with the first sprouting hope that she had actually accomplished what she had set out to do.

"I don't think Michael fancies Fiona any more than he fancies any of his other waifs." Dillian watched her with curiosity. "What happened between the two of you? I won't tell, Blanche, but I worry for you."

"Nothing happened," Blanche answered airily. "Michael was the perfect gentleman as always. It's just best if Neville doesn't know. He wouldn't understand."

"Neither would most of society," Dillian grumbled, picking up her sewing again. "You cannot go about with Michael as if he were your brother. He's not, and it's best you remember it. Michael might carry the conscience of a saint, but he's a man. Men have weaknesses of which you know nothing."

Oh, yes, she knew something of men's weaknesses. And of her own. She shouldn't risk further involvement with a man who spent his life rescuing the world at the expense of all close to him.

Blanche returned to the pianoforte and rippled the keys again.

Maybe he would go back to Ireland with Fiona after tonight. And she would make plans for the Continent.

* * *

Wearing ragpicker's clothes, sitting in a drafty attic with Fiona, Michael fingered the dainty square of perfumed lawn in his pocket. He'd found Blanche's handkerchief among his effects, reminding him of how intimately they'd shared their lives for a few halcyon days. How had he left a lady's bed to end up in this filthy attic with a nest of dangerous rebels below?

"I'm in favor of letting them all hang," Michael muttered as still another of the fools stood to speechify about the noble cause of the poor and downtrodden.

Fiona held a finger to her lips and pointed to the hole in the floor she'd been peering through. "Eamon's arrived."

Michael sighed and checked the placement of his array of tricks. They had reluctantly concluded they had no chance of talking all the radicals out of destruction, but they might end their dastardly plans by removing their munitions expert from the scene. Unfortunately, Eamon O'Connor had been remarkably elusive until tonight.

Eamon was a man of few words. The glorified speeches ended with his arrival. The leaders proceeded to give their orders. With Fiona's help, Michael could have handed this whole group over to Neville's men, but he'd promised her he would end the plot without turning the conspirators over to British justice. If she had family involved in this, he couldn't tell. He didn't want to know. The time had come to take out Eamon.

Fiona caught Michael's arm as he stood up. "They could implicate my uncle and brother," she whispered urgently, as if reading his thoughts. "Please be careful."

So, there it was. Not just Eamon, but her family, too. Nodding curtly, Michael slipped from the attic to the darkened landing.

Neville had soldiers patrolling both alley and his townhouse. The radicals in the room below didn't have a rat's chance of escaping the noose should he, or anyone else, sound the alarm about their nefarious plot. Somehow, he must convince them to abandon their plans without anyone getting killed.

He slipped down the stairs to the hall outside the meeting room.

Faded wallpaper hung in tatters from the walls of the abandoned tenement. A single sconce illuminated a darkened water stain along the ceiling. Sitting on the floor cross-legged so he seemed slight and less harmless, Michael could see layers of dust and filth and more than a few rat droppings. Fiona had lived here for weeks. He grimaced and shook his head, knowing he'd done the same. He'd hoped he was older and smarter these days.

Detaching a metal pan from the rope at his waist, he set it on the floor, then scattered a handful of dry ingredients from the chemist's into it. He wasn't a man of science, but he'd learned a thing or two from a traveling medicine show. If Eamon really knew his business, he'd have his attention swift enough.

Setting fire to the chemicals, Michael sat back against the wall and warmed his hands at the blaze. The odor would choke a sewer, but he'd come prepared with a heavy muffler perfumed with Dillian's lavender water. He'd survive.

Coughing soon ensued in the closed room beyond as Michael idly fanned the smoke in that direction. A scraping of chairs followed, and he settled into his new role.

A thin man in a frock coat frayed at sleeves and elbow appeared in the doorway. Michael knew he couldn't count on Eamon arriving first, but he'd lure him out. He scratched at the gray wig hiding his head and half his face and glanced up at the intruder. "Keepin' off from the bloody soldiers, too, ain't you? They'll likely lock us all up afore dawn iffen they dunt find their fella."

"What the hell is that you're cooking?" the man in the frayed coat demanded. "It smells like rotten eggs. Be off with you now. This place is taken."

Michael studied the tattered walls and broken windows and gave a gaped-tooth grin. "Taken by me, it is. And a few rats, likely. Grew up here, I did, 'til I got 'pressed leastways. Docks full of soldiers tonight. Must be expectin' Frenchies. Got a drop of gin on ye? Mighty cold in these old bones."

By this time, the smoke had everyone in the far room choking. A hoarse voice shouted at the thin man to shut the door. Before he could do so, a larger man elbowed past him.

Recognizing Eamon's black curls and chiseled chin, Michael threw a handful of chemicals on the dying fire. The embers roared into a blazing flame that nearly singed his eyebrows. He sat back hastily to keep his wig from going up with it.

Cursing, Eamon stamped out the blaze with his heavy boots and aimed a kick at Michael for good measure. Michael leaped to a wooden crate, and the kick merely earned Eamon a stubbed toe.

"Are ye after burnin' the place down, ye old fool?" Eamon cried in exasperation.

"Mr. O'Connor, and it is a rare plasure to be meetin' you at last," Michael responded. "A fair lady was by way of telling me yer troubles. She fears for yer worthless neck, she does, and that of her only brother's."

Both men stopped cold and stared. Michael gathered his ragged woolen coat with some semblance of dignity but kept his position on the crate. "Are ye dumbstruck then, at the thought of a fair lass lookin' after ye? She says as ye once pushed her little swing as a lad. She would not see yer neck in a noose if she can help it."

"Fiona," Eamon spat out. "I knew it! Where the bleedin' hell is she?"

"Lookin' after yer fine neck, it seems to me," Michael said equably. "As well as her brother's," he added to be honest. "The duke has a list of names and ye're all on it," he lied gleefully. "Just look out the windows. His men are after lookin' for ye now. Unlike ye silly stumps, the lass courts friends with power."

The thin man cursed and hurried to warn his coughing comrades. Eamon remained.

"I will not believe Fiona turned us in," Eamon said stubbornly.

"That she did not," Michael agreed. "But the duke has spies everywhere. As I said, the lass doesna wish ye to hang, but the duke knows your name." That should scare the fool. "He did not take kindly to your terrifying his lady cousin. 'Twas a shameless thing ye did there, O'Connor. The lady works as we speak to right the wrongs her grandfaither made."

"Who the divil are ye?" Eamon stepped forward to grab Michael's collar.

A flick of Michael's wrist sent a column of smoke soaring between them. Coughing, backing out of the smoke and wiping his eyes, Eamon stumbled into the crowd of men hastily donning their coats and looking for escape. When Eamon reached for the gray-haired apparition again, he was gone.

"Red coats in the alley," a ghostly voice reminded them from above. "Spies in your midst!"

From a distant corner of the ceiling a more feminine voice joined in cheerily, "I hear France is quite nice this time of year."

As men fled by back doors and windows, scampering across alleyways and trash bins, Eamon O'Connor dashed for the attic.

He found only a beggar's wool coat and a gray wig for his efforts.

Twenty-five

"Well, I'm happy to hear it was a lot of to-do about nothing," Dillian exclaimed as she straightened her skirt and took a seat on the sofa one mid-May morning after the crisis had passed. "Neville has had his important dinner without anyone blowing up the prime minister. Now we must think what to do about Fiona. She cannot continue running about the city like a ragamuffin."

"I'll return her to Ireland where she belongs," Michael replied absently, not looking up from the papers in front of him. Restlessly, he set aside his pen and strode to the window. To keep from clasping and unclasping his fist, he fingered the cloth in his pocket. "The radicals may have left London, but they're out there somewhere, burning with the fires of injustice. I don't suppose Neville has changed his position any?"

"You know he has not," Gavin said as he strode into the room. He kissed his wife on the forehead. "Centuries of privilege cannot be turned around overnight. And the threat of violence only makes them more stubborn. You should have let us capture the dolts, Michael. You've not made my job easier."

"It's this system of injustice that should be on trial, not those angry young louts." Michael spoke without heat, turning to face the room. "Someone must make government realize it stands on the backs of working men. When that foundation crumbles, authority crumbles with it."

Gavin ran his hand through already rumpled hair. "I can only do one thing at a time. I find the child labor law most important right now."

Before the argument could escalate further, Dillian stood up. "If you allowed women the vote, that law would be in effect now. And most of the others, I daresay. Blanche has the right of it. Men are too thick-headed to get anything done. We must work around you."

"Blanche has returned?" Michael asked.

Dillian sent him a sharp look over her shoulder. "Did you think she would not? She has missed much of the Season, but she means to make up for it. She is interviewing stewards today and plans a rout for Friday night. I understand she's expecting quite a crush."

She swept from the room, leaving Michael thoughtfully scraping his toe on the carpet.

"The invitation includes all of us. Will you attend?" Gavin broke the silence.

As if he hadn't heard, Michael gave up his toe sketching. "I've some business to take care of. Tell Dillian I'll not be in for dinner."

Since that wasn't news, Gavin stayed where he was, fretting at a loose thread in his waistcoat and frowning at the carpet where his brother had stood.

* * *

The lamp sputtered on the vanity as Blanche pulled out the last of her hairpins and idly dragged her fingers through waist length locks. She'd sent her maid to bed hours ago. She would brush out the tangle herself tonight, once she summoned the energy to lift her brush.

She didn't bother looking at the image in her mirror. She knew her porcelain doll appearance hadn't changed, except perhaps for a small smudge of darkness beneath her eyes. The pink puckered scars on her brow still remained, although mostly hidden behind a thick fall of golden waves that curled artistically in just the right places. Her eyes still shone clear and blue, her lips looked untouched. No one would know her as the wicked wanton she was from that image in the mirror. No one but Michael, anyway.

The thin chemise she wore rubbed at sensitive breasts, and with a frown, Blanche tied her wrapper tighter. It didn't help much. She felt a hollow in her mid-section that tempted her night and day. Most of the time, she could keep her hands away, but tonight, she was weary, and her fingers stroked the thin material over her abdomen. She was more aware of her body than she had ever been before in her life, now that she knew what it could do to her.

What she had done so daringly with Michael terrified her now that she was alone. The crush of people at dinner tonight had not made her feel any less alone. She'd tried talking to every man in attendance, but none affected her as Michael did.

She had no courage of her own, she'd discovered. She should have ignored Dillian's ploy and come to London weeks ago, escaping Allendale and Benington's protective custody. But she hadn't had the courage. The knowledge that Michael was nearby and hadn't come to her had sapped her confidence. Her anger at him sank beneath the quicksand of what she had once thought was the firm ground of their relationship.

Six weeks since she had seen him last. Pinching the bridge above her nose, Blanche rested her head against her hand. She had known what he was, walked straight into his arms knowing it, believing his wanderlust the ideal solution to her situation. She simply hadn't counted on him leaving quite so soon. She hadn't known she would ache for him.

Deciding she would untangle her hair in the morning, Blanche tied it back with a ribbon, blew out the lamp, and drifted toward the bed. Dropping her wrapper where she stood, she slid in between the cool sheets and tried desperately not to think of Michael's warm body filling the space next to her. She curled her fingers around the thin gold band hanging from the chain about her neck.

The room held little light, but a shadow caught Blanche's attention. Riveted, she watched the silhouette step into the pool of gray light from the window. Michael! Her heart skittered as he removed his coat and unfastened his cravat. He threw his outer garments over a chair and began unfastening his shirt. The breadth of his shoulders and the narrowness of his waist still had the power to take her breath away.

Scrambling to sit up against her pillows, Blanche pulled the sheet up to her chin.

"You're mad! You cannot come in here like this. How did you get in?"

He discarded the shirt, and even in the poor light she could see the outline of muscled shoulders and arms as he sat on the bed beside her to remove his shoes. She thought her heart might pound through her chest or just split in two altogether. Michael had never acknowledged the barrier of walls. Or family.

"Did you think I would not?" He dropped the last shoe and leaned over her, one strong hand trapping the covers on the far side of her legs. "You must think me a singularly lacking lover or without the imagination of a hedgehog. I can assure you, I am neither."

"You cannot!" she whispered, shocked, as he brushed a kiss

against her cheek. She slid down beneath the sheets. Arguing would work better from a distance. Stripped to just his trousers, Michael halted her efforts by leaning forward and crushing her beneath his greater weight. His long legs came to rest atop the covers between hers. His proximity sent chills down her spine, and heat to her cheeks.

"But I can," he reassured her, his voice a caress in her ears. "You gave me that right. Did you think I would yield it so quickly? We made vows, Blanche. I do not forsake mine."

He spoke as if words said in the heat of passion meant the same as those said in a holy church. "You cannot just appear whenever it pleases you, take your pleasure, and depart," she whispered angrily, shoving at his shoulders. The contact with his bare flesh seared her, but she fought the wave of desire. She had right on her side. She dropped her hands, just the same. "I will not be your mistress."

Michael intertwined his fingers with hers against the pillow, holding them captive. "Unless we marry, I see no other alternative," he replied without rancor, kissing the hollow beneath her ear.

His weight pressed against the length of her, his hands prevented movement, but his kiss drained all thought of fight. She turned her mouth eagerly to meet his lips. Perhaps she'd had too much wine with dinner. One kiss shouldn't decimate her will like this. She turned her head away when he lifted his mouth. "No, Michael, we cannot."

"Yes, Blanche, we can, and we will," he responded firmly, then bent to suckle at her breast through the nightrail.

Desire exploded through her.

Still holding her captive, Michael used his teeth to open her ribbons. When the moist heat of his mouth fastened over her sensitive flesh, Blanche cried out in half protest, half surrender. His tongue teased her aching nipples. "What you gave to me, you cannot take back, my love," Michael whispered against her hair as he raised his head and brushed her cheek with warm kisses. "You are the only woman I will ever know. Did you think me so fickle I would give you up easily?"

He released her hands to press her shoulders deeper into the pillows while he kissed her, and she instinctively wrapped her arms around him. She clung to the bare flesh of his wide shoulders while his mouth stole her will.

At what point the covers slipped away, Blanche couldn't say. She only knew the rough chafing of his trousers between her legs was not what she wanted there. He lifted himself obediently when she reached for his buttons, kneeling over her and lavishing her breasts with attention while she worked the fastenings. When at last she freed him from confinement, her fingers clenched convulsively around his maleness.

His moan of pleasure as she stroked him startled Blanche into an awareness that had eluded her before. She had thought herself powerless in Michael's arms, as she was powerless in all else, but she was not!

Boldly, she ran her fingers down the length of him, finding the root of his pleasure and cupping him there. With another moan, he stiffened, then leaned down to kiss her fervently.

Michael slid his hands beneath her hips, lifted her to him, and plunged deep and true between her legs. The power of his penetration stole her breath and made her weep with relief. Digging her fingers into his shoulders, kissing any portion of him she could reach, Blanche fell gladly into his wild rhythm, allowing him to carry her away on crashing waves of sensual pleasure. When at last she succumbed and collapsed, sated, Michael finally released his warmth deep inside of her, and Blanche hugged his shoulders and wept.

He kissed her tears and cuddled her between his heat and the wrinkled sheets.

"You make me feel like God," he whispered. "I think I can raise the sun and lower the moon right now."

Blanche chuckled through her tears. The sheets smelled of the musky scents of their love-making. She didn't know how she could explain them to her maid in the morning. She didn't know how she would explain Michael to anyone if he should remain. He had torn her life into tattered bits of worthless paper, but she couldn't get enough of the touch of his hand, the weight of his body, the low humor of his masculine voice. He caressed her breast, and she arched into him, wanting more.

"We can't," she murmured sadly against his ear as he kissed the corner of her mouth.

"I thought I already put an end to that foolish argument," he whispered, flicking his tongue along her earlobe. "Must I prove it again? We can, and we will."

And they did.

* * *

Dawn had not yet succeeded in throwing its rosy hues across the bedroom floor when Blanche first awoke. But the gray light preceding dawn glinted against the gold of the medallion around Michael's neck.

Still languorous from their love-making, she fiddled with the chain, brushing her fingers through the soft curls of hair on his chest. His arm around her tightened, and she sighed, stretching her legs to twine with his. Somewhere during the night, they'd divested themselves of what remained of their clothing. Lying naked in a man's arms was as close to sin as she had ever come, and she enjoyed it.

"I have to send you away," she murmured regretfully.

He stroked her hair. "I would not have it this way, Blanche," he replied, more as if he spoke to himself than to her. "I would claim you before all the world if you would let me."

She shivered in denial. They could not marry, not if she wished any control of her future. She would rather play with the chain hanging between dark male nipples. She touched one flat bud experimentally, and felt his intake of breath. All in the interest of science, she leaned over and licked the crest she'd caused to pucker with her touch.

Michael grabbed her hair and tugged her back, but not before she'd felt the muscles of his abdomen tighten and knew the thrust of his masculinity against her.

Her gaze met the muddy green of his eyes.

"I am trying hard not to scandalize our families," he said from between gritted teeth. "But I won't give you up just to appease anyone's social conscience."

Her stomach churned with alarm at the intensity of his expression. Blanche pulled back, studying him with care. Her family had never given her any experience in fidelity. Her eyes widened at the thought of Michael not leaving, as she supposed he would.

Wide, tanned shoulders appeared permanently affixed to her

lacy pillows. Over-long auburn hair brushed the top of her headboard as he sat up, his arms crossed belligerently across his muscled chest. She couldn't move this man from her bed if she tried, his posture seemed to say. Her stomach roiled even more.

"We'll talk of this another time," she said, swallowing her fear. "You'd best leave before it's light."

"And if I choose not to leave?" he asked with ominous calm.

He'd always been able to read her thoughts. Stomach churning, Blanche rolled to the side of the bed and sat up. The motion sent acid spewing upward, and with horror, she dashed for the chamber pot.

As she collapsed on the floor with the bowl, retching up last night's dinner, Michael knelt beside her, pulling the long strands of hair out of her face, and holding back the chain with his ring around her neck. They were both naked as the day they were born, kneeling on the cold floor in dawn's first light, and the reality of it embarrassed Blanche to her very core.

She couldn't hide behind the shadows of night, tucking the images of what they did away with the dawn as if they were no more than dreams. Reality had her insides heaving into a bowl. Reality was that she'd allowed this man to put himself inside her and place his seed there. Reality was bedding a man with no name, no home, and no future.

She wanted to shake off his comforting hands, but she needed the security of Michael's presence. His solidity somehow made the crash with reality a little easier. When the retching finally stopped, he wrapped her in a blanket and brought her a glass of water while she kneeled over the chamber pot, afraid to move. She concentrated on his toes rather than meet his eyes. He had long toes with fine hairs on them.

If it was possible to hear a man's hesitation, she heard it in his silence. He could not know for certain that what they had done had borne fruit. She would keep him from asking. She could still go to Europe.

"The cook must have put mushrooms in the sauce last night," she said weakly. "I have told him my stomach cannot abide mushrooms, but he will not listen. Men never do."

Michael crouched before her. He tried tilting her chin so she met his gaze, but Blanche would not. Her heart cried out in despair and protest at the unfairness of it all.

"I never knew my mother or father," he said, speaking to the side of her face. "I've never known my real name. I've always felt as out of place with Gavin's family as a cuckoo in a hen's nest."

Her heart went out to him, to the lonely, imaginative boy he must have been. But loneliness was no basis for losing her heart to yet another man who would abandon her, as he must, no matter what fine words he used. She would not be the anchor around his neck.

He took her cold hands and warmed them against his wide chest. "I vowed then, when I was very young, that I would never bring a child into this world unless I was prepared to stand by his side, give him my name, and support him in the best manner available. I have reaffirmed that vow a thousand times as I've seen the tragic results of parental neglect. I am not blind to the irresponsibility of men who take their pleasure and never consider the results. For that reason, I swore never to bed a woman until I could marry her."

Startled, Blanche's gaze flew to Michael's face. She must be misunderstanding his meaning. Still, the gold ring burning between her breasts acquired new significance.

Michael smiled. The warmth of his gaze caressed her as clearly as the touch of his hand. She huddled in her blanket while he crouched quite shamelessly naked and seemingly untouched by the cold.

"There are other ways of releasing sexual urges, and I know all of them. But in my eyes, after what we've done, we are wedded, Blanche. Whether or not the words are ever said in church or broadcast in public, you are my wife. That ring you hide is my pledge. I will never have another woman besides you. I will raise and cherish any child that comes of our joining. Do not deny me in this, Blanche. I have lived too long with this vow to break it."

Blanche scanned his face but found only Michael's open honesty. He meant what he said. The realization thrilled her. And terrified her.

He would never give up her or the child, no matter how she decided. The strength of his will made her shiver, though his position was the weaker one. She had the wealth and power. He had nothing.

Apparently reading her resistance in her silence, Michael stood up. "We will talk of this again, Blanche. For now, you'd best climb back between the covers and get warm. I overtired you last night, and I apologize. Your maid will bring you tea, and you will feel better."

"She always brings hot chocolate," Blanche grumbled as she returned to the bed. The roiling in her stomach had lessened, but she felt light-headed and weak.

He wore his shirt and trousers when he tucked her in a moment later and brushed a kiss against her cheek. She should feel relief, but it was regret that tugged at her heartstrings.

"I will see that she brings tea," Michael assured her.

The tender caress of his fingers across her brow stole her irritation. She felt coddled and loved as she never had before.

"Gavin can always find me," he reminded her. "You have only to ask."

He was gone before her sleepy brain fully registered his meaning: the blasted, wicked wretch meant to set off again without saying where he was going or when he would be back. She'd *known* he would do that, and still she could not control her disappointment.

Furious, she flung her water glass at the closed door.

When her maid stepped over the shattered pieces some time later, she carried a tray of tea and wore a bewildered expression.

Twenty-six

Michael leaned on the ship's railing and watched the Emerald Isle approach. The salt-tinged sea breeze blew his hair back from his face and tugged at the loose wool of his coat. He loved traveling, and he particularly loved the rolling green hills of this contradictory isle.

He had wanted to introduce Blanche to the wild blue skies and rippling grasses he wished he could call home. But he couldn't continue to besmirch her good name and make her an outcast in the society she preferred. He must do this alone.

And alone was how he would do it. Fiona had disappeared the night he'd told her he would be returning her to Ireland.

He would have liked to shake her for her obstinacy, but he recognized the trait he wore so well himself.

At least she'd finally trusted him with her family names. Her story of lands and title reverting to the crown when all direct male descendants were given up for dead was nothing new. Her grandfather's attempts to pass his lands through his daughter to Seamus had been doomed to failure given the political mood of Parliament toward Irish aristocracy.

But the family name she had given him—MacDermot—worried him more than he'd let on. It was a name from his childhood. As he'd told Blanche when they'd traveled to Scotland, he and Gavin had often used MacDermot as a code word, as their father had before them. He didn't like coincidences.

Michael worried about Fiona. A young girl should not wander London's streets unprotected. He'd sent word to Blanche, hoping she would trace the brat's direction and offer her assistance.

Traveling by his wits and talents as usual, it had taken him nearly a fortnight to get here. It was already the beginning of June. He hoped Fiona had not lied about her family's direction. Every moment he spent away from Blanche worried him. If Blanche took it into her head to flee London for the continent, he would have to borrow from Gavin's meager funds and follow before he lost her entirely. Or he could tell Neville of the marriage and use the duke's resources. He would do that if he must, but Blanche would not appreciate his choice.

But he had to make this journey. It was the only means he saw to end the conspirators' plots for once and all, if Seamus and William held the key that he suspected they did. In the back of his mind lingered a tiny impossible hope that he would find a clue to his own background.

Once ashore, he traveled half the breadth of Ireland to reach the place Fiona called home. Sleeping with rocks for pillows and the stars as blanket no longer held the appeal it once had. Michael wanted Blanche's warmth beside him, her laughing voice chiding him for the error of his ways. He didn't need her silk sheets or elegantly carved ceilings. He needed Blanche. He didn't like discovering he needed anyone or anything.

But the cool nights and long June days with their scuttling white clouds, scented spring breezes, and dancing flowers awoke Michael's awareness of the vast emptiness in his soul. He'd ignored the yearning for too long. He'd prided himself on his lack of possessions, on his ability to survive without asking anyone's help. Now he saw only the bleakness of his future.

When at last he reached the lands Fiona called home, Michael sat upon an overgrown stone wall and contemplated the acres of fallow field beyond. In the distance rose a crumbling stone castle and several thatched cottages. A few cows grazed in a far pasture. He heard dogs barking and the distant cry of children playing. And all around him spread emerald acres dotted with wild rose canes, fallen stone walls, and the bright dots of spring flowers. Possibilities abounded in this rich earth, but the field went unplowed, the seed unsown.

Michael wasn't blind to the comparison to his own life. He possessed everything Mother Nature could grant him, and he had wasted it on rambling rather than building. Perhaps he couldn't call it *waste*. There was no harm in admiring the natural beauty of the world. But neither had he taken that wealth and multiplied it or made it grow to aid God's children. A rolling stone gathered no moss, he reflected wryly. Nor much of anything else.

But that was neither here nor there. He must find Fiona's family and persuade them to turn from their cause. Then he could return to

Blanche and plan the rest of his life. She hadn't fooled him with her lies. He could barely suppress his panic and excitement at the possibility he might have a son or daughter in a few short months.

He ambled toward an old woman feeding her chickens, who watched his approach. "Top of the mornin' to ye," he greeted her cheerfully, taking off his flat cap and presenting her with a slight bow.

She stared at him with suspicion, threw out the last of her grain, and came forward, swinging her bucket. She looked frail enough for a good gust of wind to blow away, but only her skirts whipped around her as she stopped on the other side of the rose-bedecked fence.

"And it's not Seamus," she muttered with disappointment, looking him over closely. "I knew 'twas not. These old eyes are not so far gone as that."

Michael hid his relief. Fiona had not lied, then. Her family lived in these parts.

"Not Seamus," he agreed, "but I look for him. Is he about, then?"

"And who be ye askin'?"

That took a moment to translate, but Michael understood the question before the words. He trod dangerous ground now. "Michael O'Toole, at your service, ma'am. 'Tis Fiona who's after inquirin', though. I've word from her."

The old woman nodded. "She up and disappeared before she heard. Is she well, then?"

"Last I saw of her, a fortnight ago," Michael promised. "She's some fear for her brother, and I said I would bring word of him."

The woman shook her head sorrowfully, but the suspicion remained in her eyes. "Ye have a look of him about ye, Mr. O'Toole. How is it you come to know our Fiona? Be ye family?"

"Not unless there's an American branch."

"Gareth, the eldest MacDermot son went to America, as I recall, after the uprising," the old woman replied. "The British put a warrant on his head, and he fled, along with all the rest of them," she finished sadly, shaking her head. "All the young men, lost, including my Sean. They're all gone now, scattered to the winds."

With more than casual interest Michael inquired, "And Gareth? Does no one hear word of him these days?"

She broke the wilted head off a delphinium. "His da wore

mourning from the day he heard of the lad's death. They're all buried in foreign soil. They could not come home even in death." Her voice broke with the sorrow of it.

So much for that lead. Returning to his present mission, Michael prompted, "And Seamus? I take it he has not gone to foreign soil yet."

She gave him a sharp look at that. "It would be better for all if he had. He and that fool uncle of his are behind the bars of Dublin gaol. They'll likely hang for their troubles."

* * *

Blanche wearily listened to her great-aunt recount the evening's activities as the carriage rolled toward home. Her head pounded, her feet hurt, and her heart had shriveled into a rough pebble. It was the first of June and she hadn't heard from Michael in weeks. The dreary part was that this was what she'd expected and what she'd wanted, and she must learn to live like this.

She carried a child and the father was the worst possible choice for husband—should she want a husband, which she most certainly did not. Only weariness made her wonder if perhaps her decision was the wrong one. Michael had vowed constancy, but that was like asking constancy from a thunderbolt.

Her aunt's chatter rattled as the carriage halted and the footman hastened to let the steps down. She had spent these last weeks denying her hopes for this life within her, but she could no longer ignore the facts. Her courses hadn't run for two months now, and her occasional bouts of morning sickness had confirmed even her maid's suspicions. It was only a matter of time before the whole household knew. She would have to leave London soon.

She'd already dropped hints to Neville that she wished to visit Paris at the end of the Season. The new steward wasn't working out so well. The pressure of dealing with daily business decisions as well as keeping up society's routine was wearing her down. How would she handle the mines and factories from Paris?

She would have to leave them with Neville. She shuddered at the thought. She hated the business of wealth. As Neville rightly pointed out, she was far more concerned with people than profits.

Allowing her aunt to take the footman's arm up the stairs, Blanche lingered a moment in the street, studying the impressive stone buildings comprising her wealthy neighborhood. Gas lamps lit every corner. Well-matched carriage horses plodded sedately down the street, drawing an elegant barouche containing laughing ladies and gentlemen. A green park with centuries-old trees provided an aura of security and timelessness. Going to Paris would mean leaving all that was safe and familiar behind.

The notion terrified her, but the child growing within her gave her courage. For the child's sake, she would do anything. Michael had that much right—a child needed love and security to grow up straight and true. She could be strong enough for two.

Turning, she saw a slight motion behind the potted tree adorning the foundation.

Blanche's heart skipped a beat She recognized the face peering around the tree, holding a finger at her lips for silence. *Fiona.*

Stopping to ostensibly straighten some portion of her apparel, Blanche whispered fiercely, "The mews. I will open the rear door."

The figure disappeared as quietly as it had appeared.

Neville greeted Blanche as she ascended the inside stairs, and she concealed her impatience.

He had extended more civility than usual these past weeks, escorting her to affairs he normally scorned, aiding her in dealing with the multifarious legal papers littering her desk, expressing solicitude instead of his usual absent-minded impatience. She hoped that did not mean he courted her again. Right now, it just meant he stood between her and Fiona.

"Did you enjoy your evening?" he asked.

Garbed in black frock coat and breeches, he had apparently just returned from some court function, though he'd rumpled his golden-brown hair at some point. Blanche detected no impatience in his concerned gaze as he waited for her answer. Blanche wished she could confide in him, but it was impossible. Even Neville couldn't marry her now. His first son had to be a Perceval, heir to his title. The child she carried was an Irish O'Toole, heir to nothing.

That rebellious thought brought a smile to Blanche's lips. "The evening was abominably boring and prodigiously dull, as usual. And yours?"

Neville looked vaguely startled, then grinned in agreement. "Much the same. Do you still wish to visit Paris? Might I come with you?"

It was Blanche's turn to be startled. Neville? In Paris? She could scarcely persuade him from London long enough to oversee Anglesey. She would never in a million years imagine Neville going to Paris. The idea alarmed her thoroughly.

"Do you run mad?" she asked. "Whyever would you go to Paris?"

The disarming grin disappeared behind his usual cool demeanor. "A momentary flight of fantasy, I suppose. I must speak with you in the morning, but you look weary. I won't delay you now."

Relieved and concerned, Blanche watched him disappear into his study. Blanche retreated to her chamber and waved away her maid with a plea for some time alone. She would make certain everyone had retired behind closed doors before sneaking down the back steps to let Fiona in. She wished Michael had taught his protégé how to let herself in and out as he did.

* * *

Leaving the door of his study cracked open, Neville waited for the sound of footsteps in the hall. He'd seen the shadow hiding in the shrubbery. This time, he meant to catch the Irish bastard before he could sneak into Blanche's chamber. And then he was going to nail the bastard's hide to the wall and flail him within an inch of his life.

Twenty-seven

Fiona heard the click of the back door latch from where she hid behind the yew, but she'd seen two of the kitchen staff sitting on the steps of the servants' entrance, and she didn't dare risk creeping past them. One by one the lights in upper windows went out, then someone hissed at the courting pair from the kitchen, and the two returned inside.

With a sigh as much of weariness as relief, Fiona crept to the garden door. She wanted her own little bed again, her cracked water pitcher with the pretty shamrocks on it, the lace curtains blowing in the fresh breeze from the open window. She wanted no more of this hiding in the stench of filthy attics and alleys, eating what she could find. She'd give a year of her life right now for a good bowl of porridge. And she hated porridge.

But Seamus and William were all she had. Should they hang, she would not only be forced to this life forever, but she would have no family or home at all.

She found the inside back stairs, and stayed on the side of the treads to avoid squeaks. Not that a duke's stairs would squeak, she supposed. He probably had a man who went about all day killing squeaks. But she feared running afoul of one he may have missed.

Lost in her sarcastic thoughts, Fiona almost missed the thin line of light from the study door. She'd learned the arrangement of all the rooms in her prior visits. She knew the duke used that room, and that he'd come home early this evening. But she must go past it to reach Blanche.

She debated going to the next floor, then coming down the stairs on the other side. But that route took her too near the servants' sleeping quarters. Besides, by now the duke was probably snoring over a glass of brandy or deeply immersed in some weighty tome. He would never notice one small footstep in all this echoing vastness.

The instant she reached the line of light, the door flew open, and a hand grabbed her.

With a shriek, Fiona fought the hold, but a hard fist clutched her as the door slammed shut. Within seconds, she had her back against the door with the Duke of Anglesey scowling at her.

"What the hell do you think you're doing sneaking about like that?" he demanded. He seemed more puzzled than angry. Fiona studied the duke's aristocratically long face, trying to read his mind, but she knew too little about this man to begin to guess. Impatiently, he swept a hank of hair from his eyes. She smiled at the gesture, and surprise momentarily replaced the scowl. For a duke, he had a lot to learn about intimidation.

"I didn't want to wake your butler," she answered pertly.

"That's a pity, because now I'll have to do it when I have him call for a constable," the duke growled, leaving his guarded stance to prowl back and forth. "I'd suggest you come up with a better excuse than that. What relation are you to O'Toole?"

That seemed an odd tack under the circumstances, but Fiona shrugged it off. "None, that I'm aware of. I thought he was a friend of yours."

"Ladies do not sneak about other people's homes in the dead of night while wearing boy's trousers," he returned irritably, ignoring her comment.

"They do if they don't want to be caught," she answered honestly enough. "I think you'd best summon Lady Blanche, if you're worried about what ladies do. I don't think gentlemen usually stand behind closed doors with them unchaperoned unless they're married. Or betrothed," she added wickedly.

"You're no more lady than O'Toole is gentleman." But he looked anxiously toward the door. "Why are you looking for Blanche?"

Honesty had its limits. She didn't know this man. He represented a powerful government she despised with all her heart and soul. Even O'Toole had gone to Lady Blanche instead of the duke, and that said much when a man preferred talking to a woman instead of another man. She didn't think the duke would appreciate her family's predicament.

"Because I'm hungry and I want to go home," she answered, hedging the truth.

They both heard the footsteps in the hall. Blanche had decided to investigate. Fiona had spent too much time on the streets to mistake the indecisive look on the duke's face. She had no more desire to be caught alone with the gentleman than he did with her. With a mocking smile, she curtsied, and slipped out the door.

Blanche looked startled when Fiona emerged in the hall in front of her. She cast a suspicious look in the direction of the lighted study, but Fiona grabbed her arm and hurried back toward her chambers.

"What took you so long?" Blanche asked as they entered the bedchamber and closed the door behind them.

Fiona curled up in a satin brocade bed chair and wrapped a lacy coverlet around her to stop her shivering. "Your servants don't go to bed early," she said evasively. "I'm sorry I kept you waiting. I'm scared to death and don't know what else to do."

"Why did you come here? Why not Dillian?" Wearing a silk wrapper that flowed around her feet and hands, Blanche paced, creating a breeze of her own that billowed the frail silk.

"The marquess has no power," Fiona answered defiantly. "He is all that is kind, but he can do nothing. I need someone with the power to open cell doors."

Blanche halted and turned to stare. "Cell doors? Is Michael in prison?"

If she weren't so frightened, Fiona would smile at this blatant proof of her suspicions.

Perhaps she ought to say yes. Would that gain the lady's aid? But she couldn't lie so cruelly. Trying to remain calm, Fiona said, "Not O'Toole. My brother and uncle. In Ireland. I just heard tonight. They'll hang or waste away and die like all the others who disappear in Dublin prison and never come out."

Blanche looked stricken. She clenched and unclenched her hands, staring at the wall as if she sought the answer there. Fiona had some inkling of how much she asked of the lady. Society had no sympathy for the Irish or their causes. They certainly had no sympathy for traitors. Blanche must somehow persuade His Grace to act on her behalf, because she had no power of her own.

With a sigh, Fiona pushed from the chair. "I'm sorry. I should never have come. I just didn't know what else to do."

Blanche gave her a curt look that held her in place. "It's said that money can buy anything. We'll try the truth of that statement."

Fiona blinked. "My lady?"

"You'll sleep here tonight. I'll call a coach in the morning. We're going to Ireland."

* * *

Michael gazed up at the cold stone walls of Dublin prison and shuddered at the grim exterior. He'd spent this last week or more finding out all that he could about the prison, its workings, and its inhabitants. He liked little of what he'd discovered. If Fiona's relations were inside, they could be too ill by now to even attempt escaping. And he knew of no other way out short of escape. The system of justice here moved slowly when it moved at all.

Had he time to reach London, twist Gavin's arm, blackmail Anglesey, and turn everyone's lives upside-down until he had their promises of help, Michael would have gladly done so rather than contemplate what he did now. But bad food, unsanitary conditions, and the cruelty of prison guards shortened the prisoners' lives, even without the threat of hanging. It didn't matter whether the inmates were guilty or innocent. They died either way.

Standing in the brilliant June sun, a brisk breeze tugging at his frock coat and hat, contemplating the most dangerous endeavor of his life, Michael confronted what he was and what he must become.

He would make this his last adventure. Somehow, he must find practical employment, a permanent home, a steady life. He couldn't replace a ducal estate. But he couldn't help Blanche raise a child while continuing to risk his damned neck.

With a sigh, Michael gave the prison one last look, noted the position of the guards, then turned back to the inn where he'd left his clothes. It had taken time to accumulate what he needed. Officers in the British army did not relinquish their pretty uniforms readily.

* * *

A week from the time Fiona had told Blanche of her family's plight, the pair stared up at the imposing gray walls of Dublin prison.

"This will take a while," Blanche murmured.

"How do you mean to go about it?" Fiona whispered anxiously.

They had discussed this. Fiona didn't know as much as Blanche would have liked, and the complications of Ireland's politics didn't help. Between Irish Protestants and English Protestants and the always rebellious Catholics, there seemed any number of webs she must traverse to find the source of power. It seemed somehow simpler to just walk up to a guard and offer him a purse of gold.

Just the thought of approaching that stern-faced man made her stomach queasy. Blanche watched the approach of a British soldier down the narrow, winding street. The cheerful red coat seemed incongruous amidst the gray walls.

Something about the soldier's athletic stride arrested her attention. Since the war with France had ended, most of the officers she knew had resigned their positions. She couldn't think of anyone who wore this particular uniform. Actually, she'd never seen such a combination of red coat, black trousers, and regimental facings. Of course, she couldn't know all the regiments. But the grace and assurance with which he carried himself was familiar.

"Let's go." Fiona tugged at Blanche's shawl. "I have no wish to run into a redcoat."

"No, wait. Perhaps we can learn something. It might help knowing an officer who can come and go freely." Blanche boldly approached the officer as if she were some other woman besides herself.

And discovered the reason soon enough. Wearing a Guardsman's black shako and a foot soldier's red coat, Michael stared back at her as if she had just walked through stone walls like a ghostly apparition.

Blanche's heart pounded. Even in that disreputable uniform, he was more handsome than sin. He looked more tanned and handsome than she could remember. Drat the wretched man.

She peered at his hat. "I know the uniform matches better that way, but it does seem a trifle peculiar. Are you a foot soldier or a guard?"

His infamous grin tumbled her stomach to her feet.

"I'm a regiment of my own, one of the Regent's exclusive Guards, of course. Do you really think an Irish sentry will care?"

She sent the stern-faced man in question a dubious look. "He looks pretty imposing to me. I've been wondering if he would respond to a few gold coins."

The grin disappeared. "In your case, he would respond for a smile, and you're not going anywhere near him." He looked over her shoulder and muttered an imprecation at sight of Fiona. "The both of you best go back where you belong. I may need your coins to bail me out if this doesn't work, but I'll not have you near the place meanwhile."

That added starch to Blanche's backbone. "No, it's just fine if you are thrown in prison and left for dead, isn't it? It doesn't matter what happens to me or your child or Gavin or anyone else should you die, does it? The fact that we'll worry ourselves ill or ruin ourselves trying to free you means nothing at all. You care for no one. I should hand you directly over to them and let you hang!"

The utter shock on Michael's face snapped Blanche's mouth shut, but it was too late.

She'd spilled those things uppermost on her mind on the street, like a common shrew. With a bitter cry, she swung around to walk away.

Michael caught her arm and held her. "Don't, or you'll give me away. I'm supposed to be on official business. I cannot take a lady inside the prison while escorting prisoners. Take Fiona and find some clean clothes for her brother and uncle. I've a ship waiting in the harbor, the Sea Lion. Meet us there. Now kiss me as if we're betrothed, and be on your way."

Wide-eyed, Blanche allowed him to plant a quick peck on her cheek before marching off. As she watched, he presented papers to the guard at the door of the prison and disappeared inside without a backward look.

When the heavy doors clanged shut behind him, she fought a wave of nausea and ran for Fiona.

Twenty-eight

Blood racing, Michael presented his papers at the prison door. Blanche's little cannonball had thrown him off course.

A child! Talking his way into Dublin prison was as easy as lying in comparison to verification that in a few short months Blanche would present him with a kicking, screaming infant of his own.

The guard glanced at the official-looking papers and waved him in. Michael entered the great stone dungeon, and the door clanged shut, leaving him in near darkness. He halted, allowing his eyes to adjust. His breath caught at the stench. His duty was to get in and out of here as quickly as humanly possible. He must return to Blanche and straighten out their insane arrangement.

The next guard looked at his papers with a little more care. "What does his Royal Highness want with a pair of ne'er-do-wells like that? It's best we just hang them and rid the world of their pestilence."

With an authoritative scowl, Michael whipped the papers from the man's hands. "His Highness needn't reveal state secrets to the likes of you."

"State secrets, huh?" The guard grunted and started down a long corridor. "The only state secrets those two know involve cheating the government of their rightful due and associating with known traitors, not to mention flapping their gobs once too many times."

"Perhaps they didn't flap their tongues to the right people," Michael answered stiffly, praying his towering shako wouldn't tilt and fall off. Its precarious slant across his forehead hid half his face, and he could barely see from under it.

"If they know anything of importance to His Highness, I'll eat my boot," the other man complained. "They're rabble, no more, no less."

"They're family of an earl," Michael warned. "I wouldn't speak too loudly if I were you."

"An earl, huh? First I heard of it." A lock rattled, a door opened, and still another guard appeared.

This one looked slightly more intelligent than the first two and studied Michael's forged papers more carefully. "Why these two?" he demanded. "They've been tried and judged guilty. They're to hang at the beginning of next week."

"I don't question royal orders," Michael said stiffly.

"You damned well ought to. They don't look right to me. Where's the rest of your people? One man can't transport two."

"Seasick," Michael said with disgust. "And you really don't think I'll have trouble with puling cowards in chains, do you?"

Scowling, the guard rattled the papers and retreated to consult with still another official.

Despite the damp chill of the windowless walls, Michael began to sweat beneath the heavy furred hat. He'd counted on few in prison positions having familiarity with the royal seal or the signatures of anyone in the Home Office. He'd duplicated them as best as he could from memory. But he couldn't duplicate a seal easily and in such short time. He'd just done what he could and hoped it would pass.

A fourth man appeared carrying the papers, gave Michael a suspicious look, noted his epaulets and captain's insignia, and nodded. "These look in order, but they make no sense. The men are sentenced to hang. We need a writ to stay the execution."

"These orders were written before the sentence," Michael responded with cool authority. "Correspondence would have crossed in travel. It makes no difference. These men possess information of import concerning a plot against the government. I must transport them immediately. The hanging will have to wait."

"A plot against the government, is it now?" The fourth man scratched his head dubiously. "And when will they be returnin' for their sentence?"

"I'm just a messenger," Michael answered with impatience. "I've already told you more than I should. It's not as if I'm taking bread out of your mouth to relieve you of these two miscreants. I have a boat waiting to meet the tide. If I must delay, I will need a good reason to give His Highness."

The two officials growled at each other, sifted through the heavy vellum once more, looked Michael over again, then finally coming to some agreement, handed the orders back to him. "Matthews will fetch them. Care to share a cup of tea while we wait?"

The anticlimax of this acceptance practically drove the breath from his lungs. The last thing he wanted right now was a cup of tea. Nodding curtly, Michael accepted the offer and followed the man back to his office.

Spinning gossip for the guards' entertainment, Michael kept careful watch on the hall outside, until the arrival of the guard trailing two scrawny, ragged figures in chains. Michael stared at the younger of the two, searching for the resemblance everyone claimed, but the matted filth of his hair, the month's growth of beard, and his emaciated form made it impossible. Both prisoners stared at him with suspicion dulled by resignation. If either recognized Michael's likeness, they showed no sign of it.

"MacDermot and O'Connor?" Michael snapped.

"And what if we're not?" the younger answered insolently.

"Then we'll send you to hang in their places," Michael said without remorse. He blamed these two scoundrels for Fiona's neglect, and he owed them no sympathy.

If they blanched at this news, he couldn't tell beneath their filth. He held out his hand for the key to their chains, pocketed it, and marched smartly down the corridor, barking at the prisoners to lift their feet and move.

Impatient to escape the gloom of these cold walls and reach the sunshine again, Michael wished he could use the key and rip off the prisoners' chains to speed the process, but he could not. His new friend the guard followed him, chattering of ballrooms and London's tailors.

At the door to the outside, the official signaled more of his men. "Escort the captain to the docks. I don't expect their friends to know of the transfer, but we can't be too careful."

Cursing vehemently to himself, Michael gave the officer a curt nod of appreciation, and prodding the prisoners with his musket, pushed into the light. O'Connor and MacDermot staggered under the assault to their eyeballs after weeks of darkness, but then their shoulders straightened and they looked around with interest.

"You'll not try escaping if you know what's good for you," Michael snapped for the benefit of his accompaniment, wishing he had some way of communicating to the two prisoners that freedom lay ahead.

The older, shorter man turned and gave Michael a thoughtful

gaze, then nodded his head in agreement before moving awkwardly toward the street, dragging his chains. The younger scowled and followed.

The distance from the prison to the docks stretched at least a thousand miles, Michael decided. It surely would take them a week to traverse it.

He sensed curious eyes watching from behind curtains and doors, saw the hatred in the stances of the men standing in alleys and outside taverns. He knew nothing about the musket he carried except that it contained no ammunition. Killing didn't meet his scruples.

The prisoners stumbled and slowed as they neared the docks. Michael figured they'd hoped for rescue and saw their last chance evaporating. He prodded them to keep them moving and kept an anxious eye on the barrels and crates on the dock.

"Reckon you can handle it from here," one of his escorts said, eying the bobbing ship ahead.

Michael gladly dismissed them as he signaled for the dinghy.

"Feeling confident," the younger of the two prisoners said sarcastically. "You won't feel so when our friends arrive."

"Your friends are on board that ship out there," Michael replied in irritation. "For your own good, you'd best get yourselves on board and as far from these shores as you can go. If you try anything else, I'll slit your throat personally. Fiona's suffered enough."

That straightened both their backs. Before either could reply, a shout rang from the far end of the dock, and Michael swung around. A gang of ruffians raced down the street in their direction.

The military escort had already disappeared. Slapping the chain key into the older man's hand, Michael flung off the annoying shako and restricting coat while calculating the resources available between him and the rapidly approaching mob.

"Fey-onah's after waitin' for ye out there," Michael lapsed into dialect for the benefit of his companions. "The dinghy will take ye to her."

A bottle flew past their heads, and Michael rolled up his shirt sleeves in grim anticipation of the brawl to come. Behind him, the prisoners hastily unfastened their chains.

"There's the redcoat! Get him, men!" someone shouted.

"Silly asses," the younger prisoner muttered, lifting his chain as a weapon. "They'll have the whole bloody army after them."

The first of the rabble came within Michael's reach. He spun the top barrel from a stack, heaving it like a bowling ball at the man's feet. With a shout, the ruffian jumped aside, lost his balance on the wet planks, and fell screaming into the filthy water. The barrel rumbled onward, sending his comrades scrambling and scattering for escape.

"Jump!" Michael told young Seamus, who wielded his chain like a mace. "I'll not be able to get ye out a second time."

"Then we'll all hang together." Seamus grinned and lashed the chain, connecting with the burly torso of one who escaped the barrel.

William cursed them both, and after ascertaining the musket had no shot, swung it like a shillelagh at a ruffian leaping at them from behind the barrels. The man screamed in pain, stumbling backward into the remaining barrels. The blow tumbled the entire stack, creating a wildly rolling barrier across the dock.

"The dinghy!" Michael shouted, pointing at the shell of a boat and its lone sailor. "Let's get out of here."

The mob had regrouped to rethink their strategy, puzzled by the realization that the prisoners they meant to free fought beside the British soldier. Some still yelled curses and wielded hastily assembled weapons as they climbed the crates, simply looking for a fight, but others hung back, watching in curiosity as the prisoners willingly scrambled down to the waiting boat rather than make the break for freedom.

"They'll have a warship after us once the soldiers hear of this," William warned mournfully as the dinghy shoved off.

Twenty-nine

Wiping salt water from his face, Michael missed Fiona's ecstatic expression as she rushed into her uncle's arms. But he heard her cry of delight. The sense of satisfaction at a job well done was tempered by the knowledge that Seamus and William must flee the country.

Instead, he shoved his hair from his eyes, and scanned the deck for Blanche. Sailors in the rigging unfurled the sails so the ship could catch the rapidly retreating tide. Perhaps she'd gone below?

"Where is Lady Blanche?" Michael asked impatiently, catching Fiona between reunion hugs. The stricken look on the girl's face shot through Michael like a musket ball.

"She's still ashore," she replied as the first sail dropped and cracked in the wind. "She said she had business to tend to. She's to return shortly."

Michael cast a hasty glance at the sails, then back to the docks. They already seemed a mile apart. He saw no sign of Blanche signaling to come aboard. The riot would have delayed her.

"We can't risk waiting. The Navy will be after us shortly. Take your family to Effingham. Blanche and I will follow later." Michael signaled for the dinghy. He would row himself back.

Nervously glancing from Fiona to his uncle for reassurance, Seamus tugged on Michael's shirt sleeve. "Do you speak of Lady Blanche Perceval, sir?"

Already bouncing on his toes with eagerness to be off, Michael glanced at him impatiently. "I do. The one your cronies tried to blow up."

The lad held his ground. "Eamon had his orders. They came from high up. They're to strike the lady's mines next. The conditions are deplorable, I understand. I would not help her ilk, but for Fiona's sake, I offer warning."

Summoning one of Gavin's more vivid curses, Michael scrambled down the ladder to the dinghy. Right now, the whole bloody lot of MacDermots and O'Connors could go up in flame and he wouldn't look back.

The woman had the common sense of a maggot sometimes. Didn't she realize she looked out for two now?

Bubbling with rage and anxiety, Michael scarcely noticed the distance between boat and dock. His muscles ached from pulling against the tide, but it was an ache that brought him closer to Blanche.

Concluding chaining her to stone walls in some abandoned castle in Scotland couldn't even guarantee her safety, Michael swore again as he tied the dinghy to the dock. Glancing over his shoulder, he saw the ship and the MacDermots sail toward the horizon, taking with them any chance of knowing his origins.

* * *

"It will be my pleasure to help you, my lady, but you'll understand that a lot of the old titles have died out. This place had more chieftains and men who claimed spurious titles than there were peasants working the fields. Through the years, the Crown has organized the system a little more efficiently."

Blanche smiled sweetly at the government official behind the desk, held out her hand for his salute, and answered without a trace of the acid she felt. "I'm certain the Crown has been most efficient, but we cannot neglect true aristocracy, can we? I simply wish to see that my friends have not been unfairly treated." The stack of pound notes she had left behind to aid the official in his search should ensure that.

Wishing she could do more, and knowing her time was limited, Blanche hurried out of the government office toward the dock. Her path took her past the hotel where she had registered before finding Michael. To her surprise, the street seemed inexplicably cluttered with soldiers. She slowed her pace, gauging the situation. Several glanced in her direction as she approached, and Blanche decided she had best remove herself from view.

Before she could act, a man leaning against the wall of a nearby alley stepped forward, grabbed her arm, and dragged her into the shadows.

She didn't have time to scream before he warned, "Don't! We're getting out of here." *Michael.* Blanche sighed in relief and gladly followed his path as he hurried down the alley.

"Drat," Michael muttered when he glanced into the street

beyond the alley's end. Blanche couldn't see over his shoulder, but she surmised more soldiers strolled about.

Perhaps the prison escapade hadn't worked as well as he'd hoped. Dread roiling inside her, Blanche watched as he studied their surroundings and decided upon a door in the far wall.

He pried open the door and shoved her inside, bolted the latch, and they stood in utter darkness.

"I had every intention of wringing your neck," he murmured angrily, but his hands when they slid into her hair were gentle.

"Michael, what is happening?" she asked before his mouth descended over hers and the question disappeared into his kiss.

Michael gratefully closed his fingers in the silkiness of Blanche's hair while he drank deeply of her lips. It had been weeks .... He needed this physical reassurance that nothing had changed between them.

Recovering from the first surprise of passion, she tried shoving him away, but her efforts were puny.

"We're safe," he murmured, busying himself with the buttons of her bodice. "It's not us they're after. Yet."

He ignored her breathless questions as he single-mindedly went about his task. He needed to touch. He could feel the full swell of her breasts brushing against him, but he needed more.

The bodice opened and he slid his hands beneath the cloth. In seconds, he'd untied the ribbons of her chemise, and filled his palms with the heavy weight of her breasts. He gave a sigh of deep pleasure as he measured their new fullness.

Blanche stilled beneath his caress, but when he circled her nipples with his thumbs, she breathed a protesting, "Michael!"

"Already, you grow rounder with my child," he mused aloud, reveling in the silk of her skin against his palms. An unexpected thought leapt to mind, and he grinned. "Had I wondered how a large bosomed woman felt, my curiosity would be satisfied."

Blanche smacked at his shoulders, but he was too lost to the sensation of touch to notice. Her nipples puckered beneath his tug, and her breath came in shorter pants as he slid his palms back and forth.

"Michael, have you lost your mind? What are you doing?"

Keeping his hands filled, he kissed her ear and drank in the sweet scent of her hair.

"It's been over a month, my love. What do you think I'm doing? Or have you forgotten so quickly?" he asked teasingly. Murder had fled his mind for the moment.

"You cannot! Not here. Why are those soldiers out there? What if someone comes?"

He halted her questions with a kiss. He truly didn't care about the answers. He had Blanche in his arms again, and nothing else mattered. Again, she tried pushing away, but his tongue persuaded her elsewise. Joy swept through him as she surrendered, and her lips responded eagerly. He had waited for this woman all his life. He deserved this reward.

Having doffed his stolen coat at the docks, he wore only shirt and breeches to dilute his pleasure. Blanche stroked his chest, finding the tie of his linen and pulling it, then sliding her fingers into the opening. Just knowing she wanted to touch him drove him to madness.

Given his life, he could die within the hour. Before he left this mortal coil, he wanted to feel the swelling of his child. With haste, he tugged at Blanche's bodice, finding the tapes that released the front of her skirt. She gasped as the cool air hit her, but he wouldn't let her stay cold long. He pulled the short chemise upward, and at last, his hand found the smooth skin between her hip bones.

"The hollow is gone," he murmured with pleasure, testing the firmness of the very slight swelling there. "You are rounding already."

"Michael!" Blanche buried her face against his shoulder in embarrassment, trying to escape his prying hands, but he wouldn't allow her to demean herself with that emotion.

"We've created a child together," he said proudly, still finding it hard to believe. "It's a miracle. Don't hide your head in shame. Let me enjoy the miracle with you."

She shuddered, and Michael guessed she'd spent these last months worrying about nothing and everything. He would take that burden from her. He returned his mouth to hers and awakened her desires again until she'd wrapped her arms around his neck and pressed her belly up against him.

The very proper lady had needs as strong as his, thank all the gods and fates.

"Tell me you're mine, Blanche. Tell me you'll spend the rest of your nights in my bed from this day forward."

Blanche rubbed against him, and Michael almost lost control there and then. But now that the question had come out, he wanted an answer.

Lifting her buttocks in his hands until their hips touched, he bent and licked her nipple, knowing its arousal, feeling the changes caused by the child, and wanting — needing — acknowledgment of his place in her life. "You can't deny me, Blanche. You carry the result of our joining. I'll not let you flee to the Continent and leave me behind. Tell me now, and make us both happy."

"Michael, I can't," she pleaded. "Let's not talk of this. Please, Michael."

He might have foolishly argued, but a pounding on the latched door doused his ardor as effectively as her words. Cursing, Michael let her slide from his hands while he hastily pulled up her bodice and began fastening the buttons.

She seemed dazed, but connected enough to begin fastening her own clothing so he might rearrange his. Michael pulled Blanche in the direction of the shop and away from the pounding at the alley door. Without the shako for disguise, his resemblance to Seamus would surely set someone off.

Thirty

Blanche thought she ought to feel shame as they hurried toward the dock a few hours later. She'd behaved like a wanton, then rejected the father of her child, a man who had risked his life to return for her. She was a terrible person.

She didn't dare look at Michael. He'd donned a shabby wool jacket that hung on him like a scarecrow's leavings. They'd found the garments in the warehouse office and left coins to replace them. No one had even noticed them as they'd slipped into the street like all the other curiosity seekers.

Michael wants me in his bed every night. But even he hadn't been bold enough to suggest marriage. She owned more houses than she could count, and Michael had never bothered to create a single room for himself anywhere. So it would be *her* bed, and it wouldn't be every night. And then he would disappear one day and she wouldn't even know he was alive.

She deserved better than that. She hoped. They had nothing in common but what they shared in bed. And the child. "I thought you said the ship sailed," she said irritably as their direction became clear.

"We'll book passage on another. We're going to Cornwall instead of London, anyway. That is where your mines are, aren't they?" Apparently unperturbed by her irritation, Michael studied their surroundings.

Cornwall? Mines? The leap from her thoughts to his words took a moment. "Yes, I believe that's where they are," she said in puzzlement. "Barnaby always complained about them. He called the miners shiftless, demanding, and obstinate. He said I should sell the mines. But the offers he received didn't seem to match the profits, and I never did anything about them."

"I don't suppose you ever questioned how the mines made such high profits?" Michael asked as they stopped at the office of a shipping company.

"I thought mines were supposed to make high profits." Blanche jerked her hand from his.

Michael gave her a withering look. "Maybe you *should* let Neville handle your business affairs." He grabbed her elbow and steered her into the shipping office. "Keep quiet and let me do the talking."

He needn't sound so condescending. But she'd just rejected him. She couldn't expect him to praise her ignorance.

A few minutes later they emerged with passage booked on a ship that sailed for Plymouth in the morning. Blanche removed her arm from Michael's grasp. "My trunks sailed with Fiona," she reminded him. "I have nothing to wear."

"Fine. I've an army of redcoats in hot pursuit, no doubt an entire band of wild-eyed radicals who want their hands on my neck, a ship with possibly my last remaining relatives sailing into the sunset, and I haven't eaten since dawn. But I'll find you suitable clothes. What would you like? A proper nightdress for the bed we'll share this evening? A ball gown so you might attend some fancy function with one of the officers you flirted with today? A traveling gown for the morrow? Do tell me your fancy."

She'd never seen him this angry. Usually, he vanished when they disagreed. Her eyes widened... He wasn't abandoning her.

"You become overly sarcastic when you can't run away," she said scornfully. "I merely remarked upon the complication."

"I never said I was perfect." Giving her totally unsuitable muslin gown a glare, Michael steered her back toward the city. "You'll freeze in that thing. Why can't you wear sensible woolens?"

"It's the middle of June," she pointed out reasonably. "I've been quite comfortable all day. But the sea air is brisk in the evenings."

He didn't acknowledge her sensible explanation. He had decided to be angry with her and nothing she said would change it. Unless, of course, she said she would sleep with him every night. Then he'd come around, no doubt. Well, he'd wait until the devil crocheted doilies before she'd do that. His behavior now merely confirmed her resolve not to tie herself to irrational men.

When Michael dragged her into a tavern, Blanche decided to engrave that resolution in gold and wear it about her neck instead of his damned ring. She felt as if every man in the place stared at her. And every woman. Startled to realize women frequented these places, Blanche stared back. They didn't look like loose women. Most of them were dowdy and wrapped to their ears in shawls and wool. Her own fashionable high-waisted muslin was definitely out of place.

Michael ordered ale and dinner. Blanche stared at him. Michael didn't drink, as she had every reason to know. He ignored her stare. Seemingly oblivious of his surroundings, he sprawled in an old wooden booth with so many knife carvings in it, Blanche thought it remarkable the thing didn't fall into sawdust. Cautiously, she took the bench across from him, knowing his mind had leapt to another plane, heeding neither her nor anyone else. Michael never ignored her at any other time.

Blanche shoved that thought and its accompanying warmth away. Her placid nature made it easy for people to ignore her. Even when he was furious, Michael gave her his full attention every minute they were together, except at moments like this.

So she kept silent and let him concentrate while she examined the tavern and its inhabitants. The room stank of smoke, stale ale, sweat, and cheap perfume. Over and beyond that, she could smell frying fat. That stench alone should make her stomach queasy, but for some reason, the child within her didn't object. Gratefully, she patted her belly.

When their food arrived, Michael absently requested a pitcher of water and tackled the meal as if starved. While she sipped at the tea he ordered for her, Blanche watched as he drank from the pitcher and not the tankard of ale.

He managed his next act so smoothly, she didn't catch on until she heard a gasp from the bar across the aisle. Blanche glanced up. Michael had balanced his fork on the tip of his knife, then spun his mysteriously empty tankard on another finger as he apparently contemplated adding it to the tottering tower of utensils.

"Michael!" Blanche protested, having no desire to become the focus of attention.

He transferred his utensils to the rim of the spinning tankard and reached for her teacup. She snatched it back. Someone threw him a pewter plate. Grinning, Michael spun it on his finger as he contemplated the new configuration.

"Let's have a tune," he suggested. "This goes much easier with music."

A man in the corner who already played idly at bits and pieces of song on a hand organ gladly obliged with a few rollicking notes.

Someone with a fine tenor picked up the words. Within minutes, the entire tavern resounded with music. Plates and utensils, coins and assorted watches, fobs, and whatever anyone carried in their pockets appeared on the table. The spinning tower became a growing circle of objects juggled from hand to hand, occasionally disappearing and reappearing in odd places like Blanche's pockets or the audience's hats. The spinning circle never halted, just changed contents.

After a time, Blanche noticed the coins had a tendency to disappear and not reappear. No one protested. She supposed they considered it the price of entertainment. At one point, Michael spun the tower while drinking from the pitcher of water. After he emptied the pitcher, he joined in the song, and Blanche listened in amazement to his fine tenor. She didn't think she'd ever heard him sing before. She clapped her hands in time, and others stomped their feet.

When Michael stood up and headed for the bar, Blanche held her breath in fear the circle of plates and utensils would descend upon their heads. Instead, they distributed themselves up and down the bar in direct proportion to the number of empty tankards magically stacking themselves into an enormous tower. The crowd roared with approval, and the hat Michael had swiped from somewhere jingled with coins.

He was enjoying himself thoroughly, blast the man, Blanche thought irritably as the crowd surged between them. He knew precisely when to change his act, when the crowd's attention flagged, how to keep them adding coins to his collection. And he did it with such flair no one could complain—not even the tavern owner, who watched his tankards carefully but did nothing to halt the show. Michael's act had packed the tavern seats and filled the room, and everyone was buying another round.

A break in the milling crowd gave Blanche another glimpse of Michael. While he juggled heaven only knew how many objects from hand to hand, his gaze followed her, burning with a passion she could feel within herself.

As if reading her thoughts, Michael deposited his tankards and plates in a confusing array all across the room, balancing platters on the heads of old men and adorning the heavy shawls of young women with forks. Everyone roared as they sought the misplaced dinnerware under chairs and tables, and even the tavern keeper seemed distracted by the confusion.

While everyone watched elsewhere, Michael caught Blanche's arm, tugged her from the booth, and escaped with her into the darkness of the evening. Now she had some inkling of how he appeared and disappeared like magic.

"Where are we going?" she demanded as he hurried her down one street after another.

"To find you suitable clothing," he answered without inflection. "I'll not have you catching cold in that flimsy thing. Or giving our child a cold."

"The shops are closed at this hour," she protested.

"All the better." He grinned and steered her down a side street beside a small series of shops, found a door in a back alley, and after using his knife on the latch, he let them inside.

"Michael, this is thievery! We cannot just walk in and take what we like. Besides, it takes a modiste days to sew my attire."

"We don't have days. And we'll pay for what we take. Come here, let me see what I can find for you."

To Blanche's surprise and horror, the shop was littered with old clothes and shoes. Michael propped a high crowned beaver hat on his head and shook out a lovely cashmere shawl to drape over Blanche. Rummaging through the racks, he found a pea green wool frock coat for himself, and a serviceable blue kerseymere gown for her. Humming the tune he'd started earlier in the tavern, he retrieved several other articles, and took a final look around for more. Blanche noticed he hadn't included any night clothes in his shopping list.

"These clothes are worn," she whispered angrily. "What if they have lice or worse?"

"You'd know it by now if they did, and we can always wash them if you prefer," he answered as he poked among the shoes and hats. Finding a carved walking stick and a dilapidated carpet bag for carrying their new possessions, he emerged triumphant from the corner and counted his coins out upon the counter.

"I can pay for them," Blanche protested. "I didn't leave my purse on the ship."

The look he gave her was unfathomable in the gloom of the unlighted shop. "We're living in my world now. I'll pay our way. I don't need your coins."

She wanted to hit him over the head with his walking stick at this perversely male attitude. At the same time, pride surged through her. Michael didn't run up debts to keep himself in starched cravats. Of course, he only did this to prove he didn't need her.

Blanche gloomily accepted that knowledge as he led her from the shop. Michael had lived nearly thirty years without her or her wealth. He didn't need her—except in bed.

She glanced at Michael's wide shoulders, and felt a catch in her midsection. She didn't like acknowledging that Michael wasn't her court jester but a man with all the faults and foibles of men. He wanted her to behave as a proper wife. And now that she had her independence, she no longer had any desire for obedience.

He led her into a nondescript inn near the docks, where they would soon share the same bed. His look of both self-assurance and possessiveness as he laid a coin upon the desk warned her of his expectations.

In their tiny bedchamber, Blanche nervously inspected the small bed while Michael fastened the door and threw their new luggage beneath a chair. She waited for him to come up behind her. Instead, she heard the chair squeak. She turned to see him removing his boots.

That he didn't touch her immediately increased her tension. "The bed looks clean," she murmured, not knowing what else to say.

He nodded curtly. "I've stayed here these last nights. He keeps a clean inn."

She didn't understand his curtness or why he didn't kiss her now. Everything worked out so much easier when he kissed her. The single candle illuminated little except Michael unlacing his shirt. She wanted to unlace it for him. Her hands itched to touch his warmth again, to feel the hard planes of his chest beneath her fingers. Tentatively, she unfastened the buttons of her bodice.

He folded up the heavy frock coat he'd just acquired and threw it on the floor in front of the door. "There's water in the basin. I'll blow out the candle so you'll have some privacy."

Without the candle's light, Blanche stared in confusion as Michael settled down in front of the door. She finished unfastening the gown and washed quietly, hating herself, hating him for doing this to her. Must she beg?

Wearing just her chemise, she climbed between the cold sheets and listened to Michael's breathing. She didn't think he slept. She didn't think either of them would sleep.

"Why?" she finally inquired, finding the uncertainty intolerable.

He didn't pretend to misunderstand. "I want a wife, not a mistress. There's no use in my learning the joy of your charms only to have them taken away once we reach London. So I'll just practice abstaining now, thank you."

She wanted to kill him. She flung her pillow in the direction of his voice. "Mistress! Is that all I am? You have your nerve Michael Lawrence!"

"I'm not a Lawrence. I'm not anything. I can't give you a name or title or wealth. All I can offer is my children and my future. That's not enough. I've always known it, but I foolishly hoped we could work it out. We can't. So let's not pretend any longer."

Blanche clung to the covers and stared at the place where he lay. "What are you saying?"

He answered slowly. "I'm saying that I surrender. I won't fight you. I want to be a part of my child's life, but I'll stay out of yours. I'm sure we can arrange something."

"That's not what I want," she whispered.

"I consider us married, Blanche," he answered wearily. "It's not what I want, either. But unless you're willing to walk into Anglesey and declare me your husband, I don't see much other choice for us. Go to sleep. We'll talk of this in the morning."

Thirty-one

Michael disappeared at dawn, leaving Blanche to wash and dress in privacy. She no longer feared desertion. She knew he would return and take her to the docks. She just didn't know if she appreciated the knowledge. He considered them married — because of the child?

The queasiness had returned, and Blanche refused the breakfast Michael brought. He didn't argue but merely wrapped the rolls in clean linen and tucked them in his capacious pockets for later. Blanche wished he would quarrel with her again. She wanted an excuse to scream and stamp her feet and fling things. Instead, she coolly accepted the shawl he placed around her shoulders and took his arm so they might depart.

She could feel the tension in him. It gave her some satisfaction knowing he suffered as much as she did. As they boarded the ship, the queasiness intensified, and she insisted on finding a place on deck in the sunshine. If she must heave up the meager contents of her stomach, she would do it in the fresh salt air. Michael wrapped a blanket around her legs and sat cross-legged on the deck nearby, whittling at a piece of wood.

"What will we do, Michael?" she asked as the sails unfurled and the wind caught them. She had hoped to see more of the emerald shores of Ireland, but it seemed she wasn't destined for more than a glimpse of any other land but her own.

"We've not much choice in the matter," he answered. "We're married legally enough. We can have the vows said in church so Neville will acknowledge them. Or you can go on as you planned, have the child on the Continent and declare yourself widow. Either way, you'll not be rid of me. I have as much right to that child as you do."

"*Married?*" Blanche hadn't heard a word beyond that. She stared at him in disbelief. "*Legally?* What do you mean, *married?* I don't remember any such service. Have you quite lost your mind?" She'd wanted an opportunity to scream, but she was too stunned to react.

Michael never lied to her.

Shadows hid his eyes as he looked up from his whittling. "Married. In Scotland, it is only necessary to declare yourself man and wife before witnesses and the deed is done. We did that and more. We even have a minister who attests to our vows. England must abide by Scottish law. And there's obviously no question of annulment."

The nausea churned stronger as all the implications roiled in her mind. *Married*. She was married. To Michael. She had a vague understanding of Gretna Green elopements. But....

This just wasn't possible. She couldn't have a husband. He could go to Neville and her solicitors and demand a settlement. Even though her grandfather's trust left the control of his estate in her hands, the solicitors would consult with him rather than her. She would become a figurehead, a useless piece of flotsam adorning his house. *Her* house. He would live in her house, on her money. All because of a few words said in the heat of the moment.

"That can't be true," she protested weakly. "It can't be legal. I never agreed to such a thing. I don't want a husband."

"You've made that plain enough," he agreed. "But you're the one who came to my bed, not the other way around. I did what I thought necessary for any child we created. He has a name and a father, just as I said he must. Whether you acknowledge me or not is your decision. I'll not interfere, except where the child is concerned. And you agreed to that."

Pressing her fingers into her stomach, Blanche leaned against the cabin's outside wall and stared over the choppy waters. Married. Clenching her teeth, she reined in her temper so she didn't send Michael running.

"Fine. I never intended to marry anyway. I'll open the house in Dorset. We can go there in summers and at Christmas. I don't know how else I can give you access to the child. Neville would find it a trifle suspicious should you make free with the London house."

"I'm sure Dorset would be better for a child than London," he answered agreeably. "But don't dictate what I'll do or where I'll be, not any more than I'll tell you the same."

Ladies didn't scream, she reminded herself. Ladies didn't pick up oars and bang gentlemen over the head. Ladies merely picked themselves up and stood at the rail and retched up their insides.

* * *

The wind whipped their clothes and hair as the ship sailed into Plymouth harbor. Michael tugged the shawl more securely around Blanche and wrapped his arm around her shoulders for warmth. His wife stood as stiff as a board his arms, and he didn't feel much better. She'd scarcely spoken since his declaration. He wasn't certain he could blame her. But he'd done what needed doing, and he would hold no regrets.

As they sailed, he'd asked what she knew about the mines Eamon had warned him about. She knew pitifully little. Her grandfather must have been demented to dump such a burden on her frail shoulders. Blanche's negligent father hadn't raised her to know anything about business. She could run an enormous household and estate, but not factories and mines. She could learn, given time and proper teachers, but she had neither.

Michael didn't believe she had the inclination, either. She just stubbornly refused to admit it.

"I suggest we enter Bodmin incognito." At her silence, Michael considered doing as he pleased without her consent. But he owed Blanche an explanation. Grimly, he admitted he must learn the adjustments of married life even if she refused. "We will have a better chance of hearing the truth if we're strangers, and you'll be safe from a personal attack by the radicals."

She nodded cautiously. That was a good sign.

They hired an open carriage and driver and set out toward Bodmin while the weather held. Michael tried maintaining his distance, but the narrow carriage seat didn't allow much room, and the jiggling springs kept throwing them together. He hated thinking what the bouncy ride did to her queasy stomach.

He finally gave up, propped his feet against the driver's chair, and rested his arm on the cushion behind Blanche. When the ruts threw her into him, he tugged her against his shoulder. She settled there without complaint. It gave him an oddly protective feeling, as if he truly acted as husband, and he spent the rest of their journey imagining how it might be if he had the right to do this all the time. With Blanche, he thought he might enjoy it.

They arrived in Bodmin late that evening with clouds building on the horizon and distant lightning crackling across the sky. The driver leapt down at an inn on the outskirts of town and returned a few minutes later with news that a room could be had. Michael thanked the man, gave him some of his few coins, and let him lead the horse into the stable where the driver would sleep. He turned and held his arm out for Blanche.

"It's your choice. We can sign in under my name, or I will sleep in the public room. Either way, I suggest you take a name other than your own."

"I would feel better if you slept with me," she murmured wearily, leaning on his arm more heavily than usual.

Without a word, he signed them in under his name and led her upstairs. He ordered warm water for bathing and retreated to the tavern below for the latest gossip. He could learn more in places like this than in any solicitor's or mine foreman's office. By the time he returned upstairs, he had some understanding of the mine problem.

Blanche was sound asleep.

He wanted to snuggle down in that soft bed beside her, feel her warmth in his arms, measure the growth of his child, but he would only destroy what remained of his sanity by doing so.

He was well accustomed to hard floors. He supposed, if he applied his mind to it, he could make his fortune and buy soft beds. He'd always known himself capable of it. He'd just never had an incentive before.

Blanche woke to the sound of soft snores from the floor. She didn't think she'd ever heard Michael snore. She smiled, feeling a little less alone when she could hear him.

Bending over the side, she watched him sleep. Magician, juggler, skilled craftsman, and brilliant chameleon that he was, he looked like any ordinary man while asleep. Thick auburn hair tousled and falling over his beard-stubbled face, he slept like one exhausted. Life had honed the harsh angles of his face with hardship. Only when awake, with his mobile lips smiling and his eyes dancing did he lose that grim expression.

He woke then, instantly alert. His gaze shot to the bed.

Blanche gave him a pleased grin. She did like being the center of his attention.

He blinked and regarded her warily. "How do you feel this morning?"

"Quite well, actually. And starved."

He relaxed and propped his head up with his elbow. "The child causes you no distress?"

She pulled her hair over her shoulder and sat up, holding the sheet high. "It doesn't normally. Now that I think on it, the only time the sickness comes upon me is when I'm upset over something. I think, perhaps, your child may object to argument as much as you do."

Michael grinned and eyed her lap, though she covered it with linen. "Perhaps you should have been a little more particular in your choice of a father for the child. Just think what other bad traits the poor thing might have. You will find him wandering from his crib at six months, disappearing from the nursery at a year. And heaven forbid, he or she might have my hair. Can you see Neville's face when you come home with a red-headed infant? You had best not choose a dark-haired Italian as a counterfeit father."

The possibility that their child might resemble Michael did not displease her at all. But if it should inherit Michael's character, it would drive her mad. She wanted a docile, loving child like herself. She scowled at him. "By the time the child is grown, red hair might be quite fashionable, but if it insists on running away from home by age six, you can take care of him."

Mischief played in Michael's expression as he rose and sought the washbowl. "Fine, and if it turns out to be a stubborn little termagant, I'll hand her over to you."

"I am not stubborn. Everyone knows I'm pleasant and even-tempered." Blanche wrapped the sheet around her and tucked it in over her breasts, aware he watched her in the mirror. She gulped when he produced shaving gear and began to soap his face. He'd always done that in privacy before.

"You are stubborn and intractable and want your own way, and you sweet talk anyone until you get it. I'm not one of your blind-with-greed suitors, my lady. I know your foibles as well as anyone. But I'll willingly put up with them in return for some very admirable traits you also possess." He raised a leering eyebrow at the mirror.

She flung a pillow at his bare back, but he deflected it with his shoulder and let it fall to the floor. "I also have one other trait of which you're apparently not aware," she replied with ominous softness.

He gave her a quizzical look over his shoulder.

Blanche smiled maliciously. "A need to relieve myself every few hours while carrying your child. Out." She pointed at the door.

Eyebrows raised in surprise and chagrin, he beat a hasty retreat.

* * *

Michael watched Blanche pick at her food over the breakfast table while he tried to explain Eamon's warning about the Bodmin miners and the state of her affairs. He wasn't at all certain she was listening, but at least she hadn't bashed his brains out yet. If she hadn't done so for telling her they were married, she really was better tempered than most.

"From what I can ascertain, your mine had an accident last week that killed three men," he told her. "There have been similar incidents lately, with eleven lives lost all told. The men are claiming the owner demands every inch of the seam mined, which leaves weak or no supports at all. They believe the owner will close the mine as soon as every possible cent is removed, while risking all their lives in the process. And once the mine is closed, they will have lost their livelihoods. Some have already moved on, but those with families cannot."

Blanche raised her eyebrows, appalled. "I am not so desperate for funds that I need cost men their lives for every farthing. I cannot understand Barnaby acting under such an impression. And I have just got rid of the latest steward for making similar suggestions." She looked at him with open curiosity. "How is the mine manager paid? On the basis of profits?"

She caught on quickly. Michael produced a folded sheet of vellum from his pocket. "Since I don't have access to your records, I can't say for certain, but I would assume so. And I'm not at all certain that Barnaby didn't have some such agreement with your grandfather also. It's only reasonable to expect men to make more money when they share in the profit. Unfortunately, some men are more greedy than others, and that is likely the case here. I want to go to the mine office as Barnaby's replacement. I've drawn up a letter for your signature, appointing me as your agent. If the manager thinks I'm another Barnaby, he should tell me all I need to know."

Blanche's eyes widened. Under other circumstances, Michael would have simply forged her name and gone on. But they had to develop some means of working together, and she must trust him before they could.

"And what will you do if what you suspect is true?" she asked.

"I will order the mine closed until you can hire inspectors. If the mine actually is played out, we must locate other mines in the area you could invest in."

He hadn't realized he'd been tense until she nodded in agreement, and he relaxed.

"You signed us in as husband and wife last night," she said. "Would a man like Barnaby travel with his wife?"

Michael thought he saw the direction of her thoughts, and he considered his answer. "He could travel with his wife or mistress, I suppose. My main concern is that they not know who you actually are. Somehow, they know you and not the duke as owner, and I think you would be in physical danger should anyone recognize you. I would feel immensely better if you stayed in the room while I was gone."

"I understand your concern, but how can I learn these things myself if I must always hide behind men? I would talk to these people, too, and learn what kind of men they are."

"A man like Barnaby would not bring his wife to a mine. No man would. If I can, I will bring the manager back here for tea, and you can meet him then. You might, however, visit the village. You can learn much from talking with other women."

"I don't like it," she said, "but I understand. When do you think I can start doing this for myself?"

When the moon turned indigo and the sea dried up, Michael thought grimly. He would never let her suffer any heavy burden if he could prevent it. Blanche might be capable of making the right financial decisions, but the hard edge she'd developed lately that was required to enforce them was taking a toll.

"I think your first objective is to learn what you own and how it operates. That's an enormous task in itself. We'll find you a good teacher when we reach London."

She nodded as if accepting it for now.

Michael slid the agreement across to Blanche. "I'll find pen and ink."

Studying the paper, Blanche didn't look up. "Bring more paper. I mean to add a thing or two."

Michael didn't like the sound of that, but he went to fetch the required materials. This marriage of theirs had as much potential for explosion as the gunpowder O'Connor used so well.

Thirty-two

Michael strode into the mining office, and recognized Barnaby at once. Well, this should make for an interesting spectacle. The other man scarcely glanced up from the books he pored over, and Michael turned his attention to the second occupant of the office.

"Elmore Weatherton?" Michael inquired with deceptive composure, knowing full well the fat-bellied pompous ass behind the desk stood responsible for the deaths of eleven men.

The man rubbed at his sweating, balding head and glared at Michael. "Who's asking?"

Not for the first time, Michael wished he towered over six feet tall and wielded the arrogance of a marquess like Gavin. Instead, he smiled and pulled out the gold watch he'd acquired at a pawn shop. Along with the neatly tailored navy frock coat he'd found back in Ireland and his high-crowned hat, he knew he presented an image of wealth.

"I have precisely one-half hour for you, Mr. Weatherton. This will go much more efficiently if you cooperate." He produced the sealed vellum from his coat pocket, and laid it on the desk. "I'm Michael Lawrence, Lady Blanche's new representative in these parts. I've come for the company books."

Barnaby's head jerked up. To the man's hostile glare Michael gave a cool nod. "Mr. Barnaby. I wasn't aware you'd taken employment here."

Weatherton mopped his brow with his handkerchief after reading the letter. Blustering, he turned on Blanche's former steward. "You didn't tell me you were no longer in the lady's employ. You've no business with those books now. I'll talk with the gentleman in private."

Michael didn't want the thief near Blanche. "I have no objection to Mr. Barnaby staying," Michael said with a casual air. "I'm certain he's familiar with all the aspects of this operation. Would either of you care to acquaint me with the reason we're mining a played out seam?"

Barnaby rumbled to his feet like an overgrown bear, grabbed the paper off Weatherton's desk and scanned it with suspicion. "I'd demand to see the lady herself before I'd believe this drivel." He flung the paper back to the desk. "This man is a known impostor. He runs tame in the lady's household, but the duke never gave him any authority."

The insulting tone he used raised Michael's hackles. "I would be careful what you say about the lady, Mr. Barnaby," he said with deceptive softness. "These mines are her concern, not the duke's, and that paper is signed personally by her. If I do not receive immediate cooperation here, I have the authority to shut down this mine. Now, shall we talk or argue?"

Barnaby uttered a curse, flung the book he held on the desk, and stalked out of the office. Michael swung on his heel and hurried after.

* * *

Blanche sat in the sunshine on a bench outside a bake shop, sampling a delicious apple dumpling drenched in the sweetest cream she'd ever tasted. Pampered like this, she could almost accept Michael's assumption of her duties.

A tall, lean young man stopped and look at her before entering the darkened doorway of a tavern. Feeling shabby in her old clothes, she took a certain amount of gratification that young men might still look at her. Uncertain of the legalities of Scots law, she had a hard time thinking of herself as a married woman. Or Michael as a married man. Could one marry will o'wisps?

She had no idea how one went about talking to strangers. She'd known the villagers and farmers around Anglesey all her life, so that wasn't the same. She didn't know this town or what questions to ask. Michael was right. She didn't know enough.

The lean young man reappeared in the tavern doorway with a scruffy-looking older man. They stared in her direction with expressions that were rude rather than flirtatious. Blanche shook out her skirt and returned inside the bake shop.

The two men had disappeared by the time she emerged again. In relief, she took the direction the bake shop owner had given her for the dry goods store. She could pick up some needles and thread and make her gown a little less dull.

Blanche purchased the required materials and entered into a conversation with the wives of several of the local shopkeepers over the cost of thread, then left the dry goods store in a much better humor. How absolutely marvelous to have the freedom to go where she wished and speak to whom she wished. Perhaps marriage might have its benefits after all.

"Lady Blanche!"

Startled, she glanced up at the speaker before she remembered she was supposed to be Mrs. Lawrence. To her astonishment, her former steward hurried toward her. "Mr. Barnaby, what brings you here?"

"I must talk with you. May we go where we can speak privately?" He grabbed her arm and tried to lead her down the street.

"Mr. Barnaby, I did not give you permission to lay a hand on me." She smacked his meaty hand with her reticule, forcing him to a halt.

Over his shoulder, she saw Michael hurrying down the street. She refused the role of helpless female. The time had arrived to assert herself.

Taking a deep breath and summoning what little courage she possessed, Blanche skirted around Barnaby and smiled a welcome. "Michael! Look who's here. Perhaps Mr. Barnaby can answer some of your questions."

With casual possessiveness, she took her husband's arm.

"Michael, is it now?" Barnaby sneered. "I'm sure the duke won't be pleased to hear you're so familiar with the man."

Blithely, Blanche flapped her lashes at him. "Did you expect me to call him Mr. Lawrence like some cit? How very bourgeois of you. But I assure you Neville doesn't find my familiarity with my husband in the least unfashionable."

The muscles of Michael's arm tightened beneath her fingers. Turning to smile at him, she glimpsed the tall, lean man again, but she could only deal with one situation at a time. "Dear, this is Mr. Barnaby who once handled this nasty mine situation for me."

Michael nodded stiffly. "Barnaby. I think it best if we talk without my wife's presence. I have a few words for you."

Blanche didn't like the sound of that at all. "I'm not an

incompetent simpleton, sir. I have dealt with Mr. Barnaby these past years and more. We will all sit down and discuss the situation together. Will Mr. Weatherton join us?"

Michael glowered. Barnaby scowled.

Blanche stood firm. She might know utterly nothing about mines or men like Barnaby, but she wouldn't learn if he kept shoving her behind closed doors. She had Michael bested, and he knew it

Acknowledging defeat, Michael caught her elbow. "We'll return to the inn. Barnaby, fetch Weatherton and the books. We have matters to discuss."

Blanche released a sigh of relief when Michael hurried her toward the inn. She wasn't foolish enough to believe that Barnaby would appear with any books or that she would know what to do with them if he did. But she was fairly certain she had averted a fight.

"Are you out of your mind?" Michael grumbled as he tugged her through the inn portals. "You haven't even told Neville yet, and you're flaunting our marriage to a creature like that?"

Blanche shrugged. "It will do Neville good to learn his place in my affairs. He's not my guardian, you know. I'm of age and completely independent."

"Too independent for your own good." Michael signaled the innkeeper and asked for a private dining chamber. "You didn't even give the matter of publicly announcing our marriage any thought. What possessed you?"

Blanche wrenched her arm from his grasp and followed the innkeeper, waiting to speak until the doors of the room closed behind them and they had privacy. "I didn't want you punching Barnaby and that was the only way I could think to stop you."

For a moment, Michael looked amused, then he shoved his hand through his hair and shook his head. "You thought I couldn't handle him. I owe you no gratitude for your lack of confidence. Now we must deal with the matter of our marriage as well as the mine."

That gave her pause, but she wouldn't let him see it. She trailed her overlong skirt to the window. "You should have thought of that before you married me, although I don't expect it to crimp your unfettered existence."

She couldn't see his expression, but his curt, clipped tones conveyed his hurt.

"I am not your father. I will not leave you to fend for yourself while I amuse myself elsewhere. So you may remove that notion from your head right now."

She heard his footsteps walking away, heard the door slam behind him. She couldn't say for certain why she had said what she had. She supposed she just wanted the hurt out of the way. She really didn't think Michael could change his nature for her, even should he so desire.

* * *

When neither Weatherton or Barnaby arrived for their meeting, Michael consulted with Blanche, obtained her agreement once she understood the dangerous working conditions, then took matters in his own hands. This time, when he walked into the mine office, he confiscated the books, ordered the mines closed until further notice, and held a meeting with the miners.

Weatherton had cheated Blanche and the workers, in collusion with Barnaby. With evidence of their crimes, he would have to find the local magistrate and ask for their apprehension.

The mine needed a new manager, someone who knew the operations, knew the men, and could keep the mine operating without dishonesty. He'd already picked out a few possibilities from the crowd tonight.

His new authority didn't weigh heavy on his shoulders. He would have done the same without Blanche's permission, just in a less blatant manner. Responsibility he understood. Blanche, he didn't.

The meeting had lasted until dark. The distance from mine to Blanche stretched out interminably. Michael could hear some of the other miners talking around him as they all headed home.

Vaguely, he heard distant shouts, but his thoughts had wandered to the bed he would share with Blanche tonight. It took more than a few loud voices to intrude on that daydream. He could count the weeks and probably the hours since he'd shared her bed last.

Not until the miners around him shouted in alarm and raced ahead did Michael look up. Over the top of the trees, in the direction of the town, flame shot into the night sky.

Thirty-three

Flames leapt from the inn roof, illuminating the night sky like some magnificent Midsummer's Eve bonfire. Just as on a night previously scarred in his memory, Michael saw a crowd milling about the street, uselessly heaving buckets of water and wailing. The night he'd almost lost Blanche to an inferno filled his soul with horror.

Shouting "Blanche!" he pushed and shoved his way through the crowd. Many of the bystanders still wore nightcaps and gowns. Women and children screamed as a portion of the inn's roof collapsed, shooting another bolt of flame into the stars. Men formed an erratic line from water pump to inn, but the town didn't contain enough buckets to quench a conflagration of this scale. Michael didn't see Blanche anywhere, and his throat ached with the effort not to roar his pain.

Lungs bursting from lack of air after his run, Michael focused on the inn. If Blanche had panicked as she had after the carriage explosion, she could still be in there. The smoke boiling through the windows could already have silenced her. He shoved through the crowd. Someone still remained inside, he could tell from the shrieks.

Smoke billowed through all the lower windows. The ladders leaning against the inn roof had been abandoned, and the bucket brigade now simply flung water on those flames creeping closest to the tavern.

Fortunately, the night held little wind, and the earlier dampness controlled the spread. Still women shrieked and wept hysterically, watching the windows for some sign of life. For whom?

With wildly beating pulse, Michael scanned the windows. This wasn't Blanche's loyal staff milling about. This crowd didn't even know she existed. Surely she wouldn't risk her life again walking those burning halls searching for those left behind. He would kill her if she did.

He raced into the clearing around the inn with the men and their buckets, aiming for the one substantial ladder within sight.

"Michael! Michael, my God, you're here! The little girl! The little girl is still in there. I heard her, but I couldn't find her."

He skidded in the mud at the familiar cry. An arm full of wispy muslin and flowing gold locks fell into his embrace, clinging to him as if he were the last barrier between heaven and hell. Michael nearly choked on the thick, smoky air with his gasp of relief. Clutching Blanche's slender waist, he buried his face in her hair and tried to calm his racing heartbeat.

"I thought I'd lost you," he muttered. "I looked everywhere. I thought you'd gone rescuing servants again. I couldn't bear it one more time. Thank God you're safe."

Blanche wrapped her fingers in his waistcoat as he lifted her from her feet and crushed her tighter against him, but her hysterically whispered words didn't die. She sobbed, and her whole body shook with the depths of her anguish.

"The child, Michael. I can hear her crying. She's in there. I can't reach her, Michael."

Between gulps for air, she was shaking him with her fists. "I can't find her. And now I can't hear her anymore."

Michael saw the hysteria in her eyes and remembering her terror of fire, feared the worst. "What child, Blanche? I don't remember any child." Still, he could hear women wailing. He saw the grim faces of the men working at the corner of the inn least engulfed in flames.

"I heard her crying, Michael! I was in the garden, and fire exploded. She cried for her mama. She never stopped crying, Michael. I tried, but they wouldn't let me near."

Still uncertain that Blanche did not conjure the child's cries from hysteria, Michael held her close and tried to hear what she had heard.

His stomach clenched at the groan of the crowd as still another portion of the rambling roof collapsed. If the child existed, he couldn't leave it in that inferno.

"Where, Blanche? You must tell me exactly where you heard the screams." A few short months ago, he could have walked into that building without a qualm. But he had a wife and child now, and he couldn't imagine releasing his grip on Blanche.

"I was in the garden—there, where the men are." She didn't point but continued clinging to his lapels.

218

Michael knew where she meant. He'd seen the men feverishly concentrating on the yard beneath the oak. "Upstairs or down?" he demanded.

"Up. The fire started in our side, but it went up and did not spread across quickly. But the smoke is everywhere. She could still be alive, Michael, I know it."

He clutched her arms, insisting she meet his gaze. "Promise you will stay right here, away from the fire. You carry a child, Blanche. You can't risk our child to save another."

Michael read trust and love and hope in her widening eyes. "Promise?" he demanded. When she nodded, he released her and ran toward the burning inn.

"Does anyone know the room the child is in?" he asked of the first firefighter he reached.

The soot-blackened face turned toward the flames creeping across the rooftop. "We went in the back corner and couldn't find her. She's crippled and cannot walk, poor wee thing, so she could not go far. Perhaps it's God's wish to ease her pains."

The back corner—where the servants had rooms overlooking the tavern. The child was a servant? "Where are her parents?"

The man wiped his sweaty brow with the back of his forearm and nodded in the direction of a group of huddled, weeping maids. "The lass has no father that we know of, and the mother's no better than she should be. It's one less worry for a girl like that."

His scorn told Michael all he needed to know. Perhaps God had meant to take the child from the misery her parents visited upon her, but he couldn't give her up without trying. "I'll need someone to hold the ladder steady," he commanded as he crossed the distance between the crowd and the firefighters. The man gave him a look as if he thought him crazed, but he yelled at one of the other men to join them.

Michael grabbed a full bucket of water and doused himself, soaking his one good coat. He asked for a blanket from the stables. He'd need something wet to wrap the child in.

When the men had the ladder in position, Michael threw the wet blanket over his shoulder and began to climb. He didn't notice the crowd growing silent behind him. His entire being concentrated on that square of glass behind which waited an unconscious child. For Blanche's sake, he wouldn't believe her dead. Clenching his teeth, he reached for the window.

Blanche watched Michael's lone figure scaling the ladder. She covered the base of her throat, fighting a mounting scream. She sank to her knees as Michael knocked out the window with a blanket-wrapped arm. Smoke poured from the opening, and the fire roared louder in protest, as if he'd challenged and struck some fiery beast.

She clutched her arms over her chest in prayer, and rocked back and forth, praying for forgiveness, praying for Michael, making promises to a deity she had long forgotten. She would never call Michael fool again, though only a fool would obey her insane plea. But right now, in this moment, she saw the gallant knight she'd seen before, the one who protected her, teased her, taught her to live again.

She wouldn't ask for his love. She would just love him for himself, and let him go his own way. She wouldn't hold him back, she promised God. The world needed good men like him. Just let him live so he could go on as he had, righting small wrongs where he found them, rescuing maidens in distress.

The women in the crowd followed her actions and knelt on the damp ground, praying to themselves or aloud, all for the lives of one crippled child and a madman.

The crowd uttered a collective gasp as the fire reached the child's room. Fire couldn't consume slate shingles, but the decaying timbers beneath burned with the strength and duration of old Yule logs. Smoke poured from the holes left by collapsing slate.

One of the braver firefighters hurried up the ladder to warn Michael of the danger. Blanche stopped breathing as the flames crawled closer to the window. The leaves in the old tree leaning over the rear of the house caught fire, dropping tiny embers onto the yard. Other leaves merely shriveled from the force of the heat, then fell into the flames, feeding the blaze.

A light breeze changed the direction of both fire and smoke, obscuring the top of the ladder. Sparks danced up a dead limb, creating fiery lace against the blackness of the sky. Smoke curled and blew away, revealing the filthy firefighter carrying a limp, blanket-wrapped bundle over his shoulder.

Blanche cried aloud at sight of the limp bundle. She didn't remember jumping to her feet. She only recognized her direction when the force of the heat struck her. A man grabbed her before she could reach the ladder. Someone carried the limp child away. Blanche's gaze remained fixed on the figure framed in the window above.

Fire blazed all around him as Michael threw his long legs over the sill. Flames ate at the tree limb above him, at the roof near his head, at the window he crawled through. It caught in the sleeve of his coat, and he beat it with his hands, nearly losing his balance on the ladder. Blanche checked a scream of hysteria and prayed more fervently.

When his feet finally touched the ground, Blanche screamed Michael's name, and flew toward him on winged feet. The heat of the blaze no longer paralyzed her. Her hysterical fears vanished as she flung her arms around Michael. Feeling Michael tremble, she frantically called out for a physician. The crowd parted. Michael said nothing, merely resting his arm across Blanche's shoulders and stumbling beside her in the charred remains of his best coat.

* * *

Exhausted, mentally, physically, and emotionally, Blanche collapsed in the chair beside the bed and watched Michael sleep. The doctor had given him laudanum for the pain. Every time she looked at the bandages on his hands, she wept and wished she could suffer the burns for him. She knew his agony well.

She just wished the fire could have struck him anywhere but his hands, the hands that moved with such deft grace. The doctor feared for his ability to use them again. She'd wept a thousand tears, slept briefly, and wept some more, but still he did not wake. Blanche supposed that was for the good. He needed time to heal before he woke to the pain. He'd breathed too much smoke, scorched himself in too many places

She sat there, wiping her swollen eyes so she could watch and make certain he breathed. Eventually, she washed and changed into clean clothes someone had brought her. The whole town stopped by as the day progressed, bringing food, clothing, offering tidbits of news on the child's progress.

They called her Mrs. Lawrence and treated her with awed respect. She knew one miner or another remained stationed in the hall outside, waiting for the moment Michael woke.

She'd gradually learned what he had done at the mine. She should be furious at his high-handedness, but she really didn't care. She trusted Michael to do whatever needed doing when he woke. She just wanted him to wake. Needed him to wake. Please, God, let him be well.

Hearing a commotion outside, Blanche ignored it, safe in the knowledge that someone always guarded the door. The patient stirred at the noise. She twisted the ring she'd returned to her finger during the night. Gently, she smoothed the covers over his bandaged chest. The burn on his brow was not so deep as that on his hands, and the doctor had left it uncovered. The ugly red contrasted with the paleness of Michael's face. She'd never seen him so still.

The chamber door abruptly burst open. Blanche jerked around in surprise. Neville stalked through the doorway, followed by Effingham.

She didn't have the strength to protest the rudeness of their invasion. She merely leaned over and checked the tidiness of the bandage on Michael's hand.

That tender gesture sent Neville's temper soaring. "What the devil are you doing here?" He glared down at Michael's bare chest. "You have no right in here with this lying, conniving—"

Effingham grabbed the back of the duke's neckcloth and throttled him into silence. With a respectful nod to Blanche, he inquired politely, "How is he?"

Blanche said quietly, "The doctor gave him laudanum so he does not feel the pain yet. But he does not wake, or eat, either."

Effingham released the duke's linen. "Michael has no head for alcohol or drugs. The potion should have been diluted. He'll come around when he's ready. Michael's too stubborn for quacking to harm him."

His kind reassurance brought tears to Blanche's eyes. That she wanted to cry at a few kind words proved the extent of her exhaustion.

"You should have hired a nurse," Neville argued. "You have no place in this room. I can't imagine what you're thinking. You have no chaperone, no maid, no—"

Blanche fixed her gaze on Michael's brother. "What brings you here so soon? There's scarce been time for word to reach London."

"Did you even send word?" Effingham asked wryly. At her downcast gaze, he continued, "Your Fiona and her family appeared on my doorstep with some tangled tale of prison escapes and exploding mines. I thought His Grace's yacht the fastest way to discover the truth. Fortunately, given the situation at the mines, we thought to stop here first."

"It's a dashed good thing we did, too," Neville said harshly, his normally easygoing features distorted with anger and worry. "Had anyone else heard of this escapade, your reputation would be in tatters. Have you taken leave of your senses, Blanche? Had anyone discovered you traipsing about the countryside with this gypsy, you'd have to marry him."

For the first time in many days, a smile twisted at the corner of Blanche's mouth. Switching her gaze from Effingham to her noble cousin, she answered softly, "I *am* married to him. He's my husband."

Thirty-four

Pain shot up his arm and into his head as Michael struggled against grogginess. "Blanche," he murmured, and tugged restlessly at the covers.

A hand pressed his wrist against the bed. "She's sleeping," a familiar voice said. "She's fine. You can rest now."

Gavin. Michael's eyes flew open. His adopted brother sprawled in a chair beside his bed— a strange bed in a strange room. Gavin looked like hell. He apparently hadn't shaved in days, his hair needed washing, and his clothes looked as if he'd slept in them. Obviously, Dillian hadn't accompanied him.

"Where's Blanche?" Michael demanded, the roughness of his voice startling him.

"Your wife is sleeping."

Michael sensed the hesitancy in Gavin's words, the curiosity in his gaze, but his memory remained cloudy. What exactly had Blanche told him? "What are you doing here?" he asked.

Gavin shot him a look of irritation. "At the moment, preventing Neville from throwing you out the window. We found Lady Blanche nursing you, and His Grace had one of his rare fits." He watched Michael closely for reaction. "She declared herself your wife, and promptly took herself off to bed. It's a pretty close call what might kill you first, Neville's rage, your burns, or my curiosity."

With a sigh of resignation at Michael's non-reply, Gavin crossed his arms. "I've been waiting for the day when you brought home one of your strays and declared yourself wed, but Lady Blanche? If it's true, I must congratulate you. I seriously underestimated your charms."

Michael eased his pounding head against the pillow and stared at the ceiling. Pride welled at Blanche's public declaration of their marriage. She finally trusted him.

He couldn't lie to Gavin. Perhaps he should for Blanche's sake, but for the child's sake, someone must know. "We married in

Scotland months ago. I left it to her to make it public, or not."

During the ensuing silence Michael savored the reality. Blanche was his wife.

"Neville will croak," Gavin said flatly. "He held out hope that she would settle for him. To have that fortune in your hands ...."

"I make no claim on Blanche's fortune, or the lady herself unless she requests it. Don't expound upon it too much. How is she? The fire ...."

"We've talked to the villagers. It seems fairly certain gunpowder started a small explosion near your room. The fire burnt strongest in that part of the building, and the windows exploded before the flames took over. Apparently young Seamus's tale had truth behind it."

"Eamon," Michael answered bitterly, struggling to sit up. "Eamon O'Connor. We have to find him." He pulled to a sitting position and began the laborious task of easing his legs over the side of the bed without the use of his bandaged hands. "We can't leave Blanche alone. Have Neville send his men after a tall beanpole of an Irishman. Dark hair, green eyes, probably speaks French. Since he missed the first time, he may try again."

Alarmed, Gavin pressed Michael back toward the bed. "You're not going anywhere. I'll take care of O'Connor. You're in no shape to do anything."

Michael shook him off and glared at his useless hands. "I'm going to Blanche. O'Connor will have to go through me first."

Gavin looked at him dubiously. "You'll have to push through the miners waiting outside first. They're concerned about the mine. It seems you have acquired some influence in the matter, and the manager has absconded."

Michael scowled and worked at his makeshift toga, even accepting his brother's aid in his anxiety to reach Blanche. "Tell them they're being paid while the mine is inspected. Have them send the man down who claims he knows another seam, along with a man who can determine how to shore the place up. Set soldiers after Barnaby and Weatherton, then have the rest of them help you find bloody O'Connor."

"I'm glad I'm the one with the title and authority around here," the marquess said wryly as he finished tucking the sheet over his shoulder. "Maybe I should send in the duke so you can order him about, too."

Michael shot him a venomous look. "Keep His Mighty Grace away from Blanche. Let him do something useful for a change. Finding O'Connor should keep him busy."

"We'll find the bastard," Gavin said grimly. "And we'll hang him down the mine."

Satisfied, Michael set out to find his wife.

* * *

Michael jerked awake the moment Blanche stirred. Lying beside her, he could almost forget his pain in his pleasure at having Blanche beside him again. The bandages on his palms prevented anything more than running his fingertips along her bare arm.

Leaning on his undamaged elbow, he studied the streaks from her tears. She had whimpered once or twice as she slept, curling within herself until he'd held her as best as he could. He knew she had nightmares of the fire. He caressed the delicate bridge of her nose with an unburned fingertip.

She opened her eyes, meeting his blankly, then with comprehension and a smile. "Michael," she murmured, and it was music to his ears, worth every minute of pain.

"My lady," he said in return, admiring the blue of her eyes. "How do you feel?"

She smoothed her hand downward, and Michael followed the path of her hand with wistful gaze, longing to touch as she did.

"I'm famished. And you?" Concern lined her face, and she tried sitting up, but he held her down with the weight of his arm.

"I'll live." He studied her face with care. "Have you told Neville of us?"

Confidence tinted her voice. "I did. He will no doubt demand proof, and even then, he will demand the sanctity of the church. But he cannot change our vows."

"Will you take my name then? I have no other but Lawrence to give you. Will you mind being just a Mrs. Michael Lawrence?"

She wrinkled her nose, but her eyes smiled. "Actually, it will be Lady Blanche Lawrence. It's hard for the daughter of a marquess to give away her title. Will you mind?"

"You will always be Lady Blanche to me. A name does not matter. Will you live with me?"

Blanche brushed his raspy jaw. Amusement colored her words as she replied, "I will live with you. Where shall it be, in the hedgerows or a gypsy wagon?"

Michael collapsed against the pillow and luxuriated in this moment of pure joy before reality intruded. "We'll live anywhere you're happy." He basked in the radiance of her smile. "I just want you in my bed at night."

She began a careful exploration of his burns. "I can arrange that. What will you do when I swell to three times my size and there is scarce room for all three of us in the bed?"

The caress of her hands had focused his agony in new places. "I will sleep on the floor, if necessary. I won't leave your side."

"You lie," she replied softly, twisting her fingers in the singed hairs on his chest. "I know you too well, Michael Lawrence. You have itchy feet and they will carry you away from me often enough. You must make me one promise."

He watched her questioningly.

"You must promise to always say farewell before you go," she said, her gaze steadfast. "I will not have you disappearing like some phantom every time the urge comes upon you. If we argue, you must stand and fight, or tell me farewell. You cannot just walk out."

He'd never tried staying in one place. He liked new places, the wind in his hair, the blue of the skies above him. He would give them up for Blanche and the children they would have but it might kill a piece of him. Still, he would willingly sacrifice whatever it took to keep Blanche.

The ache in Michael's loins escalated as he considered her request. Her fingers traced tantalizing paths along his chest, circling his nipples and teasingly drawing lower. Michael condemned his useless hands to hell, longed for the bliss of her body beside his as he reassured her of his faithfulness. But he couldn't even remove her nightgown.

"I cannot imagine ever leaving you, or wanting to, but if that will ease your mind, I solemnly vow I will always say farewell." He eyed the swell of her breasts beneath the cloth. "Now, you had best go fetch your breakfast before you start something I cannot finish."

At her teasing smile, he filled with desire. This was the lovely fairy nymph of love and laughter he remembered. When her soft palm slid lower, Michael groaned aloud, and his hips rose of their own accord.

"It's been a long time, Michael. Do you think I just imagined the loveliness of those nights? Will it ever be like that again? Does bliss only come once in a lifetime?" She tugged her gown upward and discarded it over the side of the bed.

Oh, God, she was torturing him. Squeezing his eyes closed and gritting his teeth, Michael let the wave of half-pain, half-pleasure sweep over him as she nibbled delicately at his nipple while her hand played its elusive game. He glued his bandaged palms to his sides.

"Unless you wish to ride astride, I am in no condition to show you, my lady. I do believe there is only one part of me fully functioning, and I would not risk harming you or your child by using it in the manner my lascivious imagination conjures." He peeked, soaking in the splendor of the globes of her breasts before valiantly raising his gaze to meet hers.

An unholy light illuminated fine blue eyes as her hand stroked lower. "What if we're no longer good together? I would not shackle you with a useless wife."

"Believe me, Blanche, there is no way in heaven or hell that you could not please me now should you choose to do so. But by all that is holy, if you do not choose to do so immediately, I shall most likely expire on the spot."

He closed his eyes and groaned again as her fingers closed about his aching member. Sweet temptation, but he would walk through fire again for just this touch. "I cannot caress you in return," he complained.

She leaned over to ease his complaint with a kiss. "You have not burned your lips, have you?"

That, he hadn't. Wrapping his arms around her slender waist, he pulled her downward until her breasts brushed his chest and their lips merged in a hunger long denied. When she swung her leg astride him, he nearly exploded with the passion he'd carefully repressed. He plundered her mouth, sucking the sweetness from it, then bent his head to her breasts.

She moaned so seductively, Michael nearly took her right then. He suckled deeply, and was rewarded for his efforts by the glide of Blanche's thighs over his hips. Small tremors built there, rippling along his abdomen as she rubbed against him. He wanted to touch her there, prepare her, but he had only the tips of his fingers to work his commands. He used them cautiously, sliding his bandaged palm between them, tracing the ever-so-slight curve of her abdomen, finding the sensitive nub between her thighs and circling it. He couldn't hold out much longer. He felt like one of Eamon O'Connor's bombs. The merest spark would set him off.

"Michael, please," Blanche breathed in his ear as he circled her with his finger.

Not needing further encouragement, he wrapped his arms around her once more and pulled her down to cover him. She slid over him easily, adjusting her position until she understood how they fit together, taking him deeper with each movement until she sheathed him completely. Michael wanted to shout his joy and triumph as at last, he thrust his hips upward.

She had no need to ride him long for their needs were too strong. Feeling her contract around him, Michael carried her deeper, driving her to the peak and over, before he tumbled after. Despite the pain he had caused himself with his exertion, the need to stay inside her grew again. He never wanted to leave.

"Will that suffice as evidence of our pleasure for now, or should I show you more, my lady?" Michael asked with eyes closed.

She moved gently along his building desire, but blessedly, she slipped to his side and settled for resting her palm against his chest. "I think there is much we can show each other, but we have a lifetime for exploring. I think I'd best find us some food for now."

Instantly alert, Michael wished he could grab her arm. "You will not go outside this room alone. Send someone for the food. Gavin will have placed a guard outside the door."

She stared at him in incredulity. "There is someone standing outside our door?" A crimson blush colored her cheeks. "They could hear us?"

Michael chuckled. "I'm certain Gavin would have left a deaf mute out there. He's quite practical about these things."

Blanche pinched an unburned piece of his hide. "Why would the marquess post a guard outside our door? Does he fear we'll escape again? That sounds more like something Neville would do."

"The fire was deliberate, my love. Seamus warned us O'Connor and his lot meant to close the mines. I think they chose an easier route and went after us instead. It's possible he recognized you. If not, he no doubt recognized me or heard I acted as your representative. He probably thought us asleep in our bed that night."

Reluctantly, she pulled away, searching amid the covers for her gown. "I saw a man staring at me. A tall man, thin, with dark hair. Is that him?"

Michael bit back a curse and nodded. "That's him. With any luck, Neville has men looking for him. It shouldn't be long. But I will take no chances until he's caught."

She didn't have time to respond. A sharp rap on the door sent her diving for her gown. Michael awkwardly worked the sheet over him with his elbows. "Who is it?" he demanded irritably.

"You want the full title?" the duke answered angrily. "I don't have that long. I've someone here to see you."

Michael watched as Blanche glanced at the bed where he lay naked. Once her cousin saw them together, there was no turning back. He met her gaze challengingly.

Lifting her chin, she answered for him. "You cannot come in yet. I can't find a dressing gown."

The curse coming through the door was oddly muffled. Michael had anticipated a splendid explosion rather than this ominous silence. "Why don't you send for breakfast, Your Grace? The lady hasn't eaten yet." Michael wanted to add, "The lady is eating for two," but he thought it best not to push his luck.

Blanche's glare confirmed that decision. She tugged at ribbons and buttons in her hurry to make herself decent. He could tell her that the flush on her cheeks, the sparkle in her eyes, and the tousled chaos of her hair would reveal all she wished to conceal, but he refrained from teasing.

He heard the duke barking a few commands outside the door, the rush of booted feet, and what sounded oddly like a childish voice asking a question. Then Neville shouted at the door once more. "Two minutes, Blanche. I'll not linger in this hallway longer than that."

"You could go away and come back some other time," Michael called helpfully. Blanche frowned at him, grabbed a brush, and tried pulling the knots from her hair. "Who is our visitor?"

"It's me, my lady," a childish voice piped. "Are you a real lady? Mr. Neville says so."

He watched with interest as she threw open the door.

Outside stood the immaculately tailored, immensely powerful Duke of Anglesey with a small child in his arms, her thin arms wrapped around his neck, her crippled leg dangling over his once neatly-pressed sleeve.

His Grace's grimace of chagrin disappeared immediately as the child cried out at sight of Michael, "My hero! Can I kiss you?"

Thirty-five

Still chortling, Michael allowed Blanche to fuss over him as they prepared for bed. Neville hadn't been able to argue legalities while Blanche was in raptures over the child they'd saved.

Just watching his wife tug the covers around him warmed an empty place in Michael's heart. He couldn't remember anyone tucking him into bed.

"Neville will never forgive the poor lamb," he said, wishing Blanche would settle down and crawl into bed beside him. The nuisance of not having hands for touching her irritated him, but he had too many things to be happy about to dwell on it.

"He won't have to," Blanche replied. "I've talked to Mary's mother and she claims Mary belongs to her late sister and is none of her own. That's a lie, of course, but I made her sign a paper giving up her rights to the child. Mary has been hidden away for so long, she knows nothing except the fairy tales she's been told."

Michael watched her fret over the window curtains, arranging them so a breeze circulated in the stuffy room. "I cannot think where you will place a crippled child. I have difficulty enough finding homes for healthy ones."

The bed shifted as she slid in beside him. "I will take her back to Dorset with me. If I remember correctly, the house there is in need of extensive renovation. I'll hire an architect and have an addition built. I don't believe there is a separate nursery wing there now."

A separate nursery wing. Michael's mouth grew dry as he eased up on his elbow and stared at his remarkable wife. He sensed her tension and wished he could see her face more clearly. "You will stay in Dorset with Mary? It's a far distance from London."

"There's the farm in Gloucester, I suppose," she said. "It's more centrally located between the mines and mills. I thought perhaps of selling both mines and mills, but that would not guarantee the laborers a fair treatment."

"Gloucester is just as far from London, you'll remember."

"Children don't belong in London," she announced firmly.

Before he could put his agreement into words, a noise at the window prompted him to sit up and reach for the nearest weapon. *Damn*, he couldn't use his hands to grasp anything.

"Save your magic tricks for another day," came a mellow voice scarred with sarcasm from the window sill. "I'm not here to harm you or your lady. I'm here to return the favor for rescuing young Seamus and that foolish uncle of his."

Eamon. Michael freed his legs from the sheets, and pressed Blanche behind him. "O'Connor," he acknowledged. "I've meant to ask, are you some relation to Fiona's Uncle William?"

A snort emanated from the tall shadow blending into the curtains. "Somewhere back among our grandfaithers, I suppose. My mother is the O'Connor. I've not come to discuss family relations with you, although I've a few questions of me own if we had the time."

"Anglesey's in the next room. You're in trouble enough if he finds you. Blowing up the lady's carriage and the inn will see you hanged, even if you waited for her to leave."

"That's what I've come to tell you. We're working men, not murderers of innocents. We don't harm women and children. The carriage was a warning, but we never meant the lady harm. The inn is another matter. That fire destroyed a man's livelihood and endangered dozens of innocents besides the lady. We didn't do it. You'd best look to your mines and the ones who know the power of explosives. The lads say a fat Englishman has skulked about these last weeks, one that once worked for the lady. I'd take care, if I were you."

The curtains blew in the breeze from the open window. The shadow had disappeared.

"Where did he go?" Blanche whispered, wrapping her fingers around Michael's arm and hugging him close. "Are you sure he isn't some relation? Or do all the Irish perform disappearing acts?"

Seeing no purpose in pursuing O'Connor, Michael wrapped his arms around his wife, pulling her down on the pillows with him. "You may wish it, but I'll not disappear so easily, my lady. I'm here to stay."

* * *

Blanche refused to leave Cornwall while the men scoured the

area in search of Barnaby. Neville suggested she return to London in his yacht, but she reminded him she would only go as far as Dorset. He snapped his mouth shut and went off to yell at Michael.

Calmly combing and plaiting Mary's lovely hair, Blanche listened as her husband ordered a duke and a marquess about in the next room. She couldn't imagine why she had once considered Michael a harmless fool. He'd proved himself more commanding than any general. Even Wellington hadn't led an army from a sickbed.

The escape she had planned in her more innocent days she now knew as naive. Her husband had not yet taken claim of her wealth and power, but she could see that day coming unless she learned to speak up. Michael would have to grow used to argument.

Leaving Mary playing with a doll, Blanche slipped into the next room. She'd heard Neville and Effingham leave and knew a delegation of miners waited their turn. Her husband paced the sitting room they'd taken as the miners explained how they could reopen the mine.

"You'll need to prove there's enough coal in there to pay the cost of reopening," Michael reminded them. "If we cut the number of man hours and raise wages, operating costs will soar. Malcolm, can you do the figures? I've asked Sir Bryant's man to show you how he does his. I want honest numbers. If we go broke reopening the mine, there won't be funds for a new one. It's in your own interest to make the best decision."

Blanche understood that. So did the miners. They entered an animated discussion on coal prices, labor costs, and equipment that left her exceedingly bored. Michael's bandaged hands twitched at his sides. He really should rest more. His burns must plague him unmercifully, she knew from bitter experience.

As the miners consulted among themselves, she slipped along the edge of the room to stand behind Michael. Gently, she caught one bandaged hand, massaging the exposed fingertips.

Michael looked startled, then relaxed. "I'm pacing again, aren't I?"

"You'll have to replace the innkeeper's carpet," she agreed.

He brushed a strand of hair from her face. "It's better when you're touching me," he whispered so no other could hear. "Having a woman in my bed has diverted my energy."

"I came to warn you that Neville has sent our solicitor to verify the truth of our marriage. But I don't doubt you in the least. Is that very cynical or very naive of me?"

He grinned. "It's very Blanche of you. And tonight, we should continue this interesting discussion. Right now, I had best cool off a few tempers."

Voices rose loud in argument. She could not do much as yet, but she could handle this minor situation. With a smile, she sailed across the room, calling, "Gentlemen! Shall I ring for tea? Perhaps we could all think more clearly after a bite to eat."

The miners instantly quieted, and she sensed Michael's approval. She would make their unusual marriage work.

* * *

"We cannot find any trace of Barnaby or Weatherton. It's possible they took their own transportation to Portsmouth and sailed out using assumed names. We have men questioning along the docks, but this is Cornwall. They're a closed mouth lot. We're not likely to learn much." Gavin sprawled his lanky frame in an armchair.

In frustration, Michael wished he could make three of himself. He didn't like Barnaby running loose. The man had to be a Bedlamite. But he couldn't leave Blanche, and he couldn't leave the situation at the mine just yet. Blanche wanted to be in Dorset, and he didn't want her going alone. Not even three of him would be enough, he thought gloomily.

"They're undoubtedly long gone," His Grace said confidently. "Blanche, it's time you went home where you belong. You cannot continue living under these conditions."

"Blanche belongs with me," Michael retorted. "Whenever she is ready to leave, I will take her."

"I've no proof of the legality of your marriage yet," Neville pointed out. "And there's some chance it can yet be undone. I'd suggest you stay here with your pet miners until these things are straightened out."

"Like bloody hell, I will!" Michael exploded. "That's my child she's carrying. You can deny me everything you like, but you cannot deny me that child! So I suggest you accustom yourself to the idea of my being Blanche's husband."

Blanche gasped and Michael knew he'd let the cat out of the bag, as well as losing his temper. But he no longer had the option of releasing his frustrations by wandering down the road to the next adventure. He needed to learn new skills, like hammering dukes with blunt honesty.

Neville reddened with rage, spun to Blanche for confirmation, then slammed his fist into the wall.

Clasping his hands over his chest, Gavin eyed Michael and Blanche with interest. "You're both mad. A child won't make things easier. You should have waited."

Reaching for Blanche's hand, he answered without waiting for her response. "What we want of our marriage is none of your concern, Gavin."

Neville cursed while nursing his bruised fist. "You don't even have a name to give a wife. You have no breeding, no home, and no idea of the enormous responsibility of supporting the hundreds of tenants and servants under Blanche's welfare. I've watched you these last days. You've sacrificed enormous sums from this mine just to keep those whining miners happy. If you do that with all Blanche's properties, she'll be reduced to a pauper. How will you support her then? Do you have any idea how much just running Anglesey costs?"

Gavin halted both Michael's and Blanche's reply with a curt growl. "His name is Lawrence. He's my brother. That should be enough name and family for anyone. Deny it again and I'll beat you until your pretty face looks like mine."

"We married under the name of Lawrence," Blanche argued. "If means must be found to ensure that name, then send for your solicitors. If we must marry again, we will. Do what you like, but nothing will change the fact that we've exchanged vows and created a child. The hour grows late, gentlemen. If you've had enough debate, I'll ask that you leave so we may rest."

Both Neville and Gavin shut up and turned their glares on Michael. Neville, having the greater grievance, jumped in first. "If you care anything at all for my cousin, you will send her home. It's unforgivable housing her in this hovel any longer."

"I'm not going to Anglesey," Blanche finally spoke. "When I leave here, I go to Dorset."

"You cannot go to that godforsaken cottage unaccompanied! You have no servants there. I'll take you back to Anglesey while your so-called husband handles the situation here. Let him earn his keep."

Michael contemplated flinging the noble duke out the window, but his grasp simply wouldn't manage the act. "If Blanche wishes to go to Dorset, she goes to Dorset. If I wish to accompany her, I will accompany her. No amount of insult will change the fact that you've lost her and I haven't. I suggest that you speak to her very nicely if you wish to keep the money flowing into Anglesey's coffers."

Neville sputtered. Gavin spoke for him.

"The situation here must be resolved, and I trust you haven't forgotten, Michael, that your Fiona and her felonious relations are still hiding in my house with warrants over their heads. And my lady, I don't know where or how you keep your personal books and papers, but I take it they're not in Dorset. If you are expecting Michael's help in any way with the managing of your estates, he will need access to them. I will gladly accompany you to Dorset, if that is your desire, but Michael must take care of business."

"I would stay with Michael," she answered defiantly.

Both men turned to Michael, and he sat beside her, taking up her hand as best as he could. "You cannot travel with Mary, my love. And you must protect the child you carry. Sailing on Neville's yacht will be much more comfortable for you than taking those rutted roads. Go to Dorset and plan our new home while I finish here and see to Fiona and her family. Tell me what papers you require, and I'll bring those with me when I return. I promise I will come as soon as possible."

Her soft lips puckered in disapproval. Michael understood her doubts. She thought he would neglect her as her entire family had done. But she would have to trust in him. He could not play stool for her feet. In the long run, that would never work. He held his breath and waited for her to see it, too.

"And if I say no and go elsewhere?" she whispered.

"Then I'll hunt you down. Don't make it like this between us, Blanche. Trust me. You asked that I tell you when I leave, and I'm telling you now. And I'm telling you I'll return to your side as soon as possible. I don't know how to make it any more fair than that."

Biting her lip, she nodded. He could see the tears in her eyes, but she didn't let them fall.

"I'll go to Dorset," she answered quietly.

Thirty-six

Mid-August, Hertfordshire

Michael let himself in the family entrance of his adopted brother's country house. Parliament had ended weeks ago without any major incident from the radicals. Afterward, Gavin and family had repaired to their rural abode outside London and the endless renovations on the Gothic monstrosity Gavin had inherited with the title.

Michael normally preferred this more informal atmosphere where he could come and go unnoticed, only this time, the chaos awakened curiosity in how Blanche fared with her renovations in Dorset — on the southern coast, far from here.

He'd sent letters at every opportunity, even though his damaged hand made writing difficult. Blanche's replies couldn't keep up with him. He'd found a cache of them in Bodmin when he'd returned from visiting other mining operations and had nearly memorized them by now. He longed for home and Blanche.

Standing in the lower hall, Michael debated searching out Gavin in his study, but he had little humor for set downs at the moment. The healing burns on his hands itched. He'd removed the bandages, but he still couldn't use them as he wished, which increased his irritation and frustration. For a newly married man, he'd lost a good deal of his usual geniality.

He followed the direction of childish giggles and the thunder of boots to the nursery.

"That is not how it goes! Now put it right, you dolt, before the whole comes tumbling down." Fiona's distinct voice drew Michael's steps.

"This is where the dolly goes, isn't it, moppet?" a strange man's voice asked laughingly. "We would not want the others touching it, would we?"

Entering the nursery, Michael encountered an exact replica of himself holding a wooden shelf above his head with a doll on it.

Cousin Marian's toddler laughed and tried climbing his leg to reach it. Fiona bounced a chuckling infant on her knee while Marian and Dillian crawled about the bare floor painting wildflowers along the baseboards.

Michael donned an insouciant smile when the others turned their startled gazes on him. Young Seamus scowled as he studied his mirror image, just as Michael blithely studied him. There were differences, he could see now. The younger man stood a few inches taller, but he lacked muscle and looked undernourished. Seamus's hair glowed more carrot red than auburn, and his nose had a broken crook to it.

Edwina released her hold on Seamus's trouser and raced across the floor to tackle Michael. Catching the toddler, he swung her in his arms, kissing her neck with a loud noise. Over her shoulder, he watched Seamus still and Fiona hand the babe to Dillian.

"Couthin Michael!" Edwina lisped, tugging at his ears. "Horthie ride!"

"Edwina, do behave. Cousin Michael has only just arrived. We must send for some tea and allow him to rest," Marian scolded, reaching apologetically for her daughter.

Michael kissed the little girl's cheek and whispered a promise for later, then handed her over to Marian. Someday, he hoped to make a good father, but with no example to guide him, he had his doubts.

His gaze returned to the pair who so closely resembled him that he thought they must share ancestors. He greeted his adopted cousin Marian and Gavin's wife, then looking pointedly at his Irish rebels, indicated it was time to leave.

Fiona and Seamus followed him wordlessly. Like much of the mansion, the library he led them to had been stripped of its riches decades before the marquess's arrival. Gavin had sold the more valuable volumes to finance repairs. Empty display cases were now dust-free and filling with little trinkets Dillian collected from long-unused rooms. Cobwebs no longer covered the shelves of remaining books. A mahogany table too large for removal occupied the center of a threadbare carpet.

Michael took a particularly ornate ebony chair with a tattered tapestry seat. He didn't usually like sitting, but he'd traveled since dawn on top of days of traveling before that. He ached all over.

"I'm surprised to find you still here," he said into the silence.

"Where's William?"

"Arranging transport to the Americas," Seamus answered defiantly. "We have no funds of our own, but we can work our way across."

"Even Fiona?" Michael turned his attention to the waif he'd brought to Blanche so many months ago. She no longer looked a waif. She wore her hair up and a gown that fit now. Her stance still reeked of defiance.

"The marquess has graciously paid her a wage for watching the nursery," Seamus replied. "We'll find the balance somehow. She goes with us."

Michael nodded. It was best. The men had a sentence of death hanging over them. But he'd had hopes of their aid in discovering his family. He didn't think he would ever have the chance again.

He gestured to the chairs as a maid carried in the tea tray. "We've not had opportunity to talk. Has Gavin offered any hope of your sentence being commuted?"

Taking a chair as ordered, Seamus scowled. "That's not bloody likely now, is it? They'd see us all hanged if they could."

Michael sipped his tea. "You've associated with men who threatened the government. I can scarcely blame whatever magistrate sentenced you. I'm from America myself. I'm rather reluctant to wish you on my countrymen. But at least there they'll not hang you for voicing your opinion."

"But Galway is our home," Fiona protested softly. "We grew up there. Our friends and family are there. My grandfather was an earl and lived in a castle. Why must we give all that up because of our religion?"

Michael rubbed his brow. "I know nothing of politics. I know little enough of the law. I didn't think the British much inclined to hang earls if they could avoid it. But I understand the problem is that Seamus is not son of a son, but son of a daughter, and your grandfather did not get parliament's permission to pass the title through the female line."

"He had three sons. He did not think it necessary," Seamus responded gloomily. "He did not know that they would all die without leaving heirs."

"Sure and he'd hoped he would find his eldest son alive after seeing the youngest buried," Fiona offered. "He sent messengers all over America, but by the time they returned saying they found his grave, grandfather lay dying. There was no time for the petitioning of parliament. So he named Seamus his heir and deeded his estate through our mother."

"But the bloody British wouldn't acknowledge it," Seamus said angrily. "They stole our lands, our name, everything. What was I supposed to do? Say 'yes, sir, whip me some more, sir,' and kneel before them?"

Michael wished he were the robin he heard singing on the lawn so he could fly away. Blanche accused him of having no sense of responsibility, but the truth was, he had one so over-developed that he imagined he must save the world. Right now he didn't have the patience for saving anything but time. "I don't suppose your grandfather's messengers mentioned whether or not the American son married or had children?"

Seamus looked at him blankly. Fiona did her best to answer. "That was all before our time. We only have the stories. His eldest son was after fleeing the British much as Seamus must do now. He fought the British when they burned our fields and houses and condemned innocent men to death. He took his wife with him. My grandfather had them smuggled out of the country on a fishing boat. I'm thinking the messengers would have asked after a wife and child. Uncle William may know more of the story. He was courting our aunt at the time."

Michael groaned inwardly. He would have to wait for Uncle William if he wanted the whole story. He didn't want to wait. He well knew the impossibility of this lost Irish earl having any relation to him. But he'd waited a lifetime to learn of his origins.

Another idea caught him, and he played with it as he sipped his tea and consumed his tart. His gaze drifted to Fiona. She was the younger of the two by age, but as she had once told him, she was wiser in other ways. She would do well in America. She had the wit and beauty to make something of herself. He could give her references, letters of introduction. People owed him favors on both sides of the Atlantic. He could ask Blanche to finance their journey.

"How long before William returns?" Michael asked idly, still toying with his plans.

"Not until he finds a ship." Even Seamus had lost some of his defiance as he responded in a voice of doom.

"Send for him, then. I would speak with him before you leave here. I have friends in America. I can see that you travel in better style than as cabin boy. But first, I would see that there is no other choice left. I'll need your uncle for that."

Michael startled himself as he issued these commands. He sounded more and more like Gavin every day.

* * *

Blanche read and re-read the note from Michael. He was in Hertfordshire. He might as well say he occupied the moon. Rubbing the growing roundness of her abdomen, she looked up from the letter and gazed out to the lawn. Mary laughed and played with one of the village children there. The child had even managed one or two steps on her crippled limb the other day.

The physicians had said the leg too bent for her to ever walk normally, but they'd carved her a crutch and cane. The child had been a different person ever since. Blanche feared leaving her so soon would set back all the progress Mary had made. She, of all people, knew the fear and loneliness of a parent's abandonment. She couldn't chase off to Hertfordshire. The journey would take over a week if she traveled at the sedate pace required by her pregnancy.

And the likelihood of Michael being there when she arrived was very small. Sighing, Blanche folded the letter and tucked it away with the others in her desk drawer. He had given her what she wanted with the agreement that they carry his name. She should expect little more.

Of course, Michael being Michael, he had done a great deal more. He'd settled the problems of the mining operation at last. He'd even shown Neville how profits would increase should the government pass a labor law so all mines operated under the same conditions. Neville hadn't liked it, but since it affected his own pocket, he'd promised to look into the matter.

She had no idea what he was doing about the mills, but he'd sent her a man to interview for the position Barnaby had forsaken. Perhaps Michael would come home once he saw that her new steward did his job well.

With no exploding carriages or fiery inns, life had become almost sedate these past months. Looking over the foundation of the cottage's new wing, Blanche derived some satisfaction in life as it was now. She'd learned that she wasn't the adventuring sort. She liked solving problems, but she didn't like solving them at gunpoint.

Since no one had told her otherwise, she assumed Barnaby had fled the country and the radicals planned their subversion elsewhere. Riots continued in the north, but she was far out of them.

A parlor maid rushed to give her the day's post, and Blanche smiled at the sight of a letter from Ireland. She might be a homebody, but a great deal could be accomplished from home when one had enough money and connections.

Thirty-seven

It took a week for Gavin's messengers to locate William and haul him back to Hertford. But every time Michael thought to leave, another packet of papers arrived from London with still worse news of riots in the north and of labor protests shutting down Blanche's largest sources of income. He knew something of her holdings now. Although the capital invested seemed immense beyond his comprehension, the income teetered precariously based on a number of factors. He might never understand it all, but he did understand the importance of the mills.

He would have to go to Manchester. Cursing as if born to it, Michael strode helplessly up and down Gavin's lawn, clenching and unclenching his scarred fingers as best he could. The raw new skin ached. The muscles beneath did not respond as they ought. He would never juggle pennies again. He could scarcely hold a thick pen with which to write Blanche.

He breathed a sigh of relief when a tired, dusty messenger finally rode in accompanied by the older man Michael barely recognized from their brief meeting in Dublin. He nearly hauled the man into Gavin's study. Only Dillian's hasty interference reminded him that their guest deserved rest and refreshment first.

William O'Connor graciously agreed he could take a bite in the study as they talked, if he could have a few minutes in which to wash off the dust of the road. By the time he returned with hair wet and combed, Fiona and Seamus had materialized, greeting him with hugs.

Michael plowed through their happy reunion, grabbing O'Connor by the arm and shoving him into a chair. Seamus shut the study door.

"I need a few answers before I set the lot of you on a ship and out of my hair," Michael said ungraciously, dropping into Gavin's desk chair.

"You've done more than enough," the older man replied stiffly. "We'll repay you when we can. I've found a ship sailing at the end

245

of the month. We'll be on it."

Michael leaned across the desk, glaring at the man who should have kept his wards from harm but had led them into rebellion instead. "You'll send Fiona on a freighter with a hundred starving sailors for three months? Not likely. And what of your home and tenants? How do they fare without you? Did you even consider what would happen to those closest to you when you embarked on this insane plan of treason?"

"I think I have a few years on you, lad," O'Connor responded wryly, sipping at his ale. "You'll not teach me any lessons I haven't already learned. But there comes a time in a man's life when he must defend what is his or not call himself a man. I would not have involved young Seamus, but he is as hot-headed as all the fool MacDermots. It's better that he do it now while he has none of his own to weep over him when he's gone."

Fiona held her tongue, watching Michael with the same care she had since he'd known her. She would make a dangerous woman when she came of age.

Michael threaded his fingers through his hair. "That's neither here nor there. Fiona and Seamus tell me you know something of the late earl's search for his eldest son. Did he ever discover what became of the son's wife? Were there children? Could we offer a court reason to believe heirs to that estate exist?"

William chewed his bread slowly, considering the question. After some thought, he shook his head. "The old papers are in the attic. It's been twenty years and more. My memory is not keen. But I do remember the old man receiving one letter that broke him. After that, he did what he could to ensure Seamus's inheritance, then died. If the letter held any hope at all, he would not have given up so soon. The earl had a stubborn streak wider than any ocean."

Michael contemplated this news with interest, although it delivered a final blow to his hopes. The family resemblance was strong, but his mother could have been a dock whore who serviced one of the earl's sons or brothers or byblows for all he knew.

Right now, he wasn't too eager to claim kinship with the contrary MacDermots. He might not have a name to give Blanche, but he wouldn't hand her a family tainted with treason either.

"Some of those letters would indicate that the eldest son lived in America and that he had a wife, wouldn't they?" he asked idly, toying with the idea he'd developed this past week.

O'Connor caught on quickly and developed a crafty look. "That they would, I'm certain."

"And without that one letter speaking of the heir's grave, no one would know of a certainty what became of him?"

Fiona and Seamus stared at him as if he were deranged, but they listened eagerly.

O'Connor nodded. "There's just the fact that he never returned to hold against us."

"But if the heir died leaving an infant son, we can explain that easily enough now, couldn't we?" Michael drummed his fingers against the desk, waiting for concurrence.

O'Connor smiled and started to reply, but finally understanding the direction of the conversation, Seamus leapt to his feet. "Mary, Mother of God, you can't do this! You can't steal what is mine with some phony story to buy a magistrate! Faith, and I'll not allow it! The bloody English have taken all that is mine already. I'll not see it stolen twice."

Fiona swatted him. "Sit down, you dolt. They're after stealing it back, is all. Try and not be such a simpleton, will you?"

Michael grinned and relaxed for the first time in days. This is what it had once been like before the burdens of family and responsibility had fallen on his shoulders. He would come up with wild ideas and wave his magic fingers and turn the establishment topsy-turvy. He could still do it. He much preferred the anarchy of his methods than the legal ones of Gavin and Neville, but he could work them both in his favor.

"We just need a little proof, something material for the authorities besides my appearance," he said as if everyone in the room already understood his plan. "I've no birth certificate or church book to call on. From all I can ascertain, I was born in the wilds of Kentucky. But I'm sure I could locate a few witnesses willing to put their marks on a statement. Gavin's parents are dead now. They're the ones who took me in. But with a little arm-twisting, even Gavin might agree that the Lawrence family knew a MacDermot. He was too young to know much of my birth, but just the statement of some relationship from a marquess would give us credibility."

O'Connor sat up straighter, the expression on his weathered

features changing from crafty to thoughtful.

Michael pulled the tarnished coin necklace over his head and dangled it above the desk. "If you could find your way to declaring this an ancient MacDermot relic and produce witnesses to attest to it, we'll have a case that will stand in any court. Can it be treason for a man to defend what rightfully belongs to his family? If I'm truly the next earl, can they condemn my young cousin and his guardian for protecting my property? And if we can have a title to play with, we can take it before the Lords. They're not so hasty in condemning one of their own."

O'Connor snatched the necklace from Michael's hands. Examining it closely, he whistled, then tried polishing the tarnish so he could see more clearly. "Where did you find this, my son?"

Michael grinned at these blatant dramatics. The old man would convince himself in a minute or two that they'd found the new earl. People believed his illusions because they wanted to believe.

"Gavin's parents claimed I was born with it," he answered truthfully enough. As a child, he'd hoped the coin a clue to his parentage. As a man, he wore it out of habit.

O'Connor gave him an admiring look, then returned the necklace. "How soon can we can leave for Ireland? We'll need those papers."

Michael frowned. "It's not safe for either of you to show your faces there. You'll need tell me where to search."

The room erupted in an uproar. It seemed the MacDermots were not so ready to leave their homeland as they'd claimed. Allowing the winds of protest to blow out of their own accord, Michael tried to calculate some means of reaching Ireland by way of Dorset and Manchester.

A knock on the door intruded on that pleasant reverie. The Duke of Anglesey strode in, his expression grim. It didn't grow any more pleasant upon observing Fiona and Michael's duplicate.

"I'd hoped to find Effingham here," the duke said without ceremony. "I've never seen such disorder. Do they keep no servants?"

Not sitting uselessly at the door, but the duke wouldn't appreciate that sentiment. "The situation must be desperate for you to lower yourself to our presence," Michael observed. "What may we do for you?"

"You're the one I want anyway. The mill situation has become urgent." The duke glanced around at the others in the room. "Who are these people?"

Fiona stood and made a mocking curtsy. "Sure and you remember me, your holiness."

The duke's expression tightened. Sighing, Michael headed off the confrontation. "Fiona, you cannot mock those you may need for help. Go blow bubbles at Madeline and have someone pack my bags. O'Connor, write some introductions so I can act swiftly. Seamus, have a horse saddled for me."

His Irish refugees did not move. Michael could have a marquess and a duke jumping at the snap of his fingers, but this obstreperous lot of miscreants merely glared at him. Now he remembered why he used to disappear without a word to anyone.

"I have my phaeton," Neville informed him. "If the weather holds, we can take that as far as Manchester. Just pray they haven't burned the place down before we arrive."

Seeing his schemes for visiting Blanche go up in flames, Michael prayed for strength. "I must write Blanche. Give me a few minutes."

Fiona piped up. "I'll take care of that. You'll be going on from Manchester, then?" she asked carefully, not mentioning his intended destination.

Michael nodded, regarding her with suspicion but without the time to question her sudden willingness. "I will, if William will do as told."

O'Connor nodded. "See to your bags, son. I'll have letters of introduction ready before you leave."

Narrowing his eyes, Seamus glared at them all and stalked out without a word. When the room cleared of all but the duke, Michael turned his weary gaze on his nemesis. "There's more?"

Neville nodded grimly. "One of the mill managers has seen Barnaby inciting the radicals. I received this yesterday." He pulled a folded paper from his pocket and slapped it on the desk.

Michael picked it up using both hands and holding it by the edges. The crudely lettered demand was quite succinct. Put ten thousand pounds at the disposal of the next messenger, or the mills would burn. He let the paper fall.

"I generally don't kill men," Michael said calmly. "I think I could make an exception this time. I want guards sent to Dorset, just as a precaution. I'd rather not travel in your company, if you do not mind. I'll find you when you get there."

Ignoring the duke's astonishment, Michael walked out.

When the household searched for him minutes later, he had disappeared without a trace.

* * *

"Lady Blanche will help us," Fiona argued vehemently. "We cannot wait for them to stop rioters and patch up mills. We must act now. I have no warrant on my head. I can go."

"You do not know what to look for," her uncle argued.

"And you do?" she asked impatiently.

"I do," he said, "and it's not all that you're expecting. You don't know everything yet, young Fiona, so hold your sharp tongue. We'll ask the Lady Blanche's help, if we may, otherwise we'll be all the year finding transport. Seamus may stay here, but I have naught left to lose."

"I'm not staying here like a tame puppy dog," Seamus bit out angrily. "I'll take ship to the Americas and to hell with the lot of ye. I'll not play cats paw to the rogue while he steals our name and our possessions."

Fiona rolled her eyes.

"From this day forward," William said sharply, "he's the earl, and I'll not hear more of it. If not for him, you'd be dangling from the gallows tree now. He's offering you a chance to live on your own lands again. Cannot ye see that he means us no harm? He has a lady wife rich as Croesus. He doesn't need our poor homes. The bloody title means naught to us but power, and if he wields it in our favor, why should we complain?"

Seamus growled deep in his throat. "I'll endure the ploy for the sake of the land and people, but I'll not be stayin' here any longer," he warned. "It's a wonder the damned duke hasn't sent soldiers after us as it is."

Fiona grinned. "It's not as if he knows who we are or cares. Our toplofty duke has bigger things on his mind."

"And how do you know of him?" Seamus asked suspiciously. "You did not mention hobnobbing with dukes."

"That's of no moment. The sooner I reach Lady Blanche, the sooner we can have this done. Do we have enough funds for a coach, or must I walk?"

"We'll have none of that, lass. The marchioness has a soft heart. I'll ask for the loan of a carriage." William eyed Seamus critically. "It comes to mind that you may be of use to your new cousin, lad. It would not do should harm come to Michael before our names are cleared. Can we trust you to find your way to Manchester with a few of your friends? Just having the two of ye there looking alike might throw a bit of confusion into the works."

Seamus considered it for a moment, then nodded as the idea took root. "I might at that. One of us should keep our eye on him, at least. And Eamon's at loose ends."

Both Fiona and William looked alarmed.

Thirty-eight

Blanche looked up with a mixture of hope and alarm as a carriage bowled recklessly up the lane. Now at the beginning of September, the grass had turned gold with lack of rain, and the dirt road billowed with dust. The garish yellow post chaise coated the entire landscape with grit.

Checking to see that Mary still played with the new nursemaid, Blanche straightened her hat, shoved loose tendrils of hair behind her ear, and awkwardly rose from the bench where she sat reading. Her pregnancy gave her no trouble, but she was over-conscious of her size. She wished she had worn a fuller muslin, but she had not expected company. Or Michael. Hope surged at the possibility of her husband's return.

An unfamiliar man climbed out, offered his assistance to someone inside, and that small hope died. She'd known Michael had his hands full with his Irish rebels and the mills and the miners. One of his painfully scrawled scribbles resided in her pocket at all times, a reminder that he truly had not abandoned her.

"Fiona!" The young woman stepping out of the carriage seemed more mature than Blanche remembered. The stylish gown could explain the change, except Fiona carried herself with a lady's grace. This young woman even wore a respectable hat with flowers on it. And gloves.

"Lady Blanche!" Fiona hurried across the dry grass, holding out her hands. She caught Blanche's and almost danced with glee as she eyed the change in Blanche's shape. "Sure and you're looking most maternal these days, my lady. It's no wonder Michael's after pacing the floor as if he could walk the miles to Dorset away."

Blanche smiled at the image conjured. "Michael always paces when he cannot act. How lovely you look! I see Dillian's cooks have fed you well." She glanced questioningly to the man striding up the lane.

Fiona clasped the older man's arm. "This is my Uncle William. William O'Connor, Lady Blanche, Michael's wife."

Mr. O'Connor made a proper leg and bowed over Blanche's hand. He had a well-fed, country squire look about him despite the fact that his tweed coat did not match the ill-fitting trousers he wore. But she liked his gentle smile and twinkling eyes, for all they had no resemblance whatsoever to Fiona. She thought she remembered Michael telling her that Fiona's aunt was the MacDermot, not the uncle. She supposed she ought to wonder that an escaped prisoner wandered England without fear, but proximity to Michael had accustomed her to these things.

"I'm pleased to make your acquaintance, sir. If you have brought Fiona for a visit, I am eternally grateful. I have a dozen questions for you, but let me take you inside for some refreshments. The day is amazingly warm for this time of year."

"I will admit, refreshments would not go unappreciated. But we cannot tarry long, so do not let us intrude on your activities. We've come to beg a favor."

Blanche nodded. Briskly, she led them toward the cottage, indicating to the nursemaid that she see to the carriage driver. Blanche saw her guests seated in the parlor. "How are Dillian and Gavin?" she asked as if this were just a neighborly visit.

"Working hard, as always," Fiona replied, her expression tense now that they were out of view of the servants. "Michael asked that we send word. As I said, he's after climbing the walls to return, but the duke will not give him leave. There's apparently another to-do at the mills. His Grace arrived in person and dragged him off to Manchester. Michael sends his apologies and his love. Faith, and I believe he looked quite desperate when last we saw him."

For a moment, the tension eased, and Fiona spoke woman to woman, with curiosity in her voice. "He is not the same man I first met, is he?"

"Michael is a chameleon," she said in explanation. "He is what he must be when the occasion arises. How is he healing? Has he regained the use of his hands yet? His writing is almost indecipherable, and he never talks of himself."

"The bandages are off; he healed cleanly. With the scars, he's after having some difficulty closing his fingers, but mayhap that will change with time."

After the maid set the tray down and departed, Blanche finally allowed herself to go beyond the pleasantries. "Now will you tell me of this favor you must ask? Is there trouble? Tell me truthfully now. I'm not an invalid."

With sighs of relief, Fiona and William launched into the story with all its details. Blanche eyed William with suspicion when he stated the reason for his risking life and limb, not to mention his neck, by returning to Ireland. "You would declare Michael Earl of Aberdare?" she asked as they lapsed into silence. "And he has agreed? Would that make me a MacDermot, too?"

Fiona and William exchanged uneasy glances.

Blanche smiled wryly at their reaction. Michael would make her Countess of Aberdare, Lady MacDermot. Neville would have a royal fit and swallow his tongue. An Irish countess in the family. Maybe he'd write her off the family tree.

"Well, never mind about that now. First we must find some way of smuggling Mr. O'Connor into the country. And I have some information here that you might find useful. I'd thought to use it for the benefit of you and your brother, but I can see that this plan might work better. Of course, I'm having difficulty imagining my husband as an earl, but we'll jump that fence when we come to it. Where is Seamus, by the way? He's not upset with Michael for claiming the title, is he?"

O'Connor looked uncomfortable and Fiona glanced at her hands rather than meet Blanche's gaze.

Blanche could see she'd hit the bull's-eye with that question. Well, it was of little import. She'd married Michael when he had no name. The title was meaningless. What mattered was saving Fiona's home.

"I think we must have you enter the country as my man of business, Mr. O'Connor. Or perhaps you would prefer to be a solicitor? In either case, we must find you a new suit of clothes. Fiona, you will go as my companion. I think using your real name in the company of your uncle might be dangerous. And you look so much like your brother, that might cast suspicion on us. My companion can dress in a black bonnet and heavy shawls. No one will see you at all. Michael taught me that."

Looking shocked, her company protested, but Blanche had anticipated that. She carried the child easily. Mary was stronger and might accept a short absence. She saw no reason a little journey by Neville's yacht should cause any harm. And if she knew Michael, he would go straight from the mills to Ireland.

* * *

A week later, under gray Irish clouds, Blanche winced as the old wooden wagon hit still another stone, then smiled as she covered her rotund belly. Of course Michael's child would travel well.

Excitedly, Fiona bounced beside her, pointing into the mist rising from the land ahead. "There 'tis! There's the castle! We're almost there."

Blanche poked her with her elbow, and Fiona quieted. Beside them rode two soldiers of his majesty's dragoons intent on guarding the heiress to a ducal fortune. She wondered if the soldiers also spied on her traveling companions, but so far no one had questioned them. O'Connor made a fine, smooth-talking solicitor, albeit an Irish one. An Irish solicitor would more easily handle the affairs of an Irish earl.

Fiona had played the part of sedate companion as best as her lively spirits allowed. The broad-brimmed bonnet concealed her face. Enveloped in heavy black shawls, her figure did not reveal her youth.

As the wagon drew closer, Blanche admired the castle rising out of the early morning mist. Stone turrets stood proud and high against the backdrop of a gray-blue sky. She could imagine pennants snapping from their peaks in the brisk breeze. Some earl had opened up the arrow slits in the stone walls into gracious windows that overlooked the countryside. She couldn't think of a more romantic setting for a family like Michael's.

As they rolled up the lane, she could see how the battlements crumbled where their stones had been hauled away for the foundation of cottages and fences, but the romance stayed. Unlike the yellowing grass and dust she'd left behind, the land here shimmered in the morning dew, gleaming emerald beneath the sun breaking through the mist. Wildflowers ran rampant in the fence rows, and she could imagine paddocks of horses whickering welcome as they approached.

The officer riding beside them approached. "Are you certain this is the place? It looks as if naught occupies the castle but ghosts."

"There are ghosts aplenty, young man," O'Connor assured him, whipping the reins for a faster pace. "But the earl kept the interior intact. The library is a monument of his dedication to preserving his family's memory. The young MacDermots maintained it as best they could."

"I shouldn't think the new earl eager to take up a monstrosity like this," the officer observed wryly. "I do not blame him for remaining in England."

"He is on his way here as we speak," Blanche reminded them. "But business detains him. Of course, we do not have proof of his ownership as yet. That's why we are here. The American branch of the family did not revere family records so much as the Irish branch. I've observed this in other Americans. Tradition means little to them, it seems."

To Blanche's relief, the soldiers grabbed the topic of Americans in general and carried it until they reached the castle. She did not wish them questioning Michael's ownership or motives too closely.

O'Connor had disappeared into the bleak interior before the remainder of the party could pick their way over the rocks and through the tangle.

As they entered the cavernous darkness of the foyer, one of the soldiers found a torch and lit it. Fiona could undoubtedly lead them to the library, but as Blanche's companion, she could not reveal her knowledge of the estate. Besides, Blanche had the feeling that O'Connor had hurried ahead for a reason.

"How fascinating!" she chirped. "We must explore! Sally, you have read all about medieval castles. Which way do you suggest?" With that disingenuous direction, Blanche gave Fiona the reins. If her instincts were correct, Fiona would lead them on a wild goose chase for the rest of the morning.

Blanche, the rebellious, had emerged again.

Thirty-nine

Sitting on a rough chair in the far corner of a dark tavern, a felt cap pulled over his hair, Michael observed all newcomers while burying his nose in a mug of ale. He sipped cautiously, but the taste alone prevented overindulging.

His eyebrows shot up as a slender lad slipped in and blended with the shadows in the opposite corner of the room. Seamus wasn't half bad. He just damned well shouldn't be anywhere near here right now. If anyone noticed their resemblance, suspicion would raise its ugly head quick enough.

Of course, at the moment, even the lad hadn't detected him. So he hadn't lost all his talent yet. The cap disguised his hair, and the soot-blackened beard disguised his coloring. Seamus probably looked for a haughty fribble in gentleman's clothes.

Barnaby's messenger finally dragged in. The man's narrow-eyed gaze darted all about as he sidled up to the bar and called for a tankard. Michael wondered where Barnaby had gone to find such a scrawny, filthy specimen of humanity, but he supposed if one lived in the gutters, one could find rats.

The weasel on two legs standing at the bar would lead him directly to Barnaby. Michael hadn't contemplated what he would do with Barnaby yet, but wringing his neck sounded most satisfying. He might be more creative when the time came. Choking him until his eyes bulged out, then dangling him from the roof had appeal.

Michael's go-between joined the weasel at the bar. When the go-between shoved a sealed note instead of money in the weasel's direction, Michael prepared for a brawl. He relaxed when Barnaby's man merely uttered a string of oaths, grabbed the note, and shoved his way toward the door. Taking that as his cue, Michael slipped out the back entrance, down the alley, and with a direction from an urchin stationed on the corner, followed Weasel at a safe distance as he wove his way through the crowded market.

Just as he noted the man's direction, he was distracted by the sight of a striking golden head in an open carriage rolling through the crowded street.

Michael walked into a fish cart. Stumbling, he caught the cart's edge, dislodging no more than a trout or two. Flipping the fishmonger a coin, he raced through the throng of chattering housewives and cooks in the direction of the carriage. Finally reaching the carriage on a crowded corner where a dray blocked the intersection, Michael gasped with both dismay and joy. *Blanche was here!*

Michael elbowed an old woman out of his way and dashed into the street. Hopping onto the driver's step, he grabbed the carriage side, and lunged into the interior as the horses jerked into movement again.

"Michael!" Blanche screamed, while the woman beside her simply screamed.

With a grin, he dipped his cap and settled into the narrow space at her feet. "I shall cheerfully strangle you, my lady, just as soon as I've warmed my weary eyes on your beauty. My God, Blanche, you've taken years off my life. What the devil are you doing here?"

He couldn't stop grinning at her laughing eyes, more blue than the skies today.

"Looking for you, of course. I tired of waiting for you to come home, so I decided to bring home to you."

Michael rolled his eyes and shoved his hands through his dirty hair. "Now is not the time to prove your intrepidness, my lady. I want you and...." He glanced at the other passenger, and grimaced at discovering Fiona watching him from beneath a gawdawful bonnet. "I want you and your devil maiden to hie yourselves from here as quickly as you can. I haven't time to round up guards and keep you safe day and night. Go back to Dorset. I'll find you there as soon as everything is settled."

"And when will that be? After the baby's born?" Blanche asked scornfully. "I've tolerated a lot from you, Michael O'Toole Lawrence MacDermot or whatever name you choose these days, but I'll not tolerate more. Let Neville handle the mills. He owes me that. It's time you came home. Let me see your hands."

Obediently, Michael held out his hands. "Blanche, my love, take my word for it. You cannot stay here. It's not safe. You will terrify me into an old and gray-haired man if you do not leave at once."

Michael glared at Fiona. "I don't know what you've told my wife, but you'd best find some way of persuading her out of here if you know what's good for you. Join me in Ireland, if you must, but leave Manchester now."

"Oh, we've already gone to Ireland," Blanche replied blithely. "Mr. O'Connor is quite convinced he'll prove you the next Earl of Aberdare. Have you told Neville yet that I'll be an Irish countess? It should give him an apoplexy, at least."

Michael snorted at the image conjured by her words. An Irish countess, indeed. Neville would become an old and gray-haired man, too.

"I would not break the news to him just yet, my lady. He's in over his head as it is and probably scouring the streets in search of me as of this minute. You cannot know the seriousness of the situation." He thought perhaps one didn't discuss topics like killing a former man of business with pregnant ladies.

"I'll not leave here without you," Blanche informed him. "Shall we deliver you somewhere?"

Crossing his arms over his knees, Michael rested his head against them. "You may as well ruin my identity entirely by taking me back to your inn. I should imagine you'll cause a stir when you take someone looking like this to your room."

Blanche grinned impudently. "I've always wanted the reputation of a wanton. Shall I order a bath brought up when we arrive?"

Oh, gad, how he loved her, even when she drove him insane. Bowing his head in acceptance of this mad acknowledgment, Michael rested his head on his arms all the way back to the inn. He wasn't ready yet for anyone to see his eyes.

* * *

Scrubbed and naked, Michael tugged his wife into his arms, and sought the sweetness of her lips. Tenderness and lust surged through him as Blanche responded, throwing all her heart and soul into the kiss.

"This is insane," he whispered against her mouth as he cupped her breast. "I do not know if I can do this without hurting the babe, but I want you so much it will soon make a cripple of me."

Laughter bubbled as Blanche pressed closer. "Dillian assures me we can. I shall show you her letter when we return. It's a masterpiece of metaphors. She ought to write books for women."

Michael shuddered at the thought. "No, thank you. You may keep that particular masterpiece to yourself. If I must learn more about feminine anatomy, I should like to do it through experience."

He felt like a rutting bull as he pressed her toward the bed, but he was well beyond stopping now. Like a fragile flower, Blanche drifted in his arms, bending to his needs without protest. Resting her against the mattress, he rubbed his hand over the gentle slope of her belly through the sheer muslin of her nightshift. He shuddered with the exquisite joy of touching her with his bare hands.

"You've grown more wondrous beautiful since I saw you last," he murmured in amazement. "I cannot believe you willingly carry a child of mine. Just watching it grow beneath your heart like this takes my breath away." He eased the gown up, pulling it over her head so she was as naked as he.

Their eyes met, and Michael saw hers smoked with the same desire he felt. He eased her legs apart although he had not yet lifted her entirely onto the mattress. He thought they might fit more easily this way, so the burden of her belly did not intrude. Her eyes widened as she recognized his intent, but she capitulated the moment he bent and took her breast into his mouth. She gave a cry of pure pleasure and tilted her hips upward to rub against his shaft.

Michael heard her cry his name as he drank deeply of one aroused crest and moved to the other. The sound of his name on her lips drove him mad, but he wouldn't rush this moment. He would have only this once before he must send her away again.

Wrapping his arm around Blanche, he lifted her hips more securely on the bed, then knelt to take her with his mouth. Her high keening cry of pleasure decimated what control he retained. Bursting with need, Michael straightened, and plunged home.

Blanche came apart in his arms. Weeping, clutching his arms, pulling him deeper with the strength of her contractions, she drove him into a frenzy of desire. Holding her, desperately striving for gentleness, Michael fell into the dizzying spiral of her demands. Lost in her pleasure, he thrust deeply, measuring his rhythm to her cries, until finally he exploded to the music of Blanche's joy.

Later, properly situated upon the bed with Blanche cuddled against him, he marveled at the strength of this delicate female. An odd rippling sensation beneath his hand where it rested on

Blanche's belly drew his startled gaze downward. He cupped his hand around the pearl-drop shape of her abdomen, feeling the gentle movement. In wonder, he caressed the place where his child lived and moved, and a bond deep inside him pulled taut and irreversibly connected him to his wife and the child she carried.

Michael lifted his head in wonder, and Blanche's lips curved.

"He likes traveling," she informed him. "You will have to take him everywhere."

His hand trembled as he caressed her there again. The child kicked, creating a bulge in one side. The knowledge that a living, breathing infant rested there shook him so deeply he couldn't breathe. "What if he's too big? He's already too big! Dammit, woman, you can't carry anything like that until when? December? He'll tear you in two. We have to find a physician." Frantically, he rose on one elbow. "You shouldn't be here now. I have to take you back to London and the best physicians. I don't want to lose you. How could I have done this to you? I'm sorry, love, I didn't know. I wish I could take it all back."

Laughing softly, she tugged him down and Michael collapsed against her, burying his face against her throat, holding her tight while he tried burying his foolish fears.

"I feel fine. The physician assures me everything is normal. Maybe we'll have a Christmas baby. Shall we call it Holly if it's a girl?"

He knew she tried distracting him, but nothing could distract him now. He couldn't let her go. He'd hold her until the child was safe in their arms. How would he get her home? They couldn't stay here.

"Michael?" She tugged at his hair again. "Did you hear me? Shall we call her Holly if she's born on Christmas?"

"Holly. Yes." Rattled, he collapsed against the pillow and stared at the ceiling. He must be going mad.

With golden hair streaming across the pillow, she watched him with concern. "Michael, it's fine. Really. You needn't worry. Tell me what you would name a boy. If you really think to call yourself an earl, you must think of something properly noble for your heir."

Heir. My God, should he survive this, he would have an earldom and an heir. Or he would wake soon on a cornhusk cot in a cabin in Kentucky. He didn't even have a name. How could he have an heir?

Blanche giggled at his stunned expression and kissed his cheek. His jaw muscles clenched beneath her touch. Her sweet herbal scent wafted around him, and he wrapped his fingers in the long tendrils of her hair. His shaft had already arisen to the occasion, and Blanche wasn't one to let it go unnoticed.

Closing his eyes and groaning at the immensity of the universe and the laughter of the gods, Michael filled his newly-healed hands with her hair and tugged Blanche's mouth down to cover his.

Forty

Michael had no idea of the depth of his exhaustion until a frantic knock on the door in the hour before midnight left him too groggy to do more than grunt in reply.

"Michael!" Fiona's voice rang through the panel. "Seamus says as they're burning the mill!"

"It needed burning anyway," he muttered into the pillow, absorbing Blanche's warmth against his side. Dammit, Barnaby was supposed to give him another day.

"Michael! Hurry, His Grace is searching for you."

In other words, the duke didn't know Blanche's place of residence, or he'd be personally pounding at that door. With a sigh, Michael swung his legs over the side of the bed. Blanche sat up and sleepily wiped the hair from her eyes.

"What is it?" she murmured, yawning.

"Why is it no one calls me mister?" Michael complained insensibly as he reached for his trousers. "The brat stands out there shouting my given name to all and sundry. Could she not use a 'sir' or a 'mister' or something?"

"That's because no one knows which 'mister' you are today. O'Toole? Lawrence? Or have you decided on MacDermot this morning?"

"Nicholas," he declared firmly, reaching for his shirt.

"What?" Even half asleep, Blanche understood the waywardness of that reply.

"Nicholas. If the child is a boy born at Christmas, we should call him Nicholas." He tugged his trousers closed and began buttoning them.

Blanche giggled and donned her nightshift. "You are mad. What does Fiona want at this hour? Must you go?"

"Probably not. There is little enough I can do now. If I had any sense at all, I'd climb right back into that bed with you. But Fiona will most likely take a hatchet to the door should I try." Trying to speak calmly, Michael sat down in a bedside chair and pulled on his shoes.

"Michael! Are you awake? I'm coming in there if you don't answer this minute."

Michael cocked a wry eyebrow. "You see?" He turned toward the door. "Faith and you needn't scream like a banshee, Fey-onah, my own," he shouted. "Be after fetchin' that nuisance of a brother of yours and we'll ride out there."

They heard her running down the hall in reply. Michael had been in that derelict mill often enough to know they hadn't a chance of saving it.

"You can't stop a fire, Michael," Blanche whispered, confirming his fear as she climbed from the bed and pulled on a wrapper. "There'll be no one inside at this hour. Let Neville handle it."

Grimacing, he started to say something reassuring when he caught a movement at the window from the corner of his eye.

Instantly, Michael swung in front of Blanche and edged her backward toward the door. Behind him, she gasped as a man's boot appeared over the sill. A moment later, Barnaby stood there grinning, a long-barreled pistol in his hand.

"Well, isn't this nice? I didn't hope to catch both the lady and her lover." His grin tightened into a grim line as he recognized Michael. "I suppose it's your fault my man returned without the money. The lady's paying the price for that. You'll not get another farthing from that mill. If you want to keep the rest, I'd suggest you persuade the lady to sign a note I can take to the bank. I've a ship waiting for me and no wish for delay."

"Leave the room, Blanche," Michael said coldly, backing her toward the door while he kept his gaze on the enemy

"I think not." Barnaby shifted the pistol. "The lady will stay with some friends of mine until I have the cash, a sort of security against your tricks, O'Toole."

"You're a few names behind, Mr. Barnaby," Blanche said laughingly from the safety of Michael's back. "I think he's worked his way up to Earl of Aberdare now and is appropriately addressed 'my lord.'"

"Out, sweetheart," Michael warned. "He can't shoot you through me, so leave and warn Fiona. Just this once, do as I say without arguing."

"Make one move through that door and I'll blow a hole through your beau, my lady," Barnaby warned.

"You've only the one shot, nodcock," Michael mocked, knowing Blanche hesitated. "Shoot me, and the whole inn comes running. Are you planning on dragging a pregnant woman out the window and down the street with half the town on your heels?"

With relief, he felt Blanche easing toward the door. Just another few steps....

Blanche grabbed a pillow from the bed and flung it. Barnaby dodged.

Prepared, Michael seized the chair he'd sat in moments ago, His fingers wouldn't close enough to form a fist, but they could close around a chair back. He swung it hard, smashing it against Barnaby's jaw. The man groaned, stumbled sideways, then again staggered toward him.

Michael lashed out with his booted foot, and Barnaby's soft parts crushed beneath his toes. With ease, he tumbled the older man backward.

"Damn, but I felt that." A voice laughed from the same open window Barnaby had entered.

Finally, Blanche fled. Michael scowled at the grinning faces of Seamus and Eamon O'Connor. He pointed at the man writhing on the floor. "Tie him up, and you don't need to be gentle. I'm after Blanche."

Seamus climbed through the window first. "Fiona and the duke are downstairs. They've two husky men on the way up and the magistrate on his way. Eamon caught the weasely chap over at the mill."

Michael tested the strength of a bed sheet, then ripped it in half. Throwing half to Seamus, he ripped his half again. "I still think the Americas too good for the lot of you. If I didn't despise Anglesey more, I'd hand you over to him."

"Methinks his bark is worse than his bite," Eamon said quietly behind the quickly angering Seamus. "You've to learn control of that temper, lad."

Seamus ripped his half of the sheet with resounding force.

"You've a sister to look after, same as I've a wife," Michael reminded him. "If something happens to you, what becomes of Fiona?"

Eamon laughed and replied for him, "She'll marry the bloody

duke. Our Fiona lands on her feet, she does. But I'll take Seamus in hand if you can get his lands back. That is what you've told them, isn't it?"

Michael peered suspiciously at the former officer. "How do you keep the army from drawing and quartering you?"

In perfect French, Eamon replied, "The French Eamon died on the field of battle. They know naught of the Irish."

"Are you certain you're not kin to young Seamus?" he asked, tugging a knot tighter.

"We're a close knit lot, we are," Eamon enigmatically agreed.

Michael heard booted feet pounding up the stairs. "I've no idea what my wife has done in my absence, but I've given my word. I'll do what I can to retrieve the lands. Do I have your word that you'll keep the clodpole in hand until he grows up?"

Seamus offered a loud objection which Eamon promptly ended by slapping his hand over the boy's mouth and dragging him toward the window. "I'll see him occupied until you clear his name. Until next time."

Their departure coincided with the Duke of Anglesey's assault upon the chamber door.

* * *

"Neville thought you were having a fit," Blanche said several days later.

In the privacy of their Dublin chamber, Michael wore tailored trousers and an open linen shirt, adopting attire somewhere between his gentleman's pose and his street magician's disarray as he waited for the Irish court to decide their fates. He felt as if he had one foot in two worlds and a good breeze could topple him.

His Grace had stepped in as Blanche's representative in the negotiations between the mills and the workers. After Michael dragged him through the city's slums, the duke had been forced to see the workers as faces with names and starving children, and could no longer preach the profit motive so boldly.

He could almost grant that Neville would ultimately do better in the negotiations. Michael knew he leaned too far in the direction of the workers and would probably bankrupt Blanche.

"I was," he retorted to Blanche's laughter. "I think I shall slam my head against walls on a regular basis. I know I shall if you do not go home where you belong. You're like to have that babe in the midst of a courtroom."

"I'll go home when you do." His wife shrugged, then picked up a stitch of her knitting.

"And how does Neville's investigation of our marriage lines go?" he asked tauntingly, distracting himself as he paced the perimeter.

"I am very definitely Mrs. Lawrence, at least," she said with a hint of glee at her cousin's expense. "There's not a solicitor in London who can break the trail of evidence you left behind. They're working on the name problem, however. I dissuaded Gavin from signing a sworn statement that you are his brother until we have the court's decision on the MacDermots. If you change your name again, we may have to repeat our vows. The solicitors are uncertain of the legalities as yet."

"You are not sorry we married?" he demanded.

She rested her hand on the upper curve of her belly. "I had some choice?"

"You did," he answered emphatically. "I gave you two years to make choices. You chose me. You may regret your decision, but you cannot tell me you had none."

She smiled knowingly. "No, I cannot tell you that. And I do not regret my choice."

A knock at the door intruded, and William O'Connor entered. Instead of greeting the duke's daughter, as was proper, he stopped before Michael and bowed. With stiff formality, he righted himself and offered his hand. "Your lordship."

"Cut line, O'Connor," Michael demanded, resuming his pose against the mantel. He'd just discovered his hands would close sufficiently to fit around the candlesticks, but he disliked attempting the juggle with company present. "What stones have you overturned?"

The man practically danced in his shoes, rocking back and forth and eyeing him with complete approval. "Just like your great-grandfaither. Stern man, he was, but with the devil in him just the same."

"Such knowledge makes you a hundred years old," Michael answered scornfully. "We have no audience here. You needn't put on a show."

O'Connor raised his eyebrows. "The seventh earl lived to a ripe old age. I knew him well. Admittedly, I knew the eighth earl better, and his children more so, but I'll not have ye doubt me. Ye have the looks of your grandfaither, just as young Seamus does. Of course, your grandmother was a MacDermot also, a second cousin, so the line runs true in both."

Michael noted that Blanche took in this blarney with wide eyes and eager anticipation. The old man was good, but the subject too painful. "Just tell me how the court is buying this faradiddle," Michael demanded. "Will they consider my claim?"

"Of course they will consider your claim. How could they do elsewise? I've shown them the letters from your da, sent from the wilds of the Americas, giving the date of your birth and that they named you Michael after your great-grandfaither. I've shown them letters saying Colin MacDermot and his wife, Kathleen, went to America to meet the Lawrences, who were old friends of your great-grandfaither. Black sheep the Lawrences were, but the Earl of Aberdare had befriended them once, and he called in the favor."

Even though they all knew the tale had been woven from loose threads, the old man appeared to be enjoying his drama. He cackled and paced. "The Lawrences were not easy folk to find, it seems. It's a sorry tale that Colin and his wife did not catch up with them until Kathleen had birthed their son and was weak from travail. The Lawrences found a home for them in the hills between Kentucky and Virginia. But an epidemic caught the town, and Kathleen died first. Colin died nursing her, but not before he'd sent the little one away before he could catch the disease too. Of course the court believes me, especially after I showed them the picture in the old family book. They'd no choice but to believe."

"What book?" That was a facet Michael hadn't created.

"The family book," O'Connor responded impatiently. "You need only show them that coin about your neck, and they'll sign the papers recognizing you as heir to the earldom. Your lovely wife has already had the title and lands researched. They've lain in the crown's coffers since the day they were usurped. It's just a matter of transferring them to their rightful owner as soon as you present yourself."

"You found a book with my medallion in it?" Michael asked with disbelief. "You're more cunning than I thought. I'd like to see that book myself. Did you age the paper properly? Or just fit the loose page between ancient ones? You only saw the coin once. Are you certain you memorized it closely enough?"

O'Connor laughed and winked at Blanche. "He does not believe. That's what becomes of being a rogue, I suppose. The MacDermots are all liars and thieves when they have to be, but good to the heart of them."

"You should not tease him," Blanche protested. "I don't think he appreciates the humor. Let us just end this charade so you and Seamus may go home again."

William clucked his tongue at her doubts. "We must have an earl before we can plead our case to the Lords. I'll admit, I'll feel safer when I'm elsewhere than Dublin myself. But as an earl's representative, I'm someone important, and they do not see the O'Connor of Roscommon. And do not doubt that I am an earl's representative. You see before you the ninth Earl of Aberdare, Michael MacDermot, clear enough, and you, his countess."

Even though it was utter nonsense, Michael grinned and slapped his arm around his *representative's* shoulder. "Sure, and it's that glad I am to hear it, boyo. A penniless Irish earl is all that I've aspired to be. Shall we have a wee dram and drink to the auld sod?"

O'Connor threw up his hands in surrender. "You'll not mock when you see what I have to show you. Perhaps I embroidered a wee bit here and there, but it's the truth I'm tellin' now. You're that infant son the letters speak of. There's no doubt a'tall."

Michael winked merrily at Blanche. "Guess you're an Irish countess after all, my lady. Now will you take my name or must I still call you Lady Blanche?"

"Oh, Lady Aberdare is fine enough with me," she replied demurely, the laughter in her eyes visible even through lowered lashes. "Just make certain the marriage lines are clear so our son does not have all this to go through again."

Michael threw back his head and laughed.

* * *

One day later, Michael stood in astonishment before a judge addressing him as *Lord Aberdare*. He stared in disbelief at an ancient volume portraying the hand-minted coin given by the first earl to his only son. The coin matched his own in every detail, and the gilded pages of the volume were solidly bound in leather. He shook it to test it for himself.

O'Connor even brought in a family portrait of the seventh earl to prove the likeness. Michael could scarcely look at the bewigged old man's eagle eyes staring down from the painting without thinking he should fall on his knees and worship at the portrait's feet. He didn't have that kind of aristocratic blood in him.

But the evidence said elsewise. His parents had not only been married, but of the aristocracy.

Still stunned by the judge's pronouncement, Michael turned to Blanche. When she placed the deeds to his new property in his hands, he shook his head in disbelief.

"I'm really earl and must take responsibility for that whole cantankerous family?" he asked in dismay.

His wife smiled and touched the curve of her abdomen. "As well as responsibility for the family you've created."

"And between us, how many houses do we have?"

Blanche grinned up at him. "Oh, about six or so, depending on which you count."

He knew he sounded a fool, but he couldn't help it. "I've never had even one before."

Blanche's blue gaze pinned him firmly. "You promised you would not disappear without saying farewell," she reminded him.

Silently, Michael considered the enormous burden of his newly acquired derelict Irish castle, the sprawling wealth of all Blanche's holdings, and a family that now included everything from a haughty duke to a would-be traitor. Shaking his head at the absurdity, he smiled. "No problem. I shall just learn to juggle houses and families instead of pennies."

"You would walk into a burning building for me," she replied confidently.

"To keep you out of it, I would," he answered, following her toward the door.

"You're quite mad," she agreed.

Michael smiled and joy filled him again. "Aye, I've already concluded that, and 'tis a fine madness, 'tis." With the confidence of finally having a name and family, he bent and whispered in her ear as others pushed impatiently from the courtroom. "'Tis a madness called love, I believe. Have I ever told you how much I love you?"

She tilted her face up to his, serenely brushing his lips with her fingertips. "I've always known that. I've just waited for you to admit it. I love you, Michael Lawrence MacDermot, or whoever you are today. I loved you as O'Toole and I'll love you as you are tomorrow. I shall always love you. Even though I'll no doubt regret it in days to come," she added with a wry truthfulness.

To the accompaniment of his laughter, she took his arm and guided him toward the courtroom door where his new relations awaited him.

An entire village of new relations. Waiting outside the courthouse, they cheered in triumph as the ninth Earl of Aberdare and his countess stepped into the bright light of day.

Forty-one

Roscommon, Ireland
December, 1819

Outside the castle's library window a late December dawn tinted the horizon a paler gray. Mist swirled at the leaded glass, and a draft clutched at a guttering candle. The men warming themselves near the fire had gone beyond noticing.

"Give him some brandy," Neville said with irritation as he held his hands to the flames. "I cannot bear those bouncing balls another minute. With luck, he'll pass out after the first glass."

At the desk, Gavin glanced up from the papers he pored over. His gaze traveled to his adopted brother who paced up and down the lengthy stone floor, objects of assorted weights and sizes bouncing from hand to hand and occasionally off floor and wall. Gavin had confiscated a medieval dirk earlier, but harness buckles and pewter platters still circled in Michael's stiff fingers, nothing breakable. Too many of the objects still followed the earth's pull rather than Michael's.

"That's too easy," Gavin replied, returning to his papers. "Let him suffer."

Collecting all the items in his hands, Michael turned on the room as if having heard nothing of the previous conversation. "I am going up. I cannot stand it one minute more."

"Here we go again," Gavin groaned, laying down his pen. "Seamus," he called over his shoulder. "Rouse yourself, boy. I'm tired of this job. It's your turn."

Seamus lumbered in the direction of the library door. There he settled on a massive mahogany chair beneath the door bolt, crossing his arms over his chest as if the position were a familiar one.

"I rue the day I kept you from sailing off to America," Michael growled, swinging away and heading across the room. "I'll leave by way of the window."

"Do that," Neville agreed mockingly. "It's three floors above a rock yard. With any luck, you'll break your neck."

Michael flung open the leaded glass and a wintry breeze tore through the room. Behind him, his companions groaned and ran to weigh down papers, books, and other articles. "Why isn't the scaffolding on this damned side of the house?" The window slammed shut again.

"Because you didn't want to spend all of Blanche's money at once," Neville countered, dropping back to the warm chair by the fire. "You thought you'd waste it in increments, one tottering stone wall at a time."

"I could have insisted that Seamus and William live at Anglesey," Michael replied without hostility, pacing the wall and studying it as if looking for a hidden door. "More money goes into that monstrosity than here. I cannot see how even a duke can use a hundred rooms or more when he has no family of his own."

"You would see it decay until it resembled this damp rot fortress?" Neville asked scornfully. "Anglesey is Blanche's home. She's welcome to return anytime she recovers her senses and leaves you behind."

At some real or imagined cry, Michael stared frantically at the ceiling. His hands clenched. But when no other sound followed, he relaxed and regarded the irritating duke.

Neville had irked him all evening, but Michael understood the other man's habits. They both needed distraction and for Neville, argument provided it best.

"You'd best search for an heiress, Your Grace, or I'll persuade Blanche that our child needs more of Anglesey funds for his future. Or better yet, that all the mills need modernizing. The plans for the new one in Manchester are quite enlightening."

Neville growled and stretched his legs before the fire. "It will take me the next five years of campaigning to persuade parliament into accepting labor laws. I'm earning my keep well enough. I'm amazed, however, that you don't have your solicitor waiting at the door with a petition for trusteeship. With Blanche incapacitated by childbirth, you're in a position as her husband to take over the trust. You can rob us all blind anytime you like."

"I'm what?" Michael whirled around and glared at his antagonist.

"In a position to take over Blanche's trust." Neville shrugged without turning around. "Any man with half a brain in his head would have figured that out long ago. Childbirth is one of the reasons a man doesn't leave his fortune to a woman. It's much too easy for her husband to step in and take over due to incapacitation."

"Who wrote that bloody law?" Michael shouted. "Insufferably arrogant men like you I suppose!" He increased his frantic pacing. "She's not incapacitated. Not any more than a man on a drunk. If wives could take advantage of that law, they'd be in control of most of the fortunes in the country by now. I don't want any damned part in it."

Laughter tinted the duke's reply. "You just don't want the responsibility of all that money, do you?"

"That's enough," Gavin declared, flinging down his pen. "You'll be throwing sticks and stones next. The petition to address parliament is ready, Neville. Go over it, will you? If I don't pry these Irish rebels from underfoot soon, I'll turn them in to the crown myself."

Seamus hooted. "You're sore because I beat you at chess."

"No, I just want to see what's left of Oxford when you're done with it," Gavin mocked.

"I'm after thinkin' it's the Americas I'll be seein' when it comes down to it, even if I declare myself Protestant to attend your damned school," Seamus answered. "Parliament will have no kindness for the likes of me and William. And there's no justice in being cleared because we're kin to an earl and can claim our mother's religion. What of the others who languish in Dublin gaol while we go free?"

"You'll obtain your law degree and see them freed," Gavin replied coldly. "That's what this is all about. Michael is nigh unto useless at speechmaking, but you can run for his borough in the Commons. You'll have his vote and ours in the Lords. You can summon more if you apply your mind to it. Then you can emancipate all the Catholics you want."

When Michael did not argue his lack of ability at the onerous duties of Parliament, all the library's inhabitants glanced to where they'd seen him last. The fire cast shadows on an empty wall.

"Oh, damn," Gavin muttered, dropping his chair back on all four legs. "He's found a way out again."

* * *

Michael shoved open the bedchamber door. A nursemaid jumped and shrieked in surprise, but recognizing him, returned to washing a screaming infant.

He stared in wonder at the squirming pink flesh in the maid's hands, then turned to the bed.

"She's sleeping," Dillian warned from the shadows. "Do not disturb her. We would have called you when we were ready. You have no right in here now."

Michael crossed to the bed and the frail figure lying upon it, her long golden hair sprawled in tangled knots against the sweat-dampened pillows, evidence of the struggle that had gone on here this night. He ached with fear in every ounce of his body, and his hand grasped hers with a strength borne of desperation. "Blanche?"

Her eyes flickered, and he breathed deep with relief, nearly choking on the rush of air to his lungs. He sank to the chair beside the bed and caressed her brow. Her smile acknowledged his presence.

"You put me through hell," he informed her without compassion. Then with no regard to anyone watching, he cupped her breast, seeking the reassurance of her heart beat. "Don't ever put me through this again. Next time, I'll throw the lot of them from the window and come after you."

He could feel her smiling more than see it. "I'm amazed they're still living," she whispered. "They are, aren't they? I wouldn't wish to rise from childbed to clean bodies out of the library."

"I'd throw them into the moat for you," he promised. "But now that you have this foolishness of bearing our firstborn in his ancestral home out of your system, perhaps you will stay in Dorset where you belong."

"I was right to do it," she informed him boldly. "You did not even ask, you foolish man. You have a son, sir. He has every right to know his inheritance."

A son. The impact of this declaration staggered him. "The child inherits a ducal fortune, you silly goose," he reminded her, kissing her cheek and stroking the damp hair from her face. "He has no need of a crumbling Irish castle. Seamus will make this his home when he's ready."

"Nicholas must come here every summer," she informed him. "It is the only way for the people to trust him. He will represent them one day. He must know the people he represents."

This was a foolish argument but, like Neville, Blanche loved arguing. Michael loved her for her vehemence in defense of others. "I love you," he whispered. The words came more easily with a name and home to give them power.

"I might love you to the point of distraction, but not beyond. You'll not change my mind," she whispered, closing her eyes as she rested against the pillow. "Nicholas belongs here. Where is Mary?"

"I put her to bed hours ago. The madcap's learned to crawl the stairs. She'll be down here when she wakes, no doubt," Fiona murmured, as she carried a now quiet bundle of blankets to the bedside. "Would you like to meet your son?"

"What are you doing in here?" Michael asked with irritation as he gingerly accepted the bundle. "An unmarried maiden has no right in a birthing room. Your damned uncle can't keep an eye on you for a minute."

"Don't argue," Blanche whispered from the bed.

"You're a fine one to talk." Michael gazed tenderly on the tiny form in his arms. A rosebud mouth puckered and sucked. Perfect little fingers waved in the air, landing with a thud on a pug nose. For a moment, nearly lashless eyes blinked and stared up at him. Then the fist found the mouth, and the infant settled down once more. Awe struck Michael speechless.

"His hair looks red to me," Fiona said with a defiant air.

"Let me see." Blanche's voice was faint, but imperious.

Michael laid the bundle on his wife's abdomen and climbed up on the bed behind her. Settling his legs on either side, he pulled her into his arms so she could sit without need of moving herself. He lifted the infant so she might cuddle their son. "We've made a miracle," he murmured.

Neither of them took notice when a duke and a marquess barged into the room, scowling. Taking one look at the couple huddled together on the bed, Gavin stalked across the room, grabbed Dillian, and kissed her. Left alone in the doorway, Neville scowled a second more, glanced at Fiona's mocking expression, and turning on his heels, stalked out, muttering about Irish imps from hell.

The couple on the bed noticed nothing but each other.

Author Bio

With several million books in print and *New York Times* and *USA Today's* bestseller lists under her belt, former CPA Patricia Rice is one of romance's hottest authors. Her emotionally-charged contemporary and historical romances have won numerous awards, including the *RT Book Reviews* Reviewers Choice and Career Achievement Awards. Her books have been honored as Romance Writers of America RITA® finalists in the historical, regency and contemporary categories.

A firm believer in happily-ever-after, Patricia Rice is married to her high school sweetheart and has two children. A native of Kentucky and New York, a past resident of North Carolina, she currently resides in St. Louis, Missouri, and now does accounting only for herself. She is a member of Romance Writers of America, the Authors Guild, and Novelists, Inc.

For further information, visit Patricia's network:

http://www.patriciarice.com
http://www.facebook.com/OfficialPatriciaRice
https://twitter.com/Patricia_Rice
http://patriciarice.blogspot.com/
http://www.wordwenches.com

Acknowledgments

Although THE ENGLISH HEIRESS was written and purchased by a major publisher shortly after the release of THE MARQUESS, for various business reasons, Michael's book was never printed. For years I had requests for Michael's story, but I was caught up in new contracts, the historical romance market changed, and I knew the once sprawling tome would need severe editing. The story languished on floppy disks and in various paper drafts in my basement.

Then technology offered new opportunities, and I finally saw a chance to resurrect those disks and scan those drafts. I pieced together lost chapters, edited and cut, but after so much work, I still only had raw copy.

That's where Book View Café stepped in. I had two marvelous editors, Jennifer Stevenson and Sherwood Smith. They whacked at plot holes and all the old-fashioned verbiage that once adorned my Regencies and successfully pulled it into shape for modern readers. The story remains the same, but it's 20,000 words lighter and immensely more readable. I couldn't have done it without them. I owe you guys major big time!

And blessings on everyone else in the BVC co-op who made this book finally happen. No matter what anyone says, books do not mysteriously appear without a lot of hard work.

The cover was designed by the talented Kim Killion of Hot Damn Design, who always knows what I need better than I do.

Finally, I thank the many, many readers who have asked me for Michael's story so I never gave up on him. This book's for you!

The Irish Duchess

Patricia Rice

Chapter One

Finished with the news sheets, His Grace, Neville Perceval, the Duke of Anglesey drained his brandy glass, picked up his walking stick and high-crowned hat, and set out for home. He had a stack of estate papers on his desk that needed his attention. And his cousin Blanche had yet another mad scheme for improving the Manchester mills that he must discourage in some manner.

He couldn't believe he was placed in the position of acting as a bloody tradesman just to keep his wretched cousin from sinking all her coins into improbable schemes for benefiting the welfare of mankind. Mankind was scarce worth the effort.

Neville allowed instinct to guide him home while he lost himself in thought. The Anglesey townhouse occupied a rather large chunk of real estate in one of the older sections of town, one where gaslights had not yet been installed. Accustomed to the dark shadows of trees from the park, Neville gave his surroundings little notice. Even the clammy fog obscuring the pavement did not deter him. He could find his way home blindfolded if needed.

Only the sound of a footstep where there shouldn't be one finally dragged him from his reverie. One too many violent incidents in these past years of political chaos had taught him caution. Had someone followed him from the club? Why?

One of the things he had learned from Michael, Blanche's new husband, was how to act quickly and defend himself. Over the years, his lessons with Gentleman Jackson had given him a much needed outlet for frustration. Neville needed no more than the snap of a twig to jump from absentminded thought to full alert.

The scoundrel crashing through the shrubbery caught the full force of the gold-plated knob of Neville's walking stick. The second scoundrel suffered the brunt of Neville's fist plowing into his face at such an angle that his jaw fell slack. Neville cursed as still a third leapt from the bushes, and footsteps behind him indicated he'd attracted a crowd.

Giving up any pretense of politeness, he flicked open the sword in his stick, slashed at the man advancing from his side, kicked at the one rising from the street, and heard the sweet sound of a groan as he connected with his soft target. Any triumph he might have felt dissipated the moment a cudgel cracked across the back of his skull.

With a growl of fury, Neville swung and slashed at his opponent, but he'd already realized the futility. There were just too many of them.

As someone grabbed his sword and twisted it from his hand, Neville plowed his fist into still another jaw and had the satisfaction of hearing it crack before the club came down on his skull again.

This time, the Duke of Anglesey crumpled to the street, swearing as the blackness of unconsciousness threatened. He had no heir. He couldn't die.

Made in the USA
Coppell, TX
02 August 2020